WHITE FEATHERS

Susan Lanigan was born in the Irish Midlands and now lives by the sea near Dublin. Thrice shortlisted for the Hennessy New Irish Writer Award, she has had short fiction published both nationally and internationally. *White Feathers* is her first novel.

WHITE FEATHERS

Susan
Lanigan

BRANDON
AN IMPRINT OF O'BRIEN

First published 2014 by The O'Brien Press Ltd

12 Terenure Road East, Rathgar, Dublin 6, Ireland

Tel: +353 1 4923333   Fax: +353 1 4922777

Email: books@obrien.ie   Website: www.obrien.ie

ISBN: 978-1-84717-639-4

10 9 8 7 6 5 4 3 2 1

20 19 18 17 16 15 14

Printed and bound by ScandBook AB, Sweden

The paper used in this book is produced using pulp from managed forests.

The O'Brien Press receives financial assistance from

'Pray that you will not be put to the test.'

Matthew 26:41

Prologue

May 1917

The train pulled out of Eastbourne just after five. Although it was early in the evening, the sun was already turning a fiery gold, bathing the passengers in warm light until they squinted and fell silent, like insects trapped in amber, war-weary and speechless. Men returning to the front after being patched up in Summerdown Military Hospital gathered in the corridors by the half-open windows, while in one compartment, a young woman sat in the sun's direct line, letting herself become washed in the glow until she seemed as bronze as the light. She wore a simple violet calico dress and hummed a phrase from a Mozart operetta, over and over again. But she looked tired. Her body had been through a lot.

Her companion opposite stayed in shadow, for a story had been told, a story that needed an answer, for better or worse. But the woman in the light was taking her time: there was no hurry, for the story's first words still echoed between them.

It was my fault.

I

The Legacy

I

1 September 1913

Until the ticket collector arrived, the two women occupying the second compartment of the fifth carriage on the two o'clock train from London Bridge to Brighton had not said a word to each other. Mrs Michael Stewart, the older of the two by several decades and dressed in black, the excrescence of crêpe and tulle partly hiding the cracks on her gloves, had no book or newspaper or pastime to amuse her but stared straight ahead with the grim face of the chaperone on duty. Nothing stirred her, nothing interested her. Her widow's weeds were not recently acquired, yet she had lost interest in life long before she had qualified for their use.

By contrast, the younger of the two, Miss Eva Downey, sat close by the window, so close that her breath nearly grimed the glass. She squirmed on the soft upholstery of the seats and tweaked at the velveteen curtains. Sometimes she sat back and clasped the small medallion she wore around her neck. On other occasions she consulted her *Bradshaw's Railway Guide*, her other books being in the valise stowed above their heads.

Of this behaviour, Mrs Stewart indicated her disapproval though a series of tuts and sniffs, all of which Eva ignored. She was seventeen years of age, with hair the colour of straw that had not seen sun, wide-apart grey-blue eyes and a carriage that was a good half stone too heavy for the stricter kind of corset. And up until the moment the line turned towards the coast and showed the wide expanse of sea glowing in the severe autumn sun, she had never seen the English coastline, nor had she ever been on a train, apart from the Tube.

Her stepmother, Catherine, had admonished her, ''Twas gettin' on the Tube that night brought it on yourself in the first place. I'm glad Mrs Michael's keepin' an eye on ye.' Eva, feeling the familiar residual ache in her arm and remembering all too well what she had brought upon herself, had made no reply, merely turning away in disgust.

Mrs Stewart was a friend of Catherine's. Or, at least, they had known each other, back in Ireland. In London, Catherine Downey paid few calls; even after eleven years of marriage, her status was too uncertain for her to risk it. So of all the women in London she could have called on for the task of escorting Eva to her destination, only Mrs Stewart was at her disposal, for Mrs Downey could not, she declared, be expected to carry out the disagreeable duty herself. Why, the … the *injustice* of seeing off her stepdaughter to some fancy school when her own dear Grace had to stay at home! Every time the subject was broached, she became so impassioned that she lost her senses and it became necessary to administer sal volatile to revive her. In her stead, Mrs Stewart had agreed to accompany Eva from the top step of the Downeys' three-storey terrace in 35 Wellclose Square, East London, to the station at Eastbourne, where Eva would be handed over, like a package of goods, to Miss Caroline Hedges, headmistress of The Links School for Young Ladies.

Mrs Stewart was not a pleasant companion: she smelt of mothballs combined with something malformed and rotting deep within the gut. But, regardless, Eva felt only joy. She flourished her ticket at the collector, who stamped it with a smile. It was a single. She wasn't going back any time soon, thank God.

'Eastbourne, eh?' he enquired. 'Well, it's nice to see a lady as happy as you are. What business brings you there?'

Mrs Stewart immediately cut in. 'You're not to answer him.' To the conductor she declared, 'This girl's family is respectable. She doesn't talk to strange men.'

'He is the ticket collector,' Eva said, her voice like a bucket of iced water. 'It is his job to ask people where they are going.'

'And it's my job to make sure you behave yourself,' Mrs Stewart responded, rather more sharply than seemed merited.

The conductor, obviously perturbed, backed away. He was nearly out the door when Eva called after him. 'Sir, wait, please. I shan't leave your question unanswered. There is a school near Eastbourne, called The Links. I am going to attend it for a year.' She broke into a broad smile.

'The Links! Isn't that the fine school for young ladies? I've heard it's very fancy indeed. You must be quite the lady yourself to be going there, miss.' His forehead creased with the beginnings of doubt. She did not look quite right. While she was acceptably dressed, in a simple ivory habit-like dress that looked like a school uniform, she was hatless, her hair hanging limply by her sides in a thick, rather shapeless cut. She was no Lady Lavery, that was for sure. But the conductor had heard tell that the school cost north of seventy pounds a year. One had to be seriously moneyed to put that amount aside.

Eva shook her head, laughing. 'Oh, no, not I. I'm hoi polloi, I'm afraid. No, I was very kindly bequeathed a legacy by Lady Elizabeth Jenkins for this specific purpose. I met her at a—' But there, Eva bit her lip and stopped.

'Yes, that's right,' Mrs Stewart snapped. 'Don't be telling him of your disgraceful behaviour, or he won't be so nice to you any more. You should have stayed home and married Mr Cronin, like you were told to.'

'I'm sorry, miss,' the conductor said, nodding at Eva. 'I seem to have embarrassed your mother.'

Silence fell for a few heartbeats, a few clackety-clacks as the wheels passed over the gaps in the rails. When Eva eventually replied, it was with a quiet viciousness that was clearly audible against the rush of wind and the noise of the train on the tracks. 'She's not my mother, nor is the woman who sent her. My mother died when I was five years old, and there's not a woman alive fit to take her place.' And with that the smile left her face, she opened her *Railway Guide* and remained every bit as still and cold for the rest of the journey as the miserable, fossilised creature sitting opposite her.

A month ago, she would never have dreamed she would be making this journey. That day, she had been called down to the parlour and introduced to a stranger, a solicitor called Mr Phelps, who had called especially to see her. The parlour fronted onto the square, which was in a rather shabby part of town, so the curtains were often drawn to conceal the modesty of the neighbourhood; Mr Phelps seemed to be enveloped in a kind of half-gloaming.

Papa had been present, of course, as had the rest of the family, when that gentleman with the overlong trousers and florid delivery informed them that in gratitude for her work for *The New Feminist*, Lady Elizabeth Jenkins had bequeathed Miss Eva Downey the sum of seventy-five pounds for the express purpose of finishing her education. There had been a pause, which Mr Phelps, who looked too grand for the room, had allowed to lengthen beyond the point of embarrassment before saying, pointedly, 'Any questions?'

Eva's sister, Imelda, had embraced her while Catherine stood there with a face like a gate. Since the discovery of what Mrs Stewart called her 'disgraceful behaviour' two years ago, Eva's relationship with her father's wife had deteriorated from mutual distrust to open warfare. Catherine had done no more than live down to all expectations.

Grace's reaction, however, had been somewhat different. At the time, Eva's stepsister merely greeted her news with a shrug and the blood-red smirk that habitually animated her pale, lovely, suspicious face. But a few weeks later, in August, while reading *Woman's Weekly* on the sofa in the parlour, Eva had felt two hands suddenly settle on her shoulders. She had jumped. 'Grace! What do you want?'

'Stand up.'

Eva was too surprised to disobey.

'Now. I am going to stand behind you. Like this. And I want you to fall backwards so I can catch you. I need you to trust me. Just for this moment.' No doubt Grace saw Eva's shoulders stiffen, because she quickly added, 'You're leaving now, you've chosen your school, and we haven't really had much of a talk, have we? About what will happen when you go?'

'No.' Eva clenched her fist to her chest.

'The world is not a friendly place for people like us. We have to be careful not to let the mask slip. When we're excited, our Irish accents can come out. We're judged for that.'

Still Eva kept taut, lifting her chin slightly.

'You needn't shut me out, Eva. Just this once, let yourself be helped.'

There was something mesmerising about her voice. Eva let herself lean backwards.

'Further. Trust me.'

Eva leaned back further – and fell, hitting the floor with a thump on the tailbone. She exclaimed with pain, looked up and saw Grace glaring down, as if Eva had caused her offence.

'Let that be your first lesson. *Never trust anybody.*'

Eva gaped at her. Grace returned her astonishment with an elegant little moue. 'All right, so I tricked you. Don't be childish about it; those society girls aren't going to be any nicer. At least you now know what to expect.'

Slowly Eva rose from the floor. Her lower back was screaming. She was about to tell Grace exactly what she thought of her, but Grace held up a hand.

'The trouble with you, Eva, is that you're too reckless. And you know what happened the last time.' Without waiting for a reply, she exited the room with the same tight elegance with which she had entered it.

The memory of Grace's last salvo faded into the imperious hoot of the train as it pulled into Eastbourne station. Eva wasted no time in gathering her things and left the train without saying goodbye to her chaperone or even looking around to see where she might go. She was glad to be well shot of Mrs Stewart.

'Eva Downey?'

She turned to find herself face to face with an attractive, red-headed woman somewhere in her early forties. She wore a perfume Eva recognised, for Grace had the same one: a new variety called April Violets.

'Caroline Hedges. I trust you had an easy journey?' Without waiting for an answer, the woman held out her hand; her grip on Eva's fingers was soft but firm. The porter came from behind with Eva's bag. Miss Hedges made a gesture to him indicating 'outside' and said to Eva, 'Follow me.'

They made their way through the sunlit pavilion and out onto the street. The station entrance curved around a junction and at the far side a little clock tower chimed a quarter to five. Not far away, perhaps a mile off at most, Eva could sense the presence of the sea, could smell it in the air. Her anticipation only gathered pace when Miss Hedges stopped beside a small red motor car with a canopy and three wheels and indicated to the porter to bring Eva's suitcase separately; small though it was, it was still too big to fit into the space behind the seat. She leaned into the driver's seat and fetched a red checked scarf and motor hat from her glove compartment, beckoning Eva into the passenger seat as she fastened the scarf around her chin. Eva noticed that it smelled of April Violets too. Then she dragged the hat down on top of the scarf and dashed around to the rear to crank up the engine while Eva sat watching her, enthralled at the sight of a woman working a car, driving on the road.

'Oh, that's nothing,' Miss Hedges laughed, when Eva commented on her driving. 'We can do anything we want! I do encourage my pupils to bear that in mind. There is more than one way of finishing one's education these days. Did you know we teach mathematics? We are one of the only finishing schools in the country to do that.' Eva made a sound that was meant to convey polite admiration. 'Well, I'm glad you're sensible anyway. No retinue. You could nearly have fitted that case into the back of this little Carette. I thought when I saw that woman on the train with you—'

'Mrs Stewart?' Eva shuddered. 'She's my stepmother's friend.'

'So many of my girls think I'm going to put up their maids! It frightens me sometimes, to see them so ill equipped for life.'

Eva wanted to laugh. A maid? Her?

'It's hard,' Miss Hedges continued, shouting over the wind, 'to reconcile this sort of education with proper feminist principles. We do try to arrange alternatives for our less fortunate girls, who might not have the opportunity to marry.'

Oh, Eva thought, *she means me*.

'A decent career … teaching perhaps. Never did me any harm. Anyway, you've had the good fortune of enjoying this little trip,' Miss Hedges shouted, as the wind began to get up, 'since none of the other girls come in on the train. They all have private transport, so they'll be along later.'

Whereas I took the train because I'm poor.

As they left town, Miss Hedges accelerated along the country lanes. It was a bright evening after rain. Droplets on the windshield shone as the yellowing sun hit them, and trees whispered in the wind as they speeded past. Miss Hedges' hair blew out of her hat and scarf, while her attempts to make conversation were largely defeated by the rushing air and the noise of the engine behind them. Eva was too spellbound to speak much anyway. She allowed herself to feel the wind brushing past her cheek with an almost ecstatic pleasure.

They reached the school half an hour later. It was up a short, twisting driveway, a rather grand, white, two-storey house with a stern portico and a lawn out front that stretched for a good half an acre. Beyond that, a row of trees half concealed some sports pitches. On the far side, Eva could make out a whitewashed stone building, of the same height as the original house but longer, with its own entrance. This, Miss Hedges explained, contained dormitories and servants' quarters; beyond that were stables and outhouse buildings. These had been converted to classrooms; equitation was included on the curriculum but conducted off the premises.

'I bought the whole thing for a song back in 1907. It was a tumbledown wreck at the time. Some sort of artists' colony.' She did not say where she got the money from, and Eva knew better than to ask; she was already aware of being in a different world. In the six years of its operation, the headmistress continued, The Links could boast many distinguished former pupils in spite of its modest size and unpretentious rooms. *And here am I*, Eva thought, *a parvenue Irish girl with barely a spare penny to her name.*

A man came out onto the gravel driveway: Miss Hedges instructed him to take the car around the back, while she and Eva went inside. The hall was narrow and dark, with a limestone-tiled floor painted green and white, a colour scheme continued in the striped wallpaper. Eva guessed this was Miss Hedges' private quarters. Straight ahead, a small series of steps led down to the kitchen. On Eva's left was a row of coats on hooks. She reached out to touch one, a grey gabardine, brushing it ever so lightly with her fingertips. It released a smell of geraniums into the air. Her own coat, heavy on her shoulders, felt malodorous and shapeless in comparison.

'Miss Downey!' Miss Hedges called out.

Eva guiltily dropped her hand and went into the kitchen. A supper of thickly sliced bread with cheese and dripping was waiting for her, along with a mug of tea. Opposite, a place was set for Miss Hedges, with some cold meats and a small glass of white wine.

'Elderflower,' Miss Hedges said. 'From our gardens. Would you like to try some?'

'Oh, no, ma'am. I don't drink,' Eva answered, flustered.

'Oh, I think a sip just this once should be fine.' She extended the glass, and Eva took a cautious sip – then recoiled, the sharp taste jangling on her tongue and down her neck like a twisting corkscrew.

Miss Hedges took the glass away from her and smiled. 'Ah yes. Perhaps you are not quite ready to taste the sweetness of wine.' She finished the glass off herself with surprising speed. 'So, Eva Downey,' she said, when it was drained and set firmly back on the table, 'why here?'

The question caught Eva off guard. 'It was, er, on a list Lady Elizabeth Jenkins included in her will. She said you had a thorough understanding of the grounding needed for a modern woman. Lady Elizabeth was the one who—'

Miss Hedges cut her off. 'Oh, yes, I knew her, may she rest in peace.' She smiled with limited affection. 'Incorrigible old suffragette. You know her great-niece, Sybil Destouches, is here?'

'I didn't,' Eva said, surprised, 'but I've met her.'

The memory was all too sharp. Census Day, Sunday, 2 April 1911. The headiness of that glorious and endless summer, stretching from then to mid-October almost without a break. Just at the end of March, Eva had been out on a shopping trip with Catherine and Grace and had seen a young woman in the centre of Trafalgar Square in a navy corduroy skirt, waving her placard: 'Convicts, Lunatics, Women! All Three Have No Votes!' Her hoarse whisper of invitation in Eva's ear, while Catherine was trying to pull them away: 'History is happening here. Do you want to be part of it, or do you want to be a bystander all your life?'

Eva had persuaded Imelda, in spite of her rattling, lingering cough, to sneak out with her that evening on a clandestine journey to Richmond

Park, eleven miles and several changes on the Tube away from their home, to take part in a mass suffragette protest to evade the Census. They gathered across the road on Wimbledon Common to hear the woman from Trafalgar Square make a speech. Illuminated by lanterns suspended from a tent roof, she looked gaunt in the cheek, as if she lived off nothing but her own burning fervour. As Eva cheered with the crowd, stamping her feet and raising her arms to applaud, she felt as if she was on the edge of something new and exciting, something that would lift her out of the life she had known.

And then there had been the chance meeting that night with Lady Elizabeth Jenkins, that most singular of aged suffragettes, as Miss Hedges had already noted. Although she hardly knew Eva Downey from a hole in the ground, she had put her claw-like hand on Eva's shoulder and declared her in need of finishing, forthwith. 'There is something missing in you, an absence. It bothers me,' she had said. 'I'll see to it.' And then she had grumbled about how she could not get anyone to contribute to her suffragist magazine, not even one little article about skipping the Census. She looked disapprovingly over at her great-niece ... Yes, that had been Sybil.

Once supper was over, the headmistress brought Eva on a tour around the buildings, pointing out the classrooms, common room, sewing and music rooms and concluding at Eva's new dormitory. This contained six beds: as the newest pupil, Eva would have to sleep in the bed closest to the door. Even though the girls had not yet arrived, all their beds had been 'taken'.

Miss Hedges waited while Daisy, the maid, brought up Eva's case, then she handed her a mimeographed timetable and bade her goodnight.

For a moment, all was quiet except for creaks in the walls and floor-boards. Then, 'Halloo!' A voice rising up the stairs, then a sudden rush of footsteps, the door opening, the corridor light spilling in. The smell of cigarette smoke. The culprit leaning against the door jamb: a tall, hand-some girl of about Eva's own age, not in uniform, instead wearing a long, patterned, drop-waist dress. No sooner had their eyes met than the girl fished another cigarette out of her purse and bent close with the lighter. The flame caught her profile, then died out. The indoor light could not entirely dull the shade of the girl's hair, a far deeper and more magnificent red than Miss Hedges'. Eva recognised her immediately.

The smell of fresh smoke filled the room, pleasant for a few seconds before the inevitable staleness that followed. Sybil – for it was she – looked up, anxious. 'You're not going to tell on me, are you? I'll jolly well have to open the window or I'll get into ferocious trouble—'

Eva smiled. 'You don't remember me?'

Sybil took another drag and puffed out some smoke. 'Hold on. Oh, gosh, yes, I do! Richmond Park! My great-aunt took a shine to you, didn't she? Left you a bit in her will, I heard. Didn't leave me a bean, but she was generous enough to me when she was alive, God bless her. Besides, I didn't write naughty stories for her paper, and you did. Jolly good show.'

'I wanted to,' Eva said shyly.

'That's nice,' Sybil said, sounding somewhat doubtful. 'What's your name anyway, Evelyn, was it? I have a memory like a sieve.'

'Eva. Eva Downey.'

Sybil sat down on her bed, wrinkling her nose in some confusion. 'Downey ... Downey ... I'm sorry, who are your people?'

'You wouldn't know them. They came over from Ireland — that is to say, my father did, quite recently, and brought us with him.' Eva could feel her cheeks grow warm. Had Grace been right? Was it starting already?

'Ireland?' Sybil said. 'You have no trace of an accent at all.' She could not quite manage to keep her tone free of praise.

'I was not seven years old when we left Cork for good, so I would have very little of it left.' *And I work hard at suppressing the remnants.*

Sybil must have picked up the defensiveness in Eva's answer, because she shrugged and pulled on her cigarette again. 'I'm being cheeky, aren't I?' she said. 'I only meant to be curious. I like different backgrounds, you know. I get so tired of people harping on about ancestors and titles and all that nonsense. I mean, look at me. My blood is bluer than a field of cornflowers. We've been around, since, my goodness, Edward the First? Though, as far as I can remember, I think our entire lineage was only granted legitimacy because they offed the Duke of York and stuck his head on a pike. When was that, do you remember?'

Eva had no idea, but Sybil continued, 'And the worst part of it all is that everyone thinks we're French because I'm unlucky enough to be saddled with the last name "Destouches". It never occurs to them that my family go back far enough that *everyone* had French names. As it happens, I hate the French. They're so arrogant. Why, we were cycling around the Loire valley, and we stopped for a sandwich in the middle of the afternoon, and everything was shut. I could see the back of the kitchen, all the ingredients there, some bread, the most beautiful-looking goat's cheese. I said, "I'll make it myself, for Heaven's sake", but it was all, *Non, non, c'est fermé.* Oh, I do hate the French!' She stretched herself out the length of the bed, letting her booted feet dangle over the end, cigarette ash falling on the linoleum, just as footsteps and voices began to echo from the bottom of the stairs. 'You mustn't mind me,' she added, 'I do go on so. Mama says it gives her quite a headache.'

Eva let Sybil rattle on as she sat down on her own bed and pushed her suitcase underneath it. A bell clamoured down the corridor as the other girls joined them. They expressed a cursory interest in Eva before returning to their conversations. Another girl, in a uniform, walked up and down outside, the heavy bell in her hands. They would stand for prayer, then it would be lights out, according to the timetable.

Eva undressed carefully. The process of removing dress, corset, petticoat, flannel undershirt, stockings, combinations and finally underwear was tricky enough when done in private, and ten times worse in public. It seemed to take for ever, the fiddling, hooking, unhooking, secreting away the used linen. Finally, she donned a nightdress, which fell over her body like a billowing curtain. Usually Eva undressed in the dark, with only Imelda there, and she didn't have to worry about being seen, unlike now.

When they were all in their nightdresses, the girls all stood by their beds, leaving the door open to listen to the bell-ringer read a verse from *The Book of Common Prayer*. Then the thin curtains were drawn, the light turned out, and they got into bed. Eva rested her head on the thin pillow and looked at the faint light through the windows while the others settled into rhythmic breathing or light snores. It took her some time to follow them into sleep.

This is a new adventure, she thought, *and I must trust where it leads me.*

But during the night she had the old dream, the aftermath of that Census Day in 1911. The 'disgraceful behaviour'. The foul-tasting, mottled

24

ink of Lady Elizabeth's *New Feminist* got on her fingers, and the headline, 'A Jolly Night Out Hiding from the Census Man – by Miss E.M. Downey' turned into rivulets of black blood running down the paper and obscuring everything. Close by, her mother Angela, long dead, hummed lula-bye-byes, until Eva tried to look at her, come to her arms for safety – and then she fell into nothingness, blackest inky dark. The void roared, first a growl, low and indecipherable as a gale-force wind between buildings, then words: *Yehbitchyehbitchyehbitch! Bitseach!* Everything snapped into white, and in the midst of it was Grace, standing in a doorway, lips a precise, cranberry red, eyebrows arched with reproachful dismay. She was saying, 'Mama—'

Eva woke up in a thresh of sweat. Immediately the unfamiliar walls and windows of the dormitory crowded in on her, the sounds of the girls in slumber. She had to clap her hand to her mouth and bite her palm not to cry out. She brushed her eyes with the back of her hand. They were wet.

What had started that up again? It must have been Sybil, she concluded. Sybil, now lying on her back several feet away, sending light snores up to the ceiling. Meeting her must have raked over the coals.

She blinked and swallowed and waited for sleep. She would not weaken. She would not let them win.

2

The morning bell rang at six. From then on, the entire day's routine was mapped out: stripping the sheets and making one's bed, attending breakfast in a large room with a terracotta tiled floor and three long tables holding fifteen girls each as well as Miss Hedges and Miss Dunn, one of the teachers who lived in. Then Assembly, classes, lunch, more classes, followed by a brief pause in the afternoon, before study period and supper. Eva's first breakfast was a watery porridge with prunes; her lunch fatty beef and white, crumbly overboiled potatoes; at mid-afternoon, she had a cup of strong, stewed tea and sweetened bread. All the days were like this, book-marked and bookended by bells.

The classes included such subjects as domestic economy (how to control servants and balance books), posture and deportment, needlework, private music lessons for those who had requested them (inept chromatic piano scales, the thin soup of notes scraped on the wrong end of a violin bow and English sea-shanties shrieking from treble recorders echoed around the corridors most of the school day), English language and literature, French and, to Eva's initial alarm, equitation etiquette. This last was supervised by Miss Alethea Walton with the help of Mr Duncan, a rotund, taciturn man who wore belt, braces and a wide-brimmed hat. Mr Duncan also taught the much-vaunted mathematics and tended to look down at the ground when talking to women. Much to Eva's relief, she was not introduced to any actual horses, nor made to ride side-saddle. She was quite sure she would have fallen off.

It also became clear that for all Miss Hedges' emancipated principles, some of the forty-five girls under her care were treated with a more gloved hand than others. Eva herself suffered no penalty for having attained her place by gift rather than birthright, but then again she would never have taken the risks some of her higher-born fellow pupils seemed to run with impunity. She guessed that a spinster, even one as comfortably off as Miss Hedges, probably needed the business.

Since her arrival, she had been writing to Imelda at least once a week. Nothing had been done for her sister, no further education, not even some sort of training in case she didn't marry. Imelda had a weak constitution, so was left to languish at home. That she was Angela's daughter and not Catherine's did not help her cause. Eva burned with rage inside but could not write what she wanted; the letters were all examined before being passed on.

'I try to be Helen Burns,' Imelda wrote to her, a fortnight after Eva's arrival at The Links, 'given my general health. I find it helps to maintain that higher viewpoint, to trust in God and ignore more everyday inconveniences.'

'You would be better off as Jane Eyre,' Eva replied in brutal panic. 'Remember what happened to Helen.'

Both knew that Catherine would not understand the reference.

*

'Is French the only language on the curriculum?' Eva asked Miss Hedges a few weeks later when Assembly was over and students were invited to 'freely ask any questions'.

'Would you like to learn another language, Miss Downey?' Miss Hedges replied, pleasantly enough. 'Latin?'

Rhona Lewis, chiefly known as the daughter of Sir Evelyn Lewis, Marquess of Onslow, who had gone out to the Sylhet tea plantations in 1889 and had come back with a fortune which he had wasted no time in wasting on his daughter, arched her eyebrows to the fringe of her bob. 'French is the language of commerce and etiquette. It is useful and attractive to the ear. You're hardly suggesting we learn Irish?' That sort of question would have earned Eva a clip round the ear from her father, but Miss Hedges did not appear to be unduly disturbed by Rhona's insolence. The question was barbed enough; rumours of Eva's background had already begun to circulate. Sometimes, when she got excited, her accent would slip, the vowels becoming broader, the 't's softer. Grace had had a point.

'I was thinking of German, actually.'

The room fell silent.

'Really?' Miss Hedges said, in a less sympathetic tone.

'The language of Goethe, Heine, Beethoven? I cannot imagine I am the only one who should like to learn it.' Eva's voice sounded odd, too high-pitched. Trying too hard not to sound Irish was strangling her.

'You're forgetting that nobody likes to learn anything in this place except you, you strange little person,' muttered Sybil.

'Well,' Miss Hedges said, after a long moment, 'I must admire your studious spirit, Miss Downey. Of course we always seek to retain friendly relations with the Kaiser's country. Miss Hautbois, in addition to being a native French speaker, is also fluent in German. I shall speak to her about taking you for classes twice a week during the four o'clock break.'

Rhona sniggered at the idea of losing a free period. It did not occur to her that Eva was perfectly happy to not spend her spare time in the company of the other girls.

Sybil was not convinced either. 'What's with all this learning German malarkey?' she asked Eva later, when they were taking a walk around the front lawn. It was forbidden for students to walk there during the evening, a rule Sybil strictly honoured in the breach rather than the observance.

'I just thought it would be a nice idea. My mother had sheet music of Schubert's *Lieder* before it got … lost.' 'Lost' was one way of putting it. Eva knew all too well what had happened to the music; it had long ago met the same fate as everything else that had belonged to her mother. Including the piano. She would never forget seeing the gap in their once warm, friendly sitting room in Cork all those years ago after it had been taken away, barely a week after her mother's death.

'I don't read the newspapers, because it's all too depressing,' Sybil continued, 'but even I know there's a lot of tension with Germany. That's why we've to hurry up and bag the rich men, you see, before they all get called up.'

'I don't think there'll be a war,' Eva said.

'Well,' Sybil said, 'War or no war, I dare say your father is hoping you'll find yourself a rich man and get out of his hair.'

'I don't know any rich men.'

'I could help you meet some. Before it all kicks off.'

'Don't say there'll be a war.' Eva knotted her fingers and looked off down the path. She could see pear trees in the distance, the still-green pears hanging on the branches, ready for harvesting.

'Oh, I don't know,' Sybil said. 'I'm rather looking forward to one myself. There's nothing nicer than a man in uniform, don't you think? And somebody has to stop those Huns. They're building ships like there's no tomorrow.'

'They're entitled to defend themselves.'

'They'll be well defended at the rate they're going,' Sybil said caustically. 'My uncle Ferdy is prospecting out near Nairobi, and he isn't happy about it at all. He's written to my mother about it, and she insists on reading me the letters down the blower. He reckons they want to grab more of Africa. But we'll show 'em. We're building dreadnoughts to beat the band! Oh, *cave!*'

This last injunction was caused by the appearance of Miss Dunn, their religious instructor, a thickset woman with small eyes and greying mousy hair in a blunt cut. She waddled exasperatedly down the path, on the *qui vive* for anyone who might be out of bounds. Eva heeded Sybil's warning and followed her behind a laurel bush. She had suffered too often Miss Dunn's particular trick of flicking a leather bookmark on a girl's cheek. A minor assault, but it stung awhile. Sybil said that Miss Hedges used Miss Dunn to keep the girls in line because she couldn't bear not to be popular.

They completed their circuit by heading down to the netball courts. Sybil made it a point of honour never to play if she could help it. When she did, she always managed to be near the net, where she would allow through as many shots as possible, in spite of the shouts of protest from the games mistress. This made all the girls cheer. Half the class, it would appear, had a crush on Sybil – and the other half wanted to be her. Eva decided to cultivate her friendship. In a place like this, it would not hurt to have an ally.

Of all her classes, Eva's favourite was the twice-weekly 'English Literature'. The teacher, Mr Shandlin, was borrowed from the boys' preparatory five miles up the road. He was a slender and rather unkempt man, with a high, domed forehead and fine, flyaway dark hair, who fidgeted endlessly. He was possessed of a brusque manner and could be sarcastic, coming out with remarks like, 'I'm sure many of you think you are the Faerie Queene; my question was has anyone *read* it?' Sybil once declared to Eva that he must have owned no more than two suits and that she had never had occasion to see the second.

Eva had not read *The Faerie Queene*, but something mocking in his question provoked her, and she borrowed a copy from the library. Much of it dragged, but she could not help but be endeared by Britomart the female knight, who fought for Artegall and liberated him. Then she read a little bit about Edmund Spenser, its author, and was disappointed. He appeared a sneering, contemptuous sort, who believed that Ireland would never be pacified until its language and culture were destroyed. A long-suppressed loyalty sprang up in Eva's heart, and she mentioned it in class without prompting. 'Mr Shandlin, this poem – *The Faerie Queene*.'

Mr Shandlin raised his eyebrows. 'You have read it? Let me tell you, Miss … ah, Downey, that would be a first.'

'Sir, I want to know why we are reading the work of a man who advocates the eradication of an entire race. I'm talking about Ireland,' she continued, as Mr Shandlin looked ever more incredulous. 'Irish monks kept

Europe alive through the Dark Ages when Mr Spenser's race were still living in huts and fighting with clubs!'

A murmur of dissent began making the rounds. 'She's not got any call telling us we live in huts!' one girl cried, and soon all was mayhem, everyone shouting at Eva, including Sybil, while Mr Shandlin leaned on the edge of his desk, arms folded, regarding them all with a half-smile.

It was not long before Miss Hedges came sprinting down the corridor and launched into the room. 'Girls!' Immediate silence fell. She looked icily at the teacher. 'Mr Shandlin, perhaps you could demonstrate the correct manner of seating for the benefit of these ladies?'

Mr Shandlin, with a huge sigh, got off the table and sat down in his chair, keeping his posture as slovenly as possible. Some of the girls tittered at his defiance. Miss Hedges left, but all was in disarray, and Mr Shandlin dismissed them.

'I'm sorry,' Eva said dismally as she shuffled past him on her way out. 'I ruined your class.'

Mr Shandlin broke into an unexpected grin. 'Oh, don't be. You're the first person in this school who has expressed the slightest interest in anything other than being fattened for the altar. Try to get out of here, if you can manage it at all.'

'I can't,' Eva said. 'I was lucky to get in here in the first place.'

'You never know,' said Mr Shandlin, and he looked like he was about to say more, but there was a knot of girls behind Eva, poking her in the back, and she had no choice but to murmur a goodbye and move on.

Rhona Lewis cornered her later that evening. She followed Eva to the dormitory, where Eva had gone to retrieve her copy of Sturm's translations of Baudelaire, and she and her friends circled Eva's bed. 'I always knew there was something about you,' she said. 'Never telling us your background and always so careful with your accent. I could tell you were a bit fishy.' She wrinkled her nose. 'I'm not impressed, Downey.'

'I don't care whether you're impressed or not,' Eva retorted with some spirit.

Rhona's smile got thinner and wider until she was a Cheshire Cat in the middle of the room. 'Do you find it very different here, after all the potatoes and boiled cabbage you'd get back home? Oh, look, she's pretending to read. Pretending we're not here.'

Eva said nothing. Baudelaire's poor swan dragged its broken wing around the streets of Paris. Like the swan, she knew when she was outnumbered. She put the book down.

'Then again, perhaps you'd prefer some whiskey. Do your parents drink much of the stuff? Do they fall down at night?'

'You're being ridiculous,' Eva said, trying to sound solid, but her voice was full of doubt and Rhona heard it.

'Really. I don't see anyone else here thinking I'm ridiculous.'

'Sybil would, if she were here.'

'Oh, yes,' Rhona said, in a sing-song voice, 'run to Lady Muck and hide under her skirts. You could be her maid. Irish girls make very good maids when they're of a mind to do as they're told. My mother had one once, but we had to dismiss her because she *drank*.'

Eva flushed and balled her fists by her sides. If she were involved in a fight, chances were Miss Hedges would not take her side; indeed, she might expel her. Besides, she did not want to give Rhona Lewis the satisfaction of thinking that all Irish girls were thick peasants who knew no better than to lash out. But that only prompted Rhona and her cronies to try and rile her for a long time after that, only stopping when Sybil came back into the room. They kept quiet when she was there, oddly enough.

'You did bring it on yourself, you know,' Sybil told her at lunch the following day. 'You didn't have to show off and blather about Edmund bloody Spenser. It's not done to be too clever around here.'

'So I've noticed,' Eva said. 'You would think those people were eight, not eighteen.'

'You can tell them that till you're blue in the face, darling, and play Miss Superior, but there is only a limited amount I can do to help you if you insist on digging yourself into a hole.'

Eva nodded miserably. She could tell that Sybil was beginning to lose patience with her. She was beginning to lose patience with herself too. She put her hands into her smock pockets and looked down at the plain, wooden table.

'Oh, don't take on so,' Sybil said. 'They'll get bored soon enough. The clock's on already.'

'The clock?'

'Countdown to marriage. One o'clock, two o'clock, three – by the time the small hand hits six, it's ding, ding, ding, ding, ding, wifey! This place is a huddle of spinsters manufacturing wives, nothing more.'

'Spinsters? Are none of the teachers married?' Eva asked, grateful for the chance to change the subject.

'Almost none,' Sybil answered. 'Miss Hedges certainly isn't, as you know. Bit of a die-hard women's-rights person, or so she says. I'm not convinced.

I think Miss Dunn was once, but her husband died. If I had to live with her, I'd die too.'

'And the men? Do they have wives?'

'No, neither Mr Shandlin nor Mr Duncan. Mind you, we all know why Mr Duncan isn't married.'

Eva contemplated the round-faced Mr Duncan with some puzzlement. 'Well, he is no Adonis, but plainer men than he have married perfectly happily.'

'He's not the marrying kind, Eva.'

Eva looked at her, nonplussed.

'Oh, for goodness' sake,' Sybil hissed, 'he's an invert.'

'You mean he likes standing on his head?'

'Eva,' Sybil said, putting an arm around her shoulders, 'we need to talk.' Then she whispered into Eva's ear so none of their lunch companions could overhear.

'All right,' Eva said after she had finished whispering. 'I think I understand. So an invert is a man who falls in love with a man, or a woman with a woman—'

'Keep your voice down! Yes. That's it. Though it's very rare for women. Usually it's men – and please don't say it aloud about Mr Duncan, he could go to prison. Eva, what were you told about life? My mother wasn't much use, I grant you, but I had a wonderful nanny. Told me and Bo everything.'

'Bo?'

'George. My brother. Though I've never called him that, and he never calls me Sybil. To him I'm Pinkie.'

Eva looked at Sybil. She could have been a model for Ophelia in the Millais painting. 'Pinkie?'

'Obviously,' Sybil said. She looked offended, so Eva quickly said, 'Of course. But back to this invert business. Mr Duncan is one, you say. And Mr Shandlin, is he … ?'

'Shandlin? You must be joking!' Sybil laughed. 'He likes girls all right, I'd say, he just doesn't have enough money to marry one.'

'But does he not earn from his teaching?'

Sybil laughed, sweet and low. 'Not enough for someone respectable, dear.'

'I suppose a house and servants and all that does cost quite a lot,' Eva agreed, 'and the function of this place is to make us worthy of a man's paying for it.'

'Now you have it, Eva,' said Sybil approvingly. 'You're learning fast.'

3

November 1913

When the knock on the study door came, Roy Downey was sorely tempted to swear aloud. It was never any of their four servants; he had them well trained by now. No, the cranky little rap-rap-rap was always Catherine, pestering him about something trivial. Why did she do it, especially when he was so preoccupied with his clients in Ireland? He had built up a good accountancy practice in Cork, Downey & Collins, just off Church Street – and for Catherine's sake he had abandoned it all. One would think she would be more understanding.

Just that morning, McGowan, his Munster agent, had written to him warning that whatever monies he would lose due to the Land Bill's hobbling his clients would be further compounded now that the Volunteers were organising in Limerick, 'not to mention that seditious fellow Casement, with his false knighthood'. McGowan was always fluent with bad news but stagnant as the Regent's Canal at Congreve's broken lock when it came to the other kind, and his long epistolary wails drove Roy to distraction.

The door creaked open.

'What is it, Catherine? Can't you see I'm busy?'

She charged in, paying no attention to his choleric glare. 'There!' she cried, placing a letter on his desk.

'What? Am I to read this?'

'No, ye've to frame it and put it on yer wall! Of course ye're to read it!'

'You were here half an hour ago and not a word about this.'

'It came on the evening post. He has written again! He's received no answer for months now, and 'tis not on, sir.' Her face was red from being out of breath, her cheeks pink and showing the first signs of broken veins. It was those cheeks that had first endeared her to him, the way they flared with high colour when he looked at her a certain way. Her hair bound back in a strict, mousy bun, her Irish beauty, her combination of modesty and emotion – all these had undone something in him in those terrible months after Angela's death.

But her calling him 'sir' brought back too many memories. Memories of her attending both him and Angela as they sat in their drawing room back in Cork, he taking his cigar and Angela tea. Angela had died of typhoid fever in 1902; it had been long and drawn out. He had married Catherine soon afterwards. She had been poor, proud and Protestant, the widow of a butler called Nelius Connolly, with a daughter, Grace, the same age as his Eva, who had taken Angela's death particularly hard.

His sudden passion for his late wife's maid had been the one irregularity of Roy's life, causing enough scandal for him to decide to leave Cork on the night of their marriage, all three daughters in tow, none at the age of reason – and just in time, for things had gone to hell in a handbasket in Ireland since then.

He took the paper out of the open envelope, which was postmarked Limerick. It was folded into quarters, bulging uncomfortably in its pouch. The handwriting was square and unformed. Roy caught sight of the signature, 'Joseph Cronin', and sighed.

'Is this Eva's fellow? Am I to understand they're still corresponding?'

Just six months ago, in this very study, he had interrogated Eva about Mr Cronin's proposal, after much nagging from Catherine. All that morning it had been promising rain and finally the heavens had broken. Eva was silent: the room betrayed no sound but the scratch of his pen, the rather stertorous rattle of his inward breath (he was spoiling for a cold), the hard attack of rain on the long, narrow, churchlike windows and the occasional protesting crackle of a damp log on the fire. Strange, on recollection, to have it burning in midsummer, but there was a chill in that north-facing front room that could not be dispersed.

'I hear,' he said at last, folding the paper he had been scribbling on and putting down his pen, 'you have decided not to accept Mr Cronin's offer of marriage.'

'Yes, Papa.'

'Hmmm,' Roy said 'And what made you decide to refuse him? It is a big thing, you know, for a man to declare himself.'

'He seemed too old, Papa.'

'He is, what … ten years older? Hardly excessive, I would think.'

'Fourteen,' Eva corrected him.

'What?'

'He is fourteen years older.'

Roy opened a drawer and pulled out his pipe. 'Ten, fourteen, what matter? He seems well able to provide for you. A good job, clerk with the Waterford and Limerick Railway … what is missing?' In reality, he knew well what was missing. Joseph Cronin was a friend of Catherine's cousin Fred, and both men would occasionally come to visit them in London. Roy had seen enough of Cronin to be unable to fathom his wife's attachment: his glaucous, stained coat, the sound he made with his lips and tongue when he was eating something, the slow, high-pitched, grating way he spoke, as if he were perpetually on the verge of making a complaint to the deputy stationmaster of a provincial railway about a timetable mishap. Roy could not claim to know his second daughter well, but even he could see this fellow was not a match for Eva.

Besides, he was Catholic – as Catherine's forebears had been, but in the forties it was take the soup or starve, so they had converted to Protestantism for convenience. On his second marriage, keeping London society in mind, Roy had found it politic to follow suit and convert his daughters with him. Imelda's embarrassingly Romish name was the only reminder of their past.

Not that it had done much good. Catherine, for all her determination, had not mixed well. Occasionally Roy felt guilty for lifting her up socially as for all her protestations it was obvious she was not comfortable with her new status. On other occasions he felt irritated that she could not make more of an effort. Why was she so bent on matching Eva and Cronin? Because determined she was.

'He's writin' an' writin' and not a word out of her.'

Roy winced; he hated when she dropped her 'g's.

'Catherine, I wrote her refusal to him six months ago. In God's name, why are we even having this discussion?'

'Because she's not one to be saying no to a decent man.' Catherine went from pink to red. 'I have to be balancin' – balancing – the accounts, and keeping her on is expensive. She should be well married by now.'

40

'She's barely seventeen,' Roy said, 'and we're not keeping her. She's not even here!'

'No, she's not, is she?' Catherine was not to be headed off at the pass. 'She's off gallivanting in that finishing school when it should be our Grace!'

Roy put his head on his steepled hands, felt his own sweaty fingertips press on his brow. He should have known. 'We have discussed this already, Catherine.'

And they had. *Ad nauseam.* Ever since Eva had left for that school, Catherine's every gesture, her constant interruptions, the way she clattered angrily through a room without touching anything in it, had indicated her displeasure. Through trickery and bad behaviour, she declared, Eva had been rewarded with a legacy to a finishing school while Grace, Catherine's natural daughter, whose behaviour was unimpeachable, had not. As long as Eva was being finished and Grace was at home, he would never know a moment's peace. He made a palms-up gesture of defeat to Catherine. Eva's behaviour, not just consorting with the suffragettes but *writing* about it, had disgusted him as much as it had Catherine, but the funding had not been his, so he'd had little power to stop her. 'It's a matter of chance. That's all.'

'Well,' Catherine replied, her face now bloodless, 'if Grace has to sub-mit to this, it's only right that Eva marry Joseph. That'll be her "finishing". I'll see it happen, mark my words. I'll break her, if it's the last thing I do!'

Roy sat upright at that. 'You be careful,' he said, alarm flaring his unsmiling features, 'it's illegal to cause injury to a minor nowadays. I'm not having the police come around. Not after the last time.'

Catherine folded her hands in front of her, and once more Roy saw her in her former servitude, with all its false compliance, its eagerness to please that had once beguiled and now trapped him. Her eyes, once green and luminous and sharply reckoning, now looked like dried elderberries. When she spoke, it sounded far away. 'Illegal *now*, yes.'

When she left the room, he lit his pipe, warm relief flowing through him with the first inhalation of bitter tar. By God, these days he needed it more than ever.

4

As the months passed, Eva got used to some aspects of life in The Links, like the mediocre food and the custom of spending an entire class walking across a room with a book balanced on her head. Deportment was a thing with Miss Hedges. She took it very seriously. Imagine a fine string, she would say, suspended from a height, by which the back of your neck and spine should hang, in a long, graceful line. Imagine you are Coppélia, the doll in the window. Adopt that stance every time you enter a room and when you cross it, and men would respond to that inner grace. Eva, who had thought Miss Hedges a feminist, and who more often than not would find the book sliding off her head and hitting the floor with a thump, took a while to become accustomed to remarks like that. But if other girls' fathers paid seventy pounds a year to have their daughters do this, it must work …

What she couldn't get used to was the nonchalance of the girls around their teachers; girls like Ada Barton and Rhona Lewis appeared to delight in responding lackadaisically and without respect. It felt wrong to stay seated and only rise at the last moment when a teacher entered the room. One rainy January afternoon, in Mr Shandlin's class, she forgot to be like the others; she leapt to her feet the minute he somewhat belatedly rushed in, his collar looser than decorum advised, flinging his damp coat on the hook. A brace of titters immediately followed in her wake, and Eva sat back down, red-faced, feeling like an utter fool.

'Good afternoon, ladies,' said Mr Shandlin. 'Nice to know at least one of you is glad to see me.' Eva could happily have throttled him. 'Now. The Tennyson. Page thirty-four.' The class groaned, as they had groaned their way through Shakespeare, Milton, Dryden and the Romantics. One time – it might have been during *Paradise Lost* – Sybil had so irritated Mr Shandlin that he had shouted at her, 'Tell me, Miss Destouches, does it take diligent practice to become this stupid? For I refuse to believe you were born that way.' Today, he merely shrugged and muttered, 'Pearls before swine.'

For some perverse reason, he asked Ada Barton to read out the poem he had chosen, 'In Memoriam A.H.H.' It was sad and beautiful, mourning the loss of a friend … and Ada killed it stone dead. She read the verses in monotone while every now and then Mr Shandlin would interrupt to ask questions, the rest of the time balancing on the edge of his desk, grabbing onto the edge with his hands, his feet dangling. He did not look like the type to respond to inner grace, or even to know what it looked like.

He tolerated Ada's recital until she reached, 'The sad mechanic exercise, / Like dull narcotics, numbing pain', perhaps because the words came too close to the truth, finally cutting her off with a 'Thank you, Miss Barton', and Eva thought he would add, 'you have delighted us long enough', like Mr Bennet in *Pride and Prejudice*. That was followed by a brief attempt to discuss last week's reading of *The Mayor of Casterbridge*, an assay that met with obdurate silence. Eva had an opinion, or several, but was not going to speak up; she had learnt her lesson from the Edmund Spenser debacle.

'All right,' Mr Shandlin sighed, evidently giving up, 'let's discuss your task for next week. Keeping to our late-last-century novelists, is anyone here acquainted with the work of Count Tolstoy?'

Eva started to put up her hand but stopped herself and put it down again. The rest of the class did not move.

'Miss Downey?'

'Er … no, sir,' Eva lied. 'I've never read anything by him.'

'Quite.' Mr Shandlin smiled and did not pursue the point. 'For those of you not familiar with Tolstoy, which may or may not include Miss Downey, I would like you to read this', and he handed out mimeographed sheets to the class. 'It is a short story by the very gentleman himself, titled "What Men Live By".'

Sybil picked it up and looked at it, unimpressed. 'What sort of question is that, Mr Shandlin?'

'It's not a question, Miss Destouches, it's a moral. You can answer it nevertheless, in no fewer than a thousand words, for this time next week.'

'Aw, Mr Shandlin.'

'Sir, we've a heap to do.'

'You seem to think I have no knowledge of your timetables,' Mr Shandlin said drily. 'I'm fully aware of how much you have to do, which is remarkably little.'

A rumble of protest rose, which he quelled by raising his hand. 'One more thing: when you squeeze a little time in between your incredibly busy schedules to write, tell me what you think. Be honest. Because it's no fun for me to go home in the evenings and read the same predigested stuff fifteen times. So, original thought, I beg you. Please.'

Rhona Lewis shot up her hand.

'Sir, I should like to tell you what *I* think.'

'Please go on, Miss Lewis,' said Mr Shandlin, with a heavy sigh.

'Sir, this class is English Literature. That's what I was expecting when I read the prospectus. I don't understand why foreign authors should be included. Surely you've made a mistake?'

Eva nearly gasped aloud. Even for Rhona Lewis, that was rude. Mr Shandlin looked taken aback too, so much so that he did not respond immediately but put his forehead in his hands for a moment. 'Because,' he said at length, starting to pace up and down the room, 'Because … should you find yourself, Miss Lewis, some time from now, in a large, well-appointed drawing room, wearing whatever elaborate, gaudy outfit best fits your purpose, and a landed Russian count crosses the floor, captivated by the sight of you, and you strike up a conversation, then in the train of that conversation you are asked, "What do you think of our great master Tolstoy?" and you look at him with sheep-like eyes and reply blankly, "I have never heard of him", and he says, "What about Lermontov? Pushkin? Chekhov?" and you say, sweet as a doe, "I have never heard of any of them either", and his face shuts down, he pleads his excuses and moves on to someone else, thereby ending with a stroke your hope of wearing furs in the snow, riding in a *droshky* and being presented to the Tsar, when that moment happens, Miss Lewis, you will not be able to turn around and blame this establishment, or my teaching. Does that answer satisfy you?'

Another pause, as long as death. It was as if every girl in the room were holding her breath. Eva had to suppress the urge to laugh. Sybil winked at her.

'Yes, Mr Shandlin,' Rhona said at length, in a small voice.

'Good. I'll look forward to hearing your thoughts on the topic, Miss Lewis. One thousand words, remember.'

The clang-clang-clang of the bell rippled down the narrow corridors and around every corner of the building. It was time to change class again.

'Good golly,' Sybil said afterwards, 'that was some speech. I have to warn you. Don't ever get old Shandy into a bad mood, Eva. He'll chew you up and spit you out, just like he did right there.'

'Oh, don't you worry,' Eva said. 'He won't know I exist. I plan to stay as invisible as possible from now on.'

Tell me what you think, Mr Shandlin had said. Eva sat in the small, cold library, far away from everyone else, shawl around her shoulders and clasped at the front by a brooch, pen hovering over the blank page, pink-shaded kerosene lamp lit, ankles crossed and feet entangled with the legs of her chair.

Since the beginning of term, she had written hundreds of words, thousands, but never once had she revealed what she thought about anything. Sybil was surely right; it was better that way. Mr Shandlin's request was nothing more than a trap, like all the other ones strewn in her way over the years. If she did tell the truth, if she did open her heart, she knew one thing from experience: she would pay for it handsomely.

The fracture in her arm had healed awkwardly. It was as though the limb held the memory of what had happened, even three years on. Writing got you into that mess, it reminded her, sending bolts of white pain through her arm to reinforce its message, and writing won't get you out of it. Imelda had warned her not to write that article about the Census and their illicit night on Wimbledon Common. Eva had ignored her and had written 'A Jolly Night

Out Hiding from the Census Man' for Lady Elizabeth Jenkins, and look what had happened. Even now she was having nightmares about it.

She thought, *Send him back the usual pieties and be done with it.*

But was she to be silent all her life? She supposed so, sighing and pulling down R. H. Benson's book of religious essays to find a suitable quote so that she could write an unexceptionable piece, like all the ones she had written before. And put down her pen before she had even started. It just would not do. He had got to her.

'Damn it,' she said to the empty room. Then, to him, absent: 'You asked me to do this. So don't come shouting at me if you don't like the consequences.'

So, one thousand words of honest thought about what men live by. Never mind that she wasn't even a man. Had that not occurred to Mr Shandlin when he had assigned the topic? Well, it would jolly well have occurred to him by the time she was finished! She pulled out a few foolscap sheets, abandoned the pen she was using and took up her favourite fountain pen, the one that made writing flow well but that got ink all over her fingers. Then, at the top of the first page, she wrote, 'What Men Live By' and sat for a while.

Then she added: 'Not by higher principles, that's for sure.'

And then she wrote. She wrote about Nietzsche, the Nihilists who lived for nothing, Disraeli's reforms, Gladstone's evangelising and, of course, Tolstoy, that embittered aristocrat who loved peasants in an abstract sense but hated his wife. She wrote sentences that were the length of paragraphs, with clauses unfurling like flags on a ship. She wrote without caring, hardly even stopping, her arm hurting at first, the pain hitting a high threshold and then miraculously abating even though she was cramping her wrist, she was writing so fast. And still she had only reached seven hundred and fifty words, by the reckoning of an inky finger counting down the lines. She was just about to cross out a sentence rejecting the existence of God when bells rang up and down the corridors, announcing supper.

She washed her hands and wandered into the refectory, dazed and elsewhere and joined in the collective 'For what we are about to receive' and received it without complaint, regardless of taste or quality. She had no idea what the other girls were talking about, hardly knew they were there. She could not wait to get back to the library.

After supper, looking over the essay, Eva decided to leave that last sentence just as it was. If it offended Mr Shandlin's fine sensibilities, he would have to lump it; he, after all, had chosen the topic. But after that spirited comment, she felt herself grind once again to a full stop. She realised why very quickly: her next paragraph was going to refer to the act, to how a man and a woman consummated their marriage.

Sybil was right: she really knew nothing. Thanks to some quick reading and Imelda's explanations, she understood what her menstrual periods signified. But the rest of it all seemed so theoretical. Apart from a warm confusion Eva sometimes felt around her father's friends, with their greatcoats and moustaches and oaky smell, or the boys in the Christian fellowship Imelda used to attend, she knew nothing of what happened between women and men. What could she write? And was it wise at all, to write about such things?

Tell me what you think, he had said.

And she had. There was no going back now.

By the time the rest of the girls started their essays – a day before they were due – Eva's was finished, drafted and edited. Seven hundred words too long, but it would have to do.

After she had handed it in, she began to feel some delayed shock at what she had done. Her heart knocked about in her chest, and she was almost tempted to sprint down the corridor after Mr Shandlin's retreating back and flag him down before it was too late. She wondered if on receipt of her essay he would complain to Miss Hedges about its content, and if the headmistress would expel her. Her mind went wild with melodramatic scenarios. But there was no point in worrying. *Alea jacta est*; the die was cast.

Eva told Sybil about her misgivings, but Sybil was sanguine and did not seem to think there was any risk. Eva, however, remained agitated for the rest of the afternoon, much to Sybil's annoyance. 'You're like an India-rubber ball today,' she complained, as they finished prayers. 'Bounce, bounce, bounce.'

'Sorry,' Eva said.

'You're so preoccupied you haven't even noticed I'm upset.' It was true; Sybil looked uncharacteristically distressed.

Eva felt immediately guilty. 'What's happened?'

'My brother's joined up.' Sybil was grim.

'In the Army?'

Sybil nodded. 'He's going to the Officer Training Corps at the moment and hopes to be in the 3rd Royal Worcesters by summer.'

'Hasn't he always wanted to be a soldier?'

Sybil shook her head. 'Oh, not he. Bo wouldn't fight a wet sheet on a clothes line. He's only going because he thinks there'll be trouble and it's his duty to get involved. Oh, Evie, I'm terribly anxious.'

Eva put her arm around Sybil's shoulders. 'Nobody's fighting, though, Syb. You're worrying too much about something that might never happen.'

Sybil sighed. 'You're probably right. But it's just so out of character for him. My mother is going out of her wits. She's trying to get me to change his mind. As if he'd listen to me! This is all my fault. There was I, wittering on about fighting the Hun and our great Navy and the dreadnoughts … I wish to God I'd kept my silly mouth shut.' She looked anguished.

'It'll be all right, Sybil,' Eva soothed, at a loss for anything else to say.

Sybil heaved herself to her feet. 'You're quite right. I'm worrying over nothing. I don't know why, but I get the jitters thinking of all this war stuff. How about you, Evie? You're not still worried about that silly essay, are you?'

Eva said nothing. After Sybil's confidences, she felt foolish.

'Come on,' Sybil said affectionately, 'even if you have written the most frightful rubbish, Mr Shandlin isn't going to tell on you. He likes you, as far as I can tell. Now why don't we talk about something nice?' And with the dexterity of a true aristocrat, she manoeuvred the conversation onto the botany walk they were due to take the following day. Eva was happy to follow her lead.

5

Mr Shandlin's class was in the afternoon. Then Eva would know for better or worse. More than once during the morning she jabbed a needle into her left index finger while embroidering a peacock into a tapestry. She did not want to think about black and turquoise threads for the eyes of the tail. She just wanted to get the day over with.

She arrived early for the afternoon class and made sure she was sitting down low in her seat. If she could have, she would have made herself invisible. Mr Shandlin arranged for the essays to be handed out first thing. 'I think you will find,' he announced to the class, 'there are gaps in discursive thinking and writing skills that some of you might need to cover, but, overall, an adequate effort. Now, I believe we have some further work to do on Hardy, so can we resume at our last point where, if I recall correctly, Mr Henchard's marital life is about to get somewhat complicated?'

Eva ignored his instruction and instead turned the pages of her essay, her chest constricting with excitement and fear. She looked at the start, the margins, then at the end. Nothing. No comments, no circles in red ink, just a quick scribbling of the date at the end. She swallowed, tasting sulphur. All around her, others were turning pages. She could see red marks, spelling corrections, elaborate comments in the margins. But nothing on hers, even though she looked, and looked again.

The disappointment was overwhelming. She wasn't even scared any more, not now. Bitter tears of rage simmered in the corners of her eyes.

'Miss Downey, could you open the book, please?'

'But—' Eva began.

'Now, please, Miss Downey,' Mr Shandlin said, looking even more bored than usual.

Eva felt that rage would overpower her. This was not fair. For the second time in her life, she had taken a great risk. She had put everything into that essay and he had just – dismissed it. And her.

She opened her book, flicking and rustling the pages. She considered ripping them out and throwing them in the air. That Mr Shandlin, he really didn't care about any of his students. He was just doing it for the extra money; he thought they were all fools, rich, ignorant fillies. 'Pearls before swine' indeed! Well, she wasn't a pig! Eva breathed noisily and furiously. To hell with him if he heard her. *To hell with him, to hell with him, to hell with them all!*

How long that half hour seemed to last, how relentlessly the Mayor of Casterbridge headed for perdition while Eva sat and seethed. Finally, the bell once more. Thank God, now she could go. She would not show her feelings here, in front of that man.

But as she jerked her chair backwards, a perceptible shadow fell over her desk. 'Miss Downey.'

'What?' Eva, shocked, forgot her manners. Half standing, she stared up at Mr Shandlin, her heart beating wildly. She could barely make out Sybil in the background, eyes wide with alarm.

'I was wondering if I could have a word with you before your next class.'

'I'm sorry, sir. Yes, of course.'

'This …', picking up the pages from her desk and tapping them with his finger, '… your essay.' For the first time she noticed his hands, the fingers short and rounded, the nails square, slightly bitten. His eyes, too, as he put the pages down; they were dark brown, but she had only seen them alert and occasionally furious. Now they were black as deep rock pools, in a face hollow and gaunt as fever. The noise of the departing girls faded, the clang-clang-clang of the bell too.

'Yes,' she said, more to fill the silence, since she was too nervous to speak further.

'It's the best-written piece I've read in a long time,' he said abruptly, looking away from her at the fanlight above the classroom door.

'Thank you, sir,' Eva stammered. *Don't cry, don't make a fool of yourself.*

'You have a remarkable faculty of logic. I have never read anything like this from any of my students before.'

'But you left no comment on it, sir,' Eva said quietly.

'No,' Mr Shandlin said, 'I did not.'

'Yet you liked it.'

'Exceedingly so.'

'Why did you not write that on the sheet?'

'Comment would be superfluous. When one has nothing to add, one should say nothing.' He sounded almost angry. 'I have little to teach you, I fear.'

'I'm sure that's not true.'

He took a piece of chalk from his gown pocket and twiddled it about in his hands. Eva noticed that in contrast to his languid behaviour, his hands were never still; there was a nervous energy about him.

'You told me—' she started, then stopped.

'Do go on.'

'You told us to say what we thought. So I decided I would do that.' Eva had to swallow to stop her teeth chattering. But, to her surprise, he broke out into a wide smile that made his features, which tended to severity, look gentle.

'You most certainly did not stint on honesty, Miss Downey. You told me what's what, and no mistake.'

'I was very worried. I know people always say "be honest", but they don't mean it. They don't want to hear truthful opinions.'

'No, I meant it – with all my heart.' He was still smiling. Eva was beginning to feel uncomfortable at his gaze and relieved when he dropped it.

'Do you write much, Miss Downey? Poetry, stories – any of that kind of thing?'

'No, not at all,' Eva lied. 'A poem or two once, but they weren't any good.'

'That I find hard to believe,' Mr Shandlin said. 'A style such as yours does not spring fully formed from the waters like Aphrodite. In my experience it is nurtured through long practice. And emotional honesty.'

'Well—' Eva said, then stopped.

'Well, what? Miss Downey, there is nothing more irritating than somebody who prefixes a sentence with "Well" then refuses to elaborate further. It is like a jagged tooth in one's mouth.'

'You might disapprove of what I have written.'

'I might,' he said, 'but so what? I'll disapprove even more if you don't tell me right this minute what it is.'

'I had an article published in a suffragette magazine. About evading the 1911 Census.'

'Oh? And how did you manage to do that?'

'I attended a suffragette gathering in Wimbledon Common when I was fifteen, and then I wrote about it.'

He whistled. 'Did you indeed? You little monkey!'

Her arm began to throb again. 'I believe my right to vote is a serious matter, sir.' Oh, now she had gone too far! He would surely be angry with her. But instead he looked thoughtful.

'It is serious, you are right,' he said, half to himself. 'It is! I am sorry I joked about it.' Then he continued, less confidently, 'I do not write such things myself but I have taken the occasional foray into literary criticism. I have a few articles in print. I believe Miss Hedges insists on keeping some of them in the library. I should have written more, but I am an indefatigable sloth …' He seemed to become even more interested in his feet. Then, before he could elaborate, the bell-ringer walked past the classroom for one last reminder of class change. Clang-clang-clang! Mr Shandlin put the chalk back in its place under the blackboard and picked up the essay, folded it and put it inside his battered brown satchel with the rest of his books.

'I suppose it's Flower Arranging next. Far be it from me to keep you.'

'My essay?' Eva reached for the buckle on his bag, but he smiled and gently knocked her hand away.

'No. I will keep it for the present, I think.'

Eva just nodded. He was behaving bizarrely now, so there seemed little point in questioning him.

'You are still here, Miss Downey.'

'I have not been dismissed.' That came out more pertly than she had meant it.

He raised his eyes to heaven. 'Eva. You can go now.' As she ran to the door, she could hear him laughing. 'I want more writing from you,' he called after her retreating back. 'More, do you hear?'

Sybil had stayed a discreet distance away. It would not be right to abandon Eva if she were really in trouble – though she never thought that was the case. Mr Shandlin was not a small-minded man and would hardly punish Eva, the only one who bothered paying attention in his class, would he?

'Sybil!' Eva exclaimed, seeing her. 'Are you waiting for me?'

'Yes, dearie. I was worried about you. I thought there might have been some trouble – was there?'

Eva shook her head.

'So he's not going to report you to Miss Hedges, and you aren't going to go home in disgrace?'

'No, not at all.'

'Did he even give you lines, for goodness' sake? What went on in there?'

When Eva told her, Sybil's look of incredulity deepened. Eva could not blame her. Had she not been there, she would not have believed it herself.

'I've never heard of him praising anyone like that,' Sybil said at last. 'He must have a very high opinion of you indeed. And keeping your essay for himself! What's that about? Is he missing some bedtime reading? Does his landlady not bring him cocoa?'

'I don't know,' Eva said, laughing, 'but I shall have to make sure I only ever write on loose paper so I don't lose a whole exercise book to him next time.'

'Next time?'

'He wants more … essays, I think.'

'Does this mean we all have to write them?' Sybil asked in alarm. 'Because I will not be pleased if I'm forced to do that.'

'No,' Eva said. 'Just me, I think.'

Sybil made a breathy noise, something between a sigh and a huff. 'That's very odd, Eva. Then again he is a bit odd, isn't he?'

'Definitely,' Eva laughed, then stopped.

'What is it?'

'Nothing.' She had just remembered. When he dismissed her, he had called her by her first name.

6

3 March 1914

Dearest Imelda,

I hope this letter finds you well. Things here are the same. Except that Ada Barton is leaving to get married next month, to a Mr Colquhoun who is much older than she is and an equerry at court. They say they want to hurry it up because of the rumblings in Europe. On that subject, Sybil's brother is going through parade drill in Cardiff. They're horribly strict. One second lieutenant called his captain by his first name when they were in the mess, and another officer overheard and made him stand out in the yard half the morning while the rest of the company marched around him. And the second lieutenant and the captain were friends at school! That sounds ridiculous to me – how on earth is one supposed to fight a war when trying to remember the correct title for one's superior officer? The enemy would have burned down the city by the time one had it right.

I'm quite busy with my literature classes, for my reading list has doubled. Mr Shandlin thinks it would be beneficial for me to read poets and essayists who are 'in the now' – his words – rather than the stuff we've been doing so far. He feels that the curriculum as it stands is a bit unadventurous for a mind like mine. (Those are his words, Imelda, I make no special claims for my intellect.) He just said this to me once and handed me a sheaf of mimeographs – he guessed correctly that the library would be inadequate – with all the poems I needed. Meldi, I didn't know what to say. He must have gone to some trouble. I tried to thank him but he waved me away and walked off. He can be very strange.

It doesn't stop with poets either. I have just finished reading a short story by a girl called Katherine Mansfield. She is from New Zealand and has written stories about Germans, and Mr Shandlin thinks she is going to be a very great writer. The story he showed me was in a magazine, and it is called 'The Woman at the Store'. The style is uncommon, Meldi! So strange and sad and brutal. It is not a universe I recognise but it's one of the most powerful, real stories I have ever read. Then there is *The English Review* – he has a subscription to it and lets me read it when he is finished. So far I have seen only two issues, but the stories there are so varied and interesting. I found one of his articles in an issue in the library about a poet called T. E. Hulme and the emergence of a new poetic style. It was very well written, if dry – but when I mentioned it, he clammed up completely and refused to discuss it any further.

The strange thing is, Meldi, he rarely speaks to me, just clips little comments on lined notepaper to the pages telling me to write a piece about some aspect or other. He never comments on what I hand up either, but the one time I forgot (on purpose!) he left a piece of paper on my desk. It said 'Miss Downey, I do not hand out such materials as a diversion or a joke. Please ensure that you comply with all such requests in future.' Oh, I felt about three foot tall, I tell you. I cannot fathom the reason for his behaviour. Perhaps he feels honour-bound to help me but doesn't really like me. That's the only explanation I can think of, though it doesn't seem to make any sense.

The whole school is buzzing with the news that we are going to a social on April 3rd – a dance with the boys from Marlborough College. Apparently there was a terrific row about it still being Lent – but Miss Hedges prides herself on being a freethinker who doesn't care about such strictures. We will have dance cards and a band, but we won't be going to Stowe for the dance, as it's too far away. Miss Hedges has hired a private house near Winchester – she's also promised to bring us on a tour of the Cathedral. It is like a preparation for being 'out', though Sybil says that as far she's concerned she was 'out' ever since she left her mother's womb, which brings me to my request.

Meldi, I've just found this pattern for a beautiful evening dress in a magazine. It's by Lucile and made out of organza silk with a wonderful metallic sash. I'd put it in the letter and show you but it's from one of Sybil's magazines, and I don't think she'd want me to tear it up. I've drawn a little sketch over the other side. Do you think there would be money available to have it in for the Friday before Easter? I know it sounds like feminine avarice – but I want it. And I've not even included the sleeves!

Darling Meldi, I hope you don't think I am too selfish talking about clothes when you are at home and alone. It's hard when I haven't seen you since Christmas. I hope you are learning French well and remember all your verbs. I am learning German too, and enjoying it, in spite of the lack of enthusiasm from Miss Hedges, Rhona, Sybil et al.

Viele liebe Grüsse, as they say,

Your loving sister

Eva

6 March 1914

My dear Eva,

I am so sorry about the delay in replying; everything was at sixes and sevens here. Mother was agitated because the butcher's bill was a day later than usual and she had not put it in her monthly calculations. Which is a round-about way of saying that I am afraid the cost of the material for your dress is prohibitive. Why, the kind of voile that would suit the pattern you sent is a half crown a foot, not to mention the insertion! That is all according to Mother. Such a pity, because it is a lovely dress. I am so very sorry! Mother says you have enough materials and should manage. I wish I could help, I feel wretched about it.

I am well, though I have a cough here and there. Dr Fellowes is so much nicer these days. Remember the examinations with that steel speculum down my throat and the horrible tar drink? I thought I would choke.

Father is well too. He is here more often. Apparently a lot of these Acts of Parliament concerning Ireland mean that his business is not so involved. I did ask about the dress for you, but he was very reproachful, and told me in future to go directly to Mother about these matters. I think it's probably better to do it that way in future, in order not to displease him.

You write a lot about this Mr Shandlin. He seems like a very interesting character. I find it inconceivable that he would dislike you. Perhaps he values you and finds it hard to say so.

Anyway I had better finish this letter as I am getting too tired and I will doze off in the middle of the next sentence.

All my love and kisses,

Imelda

7 March 1914

Dear Bo,

Drop your silly bayonet and stop this parading around because this is an EMERGENCY. I need about ten feet of voile at 2s 3d a foot, and the strip is to be 44 inches wide. (Yes, yes, I know you're a man and how can I ask you to run such womanish errands. Et cetera.) You can get it in Conklin's, I presume they have a store in Cardiff?

I would never dream of asking you, but it's urgent, and I've no spare loot. My friend's stepmother has decided that Cinderella can't go to the ball. She's putting a dashed brave face on it but I can tell she's really upset, no matter how often she says 'I'm perfectly fine, Sybil'.

Look, I know it's a bit much asking a man to walk into a fabric shop, but I swear if you do me this one little, little favour I will do anything for you, be forever grateful *and* you would make a sad girl very happy! Think of it as Needful Charity Work. Don't they have that in the Army, or what are you good for?

Lots of love,

Pinkie

9 March

Dear Pinkie,

Who the blinking blazes is Cinderella and what's she got to do with your letter? (Also: I am now the laughing stock of my whole platoon. Thank you very much for that!)

Bo

10 March

Dear Bo,

Cinderella is my friend, you idiot. The one who needs the dress. Do you even read my letters? Just tell your CO I'll make sure he gets a frilly dress if you don't comply.

Pinkie

10 March

Dear Pinkie,

Well, thanks for nothing, my dear sister. After your last letter, I am no longer the laughing stock of my platoon ... No, more like the entire battalion! Mind you, I showed them a picture of you and they relented somewhat. To the point where it got a bit much. I am your brother and there is only so much of that kind of talk I will tolerate. Is this girlie Eva as fetching as they seem to think you are?

The material is on its way. My forgiveness might take a bit longer.

11 March

Dear Bo,

Oh, I knew you would, I knew it, I knew it. Thank you so much! I can't tell you how grateful I am. Just remember that it was worth it. Remember: Help the Needy!

Love, Pinkie

P.S. She is not a standout beauty, but in the right dress she draws the eye.

11 March 1914

Dear Miss Downey,

I thought this spare copy of Rupert Brooke's *Poems* might be of interest to you. Brooke is one of our foremost young poets, a man of great promise who can surely only go from strength to strength. Some of his poems are rather derivative, you will find; others transcendent. It is quite a recent collection, just three years old. His style is reminiscent of my friend Gabriel Hunter's, a poet we will hear more of in the future. You might have a read of it. I would be interested to hear your thoughts, summarised in 500 words or less.

Respectfully yours,

C. Shandlin

'Eva,' Sybil said, 'look.'

Eva looked up. Sybil was carrying a brown paper parcel by the strings.

'What on earth is that?'

'It's for your dress, of course.'

'My dress?'

'Cinderella is going to the ball,' Sybil announced, sitting on the bed beside Eva. 'Have you a penknife?'

'Er … no.'

'Right. Well, it's a waste of paper, but there's nothing else for it.' She ripped at the parcel and tore it open. A soft, filmy fabric poured out. 'Here,' she said, putting it into Eva's hands. 'Feel.'

Eva let the material slip through her fingers. It slid between them, over her hands. She clasped it in bunches, then let it go. It was filmy to the touch, slippery, soft and shining. She shook it out into a square, a reflecting grey colour. There were also two strips of mink fur. Eva caressed them gently, as if the mink were still alive.

For a moment she couldn't say a word. Sybil had done this for her. 'Syb, how much did this cost? How can I ever repay you?'

'Well,' Sybil said, 'there is something, as it happens.' She looked a bit awkward.

'Go on.'

'Miss Hedges pulled me in for a talk the other week. She says that I'm close to failing some of my classes. She'll be on to the Mater for sure, and I won't hear the end of it. The next time we get an essay like that Tolstoy lark I need you to help me out.' She crouched so that she was looking Eva in the eye. 'I can't do those essays, but you can. And I can sew this for you and make it into the most marvellous dress you have ever seen or imagined and Princess Eva shall go to the ball!'

'Wait a minute,' Eva said, 'you want me to help you cheat?'

'Oh, Eva,' Sybil laughed, 'everybody cheats. Unless they're frightfully clever, like you are. Some day you'll do it too.'

Eva was torn. She knew that behind the bravado Sybil really did suffer in class. 'All right then. I'll see if I can imitate your rather … inimitable style.'

Sybil's eyes shone with relief. 'Eva, dress or no dress, I will not be able to thank you enough for this if I live to be a hundred.'

'Steady on,' Eva grinned. 'It's fine. But are you really going to sew all this? For me?'

'Why not? I sewed my own jacket, even the leather patches on the elbows.'

Eva loved Sybil's long, flared, green velour jacket, though by fashionable standards it shouldn't have worked. Too mannish, some jealous classmates whispered, and a bit angular. Eva disagreed. On Sybil, with her height and red-gold hair, it looked perfect. Her beauty looked out of place in flounces and hats. But a jacket was one thing. A full ball gown was another matter entirely.

'Eva, don't look so horrified. Trust me, when it comes to a needle and thread, I know what I'm doing.'

'Do you not get a dressmaker to do it?'

'Oh, at home I have servants for that. But I enjoy it. It's nice to learn a skill and feel useful. Give me a few weeks and I'll create something for you beyond a fairy godmother's wildest dreams.'

She was as good as her word. Eva felt slightly guilty whenever she passed the sewing room out of school hours and heard the creak of the machine wheel. But after Sybil insisted repeatedly that she did not mind, to the point of being irritated when Eva asked, Eva relaxed and accepted the favour. All she had to do in return was Sybil's homework. That would be easy.

7

The following Monday at Assembly, Miss Hedges announced that there would be a concert in Eastbourne that weekend. A local choral group would be singing motets and Bach cantatas for the Lenten season. Eva put her name down. She had always loved the sound of the choir at mass. In the hallowed, hushed space, the smell of frankincense wafting as the censer swung to and fro, she was reminded of her mother, her face forever turned towards her yet forever blank.

Imelda remembered more about their mother, being older, but seemed to feel Angela's absence less acutely than Eva did. And how frustrating it was when Eva asked Imelda what Mama had been like and she could provide only vague answers, unsatisfactory for a longing as bottomless as hers. Why did she not remember the details? The smell of clove oil before bedtime; the moments sitting in the church with the light catching the ever-moving beads in Angela's fingers; the rather heavy-set face bent over the piano keys, until she would lift her hands and turn around with a smile? That last memory was a fantasy Eva had invented: she could not remember if her mother had smiled or not. All she remembered were the way the fingers hit the keys and the room all singing.

Only one other girl, Mina Williams, had shown an interest in attending the concert. Large and shy, Mina would sit at the back of the class, her eyes hidden behind opaque spectacles. Her state of permanent bewilderment pleased Miss Dunn and irritated Mr Shandlin in equal measure – the former mistaking it for piety, the latter considering it mental laziness. Eva had witnessed him needle her, sometimes to the point of tears, and wished herself a more compassionate person who might condemn his impatience rather than sympathise with it. She wished for Mina's own sake that the girl could be less self-conscious, but such things are often deeply bred. Eva knew that much from experience.

Saturday started blowy and cold, the kind of weather that had hair in one's face very quickly if pins weren't fastened down with a vengeance and a tight-fitting hat wedged over them. Eva thankfully did have such a hat, as well as a rather fetching pair of red leather gloves which she had stolen from Grace's room last Christmas. Paired with a long gabardine frock coat, the ensemble was quite passable, though well worn.

She and Mina made desultory conversation as a silent Miss Hedges drove them to Eastbourne. Since Mina mostly responded in monosyllables, Eva eventually grew bored and took the Rupert Brooke poems Mr Shandlin had given her from her coat pocket, opening the book at a random page and immediately wishing she hadn't, particularly as Miss Hedges was driving rather fast over a rough stretch of road:

> Do I forget you? Retchings twist and tie me,
> Old meat, good meals, brown gobbets, up I throw.
> Do I remember? Acrid return and slimy,
> The sobs and slobber of a last year's woe.
> And still the sick ship rolls. 'Tis hard, I tell ye,
> To choose 'twixt love and nausea, heart and belly.

Who on earth writes poems about vomiting? Eva thought to herself, putting the book aside once more.

On arrival at Eastbourne, Miss Hedges parked the car, and they crossed the little square to the church. As they approached the heavy wooden double doors, one of which was wedged open, the sound of a choir spilled out. Miss Hedges swept Eva and Mina in ahead of her with a frown.

The choir's conductor was, unusually, a lady, who made wide, sweeping gestures that might or might not have corresponded to the time signature but kept her singers in time reasonably well. The church was about three-quarters full. Occupying the first two rows of pews were several dozen boys in blue blazers, aged, as far as Eva could tell, between twelve and fourteen. And with them, head nodding to the rhythm of the choir's singing, sat Mr Shandlin.

Eva started; she had forgotten about his other job. For some reason she could not elaborate to herself, she was reluctant for him to see her with the book of poems; she thrust it in her coat pocket. She tried not to shiver in the draught that blew up the aisle of the church and winkled its way under her blouse.

Mr Shandlin was having some trouble disciplining his charges, Eva noticed, more than once having to get up out of his seat to admonish boys who either looked like they were playing a game or who were whispering over the performance. Then he would sag back into his seat, exaggerating his usual posture until his head was almost hanging off the back, but always with one limb twitching or dancing to a pattern, whether a foot or a hand.

The third time he rose to correct his boys, he turned around and noticed them. Eva wanted to hide, even though they were there with Miss Hedges, and perfectly legitimately too. Mr Shandlin nodded at them briefly; he was too preoccupied to pay Eva, Miss Hedges or the hapless Mina Williams much attention. Eva gripped the book in her coat pocket.

After an hour, the conductor called an interval. Her voice was surprisingly quiet, out of kilter with the drama of her gesticulations. Miss Hedges announced her intention to stay put during the break. The conversation from the boys in the front grew louder.

'If you don't mind,' Eva said to her two companions, 'I would like to get some air.'

They didn't mind but did not move either, so Eva got up and slid past them, out to the small vestibule. The wind made its way in there through the door, stronger than the draught inside, making her shiver. She was about to go outside all the same, liking the strong wind even when it was cold, when a familiar figure slipped through the entrance and joined her, coat tails flapping.

'Hallo, Miss Downey!' Mr Shandlin said cheerfully. 'Didn't know you were a church haunter, or did Miss Hedges get you to come along for company? Miss Williams is a young lady of irreproachable character, I don't doubt, but I would not choose her for her skill in rhetoric. Or any other conversational skill, now I come to think of it, but perhaps that's excessively uncharitable of me.'

'It is rather, sir. I chose to come. I like choirs.'

'Really? I didn't know, but it shouldn't surprise me. I like them too, which only makes it more painful that I have to attend their concerts with that lot.'

'Shouldn't you be attending to them now, sir?'

Mr Shandlin raised his eyebrows. 'I am boring you already, Miss Downey. I must be improving with age.'

'No, no, sir, not at all.' Eva coloured. 'I was just wondering how … manageable they are.'

'Oh, they're beasts,' Mr Shandlin remarked off-handedly. 'They are not fit to be left for five minutes. But if I worried about that I would worry about how these boys will eventually be running the British Empire – and that would keep me awake at night in cold sweats. Are you all right, Miss Downey? Is there something wrong with your coat?'

Eva had just remembered that the book was in her pocket and that if she didn't do something quickly, he would spot it there and perhaps wonder why she was in the habit of carrying it around on her person. 'No! No, I'm all right, thank you.' She was abrupt, but not abrupt enough, for it was clear from his glance that he had indeed spotted the volume. His face broke out into another of those unexpected smiles.

'Ah,' he said, 'the Brooke.'

'I—' Eva blushed with embarrassment.

'Tell me, which poem do you prefer?'

'Not the one where he's getting sick on the boat, that's for sure.'

Mr Shandlin thought for a moment, then his brow cleared. 'Oh, that one. Well, I disagree with you. Do you really think poetry is just hearts and flowers? Have you not read the *Iliad*?'

'Well, I—' Eva broke off. Inside the church, the choir were starting again. A chord sounded on the organ, presumably to give the choir their notes.

'Better go back in,' Mr Shandlin said, turning.

Eva shook her head. 'Wait … listen …'

She recognised the piece immediately. Palestrina's *Sicut Cervus*, in four parts. Voice after voice overlapped, a series of waves, impersonal and clear as an announcement in a public square, an announcement that would carry through the streets, divine and distant. The music overwhelmed the singers, grasping them with something more than the sum of their parts. Eva was caught in this new ecstatic carousel and became quite lost because she saw beyond it to something she had tried to see for the past seven years: her mother Angela's face, lifted away from her, the sun shining on the beads she threaded through her fingers. Just for a moment.

Ita desiderat anima mea ad te Deus. She was crying, she knew it, but she did not care. The voices rose and fell, rose and fell. She remembered where she was, and that Mr Shandlin was watching her. Out of the blurred corner of her eye she could see his raven shadow in the doorway, unmoving. It was very unusual for him to be so still. She pulled out her handkerchief and rubbed at her cheeks. When she looked in his direction again, she saw that he was indeed regarding her – in a fixed, odd way.

Then he said, in a not altogether even tone, 'Have I caused you distress?'

'No, Mr Shandlin,' Eva said, folding her handkerchief and putting it away. 'It is nothing to do with you. I forgot myself. Forgive me, please.'

'You've done nothing for me to forgive,' he said, 'but I wonder what is troubling you.'

'I was thinking of my mother. She loved music. I have this recurring dream about her, and it's always in a church.' Now she had started, Eva could not stop. 'She died when I was five years old. Whenever I have the dream, she turns to me, and where I should see her face, all I can see is a blank. The more I try and remember, the further the memories flee. Even my dreams won't let me have her.' She stopped abruptly. Why did she do things like that, tell things when she should be discreet? It was unwomanly and showed a lack of restraint.

'I am very sorry.' He was gentle. Then, 'I know what it's like.'

Eva looked at him questioningly.

'Twelve years ago, I lost my brother.'

'My sincerest condolences, sir.' To her own ears, the words sounded flat and insincere, but he did not seem to mind.

'Thank you. It was during the South African war. He was killed in a guerrilla ambush near Tweefontein. They attacked when he was in one of the blockhouses and … well, he was unlucky that day. Or so it said in the letter they sent my mother. He died on Christmas Day.'

Eva tried to imagine what it would be like to read such news in a letter, or in a telegram. How someone's face would change as they read the words. What a terrible thing to happen to a family! Her arm began to ache again.

'When you said, "My dreams won't let me have her",' he continued, 'I knew straightaway what you meant. My dreams do let me see him – sometimes even speak to him. But I can never *have* his company again. Part of you just stops and never goes on. It's still raw, that's the devil of it.' He spoke these words levelly but directed his gaze entirely upwards, to the roof.

Eva was dumbstruck, her heart full of sudden, sweet pain. He understood all too well, and it hurt. Something broke loose in her like a raging river. Her next question tumbled out of her mouth before she could stop herself. 'What is your name?'

He was startled out of his reverie. 'My … pardon me? You mean my first name?'

'Yes.'

'Christopher. Why?'

'N-no reason.' She wished the floor would fling up its tiles, form a quick hole and swallow her up. What had she been thinking, asking him his name like that? He would think her quite cheeky.

'Do you plan to use it on me, Miss Downey?'

Oh, God, he was smirking. Time to pull up the drawbridge. But even as the thought crossed her mind, he noticed the change in her and suddenly pointed at her arm. 'You're doing it again.'

'Doing … what?'

'That thing you do. You grasp your arm with your hand and shrink away, as if someone were about to attack you. No, don't deny it, I've seen you do it. In class! Several times! It disconcerts me. Do I frighten you?' he said, with a smile.

'I'm not frightened.' Eva let her arm fall to her side.

'Then … what is it?'

Oh, God, Eva thought, *please don't.* 'I was injured.' The words came out before she could stop herself.

'How?' His eyes bored in on her, black as obsidian in the half-light. Eva could not answer him, could not think of a casual-sounding excuse. Say something of no consequence, that was all she had to do, and she couldn't manage it.

'How,' he repeated, 'were you injured?'

There was no more looking at the roof now, or past the back of her head. No, now he was full-on staring at her, his lips parted as if he were about to say something but could not quite form the words. Her skin felt prickly, and her heart began to knock about unsteadily in her chest.

The night when Catherine found out about the article in *The New Feminist*. The night when she found out about everything.

Catherine, waiting by the door. On the sight of Eva, transforming into a moving column of flapping skirts and pink-cheeked rage, chasing her around the house, screaming. Doors closed, family fleeing to the library, parlour, bedrooms, anywhere. But no escape on the landing, half-filled by an absurd pine console which stood flush against the wall, topped with a vase of pale pink carnations. There, Catherine belted her with a wooden spoon, then, when Eva wrenched it out of her hands, with her bare fists. In the face, the belly, the breasts. Then, with a low growl, grabbing Eva's wrist and leaning forward as the spoon fell with a rattle, smashing her forearm against the edge of the console again and again – until it cracked. *It hurt, it hurt, it hurt so much, oh God …*

'How dare ye! Skippin' on the Census and runnin' round with them suffragettes!'

And Grace, looking on with that worried expression, as the vase lay on the floor, carnations scattered everywhere. 'Mama – I think you did break her arm.'

How could she describe that to anyone? 'Please, sir,' Eva said, trembling, 'it was at home – please don't ask me any more.'

He flinched, as if she had struck him – and when she saw him do it, a wave of shame convulsed her. She had striven never to even hint about what had happened that day. It felt dirty and dishonourable. All she could see on his face now was horror. He would run away from that smearing place, surely, back to his own world, free and open, where there was nothing noxious in the air. Who wouldn't?

But all he said was, 'I see.' Then, a moment later, he spoke again, so quietly that in her shame and with the wind blowing a low, mournful note through the porch and antechamber, she almost didn't hear him. 'I always thought there was a sadness about you, in your eyes, the corners of your mouth – even when you laughed, there was always an untouchable sadness behind it. Now I know why.'

The endless counterpoint of the choir swelled up and filled the silence. The base note of the Palestrina piece and the veering off-note of the moaning wind together formed a discord. Eva felt naked in the presence of that wind, exposed by Mr Shandlin's words – exposed, tattered, cheap. She longed to be as innocent as those singers, free of other people's horror or, worse, pity.

The choir finished, and another noise rose up over it. Mr Shandlin's pupils had at last noted his absence. He, for his part, appeared to be waking from a trance. Once more alert to his surroundings, he glanced anxiously in their direction. But still he did not go in.

Finally Eva said, to try and break the atmosphere, 'May I have my book back?'

He held it out, and she took it, not without a bit of resistance from him. 'I will take care of it, sir.'

'I know you will, Eva.' Her name, again, like that. He sounded sad.

'We should go in now,' she said.

'Yes,' he said, taking her lead, 'I believe the monsters might have flown a biplane through the entire choir. It would be entirely form for them. I should make sure they crash-land with some dignity. Ladies first.' Once again he was full of his earlier bonhomie, but now it was a little too hearty and forced. He seemed to be putting distance between them.

Eva slipped back in the door and rushed to her seat, where Miss Hedges greeted her with a frown and Mina Williams with a flat stare. A respectable interval later, Mr Shandlin loped down the aisle and settled in beside his restive class just in time for the start of 'Onward, Christian Soldiers', where the choir once again reasserted their provincialism with flat accents and flat notes in a deadening unison, the boys buzzed with chat and tomfoolery, Mr Shandlin waved his hands around his head as if his pupils were a plague of locusts tormenting him, Eva sat with Miss Hedges and Mina Williams, and the strange magic of the Palestrina altogether disappeared.

8

24 March 1914

Dearest Eva,

I have some news: I can collect you for your half-holiday next weekend. It will be so good to see you again! Taking the train is out of the question for me at present, for fear of infection, but Mother's cousin Fred is over from Ireland, and he has agreed to motor down to Sussex so that I can see your school, and we can go back to London together. He won't be free till mid-day, so if you can wait till three, you can travel with us!

I have given this letter directly to Fred and have not sent it by the usual means, if you understand me. I am concerned about Mother. She keeps muttering about 'paying Mr Cronin a visit and straightening things out'. I fear she has not given up the idea that you and he might be married. Fred has no idea of this letter's contents, and he is an honourable man; he will not read it. But I won't write any more about that because I know it upsets you. I am sure that once you are 'finished' you will have your pick of many gentlemen.

Do you know there are suffragettes out on Trafalgar Square again? I read it in the paper and straightaway thought of you. These women are a new group, calling themselves the East London Federation of the Suffragettes. They allow men to join, and Mrs Pankhurst doesn't like that at all! Anyway, a whole lot of them got arrested last Sunday. They started hitting police-men over the head with ropes knotted together like lifebelts. Which doesn't sound too bad, but they had lead mixed into the rope. I imagine those poor policemen got quite a headache.

I also have some news about Grace: she has a serious beau. His name is Alec Featherstone, but Grace prefers that we call him 'Captain', because he is a serving officer in the 11th Hussars. His unit were inspected by the King the other day, and, to impress Grace, he rode to our house in full parade, and oh! he looked magnificent in his red coat with its immaculate white sleeves, the bronze helmet and plumes and the braided ropes that fell around his neck. (Hopefully with no lead mixed in!) It is very special indeed to be a cavalry man, they are such a cut above the ordinary infantry, Grace says. Nelly was rightly annoyed though as there was nowhere to put the horse and he just stood out in the street, so the visit did not last so very long.

Please do answer soon. I am so looking forward to seeing you!

Much love,

Meldi

Eva and Sybil were watching a hockey match, Sybil gazing at one player in particular, a tall girl on the opposing team named Patricia Arnason, who wielded the stick with deceptive lightness as she weaved and sidled past her long-skirted markers.

'Isn't she magnificent?' Sybil breathed as Patricia, with hardly more than the slightest turn of the wrist, scored against the home side. The ball slammed past the wide swing of the goalkeeper's stick, evaded her clumsy attempt to run after it and came to rest in the corner of the net. This last goal, so carelessly delivered a bare minute before full time, won the match, and the players gathered at the centre of the pitch to shake hands.

'I wish I could play like that,' Sybil sighed.

'You've never had much interest before now,' Eva said tartly. 'I'm not an expert, but I'd imagine if you wanted to play like Miss Arnason you would need some practice.'

'If I practised till my fingers were chafed holding the stick, I'd never be anything like as good as her. She's a natural. How can you not admire her?'

'She's very good, I'm sure, but … I'm not that interested in hockey.'

'But neither am I,' Sybil said to herself in low puzzlement.

Eva was about to ask her what she meant, but Sybil had half turned away, sitting on the narrow bench, her knee drawn up, elbow resting on it and chin jutting forward between her thumb and forefinger. She was obviously perturbed about something.

The players were beginning to disperse, and the rest of the watching girls were following them back to the school. Only Patricia Arnason lingered, occasionally looking towards the stand. Eva didn't mind waiting. She took her letter from Imelda out of her pocket and read it again. It worried her to hear of Catherine's harping on about Mr Cronin. For all that she had said 'no' often enough and that her father had conveyed her refusal, Eva knew who held the power in that house.

Although Sybil did not look in Eva's direction, she must have noticed the letter, because she enquired, without taking her eyes off the girl on the pitch, 'That from a suitor? Has Eva got herself a man after all?'

'Oh, no,' Eva laughed, then frowned. 'Well, I hope not.'

Patricia Arnason was the last to leave the pitch. Passing where they sat, she smiled at both of them, and Eva raised her hand in greeting, but, to her surprise, Sybil ignored her completely. Patricia looked as surprised as Eva at Sybil's rudeness, and not a little discomfited, but she brushed it off, walking away with an easy, powerful lope. Sybil did not take her eyes off her retreating back. Without turning around, she said to Eva, 'Tell me about him, then.'

'He is a friend of my stepmother's,' Eva said, 'whom she was trying to persuade me to marry when your great-aunt died and saved me.'

'Really? I take it that he is unsuitable?'

'In every way,' Eva said with sudden passion. 'He's nearly twice my age and could pass for three times that—'

'Has he an occupation?'

'He's a clerk in a railway station in Limerick. He visits us in London a few times a year and constantly pays attention to me, but he's got nothing to say. When he does open his mouth, his voice has this high-pitched, disagreeable wobble, and his lips are wet and shiny. He calls me *Miss Eeeeveeeeeeehhhh* in this long, drawn-out whine. And, oh Sybil, his eyes! They are so watery and rheumy. And he smells of meat. I don't know why, he's not a butcher, but there's no scrubbing the smell of it off him.'

'I see,' Sybil said. 'You lost me at "railway clerk", but go on.'

'Indeed and I shall,' Eva said, anger making her words tumble out. 'When he's about to say something, he always prefixes it with a sniff. A dry, miserable little sound that sucks the life out of any room he's in. And then whenever he sees a stray dog, a mean little look crosses his face and he'll kick it. Oh, Syb, when I last saw him, he shook my hand: it was cold and clammy. His fingers slid off mine. I swear my own were damp afterward. And he *sniffed*.'

'So,' Sybil said, 'you don't like him then?'

'I despise him.'

'Then you can't marry him. Stands to reason. Besides, there's no point finishing you just for a railway clerk. Waste of my aunt's money, frankly. What's wrong with your stepmother, has she got mercury to the brain or something?'

'She doesn't like me.'

'I can see that,' Sybil said. 'And your own mother, is she——?'

'She died a long time ago. I was very young.'

'Oh, sweetheart, I'm sorry. Even if it's long ago, you still remember.'

'That's what *he* said,' Eva said without thinking.

'Who did? That railway fellow? Sounds as if he's got more sense than you give him credit for.'

'No, not him. When I was at that concert last weekend,' Eva said, heat rising to her face, 'Mr Shandlin was there with the boys from his school. I went out at the interval to get some air, and he was there too, then the choir started singing some music that reminded me of my mother. I got upset and made a fool of myself and started crying.'

'Oh,' Sybil cried, 'and you told *him*? He's just about the last person I would ever tell anything to do with my personal life. I hope he was decent about it and didn't start quoting some more wretched Tolstoy or Swinburne or whatnot.'

'Oh, no, Sybil, he was so kind to me. And I was terribly embarrassed. But he was very understanding. He's different outside class, much gentler.'

'Maybe towards *you*,' Sybil said, frowning. 'I've noticed that lately. It's becoming quite marked.'

Eva opened her mouth to protest.

'Never mind that.' Sybil, seeing Eva's discomfort (a discomfort that confirmed a nascent suspicion of hers), changed the subject with her usual deftness. 'I wonder if there's any chance of getting into the hockey eleven for the next match?'

'I would say it'll be a cold day in hell before you're picked, Sybil. Sorry.'

'I disagree,' Sybil said equably. 'You would be surprised what I can do when I put my mind to it.'

'Perhaps,' Eva said, 'but this match is over, and it's a little chilly. Shall we go back inside?'

The half-holiday was preceded by an German lesson Eva had chosen to take. As she recited verb conjugations while a bluebottle repeatedly flew against the closed window, she couldn't remember why she had. '*Hilf mich,*' she said absent-mindedly.

Miss Hautbois frowned. '*Hilf mir,*' she said. 'It takes the dative case. You know this.'

'Of course. I'm sorry.'

Half an hour, one released insect, and ten conjugated German verbs later, she wandered out on the lawn where pupils and staff were gathering. She was in no rush herself. Imelda wouldn't be there until three and it was only half past twelve. As the bell rang once more, the side door opened and Mr Shandlin strode out, in his habitual black, making some odd sounds as he goose-stepped across the lawn as if he were a soldier. It took Eva some time to realise that he was singing, in a thin, loud, rather tuneless baritone, swinging his satchel back and forth, almost hitting a few people. As he approached, Eva could make out the syllables, for God knew he was intoning them loudly enough: '*Confu-TA-tis! Ma-le-DIC-tis! Flam-mis AC-ribus ad-DIC-tis!*'

Rhona Lewis appeared in a dropped-shoulder dress with three flounces. She stood directly in his way so that he barrelled to a halt, his bag still swinging forward with the momentum from his earlier stride and narrowly missing her shin. 'I must say you look very silly, Mr Shandlin,' Rhona said, 'and you sound even sillier.' She hadn't forgiven him for the Tolstoy incident.

'I am in high good humour, Miss Lewis,' he said, 'because today is that rare jewel in my life: an afternoon off. I've had two classes this morning already, a good seven miles apart, and I'm done with school. Indeed, in about' – he checked his watch – 'forty-five minutes, I will be in a motor heading out to Dorset with my friend at the wheel, my hat whipped off my head by the wind. So you will forgive me if I seem in more exalted spirits than usual. Did you want to speak to me about something?'

'No, sir.' Rhona gave him a look that would have curdled milk. 'I wanted to see Miss Hedges.'

'Then why don't you try her office instead of standing here like a lemon? Hello, Miss Downey.' He nodded at Eva, hardly glancing in her direction. *Very proper*, she thought. *So there, Sybil.* Meanwhile, Rhona scowled and flounced away towards the school entrance, her dress flapping importantly behind her.

'Ah,' he said, turning to Eva, 'I see Miss Lewis has gone and the sun has returned. Hurrah, three cheers!'

'They say it might rain later. But for now it's pleasant, yes.' Eva tried to be diplomatic.

'Oh, don't say that. It's not allowed to rain on my half day, I won't have it. I'm just about to get on my bicycle and head to my rooms to wait for Gabriel. Are you meeting anybody yourself?'

'My sister Imelda is coming, but not until three; we shall travel to London this evening.'

'I see. That sounds very pleasant. By then I shall be far away, at an encampment near Lulworth Cove, surrounded by charming individuals of both sexes discussing poetry and philosophy, and quite forgetting all of you, I daresay.'

'Perhaps you should hurry up, then,' Eva said with a grin. 'How far away is your house?'

'Oh, no more than five miles. It's in Heathfield. You know it?'

'I know where it is.'

'Well, then. It won't take me long to get there.'

Eva nodded politely, but she thought he was rather cutting it fine. Not that it was any of her concern. 'I have to go, Mr Shandlin. Have a good weekend.'

'But you're not leaving till three!' he exclaimed, 'and did I not promise you a copy of the *Iliad* some time back? When we met in that church and you were …' He stopped, presumably not wishing to embarrass her.

'I remember you mentioned it,' Eva said, 'but you didn't say anything about giving it to me.'

'Did I not? I certainly intended to. Why don't you cycle over with me and I'll give it to you now?'

'What, to your house?' Eva said, astonished.

'No, to the moon. Yes, to my house, where else? It won't take that long. You can ride a bike, can't you? Becky isn't using her bicycle, look over there.'

Becky was the kitchen maid; Eva suspected she would not take kindly to the appropriation of her bicycle. 'Yes, but—'

'It's all right. She won't be back until four.'

How Mr Shandlin knew the servants' movements Eva had no idea; it was surprising the quantity of information he managed to divine about his surroundings while seeming oblivious to them.

'Come on,' he said, 'while the rain holds off.'

Still she demurred. 'I shouldn't.'

He arched an eyebrow. 'Why not?'

Eva found that she could think of no answer that would not offend him. Besides, what was wrong with a bicycle ride? Mr Shandlin was right. Why not give it a try? So she found herself wheeling Becky's bicycle down the driveway, cautiously looking around to see if any disapproving presence might stop her. But the windows looked on blankly.

The saddle was far too high and the pedals rebelled at her approach, gashing at her ankles, banging her left calf through her stockings. She exclaimed loudly and rubbed the sore spot. 'Christ! Hell! Damn!' That was going to bruise, badly. She pushed the pedal roughly backwards, letting the chain rasp. The pedals did not move much. Ahead of her, Mr Shandlin had found his own bicycle, large, cumbersome and black; he hoisted his bag onto his back, tightened the strap with his free hand, put one foot on the pedal, then deftly threw his other leg over the saddle, bent low and headed off into the distance.

'Thanks for waiting,' Eva said aloud. She wondered if she should give up and go back. This whole caper of Mr Shandlin's was really rather ill advised.

But when she reached the gates, he was waiting, waving to indicate she should follow him in a left turn. Once she was on the road, she realised that riding a bicycle is not something one forgets, even if the memory is somewhat imperfectly preserved. Wobbling and uncertain at first, she soon gathered speed, the wind lifting her skirts and petticoat so that she felt it in a pleasant shock against her naked knees.

The school was in the South Downs, a series of gentle, undulating hills that never went too high or too far, making her cycle undemanding. Unfortunately she could not prevent her clothes occasionally entangling with the wheel spokes and pedals, nor her stockings getting marked by chain oil, but she found she was enjoying herself. It had been a long time since she was last out in the countryside alone, accompanied only by sunshine, witch-hazel hedges and a stirring breeze.

Several times she caught up with Mr Shandlin at a crossroads; each time he waited long enough to show her which way she should go next, before disappearing once more, further along the road.

'He's so impatient,' Eva grumbled, but even when the sun went behind a cloud for a few moments, it did not affect her good cheer. If she lost him, she reasoned, she could always cycle back. 'Tawton Lane, just off the High Street,' he had told her, but she was unsure if she would find it, he was so far ahead of her.

As it happened, the winding little road she was on joined the main road into Heathfield just past the vicarage and took her straight onto High Street. She found Tawton Lane soon afterwards, and Mr Shandlin even sooner after that. He was waiting for her at a door right next to a shoemaker's shop, his bicycle secured against the railing opposite, his fingers tapping his pocket watch. 'How did it take you half an hour? You must be the worst cyclist in the Northern Hemisphere.'

Half an hour! It had felt like barely ten minutes. As she leaned the bicycle against the wall near his, she realised what a state she was in. Her hands were covered in grease, God only knew how, and her dress, a crimson chemise, was looking decidedly muddy at the bottom. Mr Shandlin made no comment on her appearance; he merely opened the large door and indicated that she should follow him upstairs.

'I ...' She felt rooted to the spot, too embarrassed to say anything.

'It will only take me a few minutes to find this thing. Come on, I can't leave you standing out here in the street.'

He took the stairs two at a time until he reached a small landing and unlocked the door directly in front of them. Feeling shy, Eva stayed out on the landing, although she took a good look at his room through the open doorway as he busied about, searching for his Homer. She saw that his task would not be easy: piles of books on the floor nearly tripped him up in his endeavours. The whole room was a bit chaotic: a shirt cast over the back of a chair, a mug upended on a plywood counter, a full brass ashtray on the window sill and what looked to Eva like a rather hastily made bed. A bookcase near the door was full; on top, between more books and periodicals, stood a framed family photograph: the father seated, the mother standing, holding the hand of a small, dark, unsmiling boy who was so obviously a younger edition of Mr Shandlin himself that Eva was touched. The other son, fair-haired and well into adolescence, leaned on the chair next to his father, looking as if he were suppressing the urge to laugh. Mr Shandlin saw Eva looking at it and remarked, 'Ah yes. You've spotted the resemblance. Francis is the handsome one … was, I mean – I'm still alive and so is my mother.'

Eva nodded.

As he once again busied himself with his search, scuttling about the room, even poking his head under the bed, Eva could not help thinking that there was something disarming about how unabashed he was at showing her his modest circumstances. That he should live here, in this simple room that smelt of fried liver and shoe leather, impressed itself on her deeply.

He re-emerged, frowning. 'I could have sworn I left it on my desk. I do when I'm lending something to someone – I leave it on my desk with a note to remind myself. And the right translation too. Not that rhyming nonsense. And the Muse should *sing*, not *speak*. I see you still won't come in, you just hover in the doorway like the Recording Angel. Is my humble abode that bad?'

'No!' Eva turned red. 'Not at all, sir. I just feel it would be more … appropriate to wait here.'

'You are very polite. I freely admit I don't keep a very good house.'

Eva puzzled over his meaning. Surely he must know that she was not staying outside from politeness? 'Does someone clean for you?' she asked.

'I do occasionally have a woman in to tidy the place, but only after I've spent several hours cleaning up for her first. The last time she arrived, Gabriel Hunter was here. We'd been up all night playing a spelling-errors drinking game with some exercises I had to correct. I had to stick my head under cold running water before I was fit to greet the lady, let alone go and teach eighteen truculent boys the finer details of the past participle.'

'I won't make any comment on that, Mr Shandlin,' Eva said, 'since it appears you were punished enough.'

'Oh, yes,' he winced, 'with every known alcoholic substance short of absinthe. And the knock on the door from the cleaning woman that woke me up ... *horresco referens.*'

'I beg your pardon?'

'It means, "I shudder to recall",' he said with a wry grin.

Eva was surprised. She had not thought he had any tendency to drink in him. Mr Duncan sometimes smelt strongly of alcohol, and, as for Miss Dunn ... it was well known that she topped up her little gin bottle regularly during the day. But Eva had never heard anything about Mr Shandlin. Then again, that encounter might have put him off.

'Come in, for God's sake, and help me find that book.'

Eva tentatively advanced a little further through the doorway, trying to ignore his gestures to sit down as he crawled into a corner, going down on his hands and knees with − there was no delicate way of putting it − his backside in the air. She hardly knew where to look.

And there was that off-key singing again, as earlier: *Con-fu-TA-tis, ma-le-DIC-tis.* Rhona was right: he looked and sounded ridiculous. Eva laughed. She meant for it to be under her breath, but he heard her and stopped mid-search, emerging from the dustiness under his bed, his hair nearly standing on end, his face flushed, and looked at her with mock indignation. 'What are you tittering at there, Miss Downey? Don't deny it, I heard you clearly.'

'Um, well, sir,' Eva struggled for words that would not be too cruel, 'your singing, it's ah ...'

'Let me tell you something about my singing,' Mr Shandlin retorted, rising to his feet and brushing the dust off his trousers. 'When I was a boy, I was sent away to school where there was a junior choir. I remember we were singing – what was it, some sort of hymn? – oh yes, 'All Things Bright and Beautiful'. I've hated that song ever since. I was somewhere in the back row, singing my little heart out, forgetting anyone else, when the choirmaster came towards me. Mr Phibbs, a really oleaginous, nasty little so-and-so. He bent down and said in that unctuous voice of his, like pouring molasses, "Well, Shandlin minor." He called me that because Francis was still alive then and we went to the same school. "You know, I don't think there's any need for you to actually *sing* at next week's concert. You can just mouth the words." I can't tell you how that made me feel. I never forgave him.'

'Oh, dear,' Eva said, trying to keep a straight face, 'that was cruel.'

'And I promised myself two things: first, when I came to manhood, I would sing what I liked, when I liked. And second, after I became a teacher, if any student of mine showed enthusiasm, I would at least try to give him a chance, or her.' He looked meaningfully at Eva.

Eva looked away from him. She felt something dangerous in the pause, and the look.

'I'm sorry I teased you about your singing, sir.'

'Oh, that's nothing. Just as long as you don't try to stop me.'

'I would never do that.' She allowed herself a smile. 'Though perhaps I might put in some ear plugs.'

'Why you little—'

He was interrupted by sounds from the street below. Somebody banged the door knocker with such violence that the whole house vibrated. A voice shouted through the letterbox: 'Hey Christopher, what are you doing up there? Self-abuse? Leave that for later and get downstairs!' That comment's effect on Mr Shandlin was immediate: he flushed red. 'Gabriel only

92

matches his charm with his subtlety,' he managed at last. He seemed to be mortally embarrassed, though Eva could not see why. He'd only been drunk the once. That hardly counted as self-abuse.

Mr Shandlin ran to the window, flung it up and shouted out into the street, 'Could you be a small bit louder, Gabriel? I don't think they heard you across the Channel!' The car hooted in response, and Eva heard cheering. Mr Shandlin shut the window and rushed around the room, piling various forgotten items into his bag. Then he stopped dead and looked at Eva. 'I never found that blasted book after all!'

'That's all right, sir, I didn't want it in the first place.'

He sighed and looked to the ceiling. 'Lord deliver me from such ingratitude, you cheeky brat.' He put his bag on the ground. 'You'd enjoy this weekend. It would be fun. What a pity you can't—' but then he recollected himself and laughed lightly, taking up his bag once more.

The man at the steering wheel of the motor car shot Eva a look as she came out after Mr Shandlin. Gabriel Hunter's smooth-skinned face was as close to a heart in shape as masculine beauty would allow. His hair was raven-coloured with a cowlick, and he had thick, red lips that looked as if they were enjoying a secret joke. He wore gold-rimmed spectacles and was altogether quite the most beautiful man Eva had ever seen; beside him, Mr Shandlin looked battered and worn. An attractive girl with waved black hair sat in the back. She looked Eva up and down with the most cursory of assessments before ignoring her and opening the door for Mr Shandlin. Eva could clearly see her gypsy-style bottle-green smock petticoat and red espadrilles. She wore no stockings.

Eva was surprised that Mr Shandlin was not sitting in front but was squeezing in beside the girl. Of course, there was no reason why he shouldn't sit in the back …

'Goodbye, Miss Downey. Enjoy your half term. Hallo there, Cressida.' Mr Shandlin shut the door and kissed the girl on the cheek. She squealed with delight. Mr Hunter craned his neck and querulously asked, 'Have I interrupted something?'

'A pupil, on an errand, that's all.' He was brusque.

The car was moving now, and he did not look back. It seemed like an odd, abrupt farewell. Why, he had been on the verge of saying he was sorry she couldn't come, and once his friends were there, he'd practically ignored her. Eva felt small and unimportant and at the same time annoyed with herself for her unreasonable feelings. There was nothing for it but to forget about it and return and wait for Imelda. Cycling against the wind, she felt the first drops of rain hit her cheeks and hair.

9

31 March 1914

Bo,

We finished the dress! Well, I finished the dress and Eva did my homework. Hats off to you for having the gumption to send on that lovely mink for sleeves, but would you believe, she wasn't having it. Wanted them plain. Well, I argued with her back and forth. Can't have them plain, I said, that's not the design. But she put her foot down. I will be able to use it for the collar of a coat I've had my eye on, but more anon – I am sure your commanding officer who is reading this will not want to hear all about girls' coats. Unless they are on actual girls, of course.

We tried it on her, and – oh, Bo, it's beautiful. Eva is not the type who looks ravishing, I'm afraid – only I get that privilege – but she did look rather remarkable. I could *not* talk her into wearing make-up. Her rotten upbringing has her convinced that only tarts and actresses wear lipstick. I'll win her round eventually.

And I must say, hurrah for Evie: she did every single one of those exercises for me, in history *and* French *and* Eng. Lit., for three weeks, when she could have been having fun (tho' I am not convinced she knows how to have fun.) I must say she has my habits down pat, not to mention my patterns of speech. All the things I never knew I misspelled she did for me. It was quite uncanny, really. Miss Stebbs the history mistress didn't spot a thing, which is unsurprising since she is utterly stupid, nor did Miss Hautbois, but unfortunately old Shandy is not stupid at all, and he eventually clicked something was up. And that was the end of our little scheme because once he found out, he humiliated Eva in class. No, really, he did. He made her stand up, shouted at her in front of everyone and said he was disappointed in her and that she had acted like a common cheat. When she tried to say something, he told her to stop talking for once in her life, that the sound of her voice got on his nerves, and that she had to fill every silence with worthless talk. Really awful stuff, Bo! I've never seen him so furious.

I tried to tell him that it was my fault and all about the dress and the bargain we made, but he just shot such a filthy look at me that my mouth dried up. Oh, Bo, when he is angry he is terrifying! It's too bad, it's jolly bad form of him to pick on her and not me when I'm the one at fault. Of course I know what's the matter with the cranky, thin-skinned so-and-so … but poor Eva? Hasn't a clue.

I'll give her this though, she kept her composure. She said not a word in reply, though he ranted at her like a crazed animal. She didn't even shake. Just stood there like a statue until he finished. I can't tell you how embarrassing it was being there in that classroom. I would rather have been in the middle of the desert in Timbuctoo with no water, that's how bad it was. Poor Eva just bent her head down and didn't look at anyone. Afterwards she walked straight out without a word, went up to the dorm and got a book out of her bedside locker.

Then – oh Bo, you'll love this – she opened the window, pulled her arm far behind her, the book outstretched in her hand. And then – whoosh!

– threw it with all her might, and it went spinning, spinning through the air down into the shrubbery. It landed in a white winter jasmine bush before slithering down to the soil out of view. Bo, she won't talk about it, but I think he gave her the book. I've seen her reading it before.

Anyway, I hope you meant it when you said Clive Faugharne was coming to the dance. I don't believe for one moment that rumour that he is 'So' – and stop spreading it around! I imagine his shyness with girls gave rise to that idea, but it's not true. He was giving me very special attention during the last Hunt Ball!

Lovelove,

Pinkie xx

1 April 1914

Dearest Eva

I just got your letter. I am sorry to hear you had an upset and hope you are feeling a little better. Thank you for enquiring after my health; I know I was a bit dicky the day we were on Eastbourne Pier, but I enjoyed it all the same. I only wish there had been more daylight to enjoy the camera obscura! But I am much recovered now.

We have all been in a tizzy lately with Mother's new interest in Mrs Humphry Ward. Have you heard of her, Evie? She is a famous authoress who lives in Oxford and who wrote lots of novels and married a history professor. She was in our district recently giving speeches for the Women's National Anti-Suffrage League. Now I know how *you* feel about them, but Mother and Grace are of a different mind and have become very keenly involved in all of this, and they insist I go along too.

I find Mrs Ward to be very martial in her speeches. She believes war will soon be afoot and that women will have to stand shoulder to shoulder with the men rather than foster division. There is a strange cast to her eyes when she talks about war, as if a blood lust has fallen over her. But I feel a bit sorry for her too, as she is effectively out of a job since the League she created has, funnily enough, been taken over by a man! That Lord Curzon is not a nice fellow, he has something wrong with his back and is forever frowning at everybody. Anyway, for all that he appears to support Mrs Ward, I think he doesn't want women to vote because he doesn't like them. I wish Grace and Mother wouldn't go to Mrs Ward's meetings because I think she is caught under his influence and that can be no good.

Good grief, this letter has gone on a bit. Just a brief note about your problems with your teacher: I would ask for God's forgiveness for your part in the whole to-do, and yours alone. You are not responsible for him. I am sure that no matter how weak mortals can be (and a man who is not in control of his emotions is surely weak), God can give you strength to forgive him – and yourself too. Also, you are not really helping Sybil by doing her work even though it appears that you are. You are preventing her from learning it herself, which is a skill she will need no matter what vocation she chooses. And, oh, now I am running out of paper (and energy!) but I hope you can accept this scrawl from

Your loving sister,

Imelda xx

Two days before the dance, a state of high excitement ruled Eva's dormitory: permission had been given at last for the girls to try on their dresses and practise their coiffures. Eva was doing Sybil's hair. She had gently swept it up and was trying to bind it with a series of bandeaux, while Sybil was looking in a spotty mirror, assessing the results. She did not yet appear satisfied.

'Here, Eva, use this, will you?' Sybil handed her a narrow band studded with imitation emeralds. Sybil's hair was, as she herself put it, 'thick and rich – like me', and needed plenty of bandeaux and pins to subdue it. Eva worked with more viciousness, Sybil felt, than was strictly necessary, jabbing and pushing at the pins as if she had forgotten that there was a scalp somewhere underneath that might suffer pain from her ministrations. It was late afternoon, and the sun was beginning a long descent. The light from the west-facing window cast a bright spot on the mirror, distracting Eva.

'Ow!' Sybil exclaimed.

'Sorry.'

'No, seriously, chum, that's the fifth time you've done that in about five minutes. How about trying to concentrate on what you're doing?'

'I *am* concentrating.'

'No, you're not. I don't think your head is here at all.'

Eva made no comment but continued to slip in smaller clips to secure the hair in just the right fashion, covering all but the lobe of the ear. It was a style that was already beginning to look dated; no wonder Sybil was bored with it – though hair like hers afforded only one alternative, that of the Pre-Raphaelite tresses, which would not be sanctioned by the likes of Miss Dunn.

'Eva, you're not saying much. Still brooding, eh?'

'I'm not. Now can we talk about something else?'

'Oh, do you have to be so snippy?' Sybil cried out in exasperation. 'Can I remind you that I'm on your side here? He was totally in the wrong.'

'I know. Hold still or I'll never have this done.'

'Eva,' Sybil said, raising her hands to indicate that her friend should stop, 'I know you are inept with anything involving titivating and dressmaking, but even you can't be manhandling me that painfully out of ignorance. You're still upset, and I don't blame you.'

'I'm fine.'

'Will you stop being so monosyllabic! I'm trying to help.'

'I know, Syb,' and Eva ruffled the hair she had so recently tried to pin down. 'I suppose I do still wonder what I did to provoke him so. It's stupid, I know, but it did hurt me.'

'Well, why don't you write him a very formal letter: Dear Sir, please stop being madly in love with me and start acting like a proper teacher, Yours et cetera.'

Eva laughed. 'All right, Sybil, but seriously.'

Sybil turned around in her chair, strands of hair dislocated by the movement falling down to her neck. 'Eva, I am being serious. He's in love with you. Absolutely besotted. I've never seen such a straight-up case of it in my life.'

Eva felt her heart beat irregularly in her chest and her breath grow shallow. 'Sybil, that's nonsense.'

Sybil clasped Eva's wrists, her hair unravelling further as the pins fell down. 'Evie, have you not seen the way he looks at you? Or, rather, the way he pretends *not* to look at you?' She imitated his eyes darting about the room. 'How about the way he singles you out, all the time, for attention?

It's so obvious. Yes, I know you're intelligent – and that's part of it. He's used to stupid people, and you came out of a clear blue sky and shocked the living daylights out of him.'

'Even if what you say is true – and it isn't,' Eva protested, blushing, 'it is only proximity that could cause it. He'll forget me quickly enough when the year is over.'

'The hell he will.'

'Sybil!' Eva was shocked.

'I'm telling you, he's beyond forgetting you. He is in too deep for that. The only question is can he keep his senses and his job. Trust me. Auntie Sybil is never wrong about men, and that man is in deep trouble.'

'Well, you're wrong now,' Eva retorted with spirit. 'Surely it is possible for a man to be interested in his female pupils' education without darker motives being brought into play?'

'If a man started writing me notes and sending me books of poems and then shouted at me like a jilted mistress for half an hour on end, I'd hardly call it "being interested in my education",' Sybil replied. 'Now, would you fetch me those pins, there's a love, and let's do this again? Properly, this time?'

Eva sighed and picked up the pins. She would need to hurry up and finish now, as their room was getting busy and more people wanted the mirror. The corridors hummed with girls rushing in and out, holding dresses up and slipping them on, sometimes with unfortunate results. The bodice on Rhona Lewis's dress was far too tight, and the fabric made a terrible ripping sound, tearing down to the buttock. Eva breathed a sigh of relief that she had herself picked a pattern flattering to her naturally rather square shape.

Sybil winked at Eva, but she didn't wink back. She was still shocked at what Sybil had told her. Sybil, engrossed in her hair, had already forgotten about it. In her mind, she was simply imparting to Eva information that had been painfully obvious to everyone else for quite some time.

When the time came for Eva to put on her dress, Sybil would not stand for being anything less than mistress of ceremonies. She lifted the dress over Eva's slip, and Eva felt the fabric pour down her back, then fall in a rush about her feet, as the material resolved itself into coherence. A brief silence fell upon the room.

'Eva Downey,' another girl said at last, 'I never thought you could look so …' Her voice trailed off.

'I'll take that as a compliment,' Eva said.

'So you should,' Sybil said. 'You look divine, and I mean it. Here. Spin around.'

As Eva turned, somewhat diffidently, the sunlight caught the silver, and a kaleidoscope of shadow and light fell on the ground. She moved another few steps to the door.

'Come back,' Sybil said, 'you forgot your shoes!'

From under the masses of crêpe paper on her bed she whipped out a simple black box with 'Peter Robinson' embossed on the lid.

Eva opened the box and gasped.

'Now, they're only on loan,' Sybil said, 'so please don't damage them.'

Eva took the left shoe out of the box and caressed the seam at the heel with her fingers. The heel itself was small enough to be suitable for dancing, while the shoe was silk and leather, patterned with grey-silver flowers, the raised petals soft as she quickly ran her fingertips over them. The straps were silk Möbius strips. Holding this wondrous, delicate thing made Eva feel heavy-handed and sweaty. She placed the shoe back in the box, much to Sybil's consternation.

'What the blazes are you doing?'

'They're so nice,' Eva said hesitantly, 'I don't want to hold on to them too long.'

Sybil stamped her own foot in exasperation. 'Eva, you clot. Put them *on*.'

So Eva raised the hem of her dress and slipped first the left shoe, then the right, over her stockinged feet. Then she straightened up, lifting the hem slightly to show off the shoes. But there was no need: it fell at just the right spot. Sybil clapped her hands in delight. 'Good show, Destouches! Nice ensemble, if I may say so myself,' she added, without much attempt at modesty.

Eva smiled at her friend's joy. 'It is beautiful. Thank you, Sybil. For the shoes, for everything.'

Rhona clicked her tongue. 'It certainly is. You had better make sure you wear it properly, Downey. I can tell from the way you stand that you're not used to clothes like these.'

Sybil made a face, but Eva couldn't have cared less about Rhona. She put the shoes carefully back in the box and closed the lid. Then she removed her stockings.

'I want to go outside,' she said.

Rhona snorted with laughter. 'Are you playing Faerie Queene again?'

'I want to feel the ground under my feet.'

Rhona squealed with derision, and Sybil looked like she was about to protest, but Eva mouthed, 'I'll be back,' and padded downstairs, the door creaking behind her as she pulled it to. The painted wood felt smooth and warm under her soles as she treaded down the stairs. Then at the bottom a few feet of carpet led her to the back door and outside.

When she lifted her skirts and gingerly trod over gravel to the uncut grass, the moisture of the dew on the blades was a welcome balm. She kept on the grass as much as possible, passing the shrubbery then crossing downhill to the small copse of elms. In the gaps between the trees, moss grew, bouncy and soft, like in the grounds of Blackrock Castle on the promontory in Cork, where her mother had brought her and Imelda to play when they were very young.

'Mama,' Eva whispered. The trees made no reply except to sigh and rustle in the slight breeze. She still could not recall Angela's face, but that was all right. Then she looked up and saw the sun shining through the cross-hatching of leaves. For the first time in weeks, she felt calm. She was struck by the realisation that it was all in the hands of God and that all would be well. No matter what happened, or where she went in the world, she was held in a pair of divine hands guiding her way. There was no rational way of knowing this, she just knew. She put her hand on one of the elms and felt the pattern of the bark beneath her palm. It seemed connected to the deep earth below, and she let her head rest against it. It comforted her and set her to rights, for a while.

Then she felt the folds of her dress brushing the grass and recollected herself. If she ruined the hem running barefoot outside, after all Sybil's hard work …! *Rhona's right*, she said to herself as she made her way back to the dormitories, *if I'm going to wear this thing, I'd better do it properly.*

10

Although there had been talk of hiring a steam bus for the journey to Winchester, Miss Hedges decided it would be too impractical; instead they were all booked into first-class carriages on each of the two trains that would bring them from Eastbourne to Winchester. They would travel as far as Portsmouth, then take the Great Western train up to Winchester and arrive at seven o'clock that evening. Sybil and Eva had the good luck to secure a compartment entirely to themselves on the first train, though Miss Hedges patrolled the corridor and looked in on them from time to time.

As the train made its way past Brighton, Sybil took out a silver case and wound up a bright red lipstick. Eva watched as her friend stretched her upper lip and inscribed a vermilion arc across its curve, then as she did the same with the lower one. She did not remind Sybil that lipstick was forbidden – Sybil knew that all too well. She did keep a weather eye out for Miss Hedges.

'Handkerchief,' Sybil commanded, and, when Eva handed it to her, she kissed it carefully, blotting and folding her lips until the cover was even. For a moment, Eva wondered if she had been right to keep her lips bare and her hair down. Sybil was forever telling her it looked too girlish. Eva was 'out' now, and she should show it. But Eva didn't feel 'out', she just felt out of place.

Sybil capped the lipstick and put it back in her purse, then remarked, 'Do you know, Evie, when we were leaving the school, I could have sworn I saw Mr Shandlin among the trees. What was he doing there, I wonder?'

Eva wanted to groan aloud. She'd had enough of Mr Shandlin. During yesterday's class she'd nearly put a crick in her neck avoiding his eye, and he was so obviously returning the favour it had been embarrassing.

'I'm sure you are mistaken,' she said. 'I didn't see anyone.'

'Hmmm,' Sybil said, rummaging for her compulsory cigarette and Ronson lighter. 'Did I tell you that I met his mother? I was walking down the avenue, minding my own business, and around he comes like a hulking black crow, with his arm craned around this old woman, steering her forward.' ('Do you mind if I open the window for a moment?' said Eva.) 'And then the two of them paused to look at me at the same time, and it was like two vultures turning their heads. Exact same profile, both of them, and four eyes on me, two brown and two blue.' ('I've changed my mind,' Eva sighed, 'it's too chilly.') 'She smiled at me, so she has better manners than her son.'

Eva wished to God Sybil would stop talking. How obvious did she have to make it that she didn't want to hear about Mr Shandlin or his blasted mother? But her friend carried on: 'A little bird told me that she and Miss Hedges don't get on at all. You do know that every Friday Miss Hedges holds a salon in the parlour of the main house? And always invites Shandlin along? The mother probably reckons she has her claws into him. Though I doubt it myself. A woman of Miss Hedges' class wouldn't end up with a fellow like him. But I'm sure you know all this.'

Eva shook her head. 'How would I know what Mr Shandlin does? I'm hardly in his confidence.' She could not keep the hurt out of her voice, and

Sybil heard it. Even in the semi-dark of the carriage, Eva could see her eyes widen with alarm as she put down her lighter.

'Oh. I see now. When I told you he was in love with you, I put an idea into your head, didn't I?'

'Of course not.' Eva turned away.

'Ye gods and little fishes! Eva, I didn't imagine for one moment it would be reciprocal. If I have put an idea in your head, for God's sake, will you abandon it? Please? No good can come of it, believe you me.'

'I haven't got any ideas in my head,' Eva said sulkily.

'Well, good,' Sybil said. 'Keep it that way.'

Not a word was spoken between the two of them for the rest of the journey. Sybil shrugged inwardly. She had helped Eva as much as she could by making the dress. She would not be able to physically drag the fellows over or make Eva forget Mr Sensitive Sunflower. Eva would have to do that herself.

After all the fuss and bother, the dance did not get off to an auspicious start. The first entry on Eva's card was a tow-haired fellow whose head was as round as the planet earth. While the string band played 'A Vision of Salomé,' he pulled her around the too-bright hall, crashing into her, urging her, 'Come on, gel', while she desperately attempted to stay away from his feet. After that, her toes smarting, came a tall boy with a pleasant, lopsided face wearing a kilt called (she thought) Clive Faugharne; he spent the whole time talking about Sybil. Then, after him, a slighter chap named David Wentworth Hopkins, who turned out to be the most promising dance of the night, talking not about horses or dreadnoughts but poetry, and with a reasonably well-educated interest.

Then a long period of nothing. Sybil joined her, two glasses of wine in her hands. 'Here, have one.'

'Is that allowed?' Eva was nervous.

'Allowed? With the crowd here tonight? I'd say it was bloody compulsory. Drink up.'

She presented the glass to Eva, who took a draught and shuddered.

'Drink! Don't look like it's a punishment,' Sybil instructed sternly, and they both downed another mouthful at the same time.

'"I punished myself with every alcoholic substance known to man except absinthe",' Eva murmured absent-mindedly.

'Eva, what are you blathering on about now? For God's sake, look sharp. Have you met anyone yet?' Eva showed Sybil her dance card. 'All right, well, that's progress. Though you can forget about Clive Faugharne. That's my territory. Anyway, I want to warn you off somebody.'

'Oh? Who?'

Sybil gestured to the far corner of the room, where three young men were in absorbed conversation. 'That one. He was a prefect at Marlborough back in '11, so he says. I thought he would be worth talking to, but when I finally met him, he didn't bother introducing himself before buttonholing me with a rant about how he was the great overlooked poet of his generation and how he should have been in the *Georgian Poetry* book that came out two years ago. And I said, "Well, that's terrible, why weren't you in the *Georgian Poetry* book that came out two years ago?" and he said it was because he wouldn't agree to do things with Mr Marsh, the editor of the book, unlike certain other people. Only he didn't say "doing things", Eva, he said something worse. I'm not saying what' – in response to Eva's questioning glance – 'all I shall say is he used the most disgusting language I've ever heard. A docker would not dream of speaking like that.' Her eyes glittered with contempt. 'He may be pretty enough, but for heaven's sake avoid him like the plague.'

But when she made out the man Sybil was referring to, Eva exclaimed and drew in her breath. 'That's Mr Hunter!'

'Mr Who?'

Eva took another mouthful of wine. 'Gabriel Hunter. He's a friend of Mr Shandlin's. Apparently he *is* very good at poetry.'

'Good *God*,' Sybil hit her forehead with the edge of her hand in frustration. 'That man is not even here, and he still manages to ruin our evening. Eva, I'm really losing patience.'

'You're the one who mentioned him on the train. I never said a word about him.'

'Only to exorcise the fellow from your head! I thought it might clear the air, but it seems I've dragged him here like a bad smell. The devil with him and his rotten friends!' She set her empty wine glass on a nearby table with some vehemence. 'Funny friendship, though, don't you think? I'd say Shandy's a good ten to fifteen years older than him. Anyway,' she frowned, 'how do you know him?'

Eva felt herself blush as she dropped her voice. 'Mr Shandlin wanted to give me a book, so I was at his rooms in town when Mr Hunter arrived—'

'Stop.' Sybil said, putting up her hand in disapproval. 'I don't want to hear any more. I don't want to know. Good Lord, Eva.'

Eva started to protest, but Sybil shook her head. 'All I can say is, Mr Shandlin has no sense of propriety. Inviting a pupil to his rooms – he could have gravely compromised you, Eva! And more fool you for going.'

Eva began a reply, but Sybil whirled around and fixed upon her such a glare that she immediately shut up and drank more wine. A few glasses later, as the band struck up 'A Thousand Kisses', she turned to look at the dancers, and her eyes met those of Gabriel Hunter himself, who had crossed the room to where she stood. Close up, he was even more handsome, but his mouth was twisted and Eva could see he was drunk. 'You're not as clever as you think you are,' he spat. 'I just want you to know I'm watching you. I know girls like you, you're all on the make. All the intelligence of a superior housemaid without the accomplishments.' Then he turned his back and walked off.

Eva gaped. 'I'm not as clever as I think I am?' she repeated to herself. 'What does that even mean?'

A while later – the wine dulled Eva's sense of time – Clive Faugharne loomed up, arm in arm with Sybil. Two facts emerged about him: he appeared to own half the Scottish Highlands, and he made bad jokes. Sybil laughed at them, quite loudly, possibly because of the first fact. Meanwhile Eva looked around for David Wentworth Hopkins in the manner of a drowning woman seeking a lifebelt, but he was nowhere to be seen.

Then it was the end, and Miss Hedges started rounding everyone up. They bade their goodbyes – well, Sybil did – and went out past the braziers into a clear, starry night.

Apart from the encounter with Gabriel Hunter, what Eva remembered most was the throbbing, in iambic pentameter, of her head from the wine – da *doom*, da *doom*, da *doom*, da *doom*, da *doom* – and how it persisted as she rested her head on her hand while the train slowly creaked and swayed its way back to Eastbourne. She wondered what Mr Shandlin had said to

Mr Hunter about her that had so provoked that man's antagonism. Then again, it could not have been worse than the things he had said to her face.

11

7 April 1914

Dear Eva,

I write to you with painful urgency. Your presence is required immediately at home, so you will leave the school next week. Imelda is seriously ill, so much so that Mother is unable to cope. Furthermore, Miss Hedges has informed me that you helped another pupil to cheat. I telephoned Miss Hedges last week and we discussed the matter in some detail. Her tact and attention left me pleasantly surprised and I am assured of her co-operation.

Eva, were you to read your bible, as Mother does, you might learn from the Gospel: 'He that is faithful in that which is least is faithful also in much: and he that is unjust in the least is unjust also in much.' Read and mark, Eva – and pray hard for your own redemption. I can no longer advise you, since you have long since proved yourself too proud and headstrong to pay proper attention. I would say one thing: a finishing school is of no use if the material to be finished is shot through with irredeemable defects from the start.

You are to take the 1.13 on Friday, and you will be met at London Bridge station.

Father

*

Sybil was furious when Eva told her the news. She lit up a cigarette right in the middle of the common room and put her feet up on the table.

'I don't think you should do that,' Eva said.

'Do you think I care?' Sybil cried, blowing out a huge, grey cloud. 'Why is he doing this, anyway? What can you do for your sister? I don't mean to be rude, but she needs a proper nurse, surely?'

'I don't think it's anything to do with Imelda.' Eva folded her arms. 'You have to understand about my family, Sybil. When my mother was still alive, Catherine − my stepmother − was our servant. Well, more my mother's servant than ours but generally responsible for the house.'

Sybil's mouth dropped open and her burning cigarette fell to the floor. 'Your father married his maid?'

'Never mind that for the moment. I don't actually care about Catherine being the maid. I care that she's a vile excuse for a human being. After Mama died, Catherine started spending nights at the house, to keep an eye on us, or so we were told. It's hard to recall: I was only five.'

'Oh, Eva. I never knew.'

'What I'm trying to say is, Sybil, my family always does things for a reason, and the reason is always to do with Catherine, and with what *she* wants. And she doesn't like me. When I got the opportunity to come to school here, and my stepsister Grace didn't, I was on borrowed time. It's a miracle I lasted this long.'

'But Evie, this isn't right.' Sybil grasped her shoulders. 'Something should be done.'

'Please don't tell anyone, Sybil. I couldn't bear it.'

'Come, sit down, sweetheart,' Sybil said. 'You look *well reet shook*, as my maid Mabel used to say when I had bad dreams.' She frowned. 'Could you try talking to Miss Hedges? Surely she'd understand?'

'No. My father has already spoken to her, and they are in total accord. Besides, I think she's gone off me,' Eva said. 'She used to invite me into her study and recommend Olive Schreiner to me in front of a nice roaring fire, but that stopped months ago. She hardly even greets me in the corridor these days.'

'Hmmm,' Sybil said, adding, *sotto voce*, 'I doubt that has anything to do with Olive Schreiner, whoever she is when she's at home. I could tell you who it has to do with, but you wouldn't thank me for it.'

Eva put her fingers to her temples. A headache was tightening the bands of tension in her skull and leaving her mouth dry. She got up. 'If you don't mind, I think I'll walk around. Be alone for a while.'

'Of course,' Sybil said. 'I'll be here. Doing my own homework for a change.'

Eva crossed the courtyard to the classrooms, dusty and abandoned for the evening, the light leaving a scrawl of dirty yellow across the blackboards and desks. She stopped outside hers, slipped in and sat at her usual desk. She felt as if something round and heavy had settled in her chest, right in her heart. Every beat felt like an effort.

She opened the lid of the desk. There the schoolbooks lay. Not hers: they had all only been on loan. The one book she had received as a genuine gift she had thrown out the window in a fit of rage. Except … there it was, just under the lid, right in front of her. Beneath *School-Girl Days: A Memory Book* and a small pamphlet of log tables, a damp spot still on the cover where it had met the flowerbed: Rupert Brooke, *Poems*. She picked the little volume up, and a loose sheet of notepaper fell out. The jerky, upright handwriting was as familiar to Eva as the static shock she always got when she touched the bedroom door handle at home. 'I thought you would like this back. – CS'.

She closed the lid again, put her head in her folded arms, and sat there without moving for a long time.

Eva had little enough time to inform her classmates of her departure. They all expressed surprise, and even Rhona Lewis seemed genuinely sorry. 'You were always an odd thing, Downey,' she observed during a deportment class, 'but you were beginning to make your way a bit.' She tactfully did not mention her fellow students' disapprobation at the *very* persistent rumours about Eva Downey and a certain teacher; Eva, with equal tact, did not mention that the book Rhona Lewis was trying to balance on her head was a recent edition of *Anna Karenina*.

Miss Hautbois was particularly disappointed. Her cheeks, which even in repose moved down her face like sands in a delta covered by rivulets of wrinkles, dropped further, and her burgundy-painted lips vanished under the folds of flesh. '*C'est dommage*,' she said softly. 'You were getting on a little well with the German, too.'

Eva shrugged. She could not help it; the Gallic mannerism was contagious. 'I dare say I will never speak a word of the language again. I will probably forget it all.'

Miss Hautbois jabbed a claw-like index finger in the air. 'You – will – not – forget. You never know, maybe some day you will find you need it again. Nothing learnt is wasted. Remember that, Miss Downey.'

'Yes,' Eva said, 'I will remember.'

To her surprise, Mr Duncan stopped her in the corridor to say he regretted hearing of her departure, though she had said nothing to him about it. He spoke softly, with a slight Northumbrian burr. For him to stop her and speak to her was sweet, for he was tremendously shy. She wondered again about what Sybil had said. So slow, deliberate, ruminant – it was hard to imagine him excited or passionate about anybody, let alone a member of his own sex.

She had not seen Mr Shandlin yet, but he would be there on Thursday, as usual. That day, she found him rushing between buildings, his body bent forward as it often was when he was in a hurry. She nearly had to grab his coat to get his attention. 'Yes, what is it?' he said irritably, then, upon seeing Eva, a slightly gentler, 'Hello.'

'I wanted to thank you, sir.'

'For what?' He looked mystified.

'For giving me the book back.'

'Oh, yes, that.' He made a gesture akin to brushing a fly off his coat. 'I need to be somewhere—'

Eva blocked his way. 'I didn't want to go and not say goodbye. You've probably heard I'm leaving tomorrow. I just wanted—'

'I beg your pardon,' he interrupted, 'you're doing *what* tomorrow?'

'Leaving,' Eva repeated.

'But you can't. You … Why?' The shock on his face was genuine.

Other pupils streamed past them, and they were starting to form a little island in their midst. Mr Shandlin twisted about, his head jerking like a crow's. He had the air of a man watching his back with insane care. He bent down to her and murmured, 'I need to talk to you. Not here, not now. Over there' – he made a gesture at the rhododendrons that grew near the driveway and created a secluded space – 'in half an hour.' Then off he went again, before she could argue, almost leaving a breeze in his wake.

Half an hour later, Eva was standing in the damp moss, hidden from the lawn by the rhododendrons. Had he truly meant it or had she misheard him? But then she saw him cross the lawn. He crashed past a bush, snapping a twig, then reappeared a few feet away from her. 'There you are!' he said, obviously relieved. 'Now. Tell me, what's all this nonsense about you leaving?'

'My father has ordered me home. Miss Hedges says she cannot keep me here against his wishes.'

Mr Shandlin shook his head in astonishment. 'Is he aware of how well you are doing? It's come up as discussion, believe me. I find it hard to understand why he would want you to leave now.'

Eva felt a shard of anger lodge in her heart. She wanted to tell Mr Shandlin that her father would have no interest in her academic prowess. But they had so recently argued, she and he, that she did not know how to continue. She could not forget his words. *You get on my nerves. You fill every silence with worthless talk.*

'My sister is very ill, and I've been summoned home to take care of her,' she said at last.

Immediately his expression softened. 'Oh, my poor girl. I am so sorry.' He moved towards her but then paused mid-step and drew back. 'Will she be all right, your sister?'

Eva was taken aback at his compassion. Then she remembered that the thought of a sibling in danger would be near to his heart. 'I think so, thank you, sir.'

'I am glad.' He nodded gravely and was silent for a moment. Then he burst out, 'I can't believe it! You're thriving here; everyone can see it.'

'My father discussed my cheating with Miss Hedges. Sybil's homework.'

'Oh, God.' He put his hands to his face. 'No.'

'I presumed you had told her. I presumed you knew I was leaving.'

'Of course I didn't know!' Mr Shandlin cried. 'And, I can assure you, I did not say one word to Miss Hedges about that whole affair. It never crossed my mind. I know I behaved abominably, but I would never do that. Caroline – Miss Hedges – keeps a tight leash on her prefects. I'm sure one of them told her. Not I, heaven knows I feel bad enough about my conduct without compounding it by getting you in trouble.' He was pale, and Eva could not help but feel a stab of pity for him.

'I believe you, sir.'

'Thank you.' He exhaled. 'I'm so sorry, dear girl.'

'What for?'

'I should not have spoken that way to you,' he said softly. 'It was wrong of me. My vanity was offended, and I tried to hurt you in retaliation. That's how childish it was.'

She bit her lip and stayed quiet. Somewhere nearby a nuthatch called out, *twee-twee-twee-twee*. Mr Shandlin listened intently, then put his hands behind his back and recited some poetry:

'As the clouds the clouds chase;
And we go,
And we drop like the fruits of the tree,

Even we,
Even so.'

'Is that Brooke too?'

'Meredith, actually. "Dirge in Woods". I like Meredith; Gabriel cannot abide him. We have frequent arguments on the subject.'

'Mr Hunter!' Eva exclaimed. 'I saw him at the dance in Winchester.'

'I know,' Mr Shandlin said crossly. 'He told me he went, and I chewed his ear off for it. Stupid fool. Gabe Hunter is a dear friend, but I wouldn't have him anywhere near young women. A good rule of thumb is to ignore everything he says and everything he does as well.' He struck his palm with the side of his hand, frowning. 'But never mind him. Did you enjoy yourself at this dance? Were you the cynosure of the ball?'

'Not hardly. I drank bad wine and had a headache in iambic pentameter.'

Mr Shandlin made a face. 'Those are truly the worst kind. Though with your heritage, I thought you'd have had more of a taste for the dactyl. Diddledy-dum-di-diddley-dum—' Eva glared at him. 'Ah. Not, I see. Iambic it is then. My *head*, my *head*, my *head*, my *head*?'

'More or less. There was a viscount too, and a lot of manhandling around the dance floor.'

'Manhandling viscounts. Sounds like you were having fun, and without me.'

Eva laughed. 'It wouldn't be your sort of evening, Mr Shandlin. You don't dance.'

He looked at her, wide-eyed. 'I don't, do I not? Who says?'

Eva looked at him in astonishment.

'What step did you learn to skate across the floor with those ham-handed aristos anyway?'

'I think it was a hesitation waltz,' Eva stammered, still surprised.

'Right,' Mr Shandlin said, extending his hand. 'May I have this dance then, please, Miss Downey?'

Eva gestured around her. 'May I have some music first, Mr Shandlin?'

He tut-tutted. 'So unimaginative. You're not like that in your essays, let me tell you. I'll supply the music, if you insist.' He started humming, another tuneless melody roughly recognisable as a waltz, much to Eva's mixed horror and amusement. He could not be serious.

'Are you going to have me standing here all afternoon?' he demanded.

Tentatively she raised her right hand to meet his, and he took it, his fingers cupping hers, his grip loose. Their palms briefly met, then parted. Then he lightly grasped her shoulder with the other hand to turn her towards him. Together they lined up and pointed their feet outward. Eva had decided to tell him that this was ridiculous and that someone would see them, but he had already counted one-two-three and set off, so she had no option but to follow, her hand flat on his upper arm, feeling like an elephant as he quickly walked her backwards and then on the fifth count set her into a turn.

To her surprise, she found him quite a good dancer. They moved across the dewy lawn with surprising grace, and he kept a firm but gentle hand on her upper back. He was just a little bit stiff and faced forward all the while, whispering the counts under his breath – but compared to the cheery louts who had turned Eva's toes black and blue at the dance, Mr Shandlin's slightly hands-off approach was a relief. She forgot there wasn't any music and that she had no natural aptitude for dancing. She was just on the verge of forgetting herself, too, letting the dance take over, when she stepped onto the hem of her dress during a reverse turn and collided with him.

He smelt of cigarette smoke and, faintly, lemon verbena soap, the kind her mother used to wash her with when she was very small and sitting in a tin bath in the garden back in Cork. Even after Sybil's telling her that Mr Shandlin was in love with her, Eva had never allowed herself to imagine what it would be like if they touched, or even embraced; now his nearness caused a frisson under her skin that took away both her concentration and her balance. Her head just fitted under the angle of his jaw and she could see tiny shaving cuts on his neck and chin.

For a second she surrendered to the fall and let herself sway in the light hold of his arms, but he set her on her feet quickly, made a small sound under his breath, then remarked, 'Of course, that night you wouldn't have been tripping up all the time. You were wearing that grey, shiny thing, the one that falls down your back, yes?' He led her into the next step of the dance.

Still dizzy with sweet confusion, Eva nearly missed her cue for the cross-hesitation step. 'You saw me?'

'Now, now. Try to remember you're still dancing and leave my toes alone. I was on my way home through the woods when I saw you all gathered around the door like a flock of flamingos. I stopped to admire you all. I didn't draw attention to myself – it didn't seem appropriate.'

So Sybil had been right! 'And you saw me.'

'Oh, yes.' The hand on her back tightened a little. 'I saw you all right.'

'That's the first time you've ever mentioned anything I've worn. You never comment on people's appearance.'

'Not commenting,' Mr Shandlin said drily, 'doesn't mean I don't notice.'

'Well, then,' said Eva, 'what did you think of it? My dress?'

'My opinion is unimportant. Now stay behind me, I'm supposed to turn you here.' Eva obediently stepped back and allowed him to turn her forward. They did one more circuit before ending up where they had started, at which point he dropped her hand, bowing ceremoniously to thank her for the dance. He looked flushed and a little out of breath, Eva noticed. And all of a sudden very solemn. 'I need to speak to you about something,' he said, 'while we're here. I always intended to tell you – but I thought there would be time.'

Good heavens, Eva thought, *is he going to declare himself?* She laced her hands together at her waist to stop them trembling. She could not speak for nerves, only nod at him to continue.

'Did you know the colleges are offering scholarships to women? Somerville College in Oxford and the like? You should apply. Not this year, but the next. I might not be able to teach you any more, not officially, but I would do everything in my power to make sure you passed those exams and were accepted, as you deserve to be.'

Oh. Eva composed herself and shook her head. 'Father would never allow it.'

'You might be able to disregard his wishes,' Mr Shandlin said, 'if the fees were paid for by a scholarship. Look, Eva, I don't want to be crude, but if you decide to sell yourself the way this place trains you to do, choose a man who will support your ambitions. Or someone you can influence, so they won't try and keep you at home and lock you away from the world.' He added, almost in a whisper, 'That's not what I want for you.'

Eva was so shocked it took her some time to answer him. 'You think that's how it works?'

'Of course that's how it works,' Mr Shandlin said, in irritation. 'You go to these society events to make it clear by whom you would like to be chosen, and then they choose you. Simple. Heaven knows I've been there myself as the chooser – with remarkably little success, I might add.'

'And what about love?' The words were out of her mouth before she could stop herself.

'Love? Oh, Eva, no.' He looked at her in gentle reproof, as if she had used coarse language in his presence. 'That would be a terrible idea.'

Eva could hardly believe what she was hearing. Love, a terrible idea? Did he really think she could be paraded and sold like a prize cow at a fair? *To someone else?*

'Look,' he ploughed on, seeing her feelings on her face, if not divining their cause, 'I've taught a few girls – not many – who had a good future ahead of them, and then they fell in love – or so they described it. I've seen them since, and they're all unhappy. They married on impulse, and they are stuck with someone who doesn't understand them or give them any freedom. For a moment of infatuation they've lost everything. And they were far inferior to you. For you to end up like that ... no. Listen to me, Eva: use your head, not your heart. Find somebody who understands what you want. Promise me you will stay clear-sighted. For your own sake.'

He stopped for a moment, tired from the effort of so much talk. Eva felt unseasonably cold, and shivered, folding her arms across her chest, bunching her fists under her arms to warm her fingers. What he had just said – it was so dispassionate! Was that how he really felt about the whole business? About her?

He too seemed agitated, turning away towards a laurel bush, picking off one of the shiny leaves and tearing it in half, then quarters, then eighths, the little green fragments of leaf floating to the ground. Then picking another leaf, shredding that one too. Silence unnerved him, Eva saw. Good. She would treat him to a little more of it. If she could only stop shivering! Why, when it wasn't even cold?

He neither looked at her nor spoke again for such a long time that she wondered if she had effectively been dismissed. Her skin had cooled, a breeze was blowing, and her heartbeat was almost back to normal. She could hear voices far away, near the main building, as well as shouts coming up from the netball court. What if someone were to discover them? Not that there was anything more to discover than two silent people standing around like mannequins in a drapery.

'It may be,' she said tartly, 'that nobody will be interested in such an arrangement.'

'They will.' He was short.

'You … you make me feel like a goods parcel,' she said, with gathering rage, 'to be packaged and stamped for the travelling post and thrown into a sorting bag in Maidenhead.'

'Now, that's not fair and you know it—'

'I'm not an item of commerce, Mr Shandlin. I'm—'

'For Christ's sake!' He shouted so loudly that a murder of crows clattered off a nearby tree. The netball court fell silent. Mr Shandlin clapped his hand to his mouth, realising he might have been heard. After a few seconds' silence, the sounds resumed. He approached her. Barely a foot away, his fingers very softly lifted her chin. 'I am trying to do the right thing here.' His eyes were huge and black, his voice a whisper. 'Can't you … understand – at all?' He withdrew his fingers.

Eva clasped the medal around her neck and twisted the chain. The netball players' voices came closer, cutting the silence open with banalities about motor cars and up-dos and hunt balls.

'Goodbye, Miss Downey,' Mr Shandlin said abruptly. 'I wish you every good fortune. And please, do write once you have made your plans.' Then, in a softer tone, a little hoarse, 'Take care, dear girl.'

'Goodbye—' Eva began, but he had already turned his back and was walking away rapidly, his shoulders hunched slightly. She stood and watched him retreat across the lawn and vanish into the shadow of the building.

'Goodbye, Christopher,' she murmured to the empty air. The nuthatch replied, *twee-twee-twee-twee*, over and over again. It didn't care if anyone were listening, nor did it care about the crushing disappointment Eva felt in her heart to see him go.

II

The Decision

12

2 *May 1914*

The knock on the door was more like a dead hand than a firm rat-tat-tat; Hendricks, the valet, was always irritatingly quiet both in approach and address. Herbert Fellowes, who had just removed his shoes in preparation for bed, answered the door in his stockinged feet. 'Yes? What is it?'

'I have just received a phone call, sir, concerning Miss Imelda Downey. She's taken a turn for the worse.'

'Good Lord, again?' Fellowes said. 'I have told them time and time again what needs to be done.'

'Of course, sir.'

'Are there any more details?'

'Only that she appears to be coughing up a lot of blood, dark in colour. And that she is having – em – other problems.'

'Hendricks, man, there is no need to be coy, not at this time of night. What sort of problems? Female?'

'No, sir. Severe diarrhoea.'

Fellowes shook his head. 'This is getting bad. All right, give me five minutes to get my bag together and I'll be out.'

'I will get the car ready, sir.'

Fellowes blinked and rubbed his eyes. A man of nine-and-twenty with thick, wavy hair the colour of wet burlap, he had just eaten a moderately unsatisfactory meal of overcooked macaroni and fatty lamb cutlets and had finally been about to take to his bed and sleep the sleep of the dead. It had been a while since his last good kip; he had endured eleven house calls in the past twenty-four hours and was dropping on his feet.

Not for the first time he cursed the day he had chosen medicine as a career; you could never take a girl home for fear of being woken in the middle of the night because some old lady or consumptive demanded your attention. He should have studied law. All those fellows did was sit in Chancery, well fed and well rested, being paid huge sums for dressing up in wigs and gowns and … But Fellowes had iterated this particular train of thought many times before.

As the car pulled away from his rooms in Highbury and rattled over the London roads out towards the East End, he tried to doze, but his eye twitched and he gave up the effort. He was bad with faces, but good with names. He had placed Imelda Downey immediately, even though half the city had tuberculosis and half of that half was busy pretending it was something else. And for many of those people there was nothing Fellowes could do.

Imelda Downey was by no means a hopeless case; he had established that there was involvement in the left lung only. She obeyed all his instructions and took her medication regularly. It was just … there was something about the rest of her family that troubled Fellowes. Especially Miss Downey's younger sister Grace, her neck bending forward, black ringlets falling close enough to her full lips that she could take one in her teeth and bite it … Fellowes calmed himself. These moods always came upon him when he was tired. She was a tease, that Miss Grace Downey, forever going on about that army captain she was seeing while letting her fingers steal to the edge of her lace neckline as if beckoning him to untie the demure line of tiny buttons just below it.

And the *mother*. Always in the background, hands folded at her waist, watching the pretty daughter like a hawk. Something about her didn't fit. The profession he had chosen and which he loved so little had taught Fellowes the art of listening well, both to what was said and what was not, and there was something missing in the story of this family, though he was damned if he knew what it was.

Hendricks stopped the car and came around to open the door. The night air hit him with the full force of a wet slap. He began coughing as Hendricks silently handed him his bag. 'Sometimes I think you would be better at my job than I, Hendricks,' he spluttered.

'Quite so, sir.' Hendricks' agreement came rather too readily for Fellowes' taste.

Inside the house, the lights were on and everyone was awake. This was common enough, he remembered. Miss Grace had once disparagingly remarked, 'When she's up, we're all up.' Fellowes had not chided her: it was obvious she was fagged out, and he knew only too well how much noise and disturbance consumptives made during a bad spell. She could be pardoned for not having infinite reserves of compassion.

When he was led into Miss Imelda's room, Grace smiled at him with an incline of her head, just so; seated at the bed beside her was a girl he did not recognise, heavier and fairer, in an unflattering grey cloth bathrobe, holding Imelda's hand and looking daggers at everyone else. To Fellowes she made no acknowledgement or introduction. Imelda herself was grey-faced, her head lolling back on the pillow; flecks of dried blood still dotting her lips. She set those grey-blue, still eyes of hers on him and, too tired to speak, mouthed an apology.

'I need to examine you now, Miss Downey,' Fellowes said. This was the cue for everyone else to leave the room, but this new girl was not for moving. She guarded a tumbler of water on the bedside table and a cloth lying alongside it; when Fellowes moved towards his patient, her interposing hand and gaze blocked him. Then it became clear to him that they were sisters; indeed, this girl looked a lot more like Imelda than did Grace. They both had the same eyes.

'Eva, it's all right,' Imelda managed from the pillow.

'Are you sure, darling?'

'Yes. Dr Fellowes has done this many times before.'

Eva stood up. 'If you need anything, I'll be just outside. I shan't be further than the door.'

Imelda nodded weakly, and her sister left. The examination was straightforward enough. She was not coy: she presented her bare chest as if it were the front page of that day's *Times*. She did not protest at Fellowes' ministrations. Consumptives were sometimes like that, benignly indifferent. Or they would go too far the other way, pawing at him, hectic and flushed, even reaching up to kiss him, the sweet-sour tinge of blood on their breath making him recoil. Imelda Downey was not one of those.

When he was finished, he told her he would speak to both her parents. The father was a surly fellow with an Irish accent, though Fellowes was not too concerned about that as long as he wrote his cheque at the end of each visit. Dashed if he was going to get up and do a house call for nothing, especially when he had been just about to go to bed.

'Is everything as usual, doctor?' Imelda asked politely. It was the first thing she had said to him since he had started his examination.

'Yes, Miss Downey,' he said, 'everything is as usual.'

As he listed off the usual remedies she should take if she had a 'bronchial relapse', he had an uncomfortable feeling that Eva was listening to every word from behind the door.

'Thank you,' Imelda said; then, 'If that changes, can you let me know?'

He stopped, touched by her directness. 'Oh, I don't think there's any need for you to be anxious at present.'

As he suspected, when he opened the door, Eva – Miss Eva, he corrected himself – was standing barely a foot away. She had not bothered to dress in the meantime, nor were her manners any more prepossessing. She gave him the briefest of nods as he passed her in the corridor and continued downstairs to the parlour at the front where Catherine and Grace were waiting.

'Sit down, do, doctor,' Catherine soothed, pointing at an armchair. 'Mr Downey will be here in just a minute.'

'And – er – the other Miss Downey?'

No sooner were the words out of his mouth than Catherine made a face, her small mouth creased into her chin. Grace said, 'Oh, Princess Eva. Don't mind her, Dr Fellowes. She's in a chafing mood at the moment. She might turn up, and, then again, she might not.'

'Oh, dear,' Fellowes said, feeling the unpleasant sensation of being drawn into other people's concerns when he'd rather be drawn into the arms of a nice girl, a warm bed and a bottle of whisky.

'She is supposed to be at a grand school, but Imelda got sick, so they called her back.'

'Grace. Hold your tongue,' Catherine said, in a voice so sour it would have curdled a delivery van of milk. Grace was pursing her lips in preparation for a reply – rather pleasingly, Fellowes couldn't help observing – when Mr Downey entered the room. Now he had arrived, Fellowes could begin. He explained to them that Imelda needed to travel to Switzerland for an operation. The air was cold and dry up in the Alps, and the chances of recovery were much higher. She would undergo a procedure of plombage, that was to say, the induced collapsing and sealing of the cavities in her left lung by means of insertion of mineral oil and several acrylic balls. (Catherine hiccupped in horror.) These would be held fast in her chest and would serve to close the infected area, avoiding the spread to other areas.

'And this would be in the left lung only?' Roy asked.

'One could do similar with the right lung, for prevention's sake, but I think it might be dangerous to insert so much weight into the chest. I know the surgeon there, Dr Behrens, has a modified version of the standard operation which is less invasive in every way.'

Catherine looked at Fellowes, her eyes tiny and dead as raisins. 'And would that be expensive?'

'Mother,' Grace said reprovingly, then to the doctor, 'We want what's best for Imelda. My mother is simply anxious that we do not have the funds to bring her to Switzerland at this time. Of course, I could surrender part of my dowry for the purpose—' She lowered her head and half looked up at Fellowes with a coy smile.

'Ye won't do that! Ye'll not be givin' up yer dowry for anyone,' her mother blurted out. For a moment Fellowes was taken aback, but the tightness of Grace's breasts against that high-collared outfit she was wearing distracted him so much he was unable to marshal any sort of reply to Mrs Downey's intemperate remark. Little Irish minx! He felt certain she was keeping him in reserve in case things didn't work out with the captain. He decided to be blunt.

'Miss Imelda has consumption. For a young woman in her condition, there are not many options. I would advise you to act quickly.' He suppressed a belch.

Roy silently handed him an envelope. Fellowes immediately opened it and surveyed the cheque. He wouldn't put it past these people to see him undercharged. Still, Grace was rather lovely – that pert little smile … To his consternation he found himself becoming aroused. Hastily he stuffed the cheque in his pocket, then gathered up his bag, bid the Downeys goodnight and went to shake awake Hendricks, who was snoring loudly and loyally in the front seat of the car.

One window upstairs was still lit, the curtains open. Fellowes looked up and saw a figure in the window, standing still as a mannequin. It was Eva. She had not left Imelda's room since he had gone downstairs. For some reason, as he shut the passenger door and allowed Hendricks to drive him back to Highbury, he found himself repressing a shudder.

Dr Fellowes had recommended sun and light, so Imelda spent the next few days sitting on the daybed by the dining-room window at the back of the house. Eva was never far from her side. At that moment, she was sitting at the dining table, Woodhouse's English–Greek Dictionary flat on the table, page marked with a Cox's orange pippin. She was declining Ancient Greek nouns: *Eleutheriá, eleutherián, eleutheriás* …

The dining room was the most pleasant of the house, receiving all the afternoon and evening sunlight. Its only problem for a convalescent was that the sunlight inspired all the motes of dust on the bookshelves, ornaments and drinks cabinet to come out and dance, and Eva had to summon Nelly to open the windows to stop Imelda coughing. On a clear day like this, the air from outside was dry enough to bring some succour to Imelda's besieged lungs. Her breathing was quiet enough that day that Eva forgot she was there, until she spoke.

'What does it mean?'

Eva turned around, startled at the interruption. 'What does what mean?'

'That word you keep whispering.'

'*Eleutheriá* – it means "freedom".' Eva picked up the apple and took a bite. 'Escape.' There was a silence. Imelda had never said as much, but Eva knew she was displeased at being declared the reason why Eva had to return home. Eva had allowed too much yearning to creep into her words, Greek and English alike.

She took another bite. The flesh was soft and limp, crumbling in her mouth, its flavour so prim and lifeless it was almost pearish. It had been too long in the fruit bowl. The fruit bowl had been too long in the sun. Nothing moved around here and nothing changed.

'It's Greek, isn't it? Are you enjoying it?' Imelda asked.

'I'm finding it hard going, actually,' Eva swallowed down her apple. 'I'm not used to the characters and diacritics. And I have until next March …' Eva stopped abruptly.

'Next March for what? Oh, Evie, are you off on another adventure without telling anyone?' Imelda looked at her sister, her brows furrowed with worry. 'You know what happened the last time.'

Nobody in the family ever discussed what Catherine had done to Eva three years ago, after the night of the Census, but it hung in the air between them.

'The last time,' Eva said, her voice as cold as the sudden breeze that came in the open window, sending goose pimples rippling across Imelda's bare forearm, 'I didn't fight back.'

'Oh, Evie,' Imelda said with a sigh, 'I'm frightened they'll put you out on the street, truly I am. You need not offend Mother so much.'

'It offends *me* when you call her that,' Eva said tightly.

Imelda put her book down on the daybed, spine up. 'Eva, you have to accept the way things are. Why, I'd rather be up and about and healthy, not sick all the time. Pretending I'm happy with how it is.'

Eva did not answer. Imelda persisted. 'Whatever this plan is – it's what the Greek is all about, isn't it? And those university extension lectures you've signed up for?'

'When I was at school,' Eva answered slowly, 'I was encouraged to try for a scholarship to Somerville College in Oxford.'

'Oxford? Really? Whose idea was that?'

'My teacher's.' Eva tried to sound neutral. 'Mr Shandlin. I mentioned him.'

'Yes, I recall.' Imelda was all attention now. 'You more than mentioned him, Eva. You spoke about him a lot.'

'Well, what of it? We—'

'I've never heard you take on so about any other male person—'

'The sex difference does not come into it,' Eva started indignantly, but Imelda was not deterred.

'You were all about him. Then, suddenly, nothing. You talk about Sybil and her dances, and German lessons, and the Lord knows what, but since you came home, not a word about Mr Shandlin. Did you never reconcile with him after that argument?'

'We reconciled,' Eva said, after a brief pause, 'but we haven't been in communication. I wrote to him once and got no response.'

'I see. Yet you follow his commands faithfully enough.'

There was such pity in Imelda's tone that Eva could not look her in the eye and instead feigned a burning interest in short a-stem feminine nouns. This was interrupted when Grace barged in shortly afterwards, declaring that the place was *freezing* and would somebody please close the window immediately, and they would have to all turf themselves out soon because Alec – 'that's "Captain Featherstone" to you' – was coming after lunch. 'Oh, and Eva,' she added, 'Father wants you. Something to do with a David Wentworth Hopkins.'

13

Three days later, Mr Hopkins was sitting exactly where Imelda had been. Eva regarded him from the other end of the seat: in the light of day, he looked younger and paler than at the dance. His fairish hair, parted at the dead centre, was only betrayed in its stiffness by a cowlick, which, unlike Gabriel Hunter's, was slicked down with hair oil.

He had telephoned her father after receiving her details from Miss Hedges. Eva was gratified that he had gone to that much trouble but annoyed that he had asked Papa first rather than approaching her. When she ventured as much, he replied, 'I thought it would be proper.' He delivered these words with his back rigid; Eva had never seen anyone sit up so straight. Every time he did move, she got a blast of the Everlast cologne he had presumably splashed on his smooth cheeks that morning.

He was nineteen, a relative of the Parmenter family, well known in Kent and Sussex. Eva got the distinct impression that his relationship with them was distant enough and that he needed the connection to boost his own fortunes. He had been a pupil at Marlborough but hadn't managed to get sent up to Oxford so was now learning the ropes of the family business, coal mining in Wiltshire. All this information he delivered in a manner that implied he was serving an *amuse-bouche* before continuing to the meal proper. When he made a point of particular importance, his body would move forward and sideways, his knee brushing against hers. Then he drew a thick manila envelope onto his lap and started talking about writing poetry. Eva pretended not to notice the envelope or the segue, instead mentioning that she had just finished reading Tolstoy's novella, *The Death of Ivan Ilyich*. However, like Rhona Lewis, Mr Hopkins – 'David, please! I insist' – was largely unfamiliar with Tolstoy, finding his books 'too blasted long, really'.

'*Ivan Ilyich* isn't that long—' Eva began, but he wasn't listening and soon cut across her. The envelope wobbled on his lap as he talked about sonnets – 'You do know, Miss Downey, that a sonnet is fourteen lines with an ABAB rhyming scheme?' Eva assured him that she did. Then he finally got to his point: since she had mentioned it (she had not) he had a few in his folder; would she care to have a look? ('Why, that would be lovely.') He cleared his throat and started reading one out to her.

It was the longest half hour of Eva's life. No 'you' intruded where a 'thou' would do, no 'field' where a 'knoll' could do the job, and the only place for the longed-for heroine to linger was, of course, in a 'bower', with rambling roses climbing up the trellis. Eva was climbing the walls. And she had a headache.

Grace came in, having forgotten something, and Eva fervently hoped she would be as rude as usual, but, for once, on seeing Eva and David, she meekly excused herself and left again. Oh, for heaven's sake! Grace had never been nice, it was the one reliable thing about her, so why did she have to start now? Meanwhile, David was tapping her on the elbow. 'I'm sorry, what did you say?' she asked him.

'I said' – with some heat – 'would it please you to take a walk with me through some nearby pleasant greenery?' At Eva's blank look, he snapped, 'I mean outside!'

They walked in the warm June evening: one parentally sanctioned circuit around the greenery-free square. David waved off clouds of midges and invited Eva to tell him about herself. When she informed him that her mother had died young, he patted her arm and said, 'Should be it appropriate after such a length of time to express my condolences, please consider them offered.' This rather awkward sympathy softened Eva a little, and she explained that she had left school prematurely to care for her sister. So she was dutiful in addition to being well read. 'Quite remarkable!' Then David continued, 'You are probably wondering why I wanted to see you again. It was your interest in poetry. And your responses to my poems, so informed! You must have been excellently tutored.'

'I was,' Eva said, not trusting herself to say any more.

Then for a brief moment he went off the subject of poetry, confessing his desire – should God in His mercy allow it – to become an army officer and win a Military Cross for bravery.

'You are hoping for – I mean, expecting – a war?'

He took her hand in such a tight grip it nearly hurt. 'If there's a war, and I fight, it is for you and all English womenfolk, to preserve your safety.'

'I'm Irish by birth.'

'I'd overlook that,' he said hurriedly, 'considering everything else. Would you deny yourself my support?'

How quickly 'English womenfolk' had devolved to Eva herself, and the Empire's army to one rather gauche boy. 'You mean,' Eva said, 'you would protect me?' Mr Shandlin's words echoed in her mind: *Use your head, not your heart. Stay clear-sighted.*

'Yes, of course I would.' David relaxed his grip and took her hand more gently. His palm felt soft and damp against her fingers as they walked back down to Eva's house. At a judicious distance, he dropped his hand, but said in a low voice, 'May I call on you again, Eva?'

She looked at him a moment. He meant well, she could see that. 'Yes, please do.'

'Oh, I'm glad,' he said, smiling, 'it would be a rotten shame not to see you again, when I've so many more poems to show you!'

4 August 1914

"'It was officially stated at the Foreign Office last night that Great Britain declared war against Germany at 7.00 pm. The British Ambassador in Berlin has been handed his passport. War was Germany's reply to our request that she should respect the neutrality of Belgium, whose territories we were bound in honour and by treaty obligations to maintain inviolate.'" Roy Downey finished reading his *Daily Mirror* and put the paper down, smacking his lips. 'There you are, then. Battle stations.'

Catherine clattered her fork on her plate in excitement. 'If we're at war, does that mean Ireland too?'

Grace rolled her eyes. 'Mother, for God's sake, that's why it's called the United Kingdom of Great Britain and Ireland.' She poked at her mutton and gravy. 'I don't fancy the rest of this. It doesn't feel right to just sit here eating when there's a war on.' She pushed her plate away and vanished into the cool sanctuary of the hall and, presumably, the telephone, to talk to Captain Alec Featherstone.

After luncheon, and in the days that followed, Catherine railed at the servants: they were too giddy to concentrate on anything. All the usual routines were going west as fast as the Germans were going south – and Eva was not sorry. Sometimes she would sit out on the steps, eating a piece of bread and a hunk of good cheddar; passers-by hooted or waved, or both. War and hot weather had everyone excited. Overnight, every wall, shop, public bar and train station in London had a Notice for General Mobilisation tacked onto it. Feelings in the street ran high. One of Grace's friends suggested going over to the German Embassy, where people were throwing stones and rotten eggs at the windows, but Catherine had the sense, for once, to veto that plan.

Everything was up in the air – well, everything except David Wentworth Hopkins, who still faithfully called on Eva every second Monday, as reliable as the tramp and thud of each metric foot of his rhyming stanzas. He too was full of the excitement of war, even going so far as to start reciting 'Horatius', but his memory of Macaulay's *Lays of Ancient Rome* didn't stretch much further than eight lines so Eva was spared the rest.

A few days after war was declared, Captain Featherstone, called away to serve with the British Expeditionary Force, arrived at the house to say goodbye. Grace fawned over him even more than usual, in a manner that made Eva wince, putting her arms around his neck and calling him 'my Old Contemptible'. To Eva, Featherstone seemed too stupid to fight a war of any description, but Grace kept keen track of his progress. She bought a map of Europe, framed it at her own expense and hung it in the parlour. Since it had no glass, she could stick pins into the various points of the developing front. She had a special icon for Captain Featherstone – a little man on a horse – which moved as she read news of his regiment or received his letters. He was not a great letter-writer, he declared apologetically in one of them.

She also managed to find a hanky with the music to 'It's a Long Way to Tipperary' embroidered on it, which she endeavoured to pull out at every opportunity. 'Snot easy, fighting on the western front,' Imelda had commented. Eva had turned around to ensure she had heard Imelda correctly, but her sister sat there, sedate and demure, as if she hadn't said a word.

Captain Featherstone was dead before the month was out, hit by artillery fire while defending Le Cateau; neither his bayonet nor his horse proved adequate when faced with the German war machine. But the deepest cut for Grace was not his untimely death, it was that she did not hear of it until early September, after the memorial service had been held and another woman listed in the paper as Featherstone's fiancée. His infrequent letter-writing now had a prosaic and humiliating explanation. Grace's response was to fling herself ever deeper into martial fervour. As a coping measure, it worked: the glow soon returned to her cheeks and the light to her eye, especially when Imelda's health worsened and a house call from Dr Fellowes was required once more.

Eva was not unsympathetic. It was a rotten thing to love a man, then to lose him, then to realise he was not yours to lose. She still felt a certain rawness when she thought about Mr Shandlin, though that pain was beginning to heal. However, her sympathy for Grace was tempered by her suspicion that she had never loved Alec Featherstone quite as much as she had his rank. Eva said as much to her one day when Grace was in the middle of one of her sermons about it being Every Man's Duty to something something something and Eva had had enough of hearing it.

'At least he's done his part! What about your Hopkins fellow?' Grace snapped in reply. 'I'm warning you, Eva, you'd better hope he signs up. Do you know there's been a town crier down in Chatham ringing a bell and telling all the men to watch their step because the women are about? We'll put manners on them if they don't do their bit.'

'You needn't bother,' Eva said wearily, 'he enlisted about five minutes after they put up the posters. I think he'd have camped overnight at the recruiting station if it weren't open.'

'Good,' Grace said. 'Now all he has to do is propose to you and you'll be altogether respectable.'

David, still awaiting his orders, called on the first Monday of September, as per his usual schedule. However, on this occasion, he went to see Eva's father in his study before Eva was told of his arrival. When Father left and she was eventually allowed in to the parlour, David was standing in the middle of the room, hands on his hips. 'Eva dear,' he said, smiling, 'please sit down.'

I will and all, she thought to herself, *considering it's my house*. But she did as she was told. The air was close, and the pomatum she had put in her hair smelt strong and sweet. She regretted having used so much; it was stinking out the room. That and David's Everlast ... Imelda wouldn't be able to go in there for half an hour afterwards, poor lamb.

David was direct. War made his objective urgent; he had obtained her father's permission, and now sought hers, for her hand in marriage. He rushed over the word 'marriage' as if it were a faintly embarrassing blot on an otherwise impeccable business communication.

'David—' she interrupted him.

'Yes, Eva?'

'Will you touch me?'

'I beg your pardon?' He flinched, offended.

'Come here beside me. Take my hand again.'

'You ask that of me? You doubt that I am sincere?'

'Of course not, David. I just need you to take my hand. Is that not a reasonable request?'

David sat beside her and did as she had instructed. He held her hand very gravely and solemnly, as if it were made of cut glass and he was to weigh it.

'David,' Eva said, 'why do you want to marry me?'

He cleared his throat and stared at her. 'What a question! Well, because … because you have interesting opinions. A husband needs that in a wife, as well as the …' He turned scarlet. 'I mean simply to say that you seem to have an enquiring and intelligent nature, without being overly immodest.'

For want of anything else to say, Eva thanked him.

'And you like my poetry,' he added, with a bashful expression. 'Others … have been less understanding.'

'Indeed.' Eva hoped she looked composed.

'And now all that is missing is your consent.' He pressed Eva's hand slightly. 'A formality, but not insignificant.'

'David,' Eva said, 'I have some hopes of further study. I have reason to hope that marriage will provide me with the space and time to devote to my books.'

He sat up straight at that, looking every inch the frowning prep-school officer-in-training. 'What sort of study?'

'I have been encouraged to enrol for a scholarship to Somerville College in Oxford – the women's college. I need to learn the rudiments of Greek. I started a few weeks ago.'

'Oxford? Greek?' He dropped her hand, outraged. 'Do you mean to turn into a bluestocking?'

'David,' Eva took his hand again. 'I cannot marry someone who does not support my interests.'

His hairless upper lip trembled. 'You will be busy with our home, with our children! Read for pleasure, by all means, but more than that … I could not allow it.'

Eva could only wonder at his presumption. 'I would not have your support?'

'Of course you would have my support. But only for activities appropriate for a wife.'

'Then I must refuse. I am sorry.'

David looked at her with incredulity. 'You're refusing me?' He held her gaze so long that Eva began to doubt herself. Was she being silly? Holding on to the advice of somebody who had not even bothered to write to her, who had caused her so much pain? What did she know about these matters anyway? She had never been held by a man, not in any way that mattered.

The hum of the city continued outside; in the distance Eva could hear a tram bell ringing. David rose and looked down at her. He did not seem cross at all; his manner was quite amiable. 'Eva, I shall give you some time to reconsider and come back on Friday to hear your answer. Let's say twelve-thirty?' He patted her shoulder and smiled down at her in a brotherly fashion. Then he left before she could think of a reply.

Roy Downey banged the study table with the flat of his hand, exclaiming with surprised rage at the pain. 'What do you mean, you said "no"? You've been encouraging him all this time, haven't you?'

'It didn't feel right,' was all Eva could manage.

This only maddened him more. 'It didn't feel right? What sort of nonsense is this? What on earth does marriage have to do with "feeling right"?'

'You marry people because you love them,' Eva said, in a small voice, 'just as you loved my mother when you married her.'

A flash of pain crossed Roy's saturnine features at the mention of Angela. He paused before continuing, rubbing the back of his neck with his fingers. 'Yes, I loved her once, that's true. But Eva, we cannot support you for ever. This folly with the school, and now turning down this boy, and for what? Look at Imelda. Her world is reduced, yet she is content.'

Eva laughed bitterly. 'You think Imelda content? She is desperately unhappy, Father.'

'Well, she has the good manners to hide it!' he spat out. 'Do you know, I am still getting letters from that fellow from Limerick? Here, look.' He shuffled through one of the many piles of correspondence from Kildare and Birr and Borris-in-Ossory to show her. 'Catherine won't stop encouraging him. I have been able to hold her off, but if you keep throwing up half decent offers from good English boys …' He sighed so heavily that several yellow telegrams on top of his correspondence drifted off the pile. 'I can't risk upsetting Mother.'

'You could always just allow her to get upset regardless.'

He looked her straight in the eye, his face small, yellow, cold. 'But I don't want to,' he said softly. 'D'you hear me? I don't want to.'

There was a room in Eva's heart which had a blind on the window. For a moment, when they had spoken of Angela, that window opened, the blind cord gently tapping the glass. But now it shut down with a swift rattle.

'Mr Hopkins reassured me that he would offer his suit again. That was most generous of him. You will accept him,' Roy concluded, moving things around on his desk, 'and there will be no further discussion about it. Now, you may go. Send Grace in to me. I rather prefer her company at present.'

8 September 1914

My dearest Sybil,

I hope you and your mother are bearing up well and that Bo is getting on all right. Will he be sent off soon, do you think?

I thought you should know that before too long I expect to be engaged to David Wentworth Hopkins. I refused him at first but Papa wouldn't hear of my doing so a second time. I do not believe myself 'in love' as the Socratic philosophers would have it, but, to be honest, Sybil, for what or whom am I holding out? Things could be much worse: if I do not marry soon, Catherine may yet push Mr Cronin on me just to get me out of the house.

David comes again on Friday afternoon to press his case. Please pray for me, to any God you please.

Your friend,

Eva Downey

14

On the Friday morning, Grace invited Eva to come shopping with her and Catherine. 'You might need some nice clothes. For the afternoon.' Her dismissive tone made Eva bristle, but she was right. War or no war, Eva needed a new skirt; her blue poplin was frayed about the edges from over-use. Eva did not question why Grace would extend such an uncommon kindness. Indeed, she did not start to get suspicious until they were well past the point where the cab should have turned off for Oxford Street and the shops. They continued west for a good ten minutes after that before Eva exclaimed, 'I say, Grace, where are we going?'

'Acton.'

'To buy dresses?'

'We're not going to buy a dress,' Grace replied calmly. 'I'm bringing you here to show you something. Because of that rotten thing you said about me loving Alec's rank more than him. I let it go at the time, but really, you should have been horsewhipped for that remark.'

Eva's heart sank. She should have known something was up. Clever Imelda, to have cried off. They got out at Acton Town Hall, Catherine charging ahead. To Eva, reluctantly following Grace inside, the place, with its worn wooden floor and long plywood dais, its faint miasma of dust and paint, had an appearance of a parish bake sale. But then she saw the women, and the feathers.

The women came from all classes, the feathers from a variety of birds: pigeon, cockerel, ostrich. Along the edge of the dais, brushing the floor, a banner read 'Order of the White Feather' – and there, in mid-speech, old, dumpy, squinting and with a weak chin, stood the famous authoress Mrs Humphry Ward herself.

'She's just started,' hissed Catherine.

'… and Admiral Fitzgerald,' Mrs Ward declared – she rolled the word 'Admiral' as if it were a particularly pleasant petit four she had just popped into her mouth – 'has entrusted me to bring to you, my sisters, the message of solidarity we women must show the men who defend us at our hour of most need.'

A woman sitting in the front row fanned herself vigorously; the hall was too warm, and there was a fetor in the air from too many clothes and a lack of washing. Eva was sure she could detect the smell of menstrual blood. She felt dizzy and wondered if she could stay standing.

'Our new order, the Order of the White Feather,' Mrs Ward continued, 'has proved very successful over the past few weeks. Why, just last Tuesday, outside the Opera House, our friends the suffragettes …' – some of the audience grew restive – 'Wait! I have not finished. Those ladies stopped a good hundred fellows out of uniform and presented them with a white feather each, so they would know exactly what their womenfolk thought of them.' The tumult turned to cheering, and a wan-looking girl in a crocheted shawl had to call the females to order before Mrs Ward could resume. 'Our aim is to be watchful of our men and to make sure that none shirk that most sacred of duties. As mothers, sisters, daughters, we must offer their blood as Christ offered His to save mankind!' Her voice rose to a shriek. 'The foul Hun has perpetrated the wickedest of deeds upon our sisters in Belgium, taking away their lives, their very chastity!'

Eva felt a headache coming on. Never mind other women's periods, her own was due. She hoped it wouldn't arrive early. There was quite enough blood in this hall already.

Mrs Ward concluded: 'I would ask each woman here to seek out every man of fighting age who is not in uniform and to present him with a feather. If the men of our empire will not save women from the Hun's depredations of their own free will, then they shall be shamed into it! They shall be shamed!'

The audience stamped, clapped and cheered. Catherine, in particular, forgot herself entirely, roaring like a fishwife, a vein throbbing in her neck, her small eyes glazing over. Women shouted 'Death to the Hun!' and 'God save the King!' as Mrs Ward stood there and lapped it up, her eyes glittering. The assistants distributed the feathers. Grace took two fistfuls. One of the girls with the trays stopped beside Eva. 'Here, take one.'

Eva recognised the girl with a start. 'Don't I know you?'

She looked at Eva with cool, contained surprise. 'I don't think so, no.'

'But I do!' Eva said, 'I met you in Trafalgar Square, three years ago. You were campaigning for votes for women. You inspired me to go to the Census Night party in Wimbledon Common. I heard you speak.'

The girl shrugged. 'Oh, that.'

Eva couldn't believe it. 'Why are you giving women white feathers? What happened to giving them the vote?'

'Did you not know?' the girl said sharply. 'Mrs Pankhurst organised for a whole lot of us to be here.'

'Eva!' Grace hissed. 'Are you refusing to take a feather?'

Eva took a few feathers from the tray and slipped them in her pocket. She felt sick.

'Don't hide them away,' the girl said, eyes shining now, 'bear them in your hands for all to see, so they know your mission.'

Eva gingerly took the feathers out again, holding them at some distance.

'Forget the other business,' the girl said. 'We are at war now.'

The meeting broke up. Eva did not keep her feathers, throwing them on the ground when they were crossing the road back to the Tube station. Grace still had hers, and a man out of uniform was coming their way. Eva watched as Grace speeded up. 'For God's sake,' Eva pleaded with her, 'he's forty if he's a day.'

'Forty's not too old to fight.'

'Grace, please!' But she was off. The gentleman was, Eva guessed, not particularly wealthy. His coat was too long for the heat, his briefcase a little battered. Perhaps a commercial traveller down on his luck. Or maybe even a teacher. But Grace didn't care. She marched up to the man and declaimed in a clear, high-pitched voice, 'I hereby bestow on you this white feather for your cowardice in refusing to fight in the war. God save the King!'

The man looked at her as if she were speaking Portuguese. 'What? … What?' But Grace was so quick that by the time he was aware of what had happened, she had already pinned the white feather in his lapel. A few other women walking past noticed and began to titter.

The man glanced around, a trapped look on his face. Now the women were chanting, 'Fight, fight, fight …' while Grace folded her arms with a smile, watching her new allies. On they went, inexorable, relentless.

Something inside the man broke. He bent his head and shuffled away around the corner, his sunny demeanour of a few moments before quite gone. Catherine watched him go with satisfaction. 'Ten to one he'll enlist first thing tomorrow.'

The Tube ride home was cheerless. Even with the windows open, the carriages stank of armpits and underclothes. Nearly every station had notices saying 'Join the Army – You Will Like It – The Kaiser Won't'. Eva felt soiled by what she had witnessed. She had let that poor man walk away, shamed. What would he do that evening? Would he go home to his wife and children and tell them he had no choice but to enlist, that some thoughtless bitch had taken it upon herself to present him with a white feather? The whole business felt deeply, dreadfully wrong. The only consolation was the certainty that she would never consider doing such a thing herself.

They were running late: David Wentworth Hopkins would be waiting for her by now. She could picture him sitting, straight-backed, hands on his knees, young and severe. He would propose to her again, and this time she would accept. The thought no longer filled her with the same dismay it had done earlier that week. Marrying him would be an escape from all Catherine's and Grace's schemes. Maybe she could take Imelda away too. David had been impressed by her concern for her sister, and there was sure to be room in his house. Yes, a wife had some freedom to make these decisions. A spinster daughter? None at all.

And all Eva would have to do in return was … well, that thing they wrote about in *The Wife's Handbook*. 'Too many wives do not realise the importance, the necessity to their happiness, of proper intercourse with their husbands,' so it said. But of course that was written by an American. Eva had read the description of the act, and of the organs involved, and tried to relate it to herself and then to David, but it all seemed so strange. She could make hardly head nor tail of it, could not imagine how his young, pale body and hers would join together – and would not risk further mockery by asking. It couldn't be that bad, surely, if people had been doing it since time began?

Eva's thoughts matched the pace of the racketing, swaying train. The wedding would be a swift one since David was soon to be deployed. Then she would live in a modest but pleasant house in Cirencester and have her own room and access to a library, where she could continue with Greek and sit her Responsions examination next year, if David relented … Before she could go on any further flights of fancy, the train stopped at their station, Aldgate, and ten minutes later they were home.

As Catherine went to put the key in the lock, the door was opened from inside. Nelly rushed to meet them. 'Oh, Miss Eva, in the parlour, there's—'

Eva nodded. 'Yes, Nelly, I know.' She walked in calmly, leaving the others to fuss with hats and coats. She closed the parlour door behind her and readied herself. 'Hello, Da—' she began, then stopped dead.

Sprawled on an armchair, his collar loose, fingers tapping a slow *ostinato* on the cover fastenings, sat Christopher Shandlin. He raised the tapping hand in a gesture of ironic half-greeting.

Eva's heart kicked at her ribs like a horse about to bolt. 'Where's David?' she blurted out, and immediately she wanted to kick herself. As if he would know who David was.

'If you mean that etiolated shape of a boy who was squeaking some nonsense about marrying you,' the familiar voice responded from the depths of the armchair, 'I can enlighten you. I sent him away.'

'You did what?'

155

Mr Shandlin rose from the chair in a belated gesture of courtesy to Eva, uncoiling himself in one long and slightly creaky movement. His eyes were restless and gleaming, his fingers still moving over thin air until he finally clasped the mantelpiece, which he seemed to need to support himself. 'I told him to be a nice boy and clear off. Did I do wrong, Eva? Would you like me to summon him back?'

'*No*,' Eva said, with such feeling and incivility that he grinned broadly and his shoulders relaxed.

'Thank God for that,' he said, 'I was a little nervous.'

She sat down, a safe distance away on the other side of the fireplace, and bade him do the same. She could hardly believe he was there, yet when she dared look across at him, he had not vanished but was still sitting forward, chin on hand, watching her quizzically. He was really there. She thought she would burst with joy – and yet, why *was* he there? Why now, after all this time? 'How did you find me?' she asked him.

'How did I find you? That is a very good question indeed, given as you never answered any of my letters and there was no exchange listed for you—'

'What do you mean, I never answered your letters?' Eva responded hotly. 'I never got any, that's why!'

'Now, Eva, that is merely a Counter-cheque Quarrelsome on your part, because you know I sent them. There was the first letter, delayed as long as possible after your departure as I could manage without sitting on my hands, in other words about one day. That was a nice long one, rather rambly perhaps, but pleasant, whimsical and sentimental without being cloying. No reply. Then the second one, a little sharper, I dare say, enquiring after your welfare and hoping all was well. Nothing. Not a word. Then, the third,' and here he winced, 'a rather angry, self-pitying screed which I put in the post box before I could change my mind. Then the fourth, sent immediately after that, which was an urgent request begging you to tear up the third without reading it. After your continued silence, I thought I had best give up writing letters altogether, since all I was doing was making a fool of myself.'

'I'll see you my Counter-cheque Quarrelsome,' Eva said, 'and raise you your own Lie Direct. Since I most certainly did write to you, a perfectly polite note, requesting help with compiling a booklist for that Somerville scholarship. And when I got no reply at all from you, I—'

'What? Eva, what?'

'I was upset. To hear nothing from you.' There, it was out.

'I'll bet you were,' Mr Shandlin said softly, 'as was I, not to hear from you. And I'll bet too that someone was intervening with our correspond-ence, and I think I know who.'

Eva wanted to say something but could barely speak. He had been upset not to hear from her. He had not forgotten her. He had written her four letters. That was enough. She did not care what complicated, manipulative mechanism her family, or Miss Hedges, or anyone else had dreamed up to keep them apart.

'Anyway,' he continued, 'I thank them with all my heart, since some of those letters didn't show me at my best. Odd, though, for I definitely posted one or two of them myself: I remember putting them in the village post box.'

Suddenly Eva remembered Catherine rushing for the post, pushing past the servants with some impatience, then shortly afterwards tearing some of the letters up. Eva had thought little enough about it at the time, but now it made sense. She had been watching for Mr Shandlin's letters to Eva and destroying them as they arrived.

'I think,' she said, 'more than one person intervened.'

'Why on earth do people have to interfere all the time? Nosy parkers, all of them.' He sighed. 'But I haven't answered your question. Hunter wanted to go off on one of his trips into the New Forest and nagged me into going with him. It all ended in tears, of course. He has people falling in love with him left, right and centre but loves the only lady of the party who is engaged to someone else. And he writes sonnets about it. Lots of sonnets. I had the misfortune of hearing most of them, rendered to me alcoholically in the middle of the night. Ten per cent were rather good. The rest—' He made a gesture.

'I thought you said Mr Hunter was a gifted poet.'

'He is,' Mr Shandlin said, 'but not when it comes to prolific love sonnets. Nobody is a gifted poet in that regard. No, not even Shakespeare. His sonnets were mostly about posterity.'

'David writes a lot of sonnets,' Eva said, with a smile.

'David being that boy, yes?'

'Yes indeed. He showed me several samples.'

'Oh? Written for you?'

Eva blushed. 'Some of them, yes. Believe me,' she added, seeing Mr Shandlin make a face, 'I was not clamouring to hear them. His style is somewhat … wooden.'

Although he was still sitting forward, he seemed to relax somewhat at that. 'To continue. I wanted to look you up, but then all this happened—'

He waved his hand, and Eva nodded. There was no need for him to explain what 'this' was. 'My mother was anxious, so I went to stay with her for a while.'

'Of course she would be concerned about you going to war,' Eva said, 'because of what happened to your brother.'

'She is very worried about me, but she needn't be,' Mr Shandlin said harshly, 'because I will have nothing to do with it.'

For a moment they were both silent. The sun was shining into the room, making the long unfastened curtains look shabby and discoloured and every surface dusty. Eva could hear whispering somewhere in the corridor. Grace and Catherine would find some way of showing how unhappy they were with this slightly shabbily dressed stranger turning up out of nowhere to call on her. If that's what he was doing? Was he calling on her or 'calling' on her? Had she misinterpreted his visit? Now, looking at the ground, he appeared to want to be elsewhere.

Eva wanted to tell Mr Shandlin about the meeting she had just attended, how the women had roared as if all sense had left them. How Grace and Catherine had preyed on that ordinary man on his luncheon break from his ordinary day's work. How Mr Shandlin himself would most certainly be watched and judged for not signing up.

At that exact moment, Grace walked into the parlour, stopped short and stared. 'Who're you?' she demanded. Mr Shandlin gave her his name, with icy politeness. In response, Grace wrinkled her nose, darted a look at Eva and walked out. Her departing voice wafted back into the room like cold air. 'Mama, there's a man come in to see Eva. It's not Mr Hopkins. I don't know who he is, but he's not in uniform.'

'Mr Shandlin, I apologise for my stepsister's rudeness.'

He picked up his coat, which he had left on the seat opposite. 'Never mind. I seem to have that effect on women, particularly the pretty ones. Anyway, it was nice to see you again, Eva.'

With the realisation that he was leaving came a rising panic in Eva's throat that she might not see him again. She needed to invent some reason – anything would do – her booklist! But then, at the door, he turned around. 'I'm sorry to rush; I have a class later this afternoon and some marking to do tomorrow. Are you free on Sunday? Two o'clock? I'll take the train up.'

'Yes,' Eva smiled with relief, 'yes, I'm free.'

'Good. See you on Sunday, then.'

The front door slammed behind him, shaking the whole house. Eva ran to the window. She saw his familiar, crow-like figure striding down the road, head jutted forward. He did not look back.

11 September 1914

Darling Eva,

I am so sorry I haven't replied until now. I received your letter about David, and I have to admit I was unsure whether congratulations were appropriate, and then ... All right. I have a confession to make. I might have bumped into Mr Shandlin at a tearoom this morning when I went to Tunbridge Wells to do a bit of shopping, and I might have mentioned your impending engagement that afternoon. He demanded to know where you lived, and, Evie, perhaps I told him. Anyway, whatever I did or didn't tell him, I didn't see him for dust until he rushed back to collect his hat and dashed off again.

Oh, I do hope I haven't messed things up for you, dear Eva. I'm awake now, terrified I've turned your family against you. I won't get this blasted thing posted out till tomorrow, but please write back by first return and let me know all is well.

Your friend

Sybil

P.S. I might also have goaded him a little by asking him if he were a man or a mouse.

15

When Mr Shandlin rang the doorbell of No. 35 Wellclose Square at five minutes past two on Sunday afternoon, and stood there in a hat and long coat, looking diffident and wondering, he was greeted not by Eva alone, but by three women: Eva, Catherine and Agatha, Catherine's maid. Mr Shandlin gave Eva a questioning look, but it was Catherine who stepped forward, snarling in his face without a word of greeting. 'Did you imagine that you could just waltz in and take a girl out without a proper chaperone?'

Mr Shandlin ignored her and spoke directly to Eva. 'Does your family think I am a brigand? You did tell them who I was, didn't you?'

'Her family are right here on this doorstep,' Catherine snapped, 'and you will pardon us if we're a bit surprised that it's one Johnny-come-lately on Friday and a different one today. 'Tis — it's — a poor start, that's all I'll say.' She folded her arms and stood there, blocking the doorway. Eva did not know what to do, so she merely smiled hopefully at him. But he was not mollified. 'So, are we going somewhere or aren't we?' He put inordinate emphasis on the 'we'.

'I wouldn't go anywhere with a man unless he had some manners,' Catherine said acidly, 'and wore the King's uniform.'

Eva longed to step up and defend him, but something in her froze. Catherine was too dangerous to be crossed.

But Mr Shandlin was not similarly handicapped by restraint. 'In the unlikely event of a man in uniform ever making the request, madam, your concerns are duly noted.'

'Upon my word, sir, you are extremely rude,' Catherine said.

'Please,' Eva found her voice at last, 'can we just go? I don't care where.'

Catherine slammed the door in disgust, and Eva and Mr Shandlin made their way down the steps, Agatha walking close behind.

'Well,' he said, after a judicious interval, 'that was rather a bad start.'

Eva said nothing. She had had little sleep the night before. She and her parents had argued and argued about Christopher Shandlin; at one point, Roy had been so angry he had swept all the files off his desk. Grace had been the one to tidy them up, since he wouldn't trust anyone else near them. Eva did not want to talk about it, though, not now.

'So where do you want to go, then?' Mr Shandlin had his hands in his pockets and was walking with a slouching gait, not looking at Eva.

'Richmond Park is nice.'

'What?' he said. 'That's miles away.'

'I can't think of anywhere else right now,' Eva said, agitated. Instead of seeking to calm her, he argued some more about her choice of destination until they reached no agreement at all but wandered on desultorily until they reached the river at Tower Bridge, where a little breeze got up. Tugboats once used for pleasure now ferried coal and goods up and down the river for the war effort, while across the river at Butler's Wharf, a few boats still unloaded tea. Further on, at Bermondsey, the jam and biscuit factories poured out rusks with patriotic slogans on them. In 1911, the women workers had rebelled and poured out into the streets, clad in their furs even in the blazing sun. Eva wondered if those same workers now pinned white feathers on men, the way Mrs Pankhurst had done at the Opera House.

Mr Shandlin mounted the stairs up to the road bridge so rapidly that Eva and Agatha struggled to keep up with him. The ill-assorted trio then made their way across Tower Bridge, he striding while the girls scuttled, and eventually ended up in Southwark Park, the sight of a tea rooms considerably cheering up Agatha, if nobody else. Eva sneaked a quick look at Mr Shandlin, but he appeared to be as disappointed with Southwark Park as with her original suggestion, and she began to wonder, her heart dropping to her stomach like a dumbwaiter creaking down to the kitchen, if he were disappointed in her too.

They walked across the green, passing the bandstand with its narrow black pillars and baskets of pink asters and gerbera daisies hanging from their capitals, children playing on the grass while their nannies sat on the benches, umbrellas ready for the rain that had been threatening all day. Eva wanted to initiate a conversation but didn't dare for fear of getting shot down. It was obvious he was in a filthy mood. Agatha's head bent forward as she walked along beside them. She, too, had run out of polite observations.

'Shall we go in?' Eva said, pointing to the tea rooms.

Mr Shandlin shrugged. 'If you like.'

The three of them went inside and sat down at a table. A group of men in khaki sat at the next table; Shandlin gave them the quickest of glances. If he was uncomfortable to be seen in ordinary clothes near them, he did not show it. A waitress brought them menus, but he did not pay much attention to his. He was doing that tapping thing on the oilcloth-covered table. Eva badly wanted to imprison his fingers in hers – and not with amorous intent.

The list of cakes looked unappealing to Eva, though Agatha seemed happy enough. 'Sussex plum heavies!' she cried out. 'They're my favourite.' She clasped her hand to her mouth as if she had uttered a curse word.

'It's all right,' Eva said, 'I'll get us two. Put your purse away.' She felt a little guilty about resenting Agatha's presence – embarrassed, too, that Agatha should have witnessed that nasty little scene on the doorstep. Let her have some biscuits. At least somebody would enjoy themselves this afternoon.

'Mr Shandlin, what would you like?' she asked, hoping to break him out of his sulky reverie.

'Eva, I know you like your Jane Austen, but this isn't the last century, and we're not in school any more: you can call me Christopher.' He turned to the waitress, who had reappeared. 'The soup, please. I didn't get to have luncheon.'

'We don't do soup. This is a tea rooms only,' the waitress said smartly.

He sighed. 'Whatever everyone else is having, then. Eva, put that away, will you? I can take for this.'

'But there's really no need. I have—'

He cut her off with an impatient gesture of his hand and counted out some coins. Eva realised that she had trodden on some exposed nerve of masculine pride and closed her purse. Their eyes met; something flared in his, and, for a moment, the atmosphere changed. But then the waitress returned with plates of cake on a tray and the moment passed.

'I hate this,' he said abruptly, after a few moments' silence. 'This ridiculous process by which people attempt to get to know each other with someone else watching. Going through a set of lines in a play stage-managed by convention.'

'This cake is very heavy,' Agatha commented. 'Kinda sticks in my stummick. Begging yer pardon, miss.' She dubiously cut another morsel with a dessert fork and chewed it slowly while Eva and Mr Shandlin – she felt unable to call him Christopher – looked down at the table, at the sky – everywhere but at each other.

The miserable repast eventually coming to an end, Eva, with desperate gaiety, proposed another walk. They took the same route around the park as before, three abreast, watching as young lads on the artificial lake splashed each other with their oars, one even jumping in to retrieve his hat, the rowboat rocking violently at his leap. 'Lawks-a-mercy,' Agatha sighed, regarding them, 'but you wouldn't think there was a war on, would you?'

'You do remind us at every opportunity,' remarked Mr Shandlin *sotto voce*, in such a manner that Eva wanted to hit him. Why was he being so sullen? She should have wished the day to last forever but she just wanted to go home. Perhaps sensing her anger, he finally asked something approaching a civil question. 'How is your sister? Is she quite recovered?'

'She's better than she was,' Eva said, 'but I worry about her.'

'What is it? If I may ask?'

'Consumption.' It was the first time Eva had said the word out loud.

'Ah.' He nodded. 'I see.'

They finished their circuit at the bandstand, where, to Eva's surprise, Mr Shandlin expressed a desire to sit down for a moment. Eva followed him up the steps and sat on the bench that ran around the inner circle, Agatha beside her. 'The Three Musketeers in the Park,' Eva muttered to herself, though if he heard her he gave no indication of it. He undid his shoelaces and redid them, all without looking at Eva.

Agatha pulled on Eva's sleeve discreetly. 'Miss Eva, I just seen a friend of mine. I'll need to speak to her for just a moment.'

'I'm sorry, what?' Eva said, confused. But Agatha was walking away from the bench. 'I'll be back,' Eva said to Mr Shandlin, who merely grunted in response.

'I seen a friend,' Agatha repeated. Then she added, in a rapid whisper, 'Miss Eva, did you know Missus Catherine hit me the other week? She read some book that told her it was usual to serve newspapers on a silver dish but she never said nothing to me, and I'd just brought them in the usual way and left them there. She picked up the tray she wanted and she hit me here with it.' Agatha lifted her hair and showed a scar on her forehead. Eva exclaimed in horror. 'I plain went out cold and when I came around she was shouting at me. There was me on the floor and all I could see was the Missus' face all red and shouty. Everyone in the house is terrified of her, Miss Eva. Us downstairs heard she was in service herself, and they are always the ones that turn on their servants the worst. We know what she did to you. We still talk about it.'

'And your friend?' Eva said, after a long pause. The wind blew up again, and she pulled her coat around her.

'Miss Eva,' and now Agatha's eyes were wide open, light hazel, 'there is no friend. We – that is, Nelly and myself – we was just thinking you deserved a break. Only twenty minutes, mind.'

'Thank you,' Eva said, a little choked.

Agatha merely winked in reply, and turned on her heel. Eva returned to the bandstand, where she and Mr Shandlin were almost alone, apart from an old woman in black, slumped on the bench, smelling of strong liquor. He continued to say nothing, slouching back, half turned away from her, hands deep in his pockets. She sat three feet away from him, turning away in similar fashion. The old woman stirred and snorted in that way drunks do when a dream interrupts their stupor.

'Eva.' He called her, softly. She did not turn around. 'Eva, don't be like that. Come back here.' He patted the space beside him. She was not going to sit next to him. 'Come back.' Still she did not move. 'Ah well,' he said, 'if Muhammad won't go to the mountain—' He rose and sat beside her.

Their thighs touched, just as her knees had with David Wentworth Hopkins', but this time the feeling was altogether different; Eva had to steady herself as even that slight contact made her skin tingle. With him so close by, the heat from his body palpable, Eva felt vulnerable, as if the knots she had tied to keep herself intact were pulling away, unravelling. 'You won't look at me,' he said. 'Why, Eva? What's the matter?'

Eva was having a hard time keeping her composure. She bunched her hands. 'Why did you ask me to meet you today? You've hardly said a kind word. It would have been nice—' She stopped, not trusting herself to finish her sentence.

'I just wanted to get to know you a bit better, that's all, without getting a ten-point interrogation on the doorstep. Oh, damn it, now you're crying.' He put his arm around her shoulders and clasped both her hands with his other hand, so that he was almost facing her.

'No, I'm not,' sniffed Eva.

'Oh, I think you are, and my fault too! I've made a mess of things, as usual.' He released her hands and rummaged in his pocket, pulling out a handkerchief, uncurling her fingers and placing it gently in her palm. 'Go on. It's clean, I swear it.' He laughed nervously.

Eva shook her head. It was too much, all of this. One minute he was cold and withdrawn, and now here he was at her side, stroking the base of her thumb with his and occasionally caressing her shoulder with his other hand. His touch was so new, after all the previous months of looking and not looking, greeting and avoiding, then their parting … it took a few moments for her to compose herself.

Then she turned around and looked him full in the face. He was barely three inches away from her. The corners of his mouth twitched with the ghost of a smile. 'There you are, dear girl. Now you see it all.' Yes, Eva did see – and was shocked. How pale and anxious he was, his forehead suddenly lined and old, his eyes huge, the look of tender supplication in them. She had never seen his face so close, so it was hard to judge, but he looked desperate, almost as desperate as she.

'Mr Shandlin' – he drew back and looked ready to protest – 'Christopher' – he relaxed once more – 'I care for you. More than I should. When you're there I feel such happiness and when you're not everything seems mean and trivial. If you're just being friendly and detached and guiding me in my education, then please stop. It's not fair—' And now she was crying properly, not just surreptitious tears; now that she had said her piece, all her courage had fled: she could not look at him. To see pity in his eyes! She would rather die. But he did not let her go, or pull away, or admonish her.

'Eva, shush.' He gently brought her head to his chest. She felt his heart beat, the pulse rapid, the rhythm light-strong, light-strong. So that was where the iambic rhythm came from, all those sonnets and whatnot, that simple, repetitive motion that would continue without rest until the day you died. From the heart. She stopped sobbing and listened, and the act of listening made her calm again. Through her half-open eyes she could see a few pigeons waddling about, their coos gentle and rumbling as they picked at cake crumbs.

Part of her wanted to protest that they were in a public park, he was being too demonstrative, but then his hands were in her hair, and he kissed the top of her head – very softly – and along with that heartbeat, strong and steady and powerful, she felt his now-confident hand at the back of her neck.

Something huge inside her finally rolled away, as if Sisyphus had been allowed to let his boulder career down the mountain and stand up, unburdened and free, the air light on his shoulder. She felt so safe. And he – Christopher – felt so warm, and close. He surrounded her.

She looked up at him, and he caught her chin in his hand. Before she knew what was happening he was kissing her hairline, then her eyes, then, lightly but insistently, her lips, again and again. For such a sharp-tongued man, his lips were surprisingly soft, and each kiss seemed to leave barely a trace, the briefest of impressions. Once or twice, he exhaled heavily, like a sigh, or the sound he had made when she had crashed into him while dancing.

She wanted to respond to his kisses, though she was unsure how. She opened her eyes; his were almost closed. He looked so fierce and strange! She was about to try and kiss him back when he withdrew and opened his eyes, keeping her in his embrace. 'There,' he said, 'that detached enough for you?' He was trying to sound debonair, but his hands were trembling.

'You do like me,' she said in wonder.

He made an exasperated sound. 'Of course I *like* you, Eva. Good God above, I thought it was obvious. The question is,' he said, with some return of his earlier irritation, though he still held her fast, 'do *you* like *me?* The other day you were rabbiting on about that boy – David this, David that. It nearly drove me out of my wits hearing you use his name again and again and not ever saying mine, not once. You're so damned formal with me – every time you address me as Mr Shandlin it feels like being struck in the face with a wet towel. You were keen enough to know my name once, if I remember rightly, keen to the point of impudence. So why not use it?'

Eva laughed happily. 'Christopher—'

'That's better!'

'—you are an idiot. Can you not understand that I could call David anything under the sun because I don't care a thing for him? I was only entertaining him because my family put me under so much pressure. It makes no difference to me whether he's called David, or Mr Hopkins, or Mincing Machine, or Teapot—'

'Or Lavatory Brush, or Effluent Pipe,' he cut in, with no little spite.

'Don't interrupt until I'm finished! What I'm saying is, his name is not dear to me. I can repeat it all day without the slightest emotional disturbance. But yours … Do you remember when I told you I was leaving The Links?'

'I remember it all too clearly. I was most put out.'

'I was about to say, "Goodbye Christopher", but you walked off and left me there before I could even speak. And I had to stand there and watch you go. It was agony.'

He swallowed. 'And to walk away was agony too.'

'Why did you?'

'Oh, God – I had good intentions. It was just as I said then, I felt I owed it to you to do the right thing.'

'"The right thing"? You mean because you were my teacher?'

'Yes.' His reply was barely more than a whisper, and his grip tightened on her hand. 'You are so young, Eva, just seventeen.'

'I'll have you know I turned eighteen in May. Your advice then left me very confused, Christopher. You told me to marry someone who would support me. You didn't seem to include yourself in that category. You were so uninterested. I quite hated you.'

'I only knew – and this was quite beside any feelings I had for you – that a mind like yours ought not to be wasted. I presumed your family would get you married off pretty quickly, and I just hoped, for your sake, it would be to someone freethinking. I wanted to keep myself out of the way.'

'And yet you liked me well enough,' Eva said in wonder.

'Oh, I liked you all right, Eva Downey. I more than like you. That was part of the reason why I avoided you after my ... outburst. I knew then, you see. I could no longer be innocent of my real feelings: my God, they were nearly uncontrollable. Seeing you there in the front row each week was a torment. Dancing with you? Emily Jane Brontë would have called it "divinest anguish".' He kissed her again. 'I never had the remotest notion of falling for any of my pupils; I could not imagine a development less convenient for my sanity or my bank balance. And yet here I am. When I ran into Miss Destouches the other day and she told me you were about to marry that Hopkins fellow, I realised I would have to make a sprint for it, otherwise I would lose you. And I realised that I couldn't bear that, I couldn't bear never to see you again, never to …' He shook his head and looked down at his knees.

Eva hesitantly put her hand to his cheek, and immediately he imprisoned it in his own. She leant over to kiss him on the lips. He responded, then lowered his head on her shoulder and hid his face in her neck.

'I missed you,' she whispered.

His voice was muffled. 'I missed you too.'

The old woman started shouting something, then fixed them both with a glare. 'Shameless! Shameless! I blame the war.'

Eva looked up and saw Agatha's returning shape beyond the plane trees. 'I'll need to go soon,' she said.

He sighed and straightened up, releasing her. 'Yes, we had better. My train is in forty-five minutes.'

At London Bridge station, the waiting room was full and smelt of sweat and onions. A locomotive could be heard hooting as the remnants of smoke drifted backwards along the platform. Christopher pulled Eva to him; once again her head was resting on his chest. She was breaking every rule of propriety in the book, but God she didn't care. Agatha had her Turkish cigarettes and was happy to look the other way. 'So,' he said, 'how does this work, then? What intricate social mechanism comes next?'

'Well,' Eva said, 'I hardly know more than you, but arranging a date and a time is usually a good start.'

'I have a half day on Wednesday. May I see you then? Same time?'

'Of course.'

'Without Grace Poole?' He gestured at Agatha.

'Don't call her that,' Eva said, 'she's been very kind. You know she has to be there. Or Catherine will send someone else.'

'It's no hardship for me to leave you alone, sir,' Agatha, overhearing, chimed in with a slight frown, 'but Missus Catherine was most particular. A respectable girl like Miss Eva needs chaperoning, sir.'

'And how do I get Miss Respectable Eva unchaperoned, then?'

'Oh, that's easy,' Agatha said. 'You have to speak to Mr Roy, then propose to Miss Eva, and then you become engaged.'

'Good God,' Christopher said, frowning. 'Marriage? I have a train in five minutes – no, three.' He dropped Eva's hand and kissed her on the forehead. 'Don't worry, dear girl. We'll sort this out. Just don't marry that other chap, that's all I ask.'

'I think I can safely promise not to do that,' Eva said, smiling.

Christopher waved from the door of the waiting room and disappeared onto the platform. A shaft of sunlight fell on the tiles, and his dark form was briefly illuminated until he was lost in the crowds. Carriage doors banged shut in quick succession, then the train let out a series of loud, high-pitched asthmatic gasps as it moved out of the station. Eva watched it leave and did not move until Agatha put her hand on her arm.

16

TO THE
YOUNG WOMEN
OF LONDON:
Is your 'Best Boy' wearing khaki?
If not, don't <u>YOU THINK</u> he should be?
If he does not think that you
and your country are worth
fighting for – do you think he
is <u>WORTHY</u> of you?
Don't pity the girl who is
alone – her young man is
probably a soldier – fighting
for her and her country – and for <u>YOU</u>.
If your young man neglects his duty to his
King and Country, the time may come when
he may well <u>NEGLECT YOU</u>.
Think it over   then ask him to
JOIN THE ARMY <u>TO-DAY</u>!

14 October 1914

Dearest Sybil,

It's been such a long time! I was hoping to get to see you before your wedding to Clive, but we seem to keep missing each other. I do wish we could
talk more. It was wonderful talking to you on the telephone just after that

magical day when Christopher declared his intentions to me. I let you go on for a while sounding guiltier and guiltier at the supposed mess you'd landed me in. Thank God you did what you did, Sybil, or else I'd now be Mrs David Wentworth Hopkins and holed up in a house with his ancient sister, silently losing the will to live. God bless you for that, and Christopher for not being a mouse in the end, in spite of his moral scruples. Yes, I suppose he is quite a bit older than I – he is thirty-one – but sympathetic temperaments do make it less important, do you not think?

Mind you, sad as I am that your new activities take you away from me, I am enthralled by your latest interest in lady motorcyclists. The Spitfire Motorcycle Club sounds wonderful, and I really hope Clive doesn't mean it when he says he won't let you go on any more trips to Malvern. Can you not tell him that motorcycles may be useful for the war effort, and, besides, it helps keep you from worrying about Bo?

I suppose you've heard the Turks are in on the game now too. Grace has put a whole new row of pins on her map where they're attacking the Russians and is fretting about supply routes, as if she'd know a supply route from Adam. Christopher calls her 'The Darling', after that girl in the Chekhov story who always takes on the personality and style of speech of her current husband, except that Grace's true husband is War. I wish he wouldn't. She's already overheard him do it once and it angered her very much.

To tell the truth, Sybil, I am worried about Grace. She is getting more aggressive about Christopher, because he will not enlist. It sounds like a horrible thing to say, but privately sometimes I wish he would, if just to take attention away from us. I am ashamed of even thinking of it. It's just

… he has a stronger character than I do, but it is beginning to get to him nonetheless, and it creates an atmosphere between us. But he has never been one to swim with the current.

So that is my news. I hope you are getting on all right and that the rumble across the Channel isn't keeping you awake, or fearful.

God bless us all,

Your friend,

Eva

Eva was finding out that as far as her family were concerned, 'walking out' with Christopher Shandlin was a very different matter from walking out with David Wentworth Hopkins. No matter what she wished to do, objection after objection was raised, mostly from Catherine but with Roy and Grace chiming in. Who were his people? What about the other fellow? And why wasn't he in uniform? After she got back from that afternoon in Southwark Park, her heart afire and spirit singing, she had been sent to her room and told in no uncertain terms that she would never be allowed to see Christopher again. On hearing this, Imelda had come down from her sickbed in high dudgeon, staggered into Roy's study in her nightgown and without knocking, and said in her faint voice that Mr Shandlin was a good man and that he should at least be given a chance. Roy was so stunned – and reminded of her late mother – that he relented.

But if Catherine had been wrong-footed on the previous occasion, she was taking no chances now. Every time Eva and Christopher met, on his precious free days, they would now be accompanied by Mrs Michael Stewart, which meant that neither could bring up anything personal or intimate, a situation they both silently endured. Agatha, to Eva's horror and guilt, had been dismissed without notice. It was clear that nothing and nobody could stop Catherine running riot. Her hatred for Eva was like a lightning rod down which a tremendous built-up electrical charge travelled.

Eva did find out why Christopher had not yet enlisted. It took a while, partly because she feared offending him by asking, and partly because they were never left alone. In late October he decided that he and Eva would have a proper afternoon tea in the Criterion. 'I bet that Hopkins fellow would have taken you there,' he said when she queried the expense.

She found herself and Christopher flanking either side of Mrs Stewart on a long, chintz banquette in one of the fanciest restaurants in London. The ceiling was gold-patterned, mosaics on the walls and at one end a huge fireplace with turquoise inlays and an oval mirror stood guard over it all. Mrs Stewart appeared unimpressed. 'I've heard this place is full of inverts,' she declared.

A snatch of wan, late autumn light shot through one of the windows as Eva looked around for the inverts, wherever they might be, but she only saw people eating scones and chocolate tortes and smelt the heavenly aroma of thick, dark chocolate being poured out of a jug.

'Inverts and conchies,' Mrs Stewart added with malice.

'That will do!' Eva snapped. How dared she! Christopher did not respond to her taunt, just sat hunched and sullen, cracking his knuckles. Later, when Mrs Stewart had eaten nearly all the cakes he'd paid for and waddled off to find a 'convenience', Eva interlaced her fingers in his. 'I'm sorry for what she said earlier, darling. That was uncalled for.'

Christopher sighed and rubbed his forehead with his free hand. 'It's not just her,' he said, 'I get looks wherever I go. I'm going to have to stop working at The Links. All those girls, wondering why I'm not in uniform. The notices. The endless hectoring. "Be certain that your so-called reason is not a selfish excuse."' He recited Kitchener's quote with distaste. 'I'm under siege.'

'What *is* your reason, Christopher?' Eva asked. 'I respect it whatever it is,' she added hastily. 'It's just that giving up work – if it's come to that—'

He rummaged in his satchel, then put a page of a letter in Eva's hand, covered with writing on both sides. 'Here. I always meant to show you this, but there was never a good moment. It's my last letter from Francis. He wrote it on the 23rd, so he was dead before it got to me.'

Eva read:

… and then I reached Orange River camp and could not believe what I saw. When our troops burned out the farms and killed all the livestock, on Kitchener's orders, they also rounded up the women and children and took them here. This is not a camp for prisoners of war, Kit. This is a place designed for the express extermination of human life.

White and black, young and old, they are all kept here in tents in the midst of the rain and floods. The meat that serves for their ration is rotten with maggots and the coffee powder mixed with wood shavings. Children are on half rations, which means they cannot live. Babies are given no milk, and they die. The stench of death is everywhere. I have to admit that when I first saw – and smelt – the horror, I had to go to one side to be sick.

On a stretcher beside me a woman lay dying. Beside her the mere skeleton of a baby breathing its last from hunger. The mosquito and its malaria are everywhere. I am weeping as I write this, and you know I am not one to be overemotional. They are already spreading lies back at home, saying that our men are looking after the Boer women and their servants 'at the expense of many valuable lives and much money'.

There is a woman called Miss Hobhouse who has agreed to bring this back home for me and post it at Southampton, because they've censored everything going in and out since October. They are all frightened of Kitchener, and he was the one who thought up the whole thing. Kit, I beg you, wherever life takes you, promise me that you will have nothing to do with that man. He is incapable of the normal stirrings of the human heart, either in intimacy or compassion. Is this what it now means to be British?

'My God,' Eva breathed, passing Christopher back his letter.

'Now do you see?' His voice was unsteady.

'Yes.'

'If you're going to hitch your wagon to mine,' he said, 'you're going to have to understand what this means to me.'

'You have kept your promise,' Eva said gently, 'even if he never knew it.'

Christopher made no answer but a small noise, and turned his head. For a moment they sat in silence until Mrs Stewart returned and she let his fingers go.

Eva knew that Grace disapproved of Christopher's being out of uniform. She forbore to mention it but looked often enough at him in a sideways, twitchy way for her odium to be clear. Even so, just the day after their afternoon tea at the Criterion, when the knock on her bedroom door came and her stepsister's pale, stern face appeared around the door, Eva was unprepared for the cold, contained way Grace said, 'Come down, please. There's something I have to say to you.'

Eva followed her into the parlour, where Grace quietly shut the door. A bucket by the window smelling of borax and pearl ash compound betrayed the recent presence of the new maid, Agatha's luckless replacement. Presumably she had been about to clean the room when Grace commandeered it.

'As you know, Dr Fellowes and I have grown close in recent months. He has been most kind to me in the wake of poor Alec's death.'

Good for you, Eva thought sourly, *you certainly haven't wasted any time.*

'We are to marry in December: it is necessary to make it soon as he has just signed up for the Royal Army Medical Corps.' Something in her tone put Eva on high alert. Grace was not telling her this for nothing. 'You are aware that I agreed to sacrifice half my dowry to contribute towards Imelda's care in Switzerland. I am willing to give that portion, without reservation or resentment, to save your sister's life.' *Your* sister. The lines of battle were drawn. 'Eva, it is time for you to do your part.'

'My part?'

'I'm not paying for Imelda unless you give up that man.' The disdain in Grace's voice was like rough brick. 'You know, it's odd,' she continued. 'I really admired you. You played the game so well. You got into one of the most exclusive finishing schools in the country. That showed real initiative. But only you, Eva, could go and ruin it all by going off with one of the staff. I was so disappointed in you! And all this time since you've taken up with him, have I said a word?' Her voice veered out of control, loud and harsh. 'I watched you waltz around with that fellow and marvelled at how you let him paw you when he doesn't have a sou to his name, and not a jot of common decency or manners. No,' seeing Eva raise her hand, 'don't demean yourself by arguing. Just think on this. Isn't it a bit much to expect me to foot the bill for your sister's treatment when you don't pay a penny and dance attendance on that fool?'

Eva felt something in her tighten like the string of a bow. 'You know well that my dowry is tiny because your mother made sure yours was large.'

Grace coloured. 'And? Is that my fault? Did I personally go and steal all your money? Part of my offer is to make the situation more equitable.'

'Equitable, until it suits you to change your mind. I see,' Eva said with disgust.

The red in Grace's cheeks shrank to two angry points just below her eyes. 'Don't try and turn the tables. You're the one in the wrong here. You've brought him into our house. Have you any sense of decorum, Eva? Do you know how upset Father is, and everyone? Did it occur to you that Agatha lost her job because of your behaviour? I don't like saying this any more than you like hearing it, but I am not going to give over my dowry while you are waltzing around London with a coward.'

'He is not a coward. Not that it's any of your business, but he is a thousand times above you, he—'

'I'll tell you what he is.' Grace put her face up close to Eva's. 'He's a man who won't fight. You can say whatever you like, but in life a man gets only a few chances to prove himself. Here's his chance, right now. And he's failing. He's failing his country and his king, but never mind that, Eva, he's failing *you*. It's what a man does that matters, Eva. And he's doing nothing.' She hit her palm with her fist. 'Have you any idea how I wish I could serve my country? I'd gladly fight in his place, I swear to God. I'd get a rifle or a machine gun or whatever they wanted, and I would pound every Boche within a ten-mile radius to death. I'd do it! I'd disembowel them and watch them die with my own eyes!' She sat down, slightly winded by her own vehemence.

She really means it, Eva thought in wonder. 'So … what, Grace? What are you trying to tell me? If I don't give Christopher up, you'll withhold money from Imelda? Is that it? I'm sure you'd love to stick a feather on him while you're at it!'

A slow smile made its way across Grace's features, like a snake winding through the bushes. 'Me? Oh, no. I'm not going to give him a white feather. *You* are.'

On the Sunday of that week, Imelda had a bad episode. Eva wanted to call their father but she gestured 'no', and so instead Eva rocked and rocked her until her breathing eased and she could swallow some more mixture. She thought that after such an ordeal Imelda would want to sleep, but she remained awake and distressed. 'Oh, Eva, I thought it would be easy. I thought I was ready.'

'Ready? What do you mean?'

'For death,' Imelda said. 'So many men die at the front every day. I wonder how it happens for them. A wound, maybe just a small one, that got infected. Somebody on night duty who forgot to be careful, lit a cigarette and was hit by a sniper. Or was blown up. Or got a bullet in the stomach. Every day it happens to our men. So I thought if they go through it, maybe it won't be that bad. I mean, I won't be alone. That was what I was thinking.'

'Imelda!' Eva cried out in horror.

'But I was wrong.' Imelda's hand tightened around Eva's wrist. 'Eva, I can't face it. I'm not ready.' She began to cry weakly, too exhausted to put much power into it. 'Please, Eva. Help me. I'm not ready to die. I want to live. I can live.'

'I know, darling,' Eva whispered. 'I know.' She embraced her sister and let herself be enveloped by the warm, familiar smell of Pears soap on her neck and the raw, animal odour of the lanolin she took care to apply to her skin every day. Those smells reminded her of her mother too. When it came to living, everyone was selfish, Imelda being no exception. 'You shall go to Switzerland, and you shall live. I promise you, Meldi.'

The moon came out from behind the clouds. Eva noticed it for the first time among the street lamps. It shone onto Imelda's cheek as she turned her gaze to her sister. Her gaze was as luminous as that moon, full of trust and hope. And with it turned towards her, Eva felt as if someone had closed a door and turned a key in the lock.

'Why the secrecy?' Christopher said, concerned. 'Why did you ask to meet me here? I had a fair sprint to make it after class.'

They were in the buffet beside the waiting room in London Bridge station. Eva had managed to dig into a long-stashed pocket-money collection and send a telegram to Christopher at his home in Kent. She had been so distraught that she had just run out of the house and down to the nearest post office. 'Monday Nov 2nd, 5.30pm, London Bridge station, sub rosa STOP.' The Latin phrase meant she would be unaccompanied. It was part of their code.

'I – I …' Seeing him there nearly undid her.

'Come on, Eva, what is it?'

Grace's words were a stone in her throat. She swallowed and swallowed but they would not go away.

'Eva.' He caught her gently on the chin. 'Come on, it can't be that bad, surely?'

'Grace says that if you don't enlist I'm to present you with a white feather,' she blurted out.

He took his hand away and drew back. 'Well, you can just tell her to go away, can't you? No,' seeing Eva's face, 'no, you can't, or we wouldn't be having this conversation, would we?'

Eva explained Grace's terms. When she reached the part where Grace said that Imelda would not get the funds if she did not comply, Christopher reacted with a start, his seat juddering back with a creak. 'I beg your pardon. Continue.'

'There isn't much more. That's it.'

'It takes quite some ingenuity to be that wicked.'

Eva slid her fingers together and put her hands on the table like a steeple. 'Wicked it may be, but I have to make a choice. She is determined.'

'Choice?' he said incredulously. 'How can that be a choice? It's like dodging Scylla by throwing oneself into Charybdis! That is not a decision any human being should be forced to make. Come away with me now.' He grabbed her hands again. 'Bring Imelda. I'm not entirely friendless, you know, there are people whose help I can draw on. I can get us out of here.'

Eva's heart leapt. If she could! But then she remembered. 'I can't. Imelda needs that treatment. I have to wait until she is safely in Switzerland.'

'Switzerland? I hate to remind you, but—' He jerked his head at another recruitment poster for the Public Schools Battalions that hung lopsided on the wall.

'It's safe enough, if she goes through Italy. It's all arranged. I don't want to do anything until she has arrived there and I know she is all right.'

'I understand. It would not be right for you to break a promise to your sister because I kept a promise to my brother.' He dropped her hands. 'I'll tell you what you should do. Tell them we've broken up. I won't write to you or see you for, let's say, a month – and then see if you can write and tell me how the land lies.'

Eva bit her lip and said nothing. The waiters were starting to lay places for the evening service. People hustled in from the matinees. She thought how delicate love was, as thin as tulle or crêpe paper in a fierce gale. She had lost her mother, and now she might lose Christopher too.

Something in the agony of that moment made them reach for one another at the same time, each clutching on to the other as if drowning. His hands grasped the fabric of her coat, while he buried his face in her shoulder, leaving nothing visible but a shock of greying dark hair. She murmured into his ear that she loved him, and he responded in kind, with a flow of endearments and sweet names, too low for anyone else to hear but her.

The woman at the tea counter, pouring out cups for workmen, did not chide them. She could see from the poor girl's face that her sweetheart was going off to war and would soon have to don his uniform. It was heartbreaking, so it was, so many young girls saying goodbye to their sweethearts, never to see them again.

17

The Bad Saunau clinic was situated in Leysin, a small village in the Swiss Alps. War would make the journey circuitous: Imelda would have to cross the Channel and make her way through France, then northward through the Italian Alps, with one ferry crossing and heaven knows how many train changes before finally taking the cog railway up to Leysin. There was no guarantee Italy would stay out of the war: they had to be quick. Grace had instructed her banker to authorise the transfer to come through the following week.

Eva worried that, in spite of what they had agreed, Christopher would begin to forget her. No little notes, no tender gestures — nothing. She ached for him not only with her heart but sometimes with her body too. She dreamt that he came to her at night and lay beside her, skin to skin, as he had once described to her he would love to do. She would wake from these dreams in a fever, unable to get back to sleep.

Grace had become kinder. Separating from Christopher had caused Eva pain, and Grace saw that. Now that she had won, there was no more talk of giving him a white feather. 'You look like you've been punished enough,' she said. Eva gritted her teeth. All she had to do was keep her own counsel until Imelda was safely off to Switzerland.

On one of their walks together, which Eva felt unable to get out of, Grace slipped her arm through Eva's and wound her gloved fingers around

Eva's upper arm. It was a shame that Eva had let Mr Hopkins slip through her fingers, she said, but there were plenty of other men out there, even now with the war on, and all she had to do was use her education to procure one. There was no mention of Christopher Shandlin.

Eva listened in disbelief. *Use my education to procure a man*, she marvelled to herself, *when the only man I want to procure is the one who educated me in the first place?* But if she were honest with herself, she had to admit that it was nice to be walking with Grace, to just be an ordinary part of the family rather than the one who caused problems all the time. It was nice not to be constantly worrying of which transgression she was guilty, to wake up blameless, without that sick feeling in her gut. Though hard to get used to: Grace and Catherine were the first disapprovers she had ever known. In spite of herself, she had always wanted their approval, even craved it.

A treacherous little voice in her head started commenting, *Isn't Christopher rather unkempt? When he was close to you, didn't you wish he changed his clothes more often? Aren't his teeth a little yellow? Isn't he being inconsiderate of you, dragging you into his anti-war crusade?* There was something infectious about spending time with Grace; Eva was beginning to see the world through her eyes.

On Sunday, the family, absent Roy, who was delayed in Dublin, attended the eleven o'clock service at St George in the East. It had been a full week since Imelda's attack, and she was as well as could be expected. Grace enquired if Eva was enjoying the walk and wasn't the weather pleasant? Eva found it easy to play along, even if this new, kinder Grace still unnerved her a little. Grace enquired after Sybil, and Eva was able to tell her that she was worried about her brother, who was trying to hold the Salient at Hooge. Now that they were on the topic of war, Grace was in her element;

she knew exactly where the village of Hooge was. Their talk was almost friendly.

Their walk back from church brought them through Princes Square, past the Swedish church that had gone to ruin in the three years since Emanuel Swedenborg's body had been taken out of it and brought back to Sweden. Eva always thought it looked sad, with its circular, bricked-in panels, like something you would see on a folly. But today, as they passed it, she thought her heart might stop: Christopher was leaning against the entrance. As she passed, he lifted his head and fixed his eyes on her to the exclusion of all else. They were dark and hungry.

She had to bite on her tongue not to cry with joy. He had not forgotten her. The sight of him made her own doubts evaporate. How could she have thought such things about his teeth, or his shirts? What had planted such ideas in her head? The moment she saw him, she felt a powerful surge of love and longing, and it was all she could do not to break ranks and run after him. *I love you*, she thought, and it was like a song in the right key, a clear call in the November air.

Grace skidded to a halt. 'What did you say?'

'I said ...' Eva did not continue. Had she spoken out loud?

'You said those words' – Grace's mouth screwed up in revulsion – 'to that man. Just now. I saw him.' Christopher had by now disappeared. 'Love.' Grace spoke the word the way one would utter the filthiest obscenity. She looked as if she were about to spit a gob in the middle of the footpath. 'You lying bitch. You never meant a word of it, did you?'

'Grace—' But Grace cut Eva off. By now Catherine was puffing up, dragging Imelda with her. 'It's all right, Mother,' Grace said, digging her fingers into Eva's arm, 'Eva and I are going to settle this ourselves. I'll see you later.' Since Grace was the one person she obeyed without question, Catherine fell back and set to restraining Imelda. Grace pulled Eva around the corner, her teeth clenched, jaw set. When Eva tried to pull away, she felt long fingernails press through the fabric of her sleeve.

Their front door had been left ajar, and Grace pushed in, steering Eva into Roy's empty study and flinging her against the wall. 'You must think I was born yesterday.'

'Grace, I didn't expect to see him there. I thought he was gone for good.'

'Don't lie to me.' She was white and wild, every hissed word jabbing like the point of a spear. 'How do you think I feel? Was I about to give up half my entitlement – I even considered giving more – to find out the minute the money was gone from my hands you'd be sneaking around with that man again?'

'Oh, God,' Eva moaned. 'What have I done?'

'You betrayed my trust, that's what you did. And to think I believed you! Tell me' – Eva was surprised to hear a note of hurt in Grace's voice – 'were you both laughing at me all this time? A snigger at the servant's daughter? That would be your little touch, wouldn't it? And he'd back it up with some fancy literary allusion, thinking me too low-bred to understand.'

'No, we never—'

'Have you any idea how hard I have to work, every day? You were born respectable: I had to make myself so. It doesn't matter that people don't know the true story; I know, always, inside.' She put her hand on her heart. 'It's exhausting, having to pretend all the time. Having to work to get people's attention. Do you think I always enjoy Dr Fellowes' company or that my heart skips beats for him? Do you think I waste my time with love? I don't do what I do for pleasure, Eva. I do it for family. I do it to raise myself up from what I was born into.' Eva saw tears in her stepsister's eyes.

Grace straightened herself up and cleared her throat. 'But this isn't my beau we're talking about, Eva: it's yours.' At Eva's questioning look, she raised her eyes to heaven. 'You know what I mean.'

Yes, Eva did know, and the realisation flooded her. Her stomach constricted, and Grace watched her as she doubled up, not bothering to hide her disapproval. 'Let me make it easy for you. Who do you love more? Him or your sister?'

Eva whimpered. 'Grace, I can't—'

'Answer me!' Grace shouted. 'Which one? Him or Imelda?'

Eva felt a tight band around her heart. Grace came nearer, shouting and shouting. The whole world shrank to her mouth, pursed, shouting, flicking saliva. Him or Imelda? Him or Imelda? Him or Imelda?

Eva fought to breathe. Her heart was beating like a drum. She shook her head tearfully.

Grace folded her arms. 'Eva. I'm sick and tired of this. We all are.'

Still Eva was silent, which only enraged Grace. She let out a barnyard yell, 'God Almighty, I am losing patience with you!' The shout rebounded through the house. From the kitchen, a loud cry and the crash of a plate, followed by shouted remonstrations. Eva's lips were trembling, and the habitual ache in her arm was now a shooting white bulbous arrow. She was almost crying from the pain of it.

'All right,' Grace said, 'I'll take that as a no. I will instruct my lawyer to withdraw the transaction.' She turned smartly on her heel. Eva fell to her knees and grabbed at Grace's skirts, tearful and wild-eyed, begging her please not to do this, please don't ask her to choose, she could not, she could not. Pleading in an odd, high-pitched wail, asking Grace why wasn't she good enough, why had she never been good enough, what did she do wrong that Grace was loved and she was not? How could they ask her to do this thing? She could not bear it, no, she could not. Please let her alone, just this once let her alone.

Grace allowed herself a delicate shiver of disgust. 'Eva. Control yourself.'

The door opened. Catherine had arrived. She said nothing, but her quiet support for Grace emanated out of her tight-waisted, straight-backed body. Grace looked down at the kneeling Eva, a slight tremor in her voice which she struggled to control. 'Let me put the question differently. Do you choose to save Imelda?'

Eva remembered Imelda begging her not to let her die. And she remembered promising that she wouldn't.

Grace put a hand on Eva's shoulder and began to stroke her neck, very softly, with her thumb. Her fingertips slipped under the fabric of Eva's dress, cool upon her skin. A patient, disinterested touch. Eva rose to her feet, her knees creaking. Shock had made her breathing shallow and rapid. She could not speak. All she could do was nod her head.

'Good,' Grace said. 'You're doing the right thing.'

They calmed her down with cups of camomile tea laced with quinine, the bitter sting of the latter making her gag, then they drafted the letter together. Eva wrote that there was no need now for subterfuge. Grace and Catherine had thought about it and had decided that maybe they had been unreasonable. While Grace had strong feelings about conscientious objectors, she did not want to obstruct her sister's happiness. Most of this was dictated by Grace herself, but she nagged Eva to write it in her own style. 'That man will know if it's me,' she said. 'Make it sound like you.'

After a few drafts, Eva managed it. The letter was affectionate, with splashes of wit, and the last sentence invited Christopher to come to the house at two o'clock on Saturday, 21 November, when her stepmother and stepsister 'would be glad to receive him'.

Which, in a way, was true.

'Are you writing on the ruled paper?' Catherine interjected, her neck like a stalk as she bent over, her wattled chin with its turkey neck slightly brushing the top of her daughter's head. 'I think mostly them things don't get written on the ruled paper, sure they don't? 'Tis the fancy notepaper with the flowers and suchlike.'

'Mother, for God's sake!' snapped Grace. 'It will do. Now.' She took Eva's letter and scanned it carefully, her tongue popping out between her lips as it often did when she was concentrating. Then she moved her index finger vertically down the left-hand side of the page, then the right. 'You think people like me are stupid and don't know about acrostics,' she said, then, to Catherine, 'I don't trust her not to sneak in a coded message.' Catherine nodded. She wouldn't have known an acrostic from the winner of the Epsom Derby.

He won't be fooled, Eva told herself, as she dampened the gum on the envelope and sealed it. And then a sudden realisation: *I need him to be. For Imelda's sake.* And fooled he was. He replied quickly, underlining his enthusiastic consent. Eva hoped that he too was writing in code, that *he* would insert some sort of acrostic. She read the letter carefully but could find no hidden message in English or in Latin. Her heart sank. For all his intelligence and incisiveness, Christopher was not a man who understood social signals. And he would have a tendency to believe what he wished to be true.

She tried one last appeal to Grace's better nature, but it was pointless. Her will had been broken in their confrontation the day before, and Grace knew it. She would concede nothing: it was to happen in broad daylight, in public, and she had to be present to witness it done. The only concession she granted was that Imelda would not be told. Eva could not put that much guilt on her sister's head. All she told her was that seeing Christopher lurking like that had made Grace angry but that they had settled it between them.

In all this, Roy played little part. These days he tended to shut himself in his study, and at mealtimes he sequestered himself behind his *Times*. He spoke to Eva only once, the day before Christopher was due to arrive at the house.

Since Imelda's taking badly ill that summer, Eva had moved from their shared room into a small boxroom next door, a windowless closet once used for storing suits. It was on the door of this room that Roy knocked, then entered without waiting. Eva was surprised to see him there, still wearing his outdoor coat. His skin was sallow with tiredness. 'Mother has told me of your decision to give Mr Shandlin a white feather.' Well, at least he called a spade a spade. 'Are you all right with this, Eva?' Eva said nothing. 'I am uneasy,' he continued. 'It might reflect badly on us, especially if done in public.'

'You had better tell Grace that.' Eva's voice was hoarse.

Roy rubbed his nose. 'Grace … well, she does tend to absolutism.'

The hand he put on Eva's shoulder was heavy and ponderous but easily shaken off. His sigh briefly lifted the page of an open book on the small cedarwood box Eva stored her things in. 'What must be, must be,' he said, moving to the door again.

'Father, wait.'

He turned around.

'Why?' One word, so weighted that she did not need to say anything more. On the first-floor landing, the cistern flushed, long and loud, its roar and gurgle vibrating all over the house. Eva almost missed his reply.

'I need to keep the peace.' Then he started muttering: 'I committed myself. From the start.'

'What are you talking about?' Eva said.

He exhaled, his breath nasal, his profile stiff. 'Eva, your mother … Angela …' He didn't continue, instead sinking his chin into his coat collar: 'You were right. I shouldn't have married Catherine. It was ill judged and hasty. But I had no choice – none! And she—' The half-light from the corridor cast his face in a particular anguish, a demeanour more noble than his true nature. 'I cannot stop the wheels of fate,' he said, chafing his palms, not looking at her. Then he put his knuckles to his lips, coughed drily onto them and left the room.

By half past one that Saturday afternoon the steps to No. 35 Wellclose Square were flanked with women, ten in all, some veiled in black, war widows, some in gaudier shades, some in silk-trimmed hats, some of them standing, some leaning on the railings, others sitting – and several of them carrying a handful of feathers.

Grace looked aghast. 'For God's sake, Margot,' she snarled at one of them, 'I said "a few people". Just to ensure there were witnesses. You've brought a street party.'

'Oh, Gracie, don't be like that. A lot of the girls don't get out much these days. It's nice to have a little moment of solidarity.'

'But what about me?' Grace was white with alarm. 'What does this make *me* look like?' She marched over to the gaggle of women. 'Put those feathers away. We only need one.'

Eva was there too, but she couldn't hear what Grace was saying. They had given her more of that vile-tasting quinine concoction, and her head was spinning. 'Not so much of that,' Grace had said when Catherine brought it to her lips. 'We want her standing up.'

Blurring, sharpening, images moved. Long skirts, clicking boot heels. A convivial gathering, wouldn't you say? Flasks of tea. Carrot cake, pound cake, Battenberg – no, we don't call it that any more: sponge, sponge cake. Edie, did your cook make those? She's jolly good, isn't she? Yes, I don't know where I found her. She's a bit slatternly, but these days you take what you can get. Oh, look, there's Mason, isn't he poor Alec Featherstone's friend? You heard about that, didn't you? Rather a scandal. Poor Grace. Decent of him to come today, under the circumstances. What's he now, a second lieutenant? Major? Oh, my. Oh, and who's the wan-looking creature staring over at us as if she's got no manners? That's her. That's Grace's sister. Good gracious.

At a quarter to two, they gathered into the small space outside the servants' quarters in the basement. 'We don't want him to see us and think something's up, do we?' Margot said. Grace did not reply. She knew she had lost control over proceedings.

It was early enough for the half-hearted daylight to cast a wan, baleful glow onto the street. Advent would begin soon, with its hectic joy and a defiant resolve to make this Christmas like all the others before it. A snatch of music wafted out of a workman's café around the corner – *Don't ferget yer sod-jer lad!* A spade scraped the cobblestones as a worker shovelled horse dung into a cart. Soon he too would be gone; war would shovel him up in just the same way, with about as much respect.

Closing on two now. Then five past, ten past.

Then he was there too, his head held high, a man with nothing to hide or fear. *Turn tail. Run away. Oh, God, please.* But he didn't. He kept coming, his arms working in their usual jerky fashion. His lips were moving – perhaps he was singing again. His face was mobile and readable as always. Looking for her, seeing her and dipping his head, his brow creasing into a wordless question.

The women appeared up the basement steps, clapping and cheering mockingly. Eva had been holding on to the pigeon feather, turning it in her fingers. Grace watched her carefully to make sure she didn't break it or lose it. The feather itself was not much of a thing; it was hardly even white. If it had fallen off a bird in flight and drifted down to the street, nobody would have noticed it.

Christopher approached the house. All those women, who were they? Where had they come from? They seemed to have materialised out of nowhere, like urban nymphs. Eva stepped towards him. Still he did not see what was in her hand.

She did it quickly, without looking at him. Her fingers were trembling so hard she had no idea how she secured the thing on his lapel. The wool felt rough against her fingers. His eyes told no story. His face was something folded and put between the pages of a book. Eva felt cold ice ram through her body and up into her throat and heart.

Grace loomed behind, pale and unhappy, not exultant. One woman called out in a rather pleased contralto, 'Shame on you! Shame!' and a smattering of applause followed.

Christopher turned away from them all and walked rapidly down the street.

III

Oblivion

18

18 November 1915

From Father Samuel Knapp, ODC, to Prior Albert, Carmelite Monastery, Notting Hill

My dearest brother in Christ,

I cannot tell you how delighted I was to receive your last and know you are in good health. You speak yearningly of Palestine; I myself remember all too well the shade of the laurels, the olive groves, the glory of Haifa and the entire Mediterranean below, shimmering like a vast jewel. But, as in your case, duty has called me elsewhere.

I have served as an army chaplain for the past two years, all over the western front, and am now attached to the 2nd Irish Guards, ever since the fellow before me went down with the lumbago. It has been difficult work at times, though I know that the Lord, even now, looks over all of us with love and forgives us all our sins, in war and in peace.

My dear brother Albert, something has recently happened that preys on my mind and fair disturbs my sleep. As you heard my confession all those years ago, I beseech that you do so now. A confession within a confession, like a Russian doll! It is written in John 8:32 that 'The truth shall make you free.' So I hope it shall be in my case.

I joined this particular battalion on 30 August 1915, in preparation for a great attack that had been planned for September. It was supposed to be a secret, but the dogs in the street knew something was happening. The road to Cambrai was clogged with traffic, cavalry, supply trucks and men marching north to join their comrades. We all met at Saint-Pierre, and the men in the 1st and 2nd were in high spirits. General Haking had told them this would be 'the greatest battle ever fought'. I confess I did not believe a word of it. I'd heard of Haking, and nothing good either. He'd lost a good chunk of the New Army back at Aubers Ridge in May. Sent the pipers of the Black Watch over the line, piping away – for all the good it would do them – and the Germans had mown them down at close range with machine-gun fire. Poor fools. So I was more than a little doubtful that he would succeed here. But I could not tell anyone what I truly thought of General Haking and his talk. It is the role and duty of a chaplain to put heart into his troops and prepare them to fight a just cause, not to sow dissent and anxiety.

As often happens – my dear brother, you know this yourself! – many of the men sought me out for confidences, most of them on the same theme. I told them this: that if they must sin they were to go to the official blue and red brothels and to try to abstain from the full act. The officers were not immune either, though few of them came to me at first, not being Roman Catholics. (I could say a great deal about the C. of E. chaplains and how they conspicuously absented themselves in the thick of the action – but I won't.) I know it is not what we were taught at the seminary, nor in the Catechism, but these poor boys have little enough comfort. It is one thing to formulate doctrine when safe at home with a roaring fire and a glass of port, quite another when one ministers to men who are wet and cold, screaming with trench foot and having to watch rats run over their comrades' corpses.

I got on well with many of the lads, but there was one I could never really warm to. Which was strange because he was the most devout of the whole battalion. This private, Joseph Cronin, a native of Tipperary, had a wheedling, irritating manner, as if he always wanted something from you, even when he was merely making a statement. He disapproved of the other men drinking, or consorting with women not their wives. In theory, I should have been on his side. In practice, I found him a colder fish than ever swam in the Atlantic.

I asked him once if he heard often from his wife, and it was the one time I saw any emotion cross that long, pale face of his. I felt a dram of pity for him: for all that he stayed so tight-lipped, the pain in his face when I asked him that question told me something wasn't right there. He recovered quickly enough and said, 'Why do you want to know?' in that suspicious way he had about him. I didn't answer.

We left Saint-Pierre and marched for two days, through barely undulating countryside, the coal stacks puncturing the flatness of the place like odd black pyramids. The rumour that reached my ears was that the attack was due to start soon and that we would be using gas. My heart sank, because before then only the Germans had done this dastardly thing. It is no way to fight a war, this foul yellow curse. To see what it does to a man, blinding him, burning him … I cannot agree with it.

The morning the battle was due to start, we were still well behind the line. The men were billeted in a hay barn just outside Saint-Omer while I was back in a village house next to the staff sergeant. I am sure they all slept soundly, given the previous day's marching, but I could not get to sleep myself. I was restless about that battle, I had a bad feeling about it. I paced the room back and forth. I'm sure I drove the lady of the house demented.

The next morning, I heard nothing from the front; no messengers, runners, telegrams, nothing. I stopped at a village hotel and phoned Division, to be answered by a young officer. They'd only just repaired the communication lines. I asked him how the battle was going, and here you will have to pardon my language, for I must truthfully report what was said. 'Bloody balls-up', was his reply to me. 'Completely, from start to finish.' Well, Albert, I had a divil of a time teasing out what had gone wrong, but it came down to this: the gas people had made an utter hames of opening the cylinders. They were only able to free up about twenty of them, after running all around the place asking if anyone had a spanner. *A spanner.* By the time they did manage to let the gas off, half of it drifted back into our lines and turned the men's buttons green. I won't say what it did to their lungs and their noses and their eyes.

And the shells, don't talk to me about the shells. They were duds from America, and the ones that did explode fell into No Man's Land and on our advancing troops. Jerry might just as well have been sitting down reading the paper for all the threat we were to him – but he wasn't, he was ready to fight, and did so ably indeed, training his rifles and machine guns on the Middlesex and the King's Own and on God knows who else, and by the time he was finished there were scarce few left to keep up the attack. Hence the complete – well, just as my officer friend had described it.

When I heard all this my heart sank in my boots. For I knew that rather than give up the fight, as a man of sense would do, Haking would send a fresh batch of men in for a repeat performance. That would be us, the 2nd Irish Guards.

By the time we got to the front, it was raining and had been all day. There is something indescribable about rain in the trenches. It is not normal rain. It is not even like Irish rain, and God knows Irish rain is not normal. This rain soaks through everything. When it falls on my uniform and stains my white collar beyond recognition, it smells of mud and copper and foul death.

It didn't take much reconnaissance to see that everything had been destroyed. Communication trenches gone, front lines blown up or full of water. The raised hill we called the Hohenzollern Redoubt stood there, mocking us. We hadn't moved forward one inch.

On 27 September, Companies 2 and 3 began the attack, to no surprise whatsoever on the part of the Germans, who responded with a barrage of shells. They'd made short work of Kitchener's New Army the day before. The lads got to a disused colliery where they were supposed to 'dig in'. I tell you, Albert, if you've ever tried to put a spade in wet chalk to build a position in the pouring rain under enemy fire, I wouldn't recommend it. I'm fairly sure not a lot of digging got done that day.

As for me, I went back to oversee the next wave from 1 and 4 Companies – to put the fire into them, though I was feeling little of it myself – and there, sitting in the dugout while everyone else was on the fire-step, was Private Joseph Cronin, as dour as an egg, with his rifle cast down by his side. 'Cronin,' I said to him, 'are you not joining your friends?' He cast a glance of contempt over the whole platoon and said, 'Sure I'm not going out in that.' As if he didn't fancy a stroll in the rain! I had to reason with him for a good five minutes before I could drive it into his thick skull that taking part in this offensive with his fellow soldiers might be rather impor-tant. Finally, with a puss on him like a cat drinking sour milk, he took up his rifle again and joined his company.

Over they went, except Cronin, who fell back. As the others ran on into the firepower of the Germans, Cronin crumpled in a heap, splashing into the six inches of water at the bottom of the walls of mud, quivering and shaking. 'For God's sake!' I kicked him. 'D'you want to get yourself court-martialled?' I heard shouts approaching the position. Ours, retreating. I wasn't surprised.

One of them, an officer, jumped, or fell, into our trench. He landed on top of Cronin and swore when he saw the regimental flash on Cronin's sleeve. 'Did that man fail to go over?' I said nothing. He shook me by my lapels. 'Answer me, man! Did he fail to go over?' Seeing that I was going to say nothing, the officer turned to Cronin. 'That's it, Private, you're under arrest.' To me: 'What's his name?'

'Cronin.'

'I see. Right, men.' They frogmarched him off.

I thought no more about it as I had a lot of work giving last rites hither and yon; for the rest of the day I zigzagged about the trenches with my anointing oil, hoping to God I wouldn't be hit. The enemy were lobbing Jack Johnsons at us with all their might. The poor lads up in the Chalk Pit I couldn't reach, not that I could do them much good. I cannot describe the horror of that front line: it was littered with the dead and dying of the previous attacks: the Middlesex, Argylls, Highlanders. All those regiments, the machine guns just tore into them. Men on our wire, men drowning and bleeding in shell holes, and rats running around fat on the still-living men they were eating. It was a holocaust.

And it rained, and rained, and rained.

I nearly got knocked sideways by a shell whistling past my ear. It blasted a hole in a section of trench, cut an officer clean in half, his dead eyes still surprised, and threw a shower of mud in my eyes and mouth, leaving me blind and spitting and wiping and mercifully unable to behold the rest of the damage. I found shelter in the hole it had created and collected myself there for a while.

It was almost dark by the time I got back to our original position. There, flanked by two NCOs, was none other than Joseph Cronin. He had his head down and was rocking back and forth. The NCOs kicked him into standing up straight again. 'We had nowhere to put him,' said the officer, who I later learnt was Lieutenant Colonel Fenton, 'so we brought him back to fight. But he shows no inclination to join his fellow soldiers.'

'Well,' I wiped my brow with a decidedly soiled handkerchief, 'there's precious few left for him to join, to be fair.'

'He'll be back at battalion headquarters tomorrow when we decide the outcome,' Fenton said.

'"We"?' I said, taken aback.

'I'm the Judge Advocate of the Court Martial.' Fenton's voice was flat. I, however, was outraged. 'Hold on a minute,' I said, shouting in his ear for the drone of shells, 'you're telling me that you've arrested the fellow, he's under your command, and you're now president of the court that's putting him on trial? Next thing you'll tell me you'll be sorting his firing party while you're at it!'

The way Fenton's face sagged, I had the horrible suspicion I was right. He looked at me with a fierceness in him that reeked of despair. 'For God's sake, do you think I like this any more than you do? It stinks, from top to bottom.'

The battle went on for several weeks, but by the end of September, it was a ghost of a fight; the rest of October was nothing but futile skirmishes until the 21st, when we were finally relieved. Two days after that, at general headquarters in Saint-Omer, Cronin's fate was finally decided. Two guards dragged him out from the little room above the chemist's where they had been holding him and the battalion was rounded up and put on parade to hear his fate. A cavalryman read out the sentence as dung dropped out of the other end of his horse: Cronin was to be shot to death by firing squad at dawn the next day. The firing party would be chosen from his own company. His own company! Another rule broken, right there.

Poor Cronin fell to his knees with an almighty wail, a sound that nearly cracked my heart open. The other men looked pretty miserable, even Whelan and McGill, who had complained to me about Cronin's bible-reading and holy foolery in the past. They came to me afterwards, begging to be let off, as if I could help them. 'I don't mind killin' Fritz,' McGill said, 'but this is different. This isn't soldiering. 'Tis something else altogether.'

'I'm sorry, Jimmy,' I said, 'it's not up to me. Lieutenant Colonel Fenton is the man who makes that call.' I tell you, there were men crying that day: the prospect of killing one of their own filled them with a horror that no words of mine could displace. It made them vomit up the first decent meal they'd had in weeks. Guilt. Nothing gets to you like guilt.

Soon after I had gone to bed, Fenton's orderly appeared and told me to come: Cronin wanted me. Of course I was there straightaway. The guilt was getting to me too.

To my relief, Cronin had calmed down. The room where they were holding him was like an icebox and had no light in it, only one candle on a round table, illuminating that long face of his. I pulled up the one remaining chair and sat opposite him, reaching over and touching his hand. It was already cold, even though he was still living. 'Joseph,' I said to him, 'is there anything you need to tell me before tomorrow?'

He flinched slightly, but did not break down. 'Yes, Father. I feel a terrible burden on me.'

'Well, that's understandable.'

'No, it's not that.'

'Then … what?' I took the glass of water intended for him and allowed myself a great big gulp out of it. Churlish, I know; my throat was fierce dry.

'I'm here because of her. My wife, Eva.' And then he got tearful again, using the back of his hand to wipe his nose. 'Pardon me, Father.'

I handed him my deplorably filthy hanky. Not caring for its state, he sniffed and blew, long and wet.

'Your wife,' I said carefully when he had finished. 'You never talk about her, Joseph. Bit the head off me when I asked about her.'

'Well, I'm talking about her now, amn't I?' His voice was rough. He slammed the handkerchief down on the table, which rocked from the sudden movement. 'She hated me. I could hardly lay a hand on her without her shuddering. Do you know what she called me, Father? She would wait till I lay down with her, and then she'd whisper in my ear, like melting butter, "D'y'know, Joseph, you're a repulsive little gombeen man." In a hoity-toity accent, like a debutante! Is that anything a man's wife should say to him? 'Twas the only time I ever saw her get pleasure out of me, after she called me them names.'

'Joseph, Joseph,' I said, 'don't be telling me this. Don't be distressing yourself.'

'Well, if I don't tell you, who will ever know? It gave her joy to see me suffer,' he said. 'Father, she never loved me. Not for one second.'

I asked him then why he had married her if that was the state of affairs.

'I was mad after her, and her mam wanted it.' Cronin's face showed a new, tearless anguish. 'Her stepmam's a friend of my family, and I'd come to visit them over in England from time to time. Mrs Downey – that's the stepmam – wrote to me and told me Eva had changed her mind – nearly a year after last refusing me. I admit I was surprised at the time, as she'd said "no" to me more than once. But Mrs Downey told me that everything had been settled. There was some unpleasantness with a fella – I heard he wouldn't enlist – but Mrs Downey told me not to worry about that. She and Grace had sorted it all out.'

'And Grace is … ?'

'Mrs Downey's natural daughter. A beautiful wan, but bloodthirsty. Never stopped on about the war the whole time I was there. I swear it turned my stomach to hear her talk. Eva being only a stepdaughter, Mrs Downey never bothered much with her. I used to like to talk to her of an afternoon, or just sit and watch her reading or standing by the window. But I made a mistake marrying her. I was sold a pup, Father.'

Cronin drained the glass of water. I called the orderly and told him to get more. In the meantime, I looked at Cronin, pity mixed with revisited dislike. It was as plain as the nose on my face that his wife had been in love with this other fellow and had married Cronin under duress. And he was speaking of her as some possession to be traded.

'The day after we got married, there was not a word out of her the whole way to Wales and back home. I left her with my mother, and she never said a word to her either. And in the bedroom – well, I've just told you. I couldn't bear it any more, so I signed up. And all she said was, with a face flat as wood, "Don't blame me, I never made you." I left for training the day after that. But then I was home on leave, and the day before I went back to France, I was a man again. I had her – more 'n' once – and she could do nothing about it!'

Albert, I hate to speak so of a man facing his death, but there was something in his triumphal wail that brought bile to my throat. For that instant, I was glad he was going to die. For such an inhuman thought, I had to shake myself. 'Joseph,' I said briskly, 'I'm glad you felt you could trust me with these matters. Why don't I hear your confession?' (Of course, what was that but a confession – but how can I absolve one who is unrepentant?)

After he had finished, I stayed on. I had hardly slept the night before, so, in spite of the chill of the autumn night and the uncomfortable chair, I let my head nod onto my chin. A dream came over me, and I imagined I was in a church. The most sublime organ music played from the balcony. The place smelt of incense, sweeter and fresher than even the most potent mixtures I had burned on Sundays before my world shrank to this hellish battlefield. When I looked up, I saw the balcony was empty and I could find no source for the smell. Then the music was drowned out by shouting. Someone was calling my name: Father Knapp, Father Knapp … It was Cronin. He was wide awake. He must have been watching me the whole time I slept. 'They will be here soon,' he said.

And, indeed, a reluctant line of indigo had begun to steal its way across the bottom of the horizon. Dawn, still threatening dark, no sign of the sun. The knock on the door was quick to follow. Fenton's orderly and two guards were waiting. Cronin took a small bag and handed it to me. 'This is everything I have,' he said. 'My penknife that my father gave me on my Confirmation, my trench torch and a pen from my good friend Fred Regan and the bible from my mother. They should go back to the people who gave them to me.' His calm manner was more unnerving than the tears and knavery of the night before.

'And your wife?' I asked him.

Cronin only shook his head. His composure was starting to come apart, like threads on a loom unravelling, the warp and weft of his face at terrible odds.

'Come now,' the orderly said gently, 'it's time.'

Cronin nodded at him and extended his hand to mine. 'Thank you, Father.' I clasped his hand and moved to embrace him but he recoiled and backed away. I followed him out to where the firing party was waiting, by a walled orchard untouched by the vagaries of war. We – that is, Fenton, the guards, a medical officer and I – made our way there, in the wake of the firing party and their prisoner. I thanked God those lads were ahead of me, that I would not have to see their faces.

We assembled as detailed. Cronin was led to a spot in front of the wall, which was high enough for a firing squad to do its duty unseen. The medical officer, a dapper little chap with a curt-looking moustache, stood by, a pistol in hand. It was his job to declare Cronin dead and to finish him off if he were not.

As you know, Albert, there is a point of separation between the living and the dead. When you are following a dying person to his end, to a certain extent you walk with him, you feel with him, you could *be* him. I was with him in spirit when they tied his hands and blindfolded him as he requested. It was a terrible sight, that trembling mouth on an eyeless face, but I forced myself to keep my spirit with him. I was with him even as the firing squad raised their rifles into position. But the moment the NCO dropped his sword, before the first bullet was fired, I abandoned Joseph Cronin and became a spectator. When the bullets rang out and what had been Joseph Cronin became a blood-ridden, sagging bag, I was already detached from him. I did not want to could not – share that awful privacy of a public death. By the time the MO had dispatched one neat little bullet into his brain – a redundant exercise – I no longer trembled, for he was no longer human. That I had held his hands and consoled him no longer mattered. He no longer existed, and I did, fully, rudely, vitally. And I wanted my breakfast.

This is my confession, Albert. That I shepherded that man to an improper death. 'Verily I say unto you, inasmuch as ye have done it unto one of the least of these my brethren ...' And what did I do for him? Private Cronin was a poor soldier, and a weak man. But what we did to him that morning was inhuman, Albert, and I am diminished by my part in it. His face does not leave my mind, even when I am asleep. My sacraments seem very hollow now. I beg God will grant me the forgiveness I withhold from myself. Please answer soon.

Your (saddened, and much humbled) brother in Christ,

Samuel Knapp

19

12 November 1915

'Well, Syb,' the bonneted, leather-clad figure called out as she let the engine idle, 'what do you think?'

Sybil, Lady Faugharne, had been looking the wrong way down Gower Street when a quick, impatient toot sounded behind her. There, framed by the gateway of the Slade School of Fine Art, sat her friend Roma Feilding on the saddle of, if Sybil was not mistaken (and her experience with the Spitfire Motorcycle Club told her she was not), the latest Scott model, 550 cc, with a suspiciously empty sidecar. 'I think you expect me to get into that thing,' Sybil responded, 'and I'd really rather take a cab.'

Roma, not a woman flamboyant in her emotions, allowed herself a small smile. 'I think you could live a little.'

Sybil shot a look to high heaven but ran over to the sidecar and attempted to open the tiny door and climb in without making too much of an exhibition of herself.

'You're making heavy weather of that,' Roma observed. 'Here, let me help.' She held Sybil's elbow to steady her as she edged in one leg, then the other, aided by a delicate nudge from Roma on her calf.

It was a warm day for November, the mercury reaching fifty-five, and Sybil could feel the sweat prickle on her skin where Roma had pressed her leg. Tucking her brown, broadcloth coat into the confined, vibrating space took some doing, and there was no room for her legs to stretch. Her knees poked up over the front rim, all attempts to cover them with her coat ending in failure. 'Is this decent?' she enquired, with some alarm.

Roma laughed. 'You do surprise me, Sybil.' Then, 'I have a bonnet for you.'

'I'm not wearing one of those things, Romy, old chum. I already feel like a baby in a perambulator.'

Roma shrugged and released the brake. Crossing the road, they headed down Grafton Way and soon emerged halfway down Tottenham Court Road. Sybil could not help but notice a few people staring as Roma manoeuvred them into the middle of traffic for a right turn; it was uncommon enough to see one woman on a motorcycle, let alone two. But the breeze was up, it was a pleasant day, and it was nice to zip past everyone else while still being close enough to the ground to see them all milling about, crossing the street, going about their business. She was overjoyed when Roma, instead of continuing through the junction, took a left turn onto Marylebone Road. *We're going through the park!* she thought happily, just as the first drops of rain began to strike her cheek. Roma quickly turned her head to check that Sybil was all right to keep going; then, seeing that this was the case, she continued on through the park, skirting the lake.

At twenty-five, she was a little older than Sybil, unmarried in spite of her good looks, of impeccable connections and more economical with words than anyone Sybil had ever met. Not from shyness – no, not Roma – but from a natural, well-bred disinclination towards speaking unless either spoken to or unless she had knowledge of the subject at hand. To Sybil, whose husband rabbited on about anything that came into his head, larding it with commonplace and uninformed opinions, Roma's restraint was a gift, and her words, when they arrived, were even more treasured – particularly if they were ones of praise.

Sybil had met Roma in September, when they were both serving with the Women's Reserve Ambulance. They were detailed to the same vehicle during a zeppelin raid. Sybil, the driver on that occasion, would never forget the silence in the ambulance cab; the eerie swing of the searchlights up into the night sky and over the Thames; that ineluctable *thing* in the sky, launching mayhem and murder from its serene vantage point, still and pendulous as the harvest moon, its bombs sucking all the sound out of the air as window blinds flapped and went limp.

By the time they reached Farringdon Road, where the worst of the damage had occurred, the survivors had already been evacuated; they were left to haul the corpses in on stretchers and deposit them at the morgue in St Bart's down the road. Neither said a word for a long time, until Sybil exclaimed, 'I hope that beastly Hun gets what's coming to him … What are you doing? Are you taking *notes*?'

Roma was jotting down shorthand characters in a notebook on her knee, when the movement of the ambulance and the light allowed. She turned around and said simply, 'Always.' She was filing copy, it turned out, for *The Hendon Advertiser*, where she had a job writing captions for the gossip columns' photos. When Sybil enquired what the wilful burning and killing of civilians might have to do with society gossip, Roma stayed as cool as a cucumber, replying that one only needed a foot in the door: a woman would always be given a role of little consequence, and it was up to her to turn it into something more meaningful.

Roma was Dot Feilding's cousin, a fact that impressed itself upon Sybil since Dot – more properly, Lady Dorothie – was one of only four women chosen to join Dr Hector Munro's Ambulance Corps, which was out at the front in Belgium. Sybil had applied and had been rejected; the Women's Reserve Ambulance had been some small compensation.

After a jaunt of twenty-five minutes or so, the motorcycle and sidecar pulled up outside Sybil's London flat in Great Cumberland Place. It was difficult to believe, looking at the magnificent sweep of the terraced crescent, a rainbow breaking out behind, that London was into its second year of war. Sybil exited the sidecar with as little dignity as she had entered it; Roma waved and drove off. She had taken Sybil around as a favour only: now she had to go to work, and Sybil had a Red Cross benefit dinner to attend. Clive would not be going with her; he was up in Scotland again.

She rarely saw him during the week anyway, since his employment at the Ministry of Munitions as a 'key worker' required long hours – or so he claimed. His father's old pal Sir Laming Worthington-Evans had got him that cushy little number. The white-feather nutters wouldn't bother him, not with his 'King and Country' badge.

She was quite happy to go to the benefit dinner alone. She had thought to invite Roma, but something had stopped her. In the three months of their acquaintance, Sybil had never invited Roma anywhere. She felt like it would be an imposition to presume that someone so intelligent, so poised, would be interested in her company. At the thought of the two of them walking into the banquet hall together, Roma's dark head at her shoulder … Sybil felt a riot of emotions she could not quite process.

'Pish and tush,' she told herself as she crossed the long, brilliantly lit entrance hall with its panels, mirrors and Turkish carpets. At each recessed point stood an ornamental desk or a fake Queen Anne curio cabinet containing crystal goblets and silver trophies. The decoration was not to Sybil's taste, but since she and Clive only leased a flat upstairs and the building's owners were not disposed to clear out their own furniture, she just had to put up with it. 'Pish and tush', maybe, but as she passed each mirror and checked her reflection, she could not help but imagine Roma, with that dark hair of hers, thick and evenly parted, standing beside her.

In her bedroom, Jennifer, her new maid, took off Sybil's crumpled coat and unfastened the back of her day dress. 'I've laid out your dress here, milady,' she said. On the bedspread lay a salmon-pink silk taffeta that had caught Sybil's eye the previous week when browsing at Lucile Ltd. She liked that the colour clashed with her own hair, a combination that offended and worked at the same time. And the fabric was a far cry from the functional serge she had to wear when she was called out to drive around London when the air raids came. 'Perfect,' Sybil breathed, as if the dress were a newborn child presented for its mother's first inspection.

In the confines of her room, the heavy, floral curtains drawn against the advancing twilight, the scent of lavender from the open bathroom door making its gentle way onto her underclothes and skin, atrocity, toil and blood seemed far away.

'And your bath, ma'am.'

'Thank God.'

Jennifer unlaced Sybil's corset, and her high, small breasts dipped slightly with the relief of freedom. The whalebone left weals on her pale skin. There was some dirt on her stocking, probably from climbing into that damned sidecar. Now she was as naked as the day she was born and unabashed with it. She picked up a satin robe and made for the bath. The water was just a bit hotter than comfortable – the way Sybil liked it – and the fumes from the lavender and Epsom salts served as those special, extra felicities that made taking a bath so enjoyable. She was barely immersed when she heard a commotion outside the door. Her maid reappeared, looking flustered. 'What is it, Jenny? Is someone looking for me?'

'Er no, milady, nothing to worry about. Wilson told 'er you were not to be disturbed.'

'Her? Who is it?' Had Roma decided to skip work that afternoon after all?

'She says she knows you, milady, said she would wait.' Jenny sounded dubious. 'She didn't look as the type of person who'd know you, if you ask me. A Miss Eva Downey.'

'Eva? Here?' Sybil rose from the bath in one fluent movement, violently displacing the water. She dried herself with a towel and picked up her robe. She had not heard from Eva since last Christmas. A flurry of letters – then nothing. At the time Sybil had been offended rather than alarmed; that was until May, when Miss Hedges sent around her Annual Past Pupils' Bulletin. Sybil had looked for news of her friend, and in the marriages column read of the betrothal of Miss Eva Downey of Stepney, London, and Mr Joseph Cronin of Birdhill, County Tipperary, Ireland. She had nearly dropped the magazine in shock. What on earth? Eva hated that man! She had told Sybil so, and more than once. Where in God's name was Shandlin? What had *he* to say about all this? He was surely not a man to back down so easily; she would never forget the look on his face when she challenged him as to whether he was a man or a mouse. Miss Hedges' handmade, demure little volume offered no information on Shandlin's whereabouts; indeed, it said nothing about him at all. Enquiries to Mr and Mrs Downey were sent back with 'Return to Sender' written on them in round, childish handwriting, and Sybil had eventually given up on ever hearing from Eva again.

So it was odd indeed to see her, wearing black from head to toe and sitting in the hall, on a velveteen tuffet the colour of a cut blood orange, her hands tucked between her knees, her head barely lifting when a hastily dressed Sybil dashed down those vast, echoing steps, nearly noiseless in her slippers. When she did meet Sybil's eye, the look on her face was terrible to behold. Her hair was lank on either side, her eyes dull, as if someone had smeared a viscous, opaque substance across them. Beside her slumped a stained blue holdall with tortoiseshell handles. *My God*, Sybil thought, *what has happened to that girl?*

Then Eva spoke. 'I'm sorry, Syb. I really am. I had nowhere else to turn.' Startled by her own voice as it echoed around the hall, she whispered, 'I need your help.'

Sybil kept her tone light. 'Come upstairs and tell me all about it. I'll ring for tea. You look utterly *napoo*, as the Tommies say.'

'I've not slept in two days.'

Sybil ushered her upstairs and into the drawing room and called on the scullery maid to refresh the grate and on Wilson, the butler, to bring up tea and madeleines. She noticed that Eva stiffened to attention when she rang the bell, seeming primed to obey the orders herself. She looked out of place, Sybil thought, her confidence, her finishing, all of it gone.

When Wilson brought up the refreshments, Eva sipped gingerly at the tea but Sybil had only to turn her head a brief moment for three of the lit-tle cakes to disappear with indecent haste. *When did she last eat?* 'It's good to see you again,' Sybil ventured, trying to sound bright but only succeeding in sounding false.

'How is Bo?' Eva asked nervously. *She has not forgotten her manners, then. That's something.*

'We lost him at Neuve-Chapelle, I'm afraid.' How often had she recited that sentence? It felt unreal sometimes, as if Bo were away at school and would soon be home.

'I'm so sorry, Syb,' Eva said gently. 'He was very good to me.'

'Well,' Sybil's voice wavered. 'It all seems like such a long time ago, doesn't it? The dress, the dance … it was all another world, really. Like the most wonderful club – and now we've been kicked out for ever. Membership revoked.'

The two sat in silence for a moment. A log in the fire fell over and sparks let loose. Sybil waited: Roma had taught her the value of patience. Finally, Eva said, 'I dare say you heard that I married.'

'Yes. I saw it in Miss Hedges' bulletin. And not to Shandy! What hap-pened, Evie? I wrote and wrote and – nothing. You just disappeared.' At the mention of Christopher's name, Eva closed her eyes for one moment, which soon lengthened into several. Sybil realised that she was not ready to talk about him yet.

Then Eva came out with it: 'Sybil, I need money. I'm sorry to have to ask. I approached my family yesterday, but they turned me away.'

'Of course, sweetheart. That's—'

'You don't understand,' Eva interrupted her. 'I mean a lot of money.'

'A lot? What for?'

When Eva answered, it was as if her voice had retreated deep inside her chest. 'I've fallen for a baby, and I can't keep it. I need an abortion.'

'Your husband … ?'

'Lost at Loos. He came to see me on his last leave. You needn't say sorry, because I'm not.'

'But if you felt that way, when he was home … why did you agree … ?'

'Agreement didn't come into it.' Eva's voice was harsh as knives on gravel.

'Right.' Sybil rose to her feet. 'I need something stronger than tea for this.' She rang the bell again, and, in due time, two small glasses of sherry were set on the tray before them. The amber liquid shone as it caught the light of the fire. Sybil took a good sip; Eva left hers untouched, though she did take another cake.

'Heavens,' Sybil said, 'it's a lot to take in. It really is. When was he home on leave?' When Eva told her, she counted on her fingers. 'Oh, good Lord. You don't make it easy on yourself, do you? Evie, listen, I do want to help, but you're right, it's a lot of money to take out at short notice. I'd have to square it with Clive somehow. And it's such a beastly business, I can't … I say, have you been on to the War Office? Are you not entitled to a pension?'

Eva made the face of someone who had had cod-liver oil forced down her throat. 'Not for being married to a man who's been shot for desertion, no.'

'What?' Sybil exclaimed. 'You mean they shot him? Good God, forget the glass, I'm going to need the bottle for this. Wilson!' She rang the bell until it nearly broke. 'More where that came from, in a jiffy! Now, what happened? When did you find out?'

'He refused to fall in for the attack, and they banged him up in

Saint-Omer. I got the standard postcard from the War Office when he was court-martialled and shot. They don't do telegrams for cowards; we've to wait for the regular post. Then they sent me some effects. Nothing of any monetary value.' She drew her knees close. 'At least he's dead. I never pushed him into enlisting, but I wasn't sorry when he did go, and I'm glad he never came back.'

'Eva, that's a wicked thing to say. Take it back.'

'I shan't,' Eva said, 'and what's more, even if I had a pension and all, I'd still be looking to kill the thing.' She punched her abdomen with rage. 'I hate it. I don't want anything belonging to him inside me.'

'Eva, for God's sake, stop it! Stop it!' Sybil crossed the room and pulled Eva's fists away. 'I won't let you do this to yourself. Now, drink this – that's an order.' Eva hesitantly lifted the glass to her lips and did as she was told. Her eyes were wet with tears, and she was shaking.

Sybil was no longer in the mood to be patient. 'Eva, none of this makes any sense to me. Why did you do it? Why did you marry that man? When you loved somebody else, somebody who would have done anything for you? That day when I met old Shandlin and told him to go after you, he would have chased you to the ends of the earth – I could see it in his face. You could have got by, you and he. You could have stood up to your rotten family.'

Eva shook her head and laughed bitterly. 'Catherine swore all along she would break me. And she broke me.' Sybil looked at her questioningly. 'She kept telling me that I should marry Mr Cronin, it was the right thing – the sensible thing – to do. On and on, like weaving a spell. Of course she knew I'd obey. After what I did to Christopher, I knew I deserved no better.'

Sybil's throat tightened. The room felt heavy, as if bad magic had settled there and the fire would smoke out if she didn't open the windows. When she next spoke, it was with emphasis. 'What did you do to him, Eva?' For a long moment, Eva just sobbed into her sleeve. Then she lifted her face and told her.

'Oh, my God!' Sybil clapped a hand to her mouth.

'Grace thought he was a coward. She wouldn't release the money for Imelda's treatment unless I tried to force him to enlist. She made me choose – and I had to choose Imelda, don't you see? I had to! What would you have done if it were Bo? You would have done the same as I did,' Eva said, 'and you know it.'

There was a polite tap on the door. God bless Wilson; that would be him with the sherry bottle. 'Bring it in, please.' Sybil's voice quivered. Eva dabbed at her eyes and cheek with a grubby handkerchief. The door creaked open, and Wilson entered with a bottle in his hand. 'An amontillado, my lady, from Lord Faugharne's cellar.' He kindly kept his gaze off either woman; years of service had taught him the art of directing his address to nobody in particular.

'It's alcohol, that's the main consideration. Thank you, Wilson.'

'My lady.' He bowed perfunctorily and withdrew.

'Right,' Sybil said. 'Now, Eva—'

But Eva was not there. Sybil went into the corridor, softly calling her name. Passing the open door of her bedroom, she thought she heard something. She stepped closer – and then withdrew, quietly closing the door behind her. The door to the water-closet was open, and she had heard the sound of vomiting. She did not want the servants to know that about Eva.

She went back to the drawing room and put her face in her hands. This sex business was all so horrible; when she was a child her father had as good as left her mother and carried on with some vaudeville trollop in town and Sybil had never forgotten the shouting and crying. Bo had been her rock then. And now for Eva to go through this! She herself was lucky: Clive's few impositions on her person had been mercifully brief and unfluent, and he'd since had the decency to lose interest. Such a bloody, beastly, foul affair!

When Eva returned, a few minutes later, looking pale and shaken, Sybil had refilled her sherry glass. 'If you want,' she said at last, 'I can find a name. Someone who can help you.' At that moment, she felt nearly as sad as when she had opened and read the telegram about Bo. 'You look absolutely fagged, Evie dear. Just this morning I was cursing Clive for being away at his windblown pile of rocks up in the Firth of Forth, but it's turned out to be a blessing in disguise. You can have his room. I'll ask Mrs Phillips to see to it straightaway.'

After Sybil had left for the Red Cross banquet, looking entrancing in the salmon-pink taffeta, Eva was left alone in the capacious bedroom, her battered holdall slumped on the floor. After her long journey, she felt light-headed and shaky. But Sybil had promised help. Sybil was going to fix it for her. To know that she could hand over control … it was a deep relief.

She took off her shoes. Her stockings had sagged down to her ankles and smelt of sweat. She curled them up in a ball and stuffed them into one of the boots, then let her damp soles touch the carpet. It reminded her of wandering barefoot across the grass at The Links, and her certainty that she was protected and kept safe. She wanted to laugh aloud: how deceptive could sensations be? In her mind's eye, like a Pathé reel, the faces soundlessly rolled past: Imelda after her session with Dr Fellowes, holding her chest, the sides of her mouth flecked with blood; Christopher blanching and turning on his heel, the feather floating out of his collar and vanishing with him down the street; then, over her supine body, her arms held down, the pale, long-cheeked look of Joseph Cronin. And with him came other memories: the damp spreading its rotten roots around the walls, her skin recoiling at the fungal bloom on the sheets, the gritty air that got into her throat and settled there, the sudden flowering of pain when Joseph—

'No,' she said aloud, putting her fingers on her eyes, 'not now.'

She had interrupted Sybil at her bath, but Sybil had been kind enough to request another one for her, so she padded into the bathroom and hauled herself over the lip of the tub to bathe at her leisure. The water was warm rather than hot and Eva closed her eyes.

That night, she slept very deeply.

20

Three days later, at one o'clock, Eva was at the gates of Mile End Military Hospital, a carefully folded piece of embossed stationery from Sybil's bureau in her hand. It bore only a name, which Eva by now knew by heart: Lucia Percival. 'I heard she used to work for a Haitian woman who has a place in Beak Street. My friend Babs Fulton got herself into a right scrape a few months ago and apparently swore by this place,' Sybil had told her. 'She'll want a hefty fee of course. This should be enough.' Sybil shuddered involuntarily as she folded up the notes and put them in an envelope. She had really bitched Clive, going to the bank and withdrawing that amount. It was her account, but if there was nothing left to cover expenses for the month and barely enough for servants' wages, she would have to tell him … especially after that taffeta! She bit her lip. 'God, I hate this business. Eva, whatever transpires, please understand that I cannot be involved. It's between you and her.'

'I understand,' Eva said, 'and I'm truly grateful, Sybil.'

'There's no need for gratitude,' Sybil answered. 'I thought of what you said about choosing Bo … and it's true, I would have done.'

Mile End Military Hospital had once been a workhouse, and Eva could see the building's grim past in its functional brick and in the lines of its windows, high tower and relentless terrace. Sybil's envelope felt like live ordnance in Eva's pocket; never in her life had she carried so much cash. She hovered around the gates for a good ten minutes but nobody emerged. She would have to go in and find this Lucia woman herself.

She pushed the main doors open and immediately found herself in the middle of activity. Everywhere she looked, women floated and darted by, dressed in long tunics with white cummerbunds at the waist, grey blouses with upturned collars and white headscarves tied at the back. These, she guessed, were the Voluntary Aid Detachment girls. They seemed to be busy for the sake of busyness, rather than any useful purpose. One of them paused mid-drift, looked at Eva with some suspicion and said, 'Yaaas?'

'I'm looking for a Miss Percival.'

The girl shook her head. The implements on her tray rattled. Eva saw that it was loaded with used hypodermic syringes, surgical scissors and specula, stained dressings and sheets of cotton wool. 'Not ringing a bell.'

'Lucia. Lucia Percival.'

'Oh, I think I know who you mean. Hang on a tick.' The girl pulled a freckled, sandy-haired comrade to a halt. 'Hallo, Fay! This girl's looking for a Lucia Percival. Is that who I think it is?'

'Lucia Percival? She's on cleaning detail today. You'll find her in the building next door, probably in the corridor. Right, then second left.' Fay pointed out the double doors behind her.

'Thank you very much,' Eva said. 'What does she look like?'

The first girl began to laugh. 'You haven't met her before, have you? She's the only coloured gal in the hospital. And you'll hear her before you see her, mark my words. Could you be a dear,' she continued, 'and take these over to room 4D on your way? The instruments need sterilising, and the rest …' She smiled the sweet, assuming smile of those who know they are asking something outrageous and expect it to be done regardless. Eva, too long absent from polite society to feel confident objecting to her insolence, took the tray from her without comment.

The long corridor was punctuated by a series of doors. Her hands full, Eva had to push through each one. The tray's contents smelt of iodine and stale blood, and, since it had no useful lip, she feared some of it would get on her hands. As yet there was no sign of Lucia Percival. Then one wall of the corridor became a series of high windows, and light broke in everywhere, betraying the worn pea-green linoleum with its collection of splashes and stains. At that moment, Eva heard a voice, high on the register, pure, doleful and perfect: 'Happy birthday to me / Happy birthday to me / Happy birthday 'cause no one cares / Happy birthday to me.' The singer was still a good way away, but Eva noticed that the white uniform contrasted with her light brown skin. Yes, Eva had heard her first.

Lucia was making heavy weather of the cleaning, moving the mop around in disillusioned, ever-slowing circles, plunging it into the bucket and lifting it out, allowing it to drip indiscriminately, then pausing to lean her chin on the mop handle and look out the window in some sad reverie. After a moment, she started singing again, sublimely, each Latin syllable as clear as a bell – and as piercing as a stab in the heart: '*Confutatis, maledictis / Flammis acribus addictis / Voca me cum benedictis.*'

Eva's tray left her hands and fell to the ground with a crash, the dirty tools and flannels and cotton wool and tweezers scattering on the lino. Lucia broke off from her melody and stared at Eva. '*Mi Gad* … what is it?'

Eva could not speak. It was too much, his song from this stranger's mouth. Why had she ever thought she could come back to London? Her eyes blurring, she turned tail and fled, an angry Jamaican voice calling after her, '*Wa gwaan*? What is wrong with you?'

Outside the hospital gates, a wet wind blew up. A couple of nurses followed Eva out, complaining loudly about the ineptitude of the VADs. Army trucks clattered past, all on their way to the front or to training camps.

Eva shivered convulsively. She felt an urge to vomit again and swallowed. She stuck her hands further into the muff she had borrowed from Sybil and laced her fingers together. Fool! She'd had one chance, and she had blown it—

A hand on her shoulder spun her round: Lucia. Close up, Eva saw that she was a good head taller than her and pretty to boot, with a high forehead, wide nose and a generous mouth that looked as if it had once known how to laugh. 'Why did you run away?' Her voice was clipped.

Eva felt that stone in her chest. 'Your song. Someone else used to sing that. Someone … important. I was not prepared for it.'

'And that is the excuse you have for running off and leaving the floor all covered with dressings and syringes and things? Did you think I was going to clean up after your mess? Because, *a mi fi tell yu*—' She appeared about to reach a fortissimo of rage when she suddenly heaved a sigh. 'Ah, forget it. I'm just tired is all.'

Eva felt ashamed of herself. 'I'm sorry,' she stuttered. 'I'll go back in – I'll clean it up.'

'Too late,' Lucia said. 'I got one of those birdbrained Tollington-Smythes to take care of it. They might as well be useful for something. Besides, I need a break. I've been up since five o'clock this morning, and

I'm bunched I tell you! And …' she refocused her gaze at Eva, 'I've been expecting you.'

'So. You know.' Eva felt a wave of relief break over her. Good on Sybil for clearing the way. To have had to explain her predicament would have been a heavy task, given that they'd already got off to such a bad start. Lucia nodded. 'It was made known to me that a lady fallen into adverse circumstances would be willing to furnish a not unreasonable sum of money if I could help make her problem magically disappear.'

Eva suspected that Lucia was enjoying the cloak-and-dagger drama of it all. But she had to set her right on one thing. 'If by "fallen into adverse circumstances" you mean I shamed myself, I can assure you that is not the case. I was in Ireland—'

Lucia raised her palm to stop Eva. 'I don't want to know. Don't want to *fas inna yu* business, understand? You tell me nothing, I know nothing; makes it easier all round. I don't care if you were in Ireland or Timbuctoo—'

'Oh, happy birthday, by the way,' Eva cut in.

'What?'

'You were singing about it. That it was your birthday, and that nobody cared. Happy birthday.'

'Oh. Thank you,' Lucia replied, taken aback. 'That's mighty kind of you.' Then she looked at Eva with mock reproach. 'But you didn't bake me a cake? Why no cake?'

'I was too busy falling into adverse circumstances.'

'Not much of an excuse,' Lucia said, 'but *cha*, it will have to do. Now, to business. You will come back here at seven o'clock on Friday. I cannot get out any earlier, and you should not go unescorted. We will go together to the place, and you will meet Mama Leela. She is an experienced midwife, but she also knows the other traditional ways.' She frowned. 'Mama Leela has done this many, many times, more than you would dare believe, but there is always the risk that you will die, or end up in prison. Do you understand what I am telling you?'

'If I am not rid of this thing,' Eva said, her voice cold, 'my life is over in any case, and I shall never be free again.'

Lucia looked at her in horror and made the sign of the cross. 'You frighten me more than the *ge-rouge*, when you speak like that.'

'The … ?'

'Haitian devils. We don't hold with such heathenism in Jamaica, mind, where I'm from.'

Eva nodded, bewildered with the turn of the conversation.

'So,' Lucia continued, returning to the subject, 'you need to pay me now.'

'Fine.' Eva passed over the bulky envelope. Lucia counted the notes and frowned. 'This is too much.'

'There's money for a cab fare. To … the place.'

Lucia shook her head. 'You give it to the driver on the night.' She handed Eva back five pounds and pocketed the rest in her vast white apron. 'See you then – oh, wait. I don't know your name, star.'

'Eva.'

'Eva,' Lucia repeated, looking her up and down. Then, as Eva was turning back towards the main road to find her bus stop, '*Cha*, you look like you had one long fall from Paradise.'

*

On the Friday evening, punctually at seven, Eva was once again at the Mile End Hospital entrance, this time sitting in a motor cab. The driver had switched off his headlights, even though it was nowhere near curfew, and she had to urge him to turn them back on so that Lucia would be able to find them in the darkness. It began to rain, the droplets hovering like fine mist in the twin lights. She did not have long to wait: of all the figures walking in file out the gates, one scuttled, then broke into a run. Eva opened the door beside her, and a heavily raincoated Lucia slipped in, gasping.

'I thought I'd never get out! I was changing the dressing on one man's leg and he screamed the place down. Then he called for the sister, who is the most miserable *bakra* you ever did see, and—'

'If you can tell the driver where we're going?' interrupted Eva, hoping she didn't sound too abrupt.

'Of course, sorry. Take us back down Whitechapel Road please, and keep going from there towards the National Gallery.'

'Trafalgar Square, ma'am?' asked the driver.

'The very one! Thank you.'

Eva, a connoisseur of accents, noticed that Lucia kept hers neutral when addressing him. When they reached the National Gallery, the driver slowed down. 'Where do I go from here, miss?' he called through the hatch.

'Here is just right. Thank you,' Lucia replied.

'But—' objected Eva.

'I think it might be wiser to walk the rest of the way,' Lucia hissed.

Eva had no choice but to comply. She paid the driver as Lucia had instructed and followed her up past Piccadilly Circus and on into the rabbit warren of streets around Soho. Lucia now walked confidently, gesturing from time to time to urge Eva to hurry up. Then they were there. The halt was so sudden after all that rapid walking.

Eva recognised the neighbourhood; why, the building stood barely ten minutes from Sybil's house. They could have met in the street outside the address. Lucia took her down a flight of narrow stone steps to a basement door and rapped on it sharply in a particular rhythm that implied an agreed signal. The door was answered by a bespectacled woman with a round face and thinning hair under a white peaked cap. That and a white apron gave her the look of a nurse, but she wore no insignia. She and Lucia greeted each other. Was this Mama Leela?

It appeared not, for they were led into a room barely larger than a pantry and told to wait. Five deal chairs were arranged on either side, so close that their occupants' knees would surely have touched. A few paraffin lamps burned on a high shelf, but the light they gave was fitful. Eva could barely make out Lucia's face. In the background she could hear a faint tinkle-tinkle of a bell. The sound stopped and started with no apparent rhythm.

'Just us,' Lucia remarked. 'There've been times when I worked here I had to turn people away.' She tapped Eva's knee. 'Don't worry, star. Mama Leela is a powerful woman. When she went to Haiti she worked with a mambo priestess called Celestina Simon, the daughter of the President himself!'

Eva had never heard of Celestina Simon, nor mambo, but just as she was about to enquire, the door opened again. This new person was a woman of about fifty with a wide, light brown face and sharp eyes. She pointed to Eva. 'This she?' Her voice had a stronger West Indian lilt than Lucia's. This must be Mama Leela.

'Yes,' Lucia replied.

'Is it all settled?'

Lucia handed her Sybil's wad of notes. The woman nodded and called out to someone at the back. Eva heard once again that soft tinkle, then a little girl with jet-black skin and braided hair appeared. Mama Leela gave her some instructions in a dialect of French Eva did not understand. The girl vanished, the bell tinkling with her as she went.

Lucia took Eva's hands in hers. 'Good luck. Stay strong.'

'Are you not coming with me?' Eva said, horrified. She surely could not go through this alone. Lucia shook her head and tapped her watch. 'I have to go back. It's curfew in an hour.'

'Please stay,' Eva said. For the second time in a week, she was begging someone for support. But she could not help herself; she was mortally frightened. What if she were to die alone? That primitive thought crossed her soul like a footstep, leaving a soft, firm imprint. Lucia's face softened at her distress. 'I cannot stay now. I will come in the morning.'

'But—'

'I will come in the morning,' Lucia repeated, gently releasing Eva's hands.

'You promise?'

'You want a signed document with a big wig? Yes, I said. You will be fine and alive when I see you.'

Eva reluctantly gave in, and they said their goodbyes. When the door closed behind her, it took a few moments for Eva to focus on Mama Leela, who was speaking to her. Mama Leela's English was not fluent. 'You go here.' She beckoned Eva to follow her down to the end of the basement flat. There, to her relieved surprise, was a well-turned-out room: a tungsten light bulb hanging from the ceiling, a large, clean-looking hospital bed and a trolley containing shining, clean instruments. They looked so sharp, so brutal and butcher-like, Eva had to turn her head. The small window was locked and barred.

Mama Leela pointed to the bed. Eva lifted herself up onto it and sat there uncertainly. Mama Leela bade her remove her dress and underthings and felt about her abdomen. She clucked a few times in reproof, then stood up and looked Eva in the eye. 'Doctor have to operate. Drink not enough. Too far gone.'

Eva started to shake. 'Will it hurt?'

Mama Leela laughed. 'No, we will put you heavy asleep.' Before leaving the room, she handed Eva an itchy calico gown to change into and instructed her to lie on the bed. Eva did as she was asked. She was more scared than she had ever been in her life. How would the doctor operate on her? It would have to be something sharp, something scraping. The thought of it had her rushing to the small sink to throw up. As quick as a thought, Mama Leela was back. 'Control, control,' she chided, pulling Eva back. 'Here, drink some of this.' She handed Eva a cracked mug of something that tasted treacly at the start and bitter on the swallowing, so bitter that Eva felt a twinge all down her gut and an urge to spit it back up. But Mama Leela insisted she drink again. 'More.'

Eva shook her head. Was this woman out to poison her? Mama Leela grabbed her by the shoulder and brought the cup to her mouth. 'You must drink! My word must stand for dominate!' Eva had no choice but to trust her. She swallowed back another few mouthfuls of the vile syrup, fighting the urge to spit it back up each time. She could feel the liquid sink down into her stomach and a haze come up in front of her eyes. The older woman's face loomed in and out of view. She was chanting '*Erzulie ninnin, oh hey! Moin senti ma pe' monte', ce moin minn yagaza …*' On and on it went, that weird Haitian chant, the words twisting around themselves like ribbons as Eva found herself on the cusp of blacking out. Her tongue tasted metal at the roof of her mouth, and she was sweating and feeling feverish. And he was back in her mind's eye, her husband, Joseph, slouching, plaintive. 'For God's sake,' she shouted in her delirium, 'leave me alone! I hate you.'

But no matter what Eva cried out, still that supernal voice continued to murmur '*Erzulie ninnin, oh hey!*' while she felt the benison of a cold cloth on her forehead. Mama Leela was so close that Eva could smell the old-paper smell of her breath. Then she put something on Eva's nose and mouth. 'Breathe.'

For a moment Eva thought Mama Leela was saying 'breed', which sounded like a strange instruction from an abortionist; then she realised that the woman spoke like the Irish, hardening the 'th's. She breathed in and felt a heavy band around her head, Mama Leela's image wavering. 'Deep,' the voice commanded, sounding as if it came from the bowels of the earth. Eva obeyed. Mama Leela said something in her own tongue. 'Again,' she said to Eva, adding, 'Now I call the doctor.' Eva didn't remember what she said next.

The first thing she realised after that was wakefulness, but she couldn't quite get at it. The world was awake and calling at her, nagging her, but she could not rise to the surface: it hurt too much, it was just a few steps too many up a flight of stairs, that was all. Snatches of the *Sicut Cervus* floated in and out, broken melody and countermelody, all fuzzed and obscured; she thought once she heard Lucia's voice rising above all that brokenness, singing something entirely different, but that faded too. There was Angela, whose face always fell into darkness when she looked at it. A hand clasped hers, and she felt laughter in her heart and saw a pair of brown eyes, mocking and affectionate – she called out a name – but then lost it again.

When she opened her eyes it was morning proper; a raw blue light made the room look smaller than it had the previous night. From her supine position, Eva could see that some attempts had been made to clean her up; the sheet that brushed her legs was stainless, if worn. If anything, she wished she could see less. The light streaming through that dirty, barred window was too bright and too cruel. Then she heard someone whisper her name. It was Lucia, come in the morning, just as she had promised. 'Eva, I brought you some water.'

'Is it gone?' Eva said hoarsely.

'Yes. You sad?'

'I don't know,' said Eva, and it was true. Such rage she had felt against it, but the rage masked something else, a feeling that surged when she felt afraid and the little thing seemed to jump along with her heart. As if, were she not vigilant, she could feel attached to it. That the wall she had built around herself could collapse. Then *they* would have won.

She lifted herself, slowly and painfully, into a sitting position and took the glass. It was well timed – her throat and tongue were like sandpaper – and to her parched mouth even London water was clear, beautiful and cold. Lucia restrained her. 'Drinking water is not illegal under the Defence of the Realm Act. Slow down, 'fore you make yourself sick.'

'How long have you been here?'

Lucia shrugged. 'An hour? Two? Don't worry, I was fine. I read the paper.'

'My ...' Eva pointed to her abdomen ' ... hurts.'

'It will for a while.'

But it was too much, the pain. Eva waved away the offered bowl; she could only point at her pelvis once more. It hurt so badly that tears of pain rolled down her cheek. Lucia grasped her hand. 'Hold on, star.' Eventually, the worst stabs passed and the pain reverted to a dull ache. 'Better now,' Eva managed, not having the energy for more.

They sat together a few moments. Soon it would be time to leave, but for now Eva needed a minute or two.

'Can I ask you a question?' Lucia said. Eva, realising that she was probably trying to distract her from the pain, nodded. 'Who is Christopher?' Seeing Eva's face, she added, 'I'm sorry, I did say *no fas inna yu business*, and I meant it. But earlier you called out his name. Was it his? He the one who get you into this mess?' Eva shook her head violently. 'A man in your life, then.' A small, proud nod. That much at least she could do. 'Where is he now?'

Before Eva could answer, another round of pain overtook her. Lucia ran into the corridor and called Mama Leela, who huffed and swore her way in. 'It normal,' she shrugged when Lucia expressed her concerns. 'Stay with her for a while, is all right. But you both need to leave soon. I have other girls coming.'

Grimacing with pain, Eva stood up and started to dress. Sybil would be at home in Great Cumberland Place, waiting and anxious. Not a soul knew of this: not Clive, not Sybil's new friend Roma, nobody. Sybil, of course, would have preferred not to have known herself.

But Lucia was there and for that Eva felt a gratitude that almost moved her to tears. This Jamaican girl, a stranger, had come back as she had promised. It was, after all, a business transaction, and it had cost Sybil a pretty packet. One couldn't be too sentimental. But still …

Through the door, she could hear a woman's moan, followed by a shouted instruction to fetch Dr Hill, then another door creaking open and closing as if a breeze had caught it in a slam. And that little bell, tinkling throughout the corridor, an inappropriately childlike sound in such a charnel house. Had that little girl had any sleep? Inside the room, all was silent.

Eva realised that she hadn't answered Lucia's question. 'He went to war,' she said.

Lucia raised her eyes and hands to heaven. 'War,' she said. '*Life mash, this bloody war.*'

21

'Name, please?' The young matron sat with her elbows on the desk, her peaked cap slightly askew on her head. Eva ached to correct it.

'Eva Downey – ah, Cronin … no, Downey.'

'Would you like to tell me which it is?' the matron said, not unkindly. Behind the desk hung a felt banner bearing the name of Queen Alexandra's Military Hospital, surrounded by army propaganda posters. A heavy smell of boiled sheets and bicarbonate of soda hung in the air.

'I'm widowed, ma'am, but I use my maiden name.'

The matron nodded, the skin under her chin folding a little. A peaky, dimpled Yorkshirewoman, she did not offer condolences, merely saying, 'Right, let's save the details for now. Have you completed your first-aid training?'

'Not yet, ma'am.'

'You can start tomorrow. You'll have to fulfil that and qualify for the Red Cross before we can accept you.' Eva nodded. The matron gave her a sharp, sidelong look. 'You look young, if you don't mind my saying so.'

'I am twenty-four, ma'am.' The lower age limit for volunteering in the Voluntary Aid Detachment nursing unit was twenty-three. Eva added a year, to be on the safe side, rather than reveal her true age, a mere nineteen. The matron clearly did not believe her, but Eva was not overly anxious.

Sybil had already reassured her on that count. 'Oh, they were all Fussy Fussbudgets to start off with, but a year in and they're crying out for people. They'll not be picky, don't worry.'

The matron leaned forward and put her head on the steeple of her interlaced hands. 'You will find it difficult, Mrs – Miss Downey, if you are not accustomed to such work. I've heard that some units have trouble with their VADs. They imagine their purpose in life is to drift around the wards bringing comfort while the nurses proper have to wash the bedpans.'

'The Tollington-Smythes,' Eva said before she could stop herself.

'I beg your pardon?'

'Nothing. Just something somebody said.'

The matron's chin angled hard with disapproval.

'I am not afraid of hard work, ma'am,' Eva said hurriedly. 'My marriage taught me many skills. I can make eggs all ways, boiled, poached and fried. I can cook pigs' trotters and make soup from the jelly. And put laundry through a mangle.' This last was said with considerable pride. How strange that such a miserable, penurious year should have taught her anything at all, but it had.

The matron smiled drily. 'I'm glad to hear you're not shy of work, Miss Downey. Because I've had my fill of society girls, believe you me. This is not the Derby.' She wrote something on a slip of paper. 'Your Red Cross classes should take two weeks. There'll be a bit on home nursing and first aid. I see no reason not to put through your orders as soon as that's done, and you should be with Queen Alexandra's by the start of February. We have a lot of our boys coming back from the Dardanelles. I must warn you, they are very badly shaken up.'

'I will do my best, matron.'

'Well, then, that's settled. Welcome to the Queen Alexandra's Voluntary Aid Detachment.' She stood up and extended her hand. Eva took it. 'By the way,' she added, 'I'm very sorry to hear of the death of your husband. Was he at the front?'

'Yes. At the battle of Loos.' At it, maybe, but certainly not in it.

'You hear it so often these days. Doesn't make it any less painful.' Although she couldn't have been more than thirty-five, the matron looked as if she had seen it all. What was one more death far away when men were dying every day in her own wards? And Eva, for her part, was grateful she did not have to go into any detail about her husband's death. She took the piece of paper the matron handed her, a voucher for her new uniform, redeemable for the next month.

Sybil had done her level best to talk her out of it. 'Oh, Evie,' she said, when they were in the milliner's the day before, 'why? It's such a bore, all this nursing stuff. Ten to one you'll end up cleaning slops. And you're not cut out for it, you know you're not.'

'Perhaps,' Eva said, 'but I'm hardly cut out for anything else, am I?'

'Do you remember,' Sybil said more gently, 'that you once had ideas about sitting for a scholarship for Oxford?'

Eva went white almost to the lips. It was a moment before she spoke. 'I think we both know there's no place for that in my life any more.'

'Just because—'

'It's not only that.' Eva was harsh; she couldn't bear to let Sybil finish her sentence. 'I've no money, Sybil, and no means of earning any. If I want to support myself with any dignity, it's either war or service, and to be honest war looks more appealing.'

'Really,' Sybil said, turning away to look at a cluster of faille hats with brown silk ribbons on top, 'and there was I thinking it's nothing but a cruel and sinful waste of life.'

Of course – Bo. Eva started to stammer an apology for her lack of tact, but Sybil cut her off. 'I'm not the first to suffer, and I won't be the last. I mean, look. It's nearly impossible to find someone in town who's not wearing black. No offence, but I'm sick of it. Bo wouldn't have wanted it.'

'I understand,' Eva said, 'and I think you should wear what you want.' After all, it wasn't as if she were wearing black for Joseph Cronin.

For a moment her friend said nothing, just stood there holding the hat in her hand, her fingers crushing the silk. Eva felt wretched for her. But Sybil pulled herself together – Eva could see her do it, it took a physical effort. 'How does this one look?' she said, pushing up the short brim and allowing a few tendrils of hair to escape around her ears and forehead.

'Very attractive.'

'I would have thought you'd be rebelling against the war, not joining in.' Sybil tended to hop from topic to topic like a gadfly.

Eva smiled bitterly. 'I think,' she said, fingering the soft felt of a black-bowed hat with a wide brim, 'that for a man, if you renounce war you're a rebel, but for a woman it's the opposite. To rebel is to fight. We're supposed to marry well, be nice girls and stay out of public affairs. Every person I ever met told me this – except Christopher. He told me the opposite, but that's the man he was. Is. Anyway, they've pulled the rug out from under us. How can we marry when they've taken our men? We might as well be the rebels.'

Sybil put down the faille hat and stared at her. 'That was quite a speech.' On impulse, she put her gloved hand on Eva's shoulder. 'You still miss him, don't you?' Seeing Eva's face crumple a little, Sybil put her arm around her. 'Bear up, old girl,' she whispered. Eva nodded, blinking away her tears, then declared, 'I will, I promise. I'll not leech off you any longer, Sybil. You've been generous to me, beyond what I've a right to ask. I need to make my own way in life.'

'And that's very commendable,' Sybil said, leading her to the counter. 'But, darling, they hardly pay at all. Living quarters, whatever hellhole they might be, and some sort of honorarium, that's it. The clue is in the word "voluntary", you see.'

'I don't care. I need to get out of London and make myself useful, Syb.' Eva drew her shawl around her. 'Too many ghosts. I see them everywhere.'

'Well, you'll have to wait till I pay the man; I can't just rob the shop because you're suddenly agoraphobic.'

'I mean, I want to go to France.'

'Well,' exclaimed Sybil, as the cash register rang and the smooth jacketed assistant wrapped her purchase, 'of all the crazy ideas you've given me for signing up, that has to be the craziest of all. As if bedpans and VD and nerves weren't enough – you'll be stuck with the French! The blasted French! I can only conclude you've lost your reason, Evie.'

Eva couldn't resist a grin. 'Look at it this way, Sybil. I've lost everything else. What's reason, at the end of the day?'

'Now that,' her friend sighed, 'is a Shandlin question. In other words, it's one I have no idea how to answer.'

'Then I suppose it never shall be answered,' said Eva bleakly.

*

A week later, Eva moved her few belongings from Great Cumberland Place to the hostel on Markwell Hill where she would be staying while she worked in Queen Alexandra's. Markwell House was grim and grey, about a century old, with no decorative features to break its relentless front apart from a double-edged, unadorned pediment above the doors, which were as thick as those of a prison. Its gardens, once fine but now reduced to ragwort and dandelion, swept down the hill from where there was a magnificent view of the bend of the Thames as it continued east. The park on which it sat was a full two miles from the hospital. The rooms were long, high-ceilinged and full of draughts. Each girl had a Spartan cubicle with a thin curtain, containing a bed, a washstand and a rickety chest of drawers, and there were fifteen of these in each room.

Eva's first day, like every one that followed it, was long and hard. She rose at five-thirty, washed in cold water (the water heating was usually off), then walked to the bottom of the hill to catch a tram to the hospital. She would stand around with a clutch of girls, coats spotted with the early morning rain, watching tram after tram roll past, packed to the gills with dock workers coming in from the night shift. Finally, one of their number would give up and start walking, the rest following in a short, dismal line, carefully avoiding the passing dray carts that might splash their white uniforms with mud. An acrid stink of ordure, molasses and city detritus rose up from the Thames. Heads bent, headscarves flying in the wind, Eva's companions did not speak to one another. Like her, they were not quite fully awake.

They would walk for an hour and a quarter before reaching the hospital, Eva's insides crying out for breakfast. But the cry was to go unheard. She would not eat for another four and a half hours. Nor was she allowed to sit down at any time, especially not on a bed. There seemed to be an infinite list of rules, all infinitely infringible. Her head span trying to take them all in on an empty stomach.

On her first day, she was sent to the laundry, where she helped a small army of VADs and orderlies press and clean hospital gowns. For the first time since her arrival, one of the girls spoke to her. 'You're new here.'

'Yes, I just got my orders.'

'Why'd you join?'

'Needed the money.'

The other girl looked at her oddly, waiting for her to say more. Of course, she should have said that she wanted to 'do her bit'. It wasn't as if they were even paid that much, a miserly twenty pounds a year, that was all.

'I know somebody out there,' she said.

'Oh, you've a sweetheart?' her colleague asked, sympathetically.

'Not any more,' Eva said, a twist of pain lying against her heart, like a blade in its sheath.

'Is he dead?' The girl's voice was far softer than the pounding of the mangle and the noise of the machines and shouting, but Eva heard her clearly.

'I don't know,' she replied.

Nonplussed, the girl turned back to her work with a twitch of her nose.

Eva did not see her again after that first day. This was not uncommon, she learnt. Quite a few girls disappeared without notice. Family members, particularly parents, cultivated a sense of grievance at the loss of sisters and daughters who might otherwise be pressed into caring for elderly and infirm relatives. They would use any pretext to order the girls back home. After all, they weren't men; it wasn't as if they were doing *real* war work.

Eva had last seen her own father three weeks before, when he turned down her request for money. She had been made to wait just inside the front door in the dim hallway, drops of November rain falling from her coat onto the doormat's bristles. Then she was called in, as if she were one of the shabby-coated bankrupts he felt it his duty as an accountant to harangue, and he pulled that trick of his where he doodled at his desk to look busy. It was a ridiculous dance. Finally, when he lifted his pompous head, narrow as a ferret's, she had asked him for the money. She had not told him she wanted rid of Cronin's child. If she were fool enough to throw herself on his mercy and blurt *that* out, she had no doubt that either he or Catherine would lock her up until she gave birth.

She would not forget his response in a hurry. Did she think he was made of the stuff, he thundered. That it grew on trees? After all the trouble she had caused him with her pride and intransigence, she wanted to bleed him dry with no explanation, no thought to the others in the household? Did she not know that Grace had never been the same since that dreadful day she'd had to persuade Eva to do the right thing about that unkempt con-chie who had blackened their reputation?

Through most of it, Eva stayed silent, counting to ten over and over on fingers held firmly behind her back. But there was one insult she con-sidered it her obligation to address. 'You say Mr Shandlin blackened your reputation because of his stance on the war. I disagree with you – do not interrupt, Father, you have more than had your say – I disagree, but it is hardly relevant. If we compare by character, side by side, it is obvious that Christopher Shandlin is a thousand times the man you are – in courage, in learning and in kindness. I will always be proud of him, no matter what he thinks of me' − Eva lifted her chin − 'and I'll never stop being ashamed of you, Father.' She turned on her heel and banged the study door behind her, so hard that Catherine's little clock fell off the hall table. Ding, ding, ding, it exclaimed from the floor as her father, that wretched satrap, roared at her to come back − the nerve!

On her way out, Eva nearly ran straight into Grace, who was standing on the front step. 'Eavesdropping, were you?' she asked viciously.

Grace said nothing, though a flicker of perturbation crossed her face. She was as pale as an alabaster statue. Eva looked down and realised that her stepsister was pregnant too − visibly so. *Fast work there, Herbert.* She hated her own spite, and the way Grace looked, so silent and fragile, like a Chinese vase held together with invisible hands.

Eva went out the front door, still sailing on nerves and hunger, only to come to an abrupt halt from a sudden urge to vomit. Clinging onto the iron of the basement railings, she threw up the tea and dry cake she had eaten earlier that day when the train had stopped at Crewe, her guts heaving long after she had run out of anything to disgorge, her skirt and the pavement splashed with the sick, a map of some uncharted country in yellows, pinks and browns.

She looked up at the sky, a coal-dusted nimbostratus that spat dirty rain. Her bravado had vanished along with the contents of her stomach. She was exhausted, starving, filthy; dizzy little turns corkscrewed around her head until every limb shook. And still she stayed pregnant. Joseph Cronin's final revenge: Eva dared not think of the life inside her as anything more. She dared not think of its innocence. War did not care if you were innocent or not.

By the time she shakily pulled the doorbell at Great Cumberland Place,

Eva had already collapsed several times in the street. She had told Lucia Percival nothing more than the truth. Had Sybil not taken pity on her, she would have surely been dead by now.

The nurses and VADs broke at midday for lunch. Four hours were allotted for the latter to return to the hostel for their daily meal, before another shift until nine. Four hours was barely enough; Eva hardly had time to bolt her dinner down before it was time to return to an afternoon spent cleaning spittoons and chamber pots. She wondered why they didn't just serve the food at the hospital but was told that the food there was for the patients only. Eva couldn't help wondering why the nurses could not be fed at the same time and in the same place. But rules were rules.

She didn't hate her duties. Mindless work could be a comfort sometimes, even if it involved other people's excretions. She didn't mind the bedpans, but she did object to the endless music. All the shopworn ballads for the '*sodjer* lads' were played at top volume in every ward, and, since all the doors were left open, there was no escape from them even if one was not on ward duty. Perhaps Eva noticed it more than others, but a disproportionate number of the songs seemed to be about Ireland. If she had to hear about Irish eyes smiling (they didn't) or how it was a long, long way to Tipperary (not halfway long enough) one more time, she would march right up to the men to tell them how those lovely, soft-spoken Irish hated their guts and liked nothing better than sucking up to the Germans and getting mixed up in gun-running with them. But she never did.

By the end of the first week, she was more tired than she had ever been in her life. Even in Ireland, waking at a lightless hour, seeing to the hens and taking care of breakfast, not to mention washing Mrs Cronin and then rubbing olive oil and camphor into her slack, pale skin, Eva had not experienced such exhaustion. She slept deeply and blankly, hardly noticing the cold.

Eva suspected that Sybil was secretly relieved she was gone. Her stay at Great Cumberland Place had overlapped with Clive Faugharne's return by just one day, and the viscount had not been the jolly-tempered man Eva remembered. He had seemed ill pleased to see her and barely acknowledged Sybil's introduction. That evening, she heard the couple quarrel. Sybil's voice was modulated only by the fear of being overheard; her husband audibly didn't give a damn. 'I give you certain freedoms,' his voice flared up the stairs, 'in exchange for certain conditions. I thought that was understood. This is a joke, Sybil.'

'A joke?' Suddenly, Sybil's voice was as harsh as the chalk Christopher used to scrape down the blackboard whenever he suspected his students were not giving him their full attention. 'I'll tell you what's a joke, shall I? When I go to bed and wait for my husband, and he—' She was cut short, and Eva heard a loud crack and a scream. She leapt out of bed and pulled on her borrowed robe. She heard the servants' muted conversation on the stairwell, then a creak on the floorboards as they went back to their own rooms. This had obviously happened before. Eva wanted to run down and explain, apologise, anything that would get Sybil off the hook. But she didn't. She stood stock still in the middle of the room and realised for the first time how difficult it is to intervene in a domestic dispute. How would Sybil feel, knowing that she knew? She was a proud woman. The humiliation would hurt her worse than Clive's hand. And if the servants weren't going to get involved ... From the back of Eva's mind, as if at the bottom of a stream, she remembered Grace's voice, quiet, undramatic, admonishing. *Mama, Mama, I think you broke her arm.* Her mind was made up: she would enrol with the Voluntary Aid Detachment the following morning and have done with it.

Choosing the right hospital proved a tricky task. There were two hundred military hospitals in the Greater London area. Mile End was out. Eva had liked Lucia, her bluntness, her bravery, but Lucia, Eva's rescuer, would be a constant reminder of the dire straits Eva had fallen into, and she didn't feel quite strong enough to face that. So, after discounting the specialist VD unit at Tooting Grove and the Special Neurological Hospital in Kensington ('Loonies!' Sybil had cried dismissively), she played it safe and plumped for Queen Alexandra's Military Hospital, which she had a reasonable chance of getting into.

When she said goodbye to Sybil on the steps of Great Cumberland Place, she did not mention the bruise on her friend's cheek.

'So, it's official then. You're off.'

Eva nodded. 'Got my orders yesterday. I have to come down to Victoria Station tomorrow at six o'clock for the night ferry over to Boulogne.'

Sybil uttered a low, ladylike whistle. 'They don't hang about, do they?' They were sitting in an Aerated Bread Company tearoom on Bond Street, drinking watery, bitter coffee. Nowadays, Eva was always careful to meet Sybil on neutral ground. A place where women could sit quietly and chat over tea was ideal, not that all the women who came here were quiet; the window's upper pane was still cracked from the time a suffragette had hurled a brick at it.

Eva had never mentioned what she had heard between Sybil and Clive that night. In the months that followed, she saw less of her friend anyway, owing more to lack of time than inclination. When they did meet, she noticed that Sybil never mentioned Clive's name. She herself had run into him coming out of a club near Oxford Circus. He had nodded at her in a manner so cold it was worse than a dismissal. Eva had blanked him completely. He had no cause to be so haughty, and him a cad who beat his wife.

Sybil had followed Eva's lead and had enlisted for hospital work, though in true Sybil fashion she had managed to get a rather more exclusive billet in a small convalescent home in Chelsea with only thirty officer patients and nearly as many nurses. It was a rather gentler introduction to the realities of war and hard work than Eva's, though her sewing abilities, she wryly remarked, were being put to good use. 'They're terribly behind the times. I caused a ruckus when I told them they needed to get a proper electric machine. Roma tells me I should pick my battles, but do I ever listen to her? No, I do not.'

Sybil could never mention Roma in a casual way, Eva noticed; it always sounded forced. When Eva met Roma, she had found her very low-key. She was not a stone casting ripples in a stream; rather, she was the stream itself, slow-moving but determined to become a river in good time, whether the surrounding terrain liked it or not. But whenever Sybil spoke about her, and sometimes to her, she adopted a tone of forced gaiety. Eva had never seen Sybil try so hard to impress someone before. *And* she had given up smoking. After all her fine speeches on the topic, urging Eva to give cigarettes a try. 'Oh, Roma said my clothes stank of the smoke,' she said when an astonished Eva pressed her on it.

Eva wondered what it was all about. She remembered Patricia Arnason:

that long, confident stride off the pitch as the sun burned and set, and Sybil's refusal to acknowledge her. Something similar was going on here. Eva guessed, too, that Sybil had signed up to the VAD because Roma had volunteered for the Friends' Ambulance Unit and was going over to Dunkirk.

Roma had announced this news under the bandstand in Regent's Park. Sybil had not taken it well.

'Dunkirk!' she exclaimed. 'But … I shan't see you!' Then, recalling Eva's presence, she pulled herself up a bit. 'And how did you get in? You're not even a Quaker – or are you? Last I heard, you were a roaring Papist. Surely there's rules about that?'

'Sybil!' Eva said reprovingly.

'Mr Nevinson fixed it for me,' Roma said, pushing awkwardly at the diamanté bulldog clip that held her hair in place.

'Mr Who?'

'He's a war artist I met at the Slade.'

'A war artist?' Sybil enunciated the words with the same incredulity as she might have said 'pig breeder'.

Eva felt in the middle of someone else's quarrel and wished she could go off and feed the ducks. A bit like how Agatha must have felt, she thought wryly, back when Christopher had spent the whole afternoon sulking and she had nearly given up in despair.

Roma said nothing else, but it was obvious that Sybil had wounded her. They had walked back to the park gates in silence. Two pigeons hopped along the walkway ahead, eating bits of bread thrown at them by a child with a mop of fair hair. The child laughed excitedly and threw some more.

'When are you going?' Sybil asked.

'Two weeks' time.'

'And this Nevinson … Do you know him well?'

Roma did not answer, and Eva found it hard to blame her. What business was it of Sybil's, for God's sake?

And then, the day after Roma's news, Sybil announced her intention to enlist for the war effort, just like Eva. It was too much of a coincidence, that was all.

The field hospital in France to which Eva would be billeted was near Étaples-sur-Mer, a seaside village well over seventy miles behind the front line. During one spring afternoon in an office in Millbank, in an effort to explain the nature of their orders to Eva, two other VADs and a slightly older ward sister, the matron pointed to the map on the wall, where a snaking line crossed near the top of France. 'That's where we're holding off the Hun, just there. Those little crosses are field hospitals and clearing stations for the wounded. You're going to be here' – she moved her finger down the coast – 'just a little bit south of Calais. As you see, the front line is due east of there.'

Eva looked at the ink-black, unbroken line, traced over several times to give the effect of solidity. Dunkirk, where Roma would be tending to injured men and perhaps mixing colours for Mr Nevinson; Loos, where Joseph Cronin had failed to make his last stand; tiny Neuve-Chapelle, where poor, happy-go-lucky Bo Destouches had been hewn to pieces by close-quarter bayonetting; Le Cateau, where Grace's Captain Featherstone, majestic in his helmet and velvet braid, had fallen, one of the first victims of artillery fire, his horse lying alongside, its guts spilled open to the air. And, somewhere along that line perhaps, or nowhere at all, Christopher Shandlin.

'Yes,' she said, 'I see it all right.'

To her surprise, the men in the wards were sorry to hear of her departure. Roberts, a lanky private, missing an eye, put his hand on her arm as
she made to dress the groin wound that had reopened after surgery. Eva
hated this duty almost as much as Roberts, who bore the unbelievable pain
with fortitude, determined that he would some day sire children. For her
part, the days when Eva would have been embarrassed at tending such
injuries were long gone. 'Tell you one thing, chuck,' Roberts said, 'I'll miss
you. You were a real lady, you were. Always tried to make me comfortable.'

Eva could hardly believe her ears. There had been weeks when she had
barely noticed or cared about the men. Weeks when she had done her duty
like an automaton, mopping up the piss, cleaning the suppurating flesh,
sometimes indifferent to their howls of pain, sometimes so tired her very
being ached, not just her limbs. Her mind had often been elsewhere. She
must have done a very good imitation of caring.

She spent the rest of the day packing. She had said goodbye to Sybil
in the teashop. They had embraced awkwardly, and Sybil had murmured
'Good luck, old chum' into her ear. The other girls in the hostel were all at
work, and she was due down at the station in an hour. None of them would
miss her, nor she them. And she had nothing to say to her family.

She took a cab to the station alone. The platform was mobbed with
VADs and regular nurses. The men in uniform and parade caps with
RAMC insignia on their lapels were the doctors. They would travel separately from the nurses – all the way to Étaples. From train to ship to train,
the men and women would be strictly segregated and forbidden to commu-
nicate, on pain of dishonourable discharge.

Eva held on to her ticket and passport. Then there was a tap on her shoulder. She was barely able to turn around in the slew of people. 'Sybil! What the … ?' Gladness flooded through her, unstoppable.

'Pleased to see me? Nice surprise?' Sybil said, with her usual insouciance.

'How did you get here?'

'Got my papers – same as you. I wasn't going to let you have all the fun.' She had to shout to be heard above the din.

'How did you get them so quickly?' Eva shouted back.

'I went up and asked for them, you big booby. How else?'

Eva was left to reflect, and not for the first time, that things got done much faster in Sybil and Roma's world than in hers. But she was so pleased to see Sybil that she couldn't feel any resentment. 'Shall we try and get a seat?'

They managed to find the last seating compartment left in their carriage and squeezed in. The train rattled and shook its way across the Kent countryside to Dover, where the troopship was waiting, with several destroyers, to escort them to France.

IV

War

22

It started on a fine July day in 1916. In the woods near Fricourt, Mametz, Bazentin; in the hamlet of Ovillers, seven thousand to a field, and La Boisselle; along the Roman road that leads from Albert in the south to Bapaume in the north. Throughout the Somme valley, at seven-thirty in the morning of the 1st, the offensive began.

For several days beforehand, masses of Kitchener's New Army entrained at Étaples and left, heading north to the front line. Others followed on foot, along with processions of horses and trucks, some with red crosses on the side, to set up and maintain the casualty clearing stations. All day long, the road to Boulogne was full of marching troops, and the trains ran up and down the line, collecting more troops each time and returning empty for the next batch.

'They couldn't be less secretive,' Sybil commented, 'if they got the Brighton Pierrots to do it as a travelling theatre company. All that's missing is the one in pink playing the piano.' She mimicked the movement of hands on keys, doing a little dance.

'Less of your levity, Faugharne,' barked the charge nurse. Nobody used 'Lady' any more. Titles did not matter here – not on the surface anyway.

The field hospital at Étaples was a vast encampment of long, low huts separated from the sea by a series of sand dunes, a military cemetery with rows of wooden crosses, and the busy railway line. Once, Étaples had been a seaside holiday town; now it swarmed with military personnel. It served as a training centre for arriving British troops – and heaven knows they needed training, since the time from enlisting to engagement was getting ever shorter.

The three months since Sybil and Eva's arrival had been a period of febrile waiting. The troops in the camp drilled and drilled, carrying out long marches on the road to Boulogne, saddled with a full kit on their backs. They practised bayonetting burlap sacks at close range, their efforts arousing the displeasure of their colour sergeant: 'Call that bayonet work? Giving Jerry a bloody cuddle, eh? He needs to get what for! One – two – three – again!' The sacks would swing a few times, then hang impotently in the sweltering sun, waiting for the next onslaught.

But now it looked as if the boys would be having a close encounter with the real thing. Eva heard it from a Tommy travelling back to base with a box of provisions retrieved by his diligent quartermaster when their trench narrowly escaped a shell. 'There's a big push on, I reckon. The French have been shelling for nearly a week, some of our lads too. Should start in the next few days, I'd say.'

'Marvellous,' Eva said, 'there go my chances of getting any shut-eye.' It did occur to her afterwards that her response might have been a bit more considerate – there was rather more at stake than her sleep. But even in the trenches, men would argue about tea and cigarette rations and all sorts of things that would never bother them in peacetime. In such a way could the mind distract itself with the trivial. The truth was, her chances of a good sleep had been ruined already, before any battle had even started.

On her first night in Étaples, the air had been pleasantly warm, even this far north on the French coast. Spring was giving way to early summer. Silence would have been impossible in a camp of thousands of soldiers, but there was a deep peace humming in the air, along with the heady scent of lily-of-the-valley and the sharp smell of the sea.

When she was first shown to the makeshift Alwyn hut in which she was to live, Eva thought it was empty. She was expecting a roommate – not Sybil, alas, who had been directed elsewhere. Carefully she switched on her Orilux trench torch, one of Cronin's possessions returned to her after his execution. The beam of light swung across the hut in an arc of whitish-yellow – and stopped at a pair of eyes that stared back at her with all the affront of a domestic cat disturbed mid-grooming. The face was heavy-cheeked and the mouth thin as a crack in a wall.

'So,' the crack opened and said, 'you showed yourself at last.'

The accent was cultured, Corkonian. Eva had not heard it since she was a child. She continued to shine the torch in the woman's face, and the woman continued to stare, sitting squatly on her bunk. 'Are you sharing with me?' Eva said.

'I am, and it's no accident I'm here. Do you remember Mrs Michael Stewart? A good woman who troubled to look after you, when you gave her nothing but backchat and bad manners?'

Eva's gut constricted. She could hardly keep the torch straight. Mrs Stewart: Catherine's friend, the chaperone who had accompanied her to Eastbourne that first time and who, worst of all, had eaten a week of Christopher's wages in cake? My God, would she ever be free of them?

'I'm Breedagh Stewart, her great-niece. You may shake hands.'

Eva, more than familiar with the Irish use of 'may' as a command rather than a suggestion, put her right hand behind her back, making sure to illuminate her gesture with the torch she held in her left, so that Breedagh Stewart might be in no doubt where she stood on the matter.

'The family knows you're here, by the way,' Breedagh said, pretending to ignore Eva's gesture. 'They found out you were at Queen Alexandra's, and since I was doing the same thing up the road at Charing Cross they asked me to swing by, keep an eye on you, like. I've known Roy Downey a long time, you know. And Catherine's a lovely woman. She would drop anything to help you, really she would. 'Twas she got me and my Great-Auntie Gretta to come over to London after my two brothers died in a terrible fire, the Lord have mercy on their souls.' Her hands flew across her forehead and shoulders as she made the sign of the cross.

Eva said nothing. This gnome-like horror of an Irishwoman had put the fear of God into her.

'It's not realistic, you know, to waltz around France pretending you're somebody else. And it's very disrespectful of you to forget your married name. I made it my business to put that right with the sister.'

'It was disrespectful of my husband,' Eva commented, as if to the open air, 'to have forgotten to fight, don't you think?'

A hiss of indrawn breath. 'You think you're so smart, don't you?' The words landed like a slap. 'Let me tell you, before you insult the memory of your poor dead husband, you should think about your record with cowards. The family have told me everything about your behaviour. Everything.'

This woman is dangerous. Eva was glad Breedagh could not see her face. The heat of the night and the tension in the little hut were getting to her.

She felt her period coming on and sweat leaking through her petticoat. Stains in two places, she thought, tightening her thighs and inner muscles to contain the flow.

'Now, I've no great love for the English and their war, even if I am here. I think you did the right thing: that fella got what was coming to him. But if word got around this camp that you gave a man the white feather, even a conchie … well, soldiers tend to take that badly from a woman. Your life would be very difficult.'

'I'm going to the sister straightaway,' Eva said, trembling. 'I want to move rooms.'

'You will do no such thing,' Breedagh replied, 'if you know what's good for you.'

Eva felt like something was tightening around her neck. She knew Breedagh was right. 'Why do you care so much? Why do you hate me so?' she said at last. Her voice sounded like a squeaky version of itself.

'Don't be so childish, Eva. Nobody hates anyone. I care because it looks bad on all of us, on the community, if one of us lets the side down.' Breedagh rose and put her hand on Eva's shoulder. 'Never forget: for us Irish, family always comes first. Always.'

Nausea rose up Eva's gullet. She almost wished she were pregnant again, if only because it would have been so much easier to puke. No court martial would convict her for puking all over Breedagh Stewart, then and there.

'Now, don't upset yourself,' the voice crooned, 'you'll be needing all your strength for your first day. I have a little something you can put in your drink if you need to sleep.'

'No, thank you,' Eva answered, 'it's probably poison.'

Breedagh laughed lightly. 'Ah, would you go away with yourself? You're obviously a very imaginative young lady indeed. Well, lie awake in the dark if you must.' She stepped back to her bunk and began to undress; Eva immediately moved the torch's beam. She did not want to see any more of Breedagh than was strictly necessary.

That night was the first of many difficult ones she was to spend in that Alwyn hut, its canvas flapping in the occasional breeze as her unpleasant roommate snored her head off.

And now battle was imminent, and the charge nurse, Sister Coker, rushed about all day long, looking flustered. 'Downey, are you loitering? Where should you be?' It was her constant question: every girl under her regime had to be somewhere, or something was wrong.

'I need a drink of water, sister. I'll be straight back.'

'Mind that you are. When this first push is over there'll be plenty of work to do. Expect a fall-in tonight and tomorrow.'

Sister Coker's prediction turned out to be optimistic. When the field telephones started to ring and the divisional sergeants answered, their pale faces and abrupt instructions told their own story. All the staff of Eva's unit were summoned to a briefing. 'Downey and Faugharne, we will be moving you both to the surgical ward. Merton, you can supervise the medical ward in case of emergencies, but really it's going to be all hands on deck now. Mr Philbin, Mr Doyle and Mr Russell, if you gentlemen can be ready in Operating Theatre One—'

'The three of us?' Doyle interrupted, leaning against the room's flimsy plywood wall, gripping his forehead with his thumb and middle finger.

'Will there be room?'

'There will have to be,' Sister Coker said grimly. 'We are going to get a lot of casualties. Brace yourselves; it isn't going to be good.' Sixty thousand, somebody murmured. The word went around the camp. Sixty thousand in one day.

'They attacked in broad daylight,' Sybil told Eva later, her face haggard from horror and overwork. 'The German guns picked them off like fish in a barrel. They never stood a chance, none of them.'

'But why didn't they stop? Why in God's name didn't they stop?'

'The generals said keep going. So they did.'

'I don't understand,' Eva said wildly, 'if you keep trying to do the same thing and people keep getting killed and you don't get anywhere, why not just stop? Why kill more men?'

'Because *that's* cowardice,' Breedagh interrupted smartly, appearing from nowhere. 'Besides, it's not true to say that they didn't get anywhere. We surely have the Hun on the back foot now. The brave Ulstermen have taken the hill at Beaumont-Hamel. If we did what you said and ran away, the Hun would have the place overrun. As a woman, the thought of that makes me frightened. Very frightened indeed. And you should be frightened, too.' And off she went, serene as an ocean liner on a moonlit sea, oblivious to the submarine lurking underneath.

'She's unbelievable,' Sybil said, shaking her head.

'She's like Grace,' Eva said, 'full of declarations that she'd be fighting herself. She'd rush over to the enemy trenches and kill them all in their beds.'

'Perhaps someone should tell her,' Sybil said, with a voice heavy as stone, 'that they already tried that this morning.'

They were interrupted by the sound of bells and alarms and the call to 'Fall in! Fall in!' which meant it had started. They were directed to No. 1 Surgical Ward, which had been divested of patients before the next influx. It was silent within its walls but already the sound of the vans and the rattle of the trains on the line from Boulogne could be heard.

One moment, calm; the next, pandemonium.

Ambulances arrived in endless numbers, disgorging their loads of patients, most of whom were gravely injured and on stretchers, stitched up as best as could be done at the advanced clearing stations before being brought down to Étaples. Some walking wounded, though not many; these had to stand and wait while the more seriously injured were brought into the surgical hut and set down in a long line outside the door of the operating theatre, where Doyle, Philbin and Russell worked in boiling heat. The black and white tiled floor, so assiduously cleaned that morning with a solution of bicarbonate of soda, was soon covered in puddles of blood, fresh and congealing, into which everyone stepped, spreading bloody footprints all over the place.

Nobody cleaned up, because there was no one to do it: all the nursing staff were busy sorting the rows of groaning men, their triage basic and unspoken. Those who might live should go to theatre while those who were going to die were left to wait where they were, under few illusions, if conscious, of what was to come.

Doyle's first patient was a quiet one, at least compared to the man on the next table, who was screaming in pain at a half-lost leg while Russell tried to sedate him to the point where he could perform the amputation necessary to save his life. Eva had worked with many amputees in London and had seen the skin rupture and bleed, the drawn look of pain on the men's faces, but she had never actually been in theatre when a man got his leg cut off before. The commotion almost diverted her attention from the quiet, whey-faced Canadian under her care who had suffered an abdominal wound from machine-gun fire. Pain made him selfish; softly, obdurately, he clung to Eva's wrist, murmuring over and over, 'Please, nurse, give me a drink. I'm so thirsty. Just a little drink. Water, please, nurse, oh please.' Over and over again he begged, insensible to Eva's explanations that his injuries meant that he could not eat or drink anything.

Doyle, looming over the man, shook his head. 'I can't operate. Not until he has a stronger pulse. Give it a few moments.'

'But sir!' Eva protested. 'There's a whole division out there!'

'If I take him off now, he won't survive the wait, and you know it.'

Doyle was a tall, pale Irishman, thin as a lath, with a bald, bullet-shaped head. His demeanour defaulted to a wired alertness, as if he had drunk too much coffee, giving him a certain appeal to Eva, for she liked restless men. In fact, Doyle would not have drunk coffee or any other stimulant; he was a strict teetotaller who proudly wore a pin on his jacket and was willing to tell anyone who would listen how he had joined the Pioneer Association after being picked up out of a gutter once too often. As if determined to eschew any trace of his life as a drunk, he worked with a delicacy and precision Eva had never seen, not even in her friends' and sisters' most intricate needlework.

All his skills were lost on the dying Canadian. Doyle could not begin until the pulse strengthened, and the throb was weakening and fluttering along with the man's own life force. Blood and other matter gushed internally while Doyle and Eva stood helpless and the abdomen grew dark blue and hard to the touch. And over and over and over, the Canadian called to Eva: 'Give me some water! Nurse, please, just a sip. Nurse, it's dark, I can't see! Are you there?'

At last Doyle sighed. 'Give him some water, Downey. Sure, it can do no harm at this stage, poor craytur.'

Eva filled a steel tumbler and brought it to the man's lips. His throat bobbed faintly as he swallowed most of the water. 'Thank you, sister. You're so good, so good.' Then his breathing grew rapid and shallow. 'I can't see! Where are you?'

Eva interlaced her fingers with his. They were cold and clammy, the fingernails encrusted with black, dried blood. 'I'm here, lieutenant. I'm here.' So oddly formal, yet she would not take his title away from him.

He called out for his mother. Instinct made Eva bend down to his ear. 'It's all right, sir. She's here. She's going to take you home now.'

Doyle grabbed her shoulder and called 'Stand back!' just as the man's body went into sudden spasm, and horrible, strangling sounds escaped from his throat. A torrent of greenish, bilious gunge poured out of him onto Eva and over his bloodied uniform. It was warm, acidic, foul-smelling. Doyle put up his hand to indicate to Eva to wait – an unnecessary injunction since she was too horrified to do anything else. Then he checked the man's pulse and shook his head. 'Poor bastard. Never stood a chance. Get the next one.'

'But where do I put—'

'Just get him out of here. Go clean yourself up and then come back.' Doyle spoke abruptly, but there was something in the aggressiveness of his elbow movements that made it look as if he was fending off grief. Of course, he was right. There was nothing more he could do for this poor man, nothing any of them could do. She had probably done the most useful thing of all, sending him off with comforting words.

She called the orderlies to lift his body off the table, and they did so with speed, given that they were well used to hauling and heaving corpses from vans to graves, but also with as proper a reverence as they could muster. A moment ago he had begged her for a drink of water. Now he was dead.

With an efficiency that only shows in times of war and great need, another group brought in the next stretcher, and a new case was unloaded, live, groaning and wriggling, onto the table still warm from the last man, still stained with his blood.

Russell's amputee kept on yelling, even as the poor surgeon picked up the saw; only as he laid it onto the skin did the chloroform take effect and the howling man fall silent. Eva had to control herself not to break down at the thought of the agony he must have been in.

Many more died on the table that day. Some survived. Either way, they kept on coming. By half past one the next morning, Eva was feeling light-headed and slightly giddy; apart from quick breaks for cake and cold tea, she had not eaten a full meal since 6 a.m. the day before. Now, when a dying man laboured his last breath, she no longer troubled to tell him his mother was coming for him. Instead, she called a priest of whatever denomination was appropriate. Even the rabbi got called into service when Doyle noticed a Star of David around one dying officer's neck.

And those lives lost were the ones that had made it to the operating table. As dawn spread, more lorries came to Étaples, with a sadder load. The dead, whose comrades had picked them up in no-man's-land and had given them to the stretcher-bearers, were buried en masse with wooden crosses or cheap stones to mark their graves. A number of men had been recruited into the Chinese Labour Corps and were being trained in China for the work of war; some of them would dig graves in the fields surrounding the camp. They were not due for another few months. Nobody had guessed they would be needed so soon, so the job was done by infantrymen.

Eva knew about the dead because Doyle told her. She had not been able to leave the operating room to see for herself – he had given her enough work to keep her busy there. Surgical work did not alarm Eva; she had been watching Doyle all evening and saw how it was done. Besides, she could sew, if only serviceably. The clumsiness and unevenness that had so vexed Miss Dunn – *Good God, it seems like another life* – did not matter now when it was thick flesh rather than fine cambric through which she was pushing her needle.

When he told her about the graves, Doyle leaned back against the wall, a cigarette dangling from his lips. 'There's no way they could have got all of them. No way. Most of them are still out there. Hung out on the wire. Stuck in a shell hole turning green.'

'Mr Doyle, please.'

He closed his eyes. 'You know, I'm as bad as that Canadian chap we sent off earlier. "Give me a drink, nurse, give me a drink",' he mimicked.

'He wanted water, Mr Doyle, not the kind of drink you're referring to.'

His smile was thin and did not reach his eyes. 'True, Downey, very true. Tell me, have you someone out there?'

The question still hurt. She would never forget the look in Christopher's eyes, the way his face drained as he wrenched himself away from her and walked down the street without a backward glance.

'Oh, damn, look at you. I shouldn't have asked. I'm sorry.'

'It's all right, Mr Doyle,' Eva said. 'There was somebody once, but we parted company, and … there's a lot of water under the bridge. I don't know where he is now.'

'And you still care for this fellow, I presume?' Doyle said.

'Yes, I do. Very much.' Eva hoped he wouldn't ask more.

'I had someone too,' Doyle said. 'She got fed up of my old ways and went off. In one sense, I'm doing all this for her. Trouble is, sometimes I can't face it. I mean, look at this. Look at it.' He gestured around. 'This is hell. And I'm nothing more than hell's butcher, apron and all.' He was near tears.

'Mr Doyle,' Eva said, 'you've saved many lives tonight. You should be proud.' Doyle's head was bent. Eva saw that he was crying and trying not to let her see it.

The sister came into the operating theatre. 'You look done in, Mr Doyle. You too, Downey. Get some rest, both of you, and come back in after reveille.'

Eva stumbled back to her hut, barely able to find it, she was that tired, even though she knew the route well. The light of a paraffin lamp danced through the canvas; Breedagh must be up. Eva was past caring, almost asleep in her clothes. She took off her uniform and left it in a heap on the floor. Just this once, the hell with standards.

23

There was little let-up for the next month. As many soldiers came in from Dover as left Boulogne in hospital trains. The rattle of the night trains passing near the loose boards of the hut lulled Eva into a deeper slumber whenever she could get it, which wasn't often, partly because she was so busy and partly because of the heat, which lasted all July, hitting well over eighty degrees at its height, with rarely a day below seventy.

Sometimes she wondered whether Doyle wasn't right to compare himself to a butcher. Men were really only so much meat, and not even fresh meat at that. In the wards, the fetor of gangrenous flesh and sodden dressings was sweet, heavy and rotten in the wards. Eva had resorted to holding a handkerchief over her mouth at times, though she hated to hurt the men's feelings. She could not imagine how it must have felt to be glued to a bed by one's own sweat in such pain and fever as the sun kept up wave after wave of punishing heat. Finally, someone had the bright idea of rigging up an electric fan to one of the generators, which gave intermittent relief.

Some benign god had assigned Breedagh Stewart back-to-back night shifts. Having delivered the worst of her arsenal on the night they met, she now seemed plain out of weaponry and even occasionally tried to engage Eva in friendly conversation. Since her idea of friendly conversation was long monologues about the family farm near Kilkeen and the condition of its livestock, Eva was quite happy to pick up her book and resume wherever she had left off.

She had probably learnt more about sex from D. H. Lawrence's novels than she had from being married. Mr Lawrence had been so informative that the government had gone to the trouble of burning all copies of *The Rainbow* – or so they thought. A second-hand bookseller on the Strand had sold her an unmarked author proof, which she had now read about four times. When she read of Ursula Brangwen's attachment to Miss Inger, certain aspects of Sybil's behaviour with regard to Roma made much more sense.

Her other book, the Rupert Brooke, she would open sometimes, but only when she had the hut to herself, and not, primarily, to read the poems, for she suspected she had grown out of most of them. It was more to remember who had given them to her. That book had never left her side, not during her long journey to Ireland nor the year since. Once, in a drunken rage, Joseph had tried to throw it in the fire. Eva had slapped him so hard that her own palm stung from the blow. That was when he'd declared he would enlist the following day, and she remembered answering, 'If you do, don't blame me, I never made you.' Even now, it hurt to see that book, but it was a sweet hurt as well as a hard one, and she would not let go of it.

Breedagh was as ignorant of Eva's literary interests as she was uninterested in them, though Eva knew full well that all she had to say was that she had a dirty book and the cow would change her attitude. She would be up right behind Eva, panting down her neck in righteous indignation, in haste to read the dirty, dirty passages, to properly ascertain what a filthy dirty book it truly was. Then she would start on about the dirt and filth, not to mention the smut and dirt, and her breathing would become rapid and shallow. Eva had learnt to be circumspect about her reading material.

All through July, wave after wave of young lads were carried off on trains to the front, then waves of broken, mangled, howling beings returned to Étaples by cortèges of ambulances. Eva and Sybil did not manage to get a full day off until early August. When they did, they wasted no time heading down to the beach for a long walk. Eva wore the loose, high-collared tunic and trousers all the girls seemed to wear on their days off, which were comfortable, if slatternly by peacetime standards. Sybil preferred a more conventional dress. Whenever the breeze failed she would take her large straw boater off her head and fan her cheeks with it.

The tide was midway out, the sea rolling back and forth unconcernedly in the background, the faint sounds of artillery bombardment carrying from the north-east. Wooden depth markers stretched out along the shore. Wearing sandals, Eva felt the burning sand against her toes with pleasurable shock. She had forgotten her hat, and the sun began to burn her scalp where her hair parted. She rubbed it absent-mindedly.

Sybil broke the silence. 'I told you I was off to the front soon, didn't I?'

'Yes, you mentioned it.'

Sybil had been angling to see Roma since her arrival in France, and finally she had got her chance. The Friends' Ambulance Unit needed more drivers to collect wounded men from the front line, and Sybil had both experience and a driving licence. Roma wrote to her as often as was allowed during the restrictions of battle. To every letter she added detailed sketches, but some of the pages were taken out by the Censor. 'The injuries are too realistic,' Sybil explained when she showed the letters to Eva. She never mentioned whether Clive ever wrote, and Eva thought it better not to enquire. If he didn't, she thought, it was a poor show, when his wife was out here doing her bit for the war effort. And then, when she found herself thinking in phrases like that, Eva would shake herself. For pity's sake, she sounded like Grace.

'I'm going the day after tomorrow,' Sybil said. 'Sorry for the short notice.'

'That's all right, Syb,' Eva said, adding, on a sudden impulse, 'Sybil, whatever it is you feel about Roma, don't be afraid of it. Life is too short not to be honest with yourself. And be joyous.'

Sybil didn't speak for a moment, then said, with emotion, 'You are a brick, Evie. Thank you.'

They walked for a while in companionable silence. Then Sybil stopped. 'I say, listen.' Up ahead, where the holiday houses and the fishing boats petered out, beyond the dunes, lay a small woodland. From there, clear and undimmed by the slight breeze that moved the children's toy windmills on the fence's edge, came a voice pure and high, a voice Eva recognised instantly, with a double pain at the beauty of the song and the identity of the singer.

Here of a Sunday morning
My love and I would lie,
And see the coloured counties,
And hear the larks so high
About us in the sky.

'Why,' Sybil breathed, 'it's "In Summertime on Bredon". I've not heard that one in a while. What, Evie, what is it?'

'It's Lucia.' Eva looked straight ahead. 'The singer.'

For a moment Sybil looked questioning, then her face cleared. 'Oh. The girl who—'

'The first time I saw her,' Eva said, 'she was singing "Confutatis Maledictis" at the top of her voice.'

Sybil grimaced. She also remembered who sang that song. 'Ouch.' Then, 'Let's face it, she probably sang it a good deal better than he did.'

Eva smiled sadly. 'Oh, yes.'

Sybil put her arm around Eva's shoulders. Her hair had grown, and it fell in magnificent folds of auburn, like something out of a Titian painting. Her skin smelt of Pears soap and fresh sweat. 'You shouldn't listen to sad songs. And you shouldn't dwell on the past. Let's go back.'

'I should like to say hello to her.'

Sybil pulled away, frowning. 'Whatever for?'

'Because she was kind to me,' Eva said. 'She seemed like a nice person.'

'Eva,' Sybil pulled roughly at her dress, 'show some nous. You can't go round socialising with that girl as if the whole dreadful business never happened. You and she broke the law, in case you forgot. And what would you have in common anyway? What could you talk about?'

'Why, Sybil, the same things anybody talks about. The war. The weather. Why are you being so obstructive?'

'Because your little caper cost me a lot of money, that's why!' The singing abruptly stopped. Sybil, red-faced with sun and anger, dropped her voice only slightly to add, 'What do you think my squabble with Clive was about? Flower arrangements?' Eva felt a slow mortification spread through her. Sybil must have seen it, because the anger went out of her eyes as if someone had snuffed out a candle. 'Eva, I'm bloody mean, I'm sorry. Go talk to … whatsername. This war has bitched me completely. I can't even hear someone singing a song like that but I think of Bo, and the waste and mess of it all. I'm fit for nothing.'

A group of VADs were paddling in the shallows. Their hair down and skirts held up, they splashed noisily, their laughter suddenly loud as the breeze petered out and the air stilled. Sybil kept her hat on, pulling the brow down over her face. The sun was behind her.

'It's all right, Syb,' Eva said gently. 'I'll talk to her another time, perhaps.'

They walked back to camp in silence. Eva could not think of anything else to say; she had upset Sybil enough. And that reminder of the cost of her abortion … that had been a slap in the face. The problem was, it was true. She had been a burden on Sybil and had given precious little back, but what does one do when one must survive?

By now they had reached the camp gates and shown the sentries their papers. They walked through the camp, passing one of the medical wards on the way. Something in the corner of her eye captured Eva's attention. 'Sybil, can you hang on a tick? I need to check something.'

'Sorry, chum,' Sybil said, her nonchalance still a little false, 'I can't wait. Have to talk to the sister about tomorrow. See you later, though.'

'See you.'

As Sybil cantered off, Eva realised what, or rather who, had claimed her attention. It was a man on a stretcher in the long queue waiting outside the medical ward. His eyes were bandaged, blinded by gas. On his chest was a dressing with a small circle of recent blood. A neat wound, neater than most, not deadly, either, for he was conscious, his neck craning around as he tried to work out where he was by listening. Some familiar twist to his mouth struck her – and then Eva recognised him. It was Gabriel Hunter.

24

Within minutes, Eva was bending the ear of the duty nurse in the medical ward, pretending Hunter was an old sweetheart and swearing her to secrecy. She soon learnt that after a recent promotion to captain, he had been sent out with an advance company to organise the clearance of Trônes Wood. This effort had been successful – in the new definition of 'success' allowed by their military masters – in that they had secured their small objective, albeit with the loss of almost the entire platoon. Hunter had been fortunate to sustain wounds early in the engagement and escaped slaughter by playing dead throughout the second advance and the gas attack from the Germans, the cause of his temporary blindness. It was only when two privates attempted to move him and encountered protests from the corpse that it was ascertained he had survived the battle. And so he was dispatched, without his men, since they were all dead, to the advanced clearing station, where he was patched up pretty well before being sent back down behind the line to Étaples.

Eva, with some impatience, listened to all this breathlessly delivered information, smiling and nodding as the nurse rattled on. It was evident that Staff Nurse Yardley had taken a bit of a shine to Captain Gabriel Hunter.

It was entirely possible he hadn't changed since Eva had met him last. But he was alive and conscious, and he might know what had become of his great friend Christopher Shandlin.

She was uncharacteristically inattentive during the afternoon and evening work. 'Come on, Downey, are you with the team or are you with the team?' It was Doyle's catchphrase question, accompanied by an impatient finger-click in her face.

'I'm with the team,' she replied mechanically.

'Well, start behaving like it then. I need you to find a vein for me here. This man has terrible veins. I can't see them at all.' The man on the gurney, on the verge of death, weakly protested that there was nothing wrong with 'is veins, and he'd be thanking the good doctor not to make such personal remarks, begging her pardon, miss.

Eva made some soothing noises, but she was distracted. Her mind was riffling through the possibilities. It was possible that Hunter had no idea whether Christopher was dead or alive. If that were the case, she would be no better off. If he knew that he was dead, she would find it out in the middle of a busy ward, and there would be nothing she could do about it but pretend everything was normal. That would be the worst possible outcome.

Or he might be alive.

She had to know.

A day later, when she finally got a moment to visit the ward, she realised that it was not like a civilian medical ward at all. The men's talk was loud and friendly, especially among the group of Australians near the entrance, who were playing cards around the bed of a soldier whose leg was in traction. It was no more than a long hut, and the shade meant the light was poor, but Eva made Hunter out in one of the middle beds, his long, tapering fingers resting on the sheet. The narrow space between the beds meant that she had to move carefully not to draw too much attention to herself.

It helped that she had been listening for a while as Hunter had asked the duty VAD for a glass of water; she'd crumpled pinkly as if he'd given her a proposal of marriage and said, *yes, of course, right away.* When she reached the entrance, Eva had gently pressed a box of cigarettes into her hand and whispered in her ear; in spite of the VAD's infatuation for Hunter, it appeared to have done the trick. Eva fetched the glass of water herself.

Hunter was still entrancingly beautiful, even with his eyes bandaged, his limbs cast in all directions; the exposed knees alabaster as a Greek statue's, the dark locks of hair clinging to his forehead. But that same forehead glistened with sweat, his cheeks were jaundiced, and his lips formed a wet moue of distaste, probably at the fetid smell of the place. For a moment Eva felt pity for this man who lay there vulnerable, unaware of her presence. But the pity was mixed with fear. If he recognised her voice …

'Captain Hunter?' she began timidly, but he showed no sign of having heard her. Had she remembered his rank correctly? She tried again: 'Lieutenant … ?'

Hunter sat up as straight as if he were demonstrating Pythagoras' theorem. 'It's "Captain".'

'That's what I said the first time, sir,' Eva said haltingly, 'only you didn't hear me.'

Hunter frowned and, to Eva's alarm, seemed to be trying to recognise her voice. 'Are you the dinner lady? It's not dinnertime yet, surely? And *she* knows I'm a captain.'

It never ceased to amaze Eva how some men who distinguished themselves in war seemed in any other capacity unfit to be allowed out of doors. 'I brought you a glass of water, captain.' She had better lay his title on thick.

He wrinkled his nose but accepted the glass. 'You sound different from the last girl.' He took a draught of water before putting the glass down with a decided thump. 'This is brackish stuff. What happened to the ice I asked for?'

'Hey up, sister,' sang out one of the Australians, 'you'd better be careful. He knows how he likes his water. With oice.' The group of them put down their cards and sniggered.

'Are you serious, sir?' Eva said. 'This is a field hospital. We ensure survival, not cold beverages.' The Australians roared with laughter and applauded. So much for discretion. *You're here to gather information. Forget about everything else.*

Hunter lay back once more. 'Well, I survived, didn't I? They sorted me out further up. All I have to do is wait for these bloody bandages to come off. God knows, I've served far beyond the call of duty. I'd have been nominated for an MC if the other officers weren't all too dead to do the honours. So no, I don't think a glass of iced water is asking too fucking much, do you?'

Eva swallowed down an angry reply and simply said, 'No, sir.' She picked up the glass and was about to move away when she noticed a small hardback. She picked it up and put it back down again. 'Bridges?' she remarked, 'a little old-fashioned, isn't he, with his Miltonic syllabics and slavish adherence to classic prosody?' Or so Christopher had told her once. She had never read Bridges.

Hunter abandoned his supine pose and sat up straight again, reaching for Eva's forearm and grabbing it, just at the sore place, making her flinch. 'You're just a silly little nurse,' he hissed. 'What do *you* know about poetry?'

'Not much,' Eva concurred, hoping to calm him. But although he let go of her arm, he remained agitated. 'That sounds like something a friend of mine would say.'

'Someone who is important to you?' *Keep it in the present tense.*

'That's none of your damn business. Now get me a proper glass of water!'

Eva walked away to refill Hunter's glass without protest. It did not sit well with her to pilfer ice from the icebox that might be needed for people with genuine wounds, and she was so agitated she could hardly concentrate on her task, but she would have walked barefoot over razor blades if it led her to the truth.

A few moments later she returned to Hunter's bed. 'Your water, sir.'

He took the glass without comment and drank the water all in one go, throwing his head back and showing the clean line of that jaw Eva had first seen outside Christopher's house in Heathfield. At the same time, his Adam's apple moved under the sunburnt skin in a way that reminded her of Joseph Cronin catching fish in his boat and letting them flip about, gasping horribly, before they finally expired in a half-inch of bilge water. Such beauty and ugliness in the same body, at the same moment – it hardly seemed possible.

'Pardon my brusqueness,' he said, crunching down the ice. 'I become emotional when I think of him.'

Eva staggered backwards, feeling as if she had been kicked in the chest by a horse. *That could only mean one thing, surely? Say it, for God's sake, just say it.* But he added nothing more to his mysterious pronouncement. She didn't know how she managed the words: 'I'm sorry to hear that, Captain.'

'I am, too. He was the best of all of us. And the brightest, but he just didn't care what people thought or who the right circles were. It was infuriating.'

285

'You loved him.' She barely got the words out, her teeth were chattering so much. *Just get to the point where I know for sure.*

Hunter only sighed in response. 'He used to write poems, but he wouldn't show them to anybody. Damn it, I wanted to see them.'

That would be just like him, thought Eva, feeling the sweet jab of remembered love.

'And he was so patient with *my* efforts. I would be mooning over some girl and would write a poem, and he would force me to revise it, when all I cared about was Katie or Lizzie or Sieglinde. Damn, he was thorough. Principled, too. He was nearly a conscientious objector. I told him I thought he was mad.' Hunter smiled.

'I've been told it takes great courage,' Eva said carefully, looking at the ground so the other men could not see her face.

'Oh, yes, he would have had that all right. Then he got himself into a very nasty business with a girl at the school where he taught. An inferior, scheming creature. I write poetry about women like her, their squeamish, creaming ways—'

'Oi! I rather like a woman's ways myself!' one of the Australians interjected.

'Been a while, has it, Rog?'

The men all laughed. None of them asked Eva to excuse his manners.

'I'll have you know, my Antipodean friends,' Hunter shouted across the room, 'that bitch gave my friend a white feather.'

The Australian, who was making heavy weather of a piece of baguette, looked up, nonplussed. 'A what?'

'A white feather of cowardice,' Hunter boomed, 'habitually given by gangs of women to men out of uniform. By those who will never have to see combat themselves. Bad enough to give one to a stranger. The ultimate betrayal is to give one to someone you claim to love.'

A hiss went through the room. 'That was mighty hard on your friend.'

'And what happened to him then?' Eva cut in abruptly, her mouth dry as a salt mine, her tongue nearly sticking to the roof. She had no idea how she managed to keep her voice steady.

'Oh, he behaved like a total fool. Instead of doing it properly and signing up as an officer, he went off and enrolled in the bloody Territorials! Wouldn't take a commission. I know he wanted to sign up as a stretcher-bearer to avoid combat … but really.' Hunter shook his head. 'I never understood him. And he had such odd tastes. That horrible little queer, Brooke, I tell you—'

'Is he still alive?'

'Alive? Of course not. He died last year,' Hunter said impatiently.

Eva swayed forward, her hand landing on the mattress just inches away from him, a few strands of her hair nearly touching his face. Mechanically she straightened up. So now she had her answer.

'Typical of him to die on a nice Greek island, never lifting a finger in battle,' Hunter went on, his words roaring and dying amid a ringing haze in Eva's ears.

'How … ?' It was barely a whisper, but Hunter heard her.

'Blood poisoning. Stupid fellow got himself bitten by a fly. And now we have to hear that bloody poem up and down the place: "That there's some corner of a foreign field / That is for ever England." Sentimental nonsense.'

'Hold on a moment – you're referring to Mr Brooke?' Eva said. 'When you talk about blood poisoning?'

'Well, of course. Who else? Oh, my friend I was telling you about? No, no, he's alive all right. Poor fellow, he's holed up in a hospital on the Isle of Wight. Nobody's said it outright, but' – Hunter dropped his voice to a dramatic whisper – 'from what I hear it's a bad case of nerves.'

Eva could not have cared less about nerves. In fact, she could not care less about Gabriel Hunter. In two seconds she was at the hut doorway and then out in the open air, running, without knowing where.

'Wait! Nurse! Where are you? Nurse? I haven't finished with you yet!'

Christopher was alive. Eva's head began to throb; she could feel the pain of the blood trying to get through tight veins, that iambic hunting horn clamouring once more: a*live*, a*live*, a*live*, a*live*, a*live*.

25

Alive – and in England. Safe from danger. Eva held that knowledge like a candle in front of her, carried it with the utmost care as she went about her daily rounds. It was as if she had lived for the past two years in a thick-walled stone hut with a fireproof door and no windows. And now the door was opening, and the wind was flapping at the furniture covers, and daylight had flooded in, all at once. It was such a fierce, intense and private feeling she wanted to hug it to herself, but it was so all-consuming she longed to share it with someone too.

Sybil had left, but perhaps it was just as well she could not confide in her. Look at how she had behaved when Eva had tried to seek out Lucia. It was all very well her pontificating about forgetting the past: her brother was dead and her husband estranged. There was no unfinished business – nothing that *could* be finished at any rate. Whereas with Christopher … Sybil might try to discourage Eva from making contact again. After all, Sybil *knew*.

But how could Eva not, now that she knew where he was? When she thought of what had happened to him – invalided for his nerves – her heart felt like it would fill her chest. She had to speak to him, and about him.

Since Eva had heard Lucia Percival singing, down by the beach, the Jamaican girl had lingered on her mind. But just because she had been there at the worst time of Eva's life didn't mean she was the best person to talk to about *this*. Eva could not push confidences on somebody who was practically a stranger. And yet, when she had been in trouble before, she had gone to Lucia, even if only by default.

So she sought her out.

A few VADs from the Mile End camp directed her to another surgical ward. There was no surgery going on. More casualties from Fromelles and Pozières were due soon, but the trains had been held up – the railway had been bombed again and repairs were ongoing. The theatre was empty, apart from Lucia and a small, red-headed surgeon of about thirty, with whom she was bickering. He shouted at her in a grating Glasgow accent, 'There's naught wrong with my bishop, Miss Lucy!'

'*Cha*, you lie! Can you not see where your bishop should be there is now a hole? Right along the diagonal?' She traced a line through the air. 'If you think you win this game, you draw card on yourself, man.'

'I draw what? What sort of blether are you comin' out with now?'

'I said,' Lucia returned with some heat, 'you are fooling yourself, sir, if you expect victory.'

'Well, have it then and to hell with you!'

'I will! And it's you that'll go to hell, along with your king!'

Before Eva could wonder if Lucia were advocating high treason, the Jamaican girl walked over to the trolley behind the operating table, where, to Eva's astonishment, stood a chessboard. She picked up the black bishop and put it to one side, replacing it with a white knight. 'There – now!'

'Are you playing chess in an operating theatre?' Eva had spoken aloud. The Scotsman turned around and looked at her with undisguised hostility, his ginger eyebrows heading skywards. But Lucia brightened immediately, like a sun making a dazzling appearance after rain. She crossed over to Eva and enclosed her in a hug. 'Hallo, star! How are you? It's such a long time since I saw you last. You've lost wei—' and then, recollecting herself, 'You look well.'

'I'm all right,' Eva said shyly. 'I'm sorry, you're obviously busy. I'll come back.'

'Busy beating his bishop is all.' Lucia looked at the Scotsman with affectionate contempt. 'This is Mr Mackenzie. And this' – to Mackenzie – 'is Eva … Sorry, I don't know your last name.'

'Downey.'

'How long have you been here?'

'A few months,' Eva answered, adding, 'I didn't know you were here until I heard you singing "In Summertime on Bredon" the other day, over near the beach. I didn't see you, but I knew it was you.'

'Ah yes, that song. I love it so!' Lucia's eyes shone. 'The men here always want me to sing it for them, and it is the version by Graham Peel in G major, so it's easy for me to take it up an octave. Sometimes I drop it down to E. Either way, it always make them cry.' As if to demonstrate, Lucia touched the corner of her eye with her finger. 'It make Mr Garfield, my music teacher, cry too, but I suspect he is in love with me.'

'Yes, it was the same with my friend.'

'How would she know Mr Garfield?' Lucia said with amazement.

'No, I mean about the song. It made her sad.'

Mr Mackenzie fidgeted in the background in the manner of a man who cannot understand women making conversation not concerning him.

'She's gone to Dunkirk now … my friend, that is.' Eva added.

'Dunkirk?' Lucia said. 'My brother is there. Reginald Percival.'

'Your brother's in the Army?'

'Of course. Why, did you think he was there on holiday?' Lucia was amused. 'He's with the British West Indies Regiment, guarding aircraft. But before, he was in the thick of the fighting.' She emphasised this last with some anxiety, as if Eva might underestimate Reginald's role.

'Is he an officer?' Eva asked politely. She realised straightaway she'd said the wrong thing, as Lucia's face closed up and her eyes went cold.

'Are you being funny? Of course he isn't.'

'I don't understand … ?' Eva stuttered, at which point Mackenzie cut in harshly.

'He's not allowed, is he, Lucy? On account of being black.'

When Lucia replied, her voice had a fine edge of hurt. 'Mr Mackenzie is referring to the military regulation that forbids persons of non-European descent from becoming commissioned officers. Reggie is a mulatto, like myself, and he is a corporal. Of course, if he looked crossways at a white lieutenant, he'd get court-martialled. It happened to his friend. They shot him.'

'I am truly sorry, Lucia,' Eva said with feeling, especially for the last part.

Lucia sniffed a little. 'If it is any consolation, I would not have Reggie command my cat, let alone a company of soldiers. He is *nyaamps*, as we say, useless. But it's the principle I'm talking about, *yu nuh see?*'

'Of course I do. It's unfair.' There were things Eva could not even begin to understand, and there was no use pretending that she ever would.

Lucia's face softened. 'You weren't to know.'

'Well,' Eva said, trying to get things back on track, 'my friend who is now in Dunkirk was with me when we heard you singing the song. We both thought it was lovely.'

Lucia accepted the praise as nothing more than her due. 'I sing all the time. Mr Garfield said if I ever wanted to be classically trained, I'd have to practise, practise, practise. It is all about the breath, that is the core of it. Anyway, it is no hardship. I love it.'

'You can say that again,' Mackenzie chimed in. 'All day long, arpeggios and scales and chromatics – good God, it's like having a canary around.'

'Disregard him,' Lucia said loftily. 'He is a ginger midget, not to mention tone deaf.'

'Ginger midget, eh, Miss Percival? And as for you—'

Lucia held up a hand. 'This lady has business with me, I believe. I shall be back shortly.' She took a straw hat from the hook near the door and went outside, leading Eva around the hut's corner to a long, windowless wall where a group of VADs leaned and smoked. 'So,' she said cheerfully, 'what can I do for you this time?'

'I … need advice. I want to write to someone.' Emboldened, Eva added, 'You asked about him before – remember? The man whose name I called out when I was put under. Christopher.'

Lucia's eyes opened very wide. 'I do remember! Yes. So now finally you are going to tell me the story? Well,' she poked Eva, 'go on.' The sun shone through the brim of her hat and made little squares on her cheeks and chin.

Eva related a much-edited version of the whole tale. When she mentioned that Christopher had been her teacher, Lucia clapped her hands together and cried, 'Forbidden romance! Oh! I like!' Eva said that she and Christopher had quarrelled and hoped that Lucia would not probe further. But Lucia frowned. 'It must have been a mighty big fight, if you go off and marry someone else, and then—'

'Lucia,' Eva said, almost afraid to meet her eyes, 'I did something terrible. So bad that I really can't say what it is, so please don't ask me. I beg you.' She remembered the horror of Sybil's widening eyes, the way she had clapped her manicured hand to her mouth when Eva had confessed. 'Just let me put it this way. Sometimes the vilest things can be done by a respectable woman obeying society's customs.' The breeze freshened up and Eva's forearm goose-pimpled.

Lucia took off her hat and tilted her head to one side, regarding Eva with tender exasperation. 'In no way are you mollifying my curiosity, girl. In no way at all. And why ask me anyhow? You can write, *nuh*? What do you need me for?'

'Because I don't know where to start,' Eva said, red-faced.

Now Lucia looked bewildered. 'Where I come from, we start at the beginning. I don't know about England, maybe *oonu*, you all crazy over there.'

'But I'm not beginning. I'm resuming.'

'True,' Lucia said thoughtfully, then, '*Cha*, I like your wordplay. I am game. I'll help you write your letter.'

They were interrupted by a heavy tread on the scorched, barbed grass. Mackenzie appeared, his compact neck straining forward, face glistening with sweat. He had hardly been out in the sun five minutes and red patches of sunburn were already appearing near his hairline. Lucia began softly to chant, 'Oh, Cordelia Brown, what make your head so red / Oh, Cordelia

Brown, what make your head so red?' Mackenzie shot her a look, but addressed Eva. 'Your charge nurse is looking for you. She's none too happy that you've deserted your entire ward.'

Eva could tell from his ranging, possessive look over Lucia that it was *her* absence that was the issue, not Eva's. 'I'll be right there,' she said.

'Oh, and by the way,' Mackenzie added, 'check!'

'You make such a fuss-fuss about your check,' Lucia said loftily, 'but soon the king will be safe, and you, sir, will be in *Zugzwang* for good.'

'What's—?' began Eva.

'No move without loss,' Mackenzie and Lucia replied in unison.

'It's a Hun word,' Mackenzie noted, 'but a bloody good one.'

'It is,' Eva said, 'though my situation is the exact opposite. I have nothing to lose at all.'

Lucia smiled. 'That's the spirit. Now, you *gwaan* write that letter or what?' Her voice grew more melodious as it became more insistent. 'You can bring it straight to me, and I will give it marks out of ten for style, substance and execution.' She rubbed her hands. 'I am looking forward to this!'

'You'll be sorry. Ten to one she'll sing the bloody thing, and do a theme and variations on it,' sighed Mackenzie.

First draft

Dear Mr Shandlin,

I know it has been some time since you heard from me, and the last time being in the most injurious circumstances, which continue to haunt me and for which I must apologise again and again—

After reading that section aloud in front of Eva, Lucia proceeded no further but ripped the paper in two, then four, throwing the torn pieces into the bin, alongside bloody dressings and empty iodine bottles. 'You can't write that!' she declared.

'Why not?'

'Well, for a start, whatever it was you had your big *bangarang* about, why remind him of it right up the top? If it's big enough to keep you apart this long, it's not something you can discuss in a letter when you haven't spoken to him in a long time.'

Eva was impressed by Lucia's sagacity but was still not quite convinced. 'I need to apologise. I need to explain.'

'You need to do neither,' Lucia said firmly. 'And what's with this *labba-labba*, this "Mr Shandlin" nonsense? You loved this Christopher man. And he loved you too, so you say. Why are you insulting him by making him sound like some sort of acquaintance? That is a four out of ten. Nah, I am being generous. Make it three.'

Eva laughed weakly. 'God, you sound just like him. He was forever at me to call him by his first name.' She fiddled with her pen for a while, then said, 'I know you're right, but I need to start at the beginning. I can't just presume intimacy—' She blushed fiery red, mortified with shame. 'All right,' she conceded, 'I'll try again.'

Second draft

Dear Christopher,

Well, greetings! I expect you were surprised to see my name on the envelope. I am in France at present and there's lots of fun going on here with battles and whatnot! But I digress. I hope you are well and was wondering how you felt about meeting some time—

Eva threw that one away herself before Lucia could get to it. But Lucia, as vigilant as any company commander, retrieved it from the wastebasket. 'Just to make sure,' she said. After a few moments, she nodded and threw it back in. 'Right decision.'

'Do I get a score?'

'No, because I'm not cruel.'

Eva put her head in her hands. 'Why is this so hard?'

'Because it's important, star.'

'I'd be better off not writing anything at all. This is ridiculous.'

'Well, regret it for the rest of your life if you want to. It make no difference to me.'

Fifth draft

24 July 1916

Dear Christopher,

I hope you are well. I know it has been a while since we last spoke. I am now working as a Voluntary Aid Detachment nurse in France and have been here since May. As you can imagine it has been very busy here recently. I understand you were busy too.

Your friend Mr Hunter was here. He is now a captain. He was injured in battle, gassed and shot, but he should make a full recovery.

I learnt that you have been allowed some indefinite leave home. I have some leave in two weeks' time. Should you wish me to visit you, I would be glad to. However, I understand if you would prefer to draw a line under your past.

Yours affectionately,

Eva Downey

'Hmmm,' Lucia said, and then again, 'hmmm.'

'What do you mean, "hmmm"?'

'I mean, that looks all right. The fourth version had too much poetry in it. I couldn't let that one go out.'

'But the one before that wasn't too bad.'

'It was too long,' Lucia said, 'and full of things that weren't relevant. Put a stamp on that one and make sure the Censor gives it ten out of ten.'

'The Censor can't be as bad as you.'

Lucia shrugged, palms upwards. 'You'll thank me, mark my words.'

26

Two days later, Breedagh sailed into the Alwyn hut, holding a letter. 'This arrived for you, Downey.'

Eva grabbed it, her hands shaking so badly she couldn't open the envelope properly. She pulled off the top and, in her haste, ripped some of the page before taking it out and unfolding it. She scanned it for a moment or two before throwing it on the bed in disgust.

'What's the face on you about?' Breedagh asked as a watermarked page floated to the floor.

'Do you know what, Breedagh?' Eva said. 'Why don't I read it out to you since you're so damned nosey?' She picked the letter up again and started rattling it off in a sing-song, angry voice. '"Dear Eva, I have just learnt of your whereabouts via Miss Stewart. We have had a baby girl. Her name is Dolly. We should be delighted if you called on us when you are next in London. We should not be estranged any longer; I know you had reason to grieve, but so did I. It is time to stop this foolishness. Yr affec. sister, Grace Fellowes. P.S. I have learnt some disturbing news that I think you should hear from me in person. Please write back with return of post."'

For a minute, Eva was silent. '"Foolishness",' she said eventually, in a monotone that could have cut glass. 'That's what she thinks it is. She destroys my life and calls it that.'

Breedagh opened her mouth to start her usual enfilade of arguments defending the unity of the family, but Eva crumpled the letter into a ball and threw it at her. Breedagh bounced upright with indignation. 'I'll not tolerate such disrespect!'

'Please yourself,' Eva retorted. 'No, really.' She pulled her D. H. Lawrence novel out of her bag and chucked it on Breedagh's bed. 'Here's that book you keep trying to read over my shoulder. Have it.' Then she went out. She wasn't going to hang around to hear Breedagh surreptitiously turning the pages to the dirty bits.

When she arrived on duty, Doyle bounded over immediately. 'Downey. Need you now. Attempted suicide.' He provided a clipped, grim summary. A private in the Munster Fusiliers had learnt that his fiancée in Cork loved someone else and had shot himself in the head with his CO's revolver.

For three days, the man continued to live, but his eyes were not the eyes of a living man. The bullet had gone clean through the brain, causing such damage that he was incapable of moving his limbs. Still able to speak freely, if without sense, he repeatedly called out his fiancée's name, in a low, mournful almost-song: *Mary, Mary, Mary*. Hearing the toneless voice, seeing those horrific blank eyes, distressed Eva more than any physical wound ever could. It was cruel to keep him alive, inhuman! And yet that was what they were trained to do.

Finally, one night, somebody forgot to stanch his wound, which reopened, causing him to bleed to death. The matron summoned everyone for a lecture, but her heart was not in it. His face waxy and cool, he had a glazed peace about him, unlike the restless, half-conscious stare that had so haunted Eva as she tried but failed to avoid his sightless gaze.

All that night her sleep was broken. Between snatches of slumber, she looked up at the ceiling in the half-light. All she had to do was step outside the door and she would see stars. Her hands joined in the beginning of a prayer – then fell back by her sides. She could not find the words to address God and was wondering, for the first time, if He really existed.

The dead private was washed and taken to the cemetery. No need to mention the suicide. He had survived three days without food and water in a shell hole with some of his company. Let him die with an honourable record.

That day, Eva got a letter.

This time, there could be no doubt. The writing on the envelope was the same definite, spiky hand that had scribbled on the margins of her exercise book. The postmark was Cowes, on the Isle of Wight. The shock of seeing his writing nearly undid her. She walked out without telling anyone where she was going and once more sought out Lucia.

'Him, is it?' Lucia took the letter from Eva's hands with a sigh that poorly disguised her glee. 'I s'pose you want me to read it.'

Eva nodded.

'All … rightie.' Lucia filleted the envelope with a scalpel – Eva hoped she had disinfected it – and took out just one page.

'Where's the rest of it?' Eva fretted, hovering.

'That was all that was in the envelope,' Lucia said simply. Then she started reading, and laughed softly. 'Well, he is a *faasty* one, your fellow, that I can say for sure.'

'What does it say?' It was all Eva could do not to jump up and down with impatience.

'It says, "Dear – question mark – I must say I am most surprised to hear from you." No signature or nothing.'

'What?' Eva said. 'That's it?'

'Yes indeed. That's it. Here, see for yourself.' Lucia handed her back the page.

Eva shook her head in puzzlement and irritation. 'But what does that mean?'

Lucia closed her eyes and shook her head. 'Are you a half-*eedjiat* or what? Only one way to find out, nuh? Stop asking yourself twenty questions and answer his letter.'

30 July 1916

Dear Christopher,

I understand that my letter has surprised you. There is much I need to explain. But the decision to hear me is entirely yours, and I leave it in your hands. I am free to correspond or not correspond as you wish.

Yours sincerely,

Eva Downey

31 July 1916

Dear Miss Downey,

Many thanks for your letter and subsequent clarification. It is good to hear from you and to know that you are profitably engaged by the Great War Machine.

I have recently been released home on leave from Puchevillers casualty clearing station, where I was for the past few months. I don't know if

Hunter mentioned to you that I originally enlisted as stretcher-bearer for the 6th Brigade, 2nd London Division (that's one of the Territorials), but, given the tendency of entire divisions to get eaten for breakfast around there, I floated round and about in almost mercenary fashion, getting an entirely undeserved promotion somewhere along the line.

I am still only a lance corporal, however, which is rather *infra dig.* in the circles of your former schoolmates, I would imagine, who would never settle for anything less than a major. Puchevillers is not far from where you are, maybe seventy miles. It is strange to think you were that close to me then. In the midst of this nightmare, people from the old life have never seemed further away.

I was also in service during the engagement at Loos. Although I was stationed quite far behind the lines, there were several occasions that had me up at the front. They are not pleasant to recall.

In the end, they sent me home because I was getting a little bit twitchy. The constant droning soprano of eighteen-inch shells detonating around his head will do that to a fellow, unfortunately.

I am allowed day leave so if you do wish to visit, it would be advisable to let me know well in advance, as spontaneity is out the window, I am afraid.

Yours affec.,

Christopher Shandlin

P.S. A little bird told me that you had married. However, you are still using your maiden name. I am curious to know the reason for this?

God, it was good to hear from him. Eva read the letter again and again. She now had blissful privacy at the hut, since Breedagh had angrily requested a transfer, leaving the Lawrence novel on Eva's bed. (Eva noticed that the pages were well thumbed, particularly at certain parts of the narrative involving sex.) Her replacement was a stocky girl from Liverpool, too busy writing to her 'best boy' to care what Eva was up to. But even if Breedagh had been there, Eva was too happy to care. He had asked about her marriage. He was curious about that. Why would he care, unless … ?

'Oh, *mi Gad*, girl,' Lucia said, losing patience. 'Just ask for the leave and tell him you're coming. Look: he wants to see you. He has said it plain as black ink! He's got the shakes, nuh? If you leave it too long, he might take fright and say "no" again.'

1 August 1916

Dear Christopher,

Thank you for your kind response to my letter and willingness to see me. I am sorry about the nervous shock. I hope you will soon recover. I have two weeks' leave starting Saturday, 16 September, so should reach England on the same day if the crossings and weather are favourable.

I am happy to clear up the mystery of my name. Last year, a marriage was arranged between myself and a Mr Cronin, a friend of my stepmother's. However, he enlisted in the 2nd Irish Guards and died while the battle at Loos was in progress – the very battle you mention being involved with yourself. On his death I immediately returned to England from Ireland and enlisted in the Voluntary Aid Detachment. I saw no reason to keep my married name, which I only held very briefly.

I heard that Kitchener died when his boat got torpedoed by a German submarine. You must have been grieved to hear the news.

Your friend,

Eva

2 August 1916

My dear Eva,

I was grieved indeed to hear of the loss of Kitchener. So grieved that I dropped the stretcher I was carrying and undertook an elaborate funereal ritual known to less knowledgeable men as a 'dance'. I think the man on the stretcher survived, but it is all a bit of a blur.

'No reason to keep your married name'? Could you elaborate on that rather gnomic statement?

I am enjoying some poems by a chap called Isaac Rosenberg. I think he is going to be important. Here, what do you think of this?

> O! ancient crimson curse!
> Corrode, consume.
> Give back this universe
> Its pristine bloom.

Looks like he might take the baton from the late, lamented Mr Brooke. Poor old Rupert. I expect you've long mislaid that book in the trials of war, etc.

Regards, C.

3 August 1916

No, I never mislaid it. I keep it right here beside me and always have.

Eva

4 August 1916

Glad to hear it. Even if the poems are (on reflection) criminally naive and I made an error of judgement in recommending them to you.

See you soon.

P.S. You still haven't answered my question.

27

'You wanted to see what it was like,' Roma said. 'Well, here it is.'

'Heavens,' Sybil said, shocked, 'there's not even a blade of grass.'

She was right: no grass, nor any leaves on the trees, which were barely trees at all, merely stumps. No life, not even the song of a bird. Swathes of land churned, dead, bleak, like the surface of the moon seen through a telescope, full of craters and holes. Barbed wire on sticks, stretching on for miles and miles. The light hitting colourless land, and the tormented, broken ground absorbing it all.

They were approaching the front line.

'Shall I close the window?' Roma said. She was sitting on the right-hand passenger seat.

'Oh, do!' said Sybil heartily. 'It stinks.'

Roma only shuddered in reply and wound up the window. The overlying odours were cordite, cresol, ammonia, sewage. But the underlying odour was death, on a mass scale. It hit their nostrils and nearly burned them out it was so rank. Even with the windows closed, Sybil couldn't stop coughing.

'Can you keep quiet, please?' snapped Major Arnold Stephens from behind the wheel. 'I'm trying to drive a van full of ruddy pigeons here.' As if to corroborate his irritation, some of the birds set to squawking. Stephens had been charged with conveying an assignment of messenger pigeons from Lieutenant

Colonel Osman in the Home Office to the front line at Nieuwpoort. Osman was a notorious pigeon-fancier, and his *idée fixe* about employing pigeons in the war effort had begun to pay off, with officers noting approvingly that the little buggers appeared impervious to mustard gas and were not hampered in carrying messages by the shelling of communication trenches.

Although Sybil and Roma rarely went on driving missions, and most of these involved the transportation of the sick and wounded from various requisitioned chateaux around the area to safety at Dunkirk and beyond, they had been roped in to help with unloading the cages. Their vehicle was a supply truck, painted in camouflage, to which was attached a van the size of a wagon, and on top of that again the cages of pigeons. The whole thing looked like a top-heavy, triple-decker bus.

Apart from the pleasant diversion of having Roma's leg smack bang next to hers (Sybil was no longer under any illusion as to what drove her to follow this girl wherever she went), the journey was a little frightening, and very tedious. The van moved at an excruciatingly slow speed and had already stopped several times. The major insisted that neither Sybil nor Roma be involved in fixing any of the mechanical problems – that was men's work. 'Men's work' had got them the fifteen miles from Dunkirk to the Belgian border – in just over three hours.

Further, Major Stephens' conversation was as constant as it was dull. He shared details of his occupation as an artillery observer that nobody had requested. It was all to do with calculations and indirect fire and something called an azimuth, which sounded to Sybil like nothing more than an angel of Satan. As he droned on, Roma nudged her, and Sybil looked down at the seemingly disorganised cluster of notes on her lap. She had written:

'His MO appears to be a Battery of Boredom: from it, he will fire six-inch howitzer shells of Pure Monotony, followed by a rapid machine-gun fire of Interminable Facts until the Germans will scream for mercy – anything, anything but to have to listen to this man for a moment longer!'

Sybil had to stuff her knuckles in her mouth not to laugh out loud; she ended up snorting the laugh through her nose and sounding like a pig, which made Roma laugh too.

'I don't know what they're doing, letting giggling society girls out on a dangerous mission like this,' said Stephens primly.

As if in agreement, the sky in the distance lit up with a shell. Stephens braked violently, and half the cages lurched to the right. Behind the partition, the pigeons squawked with distress.

There'll be enough white feathers in there, Sybil thought to herself, to shame a whole army of Shandlins. She had read in Eva's letter the day before that Christopher Shandlin was still alive. She had not managed to answer it yet, because Eva's little note of reticent joy had arrived at the same time as a far less welcome communication from Clive. Viscount Faugharne had written to tell Sybil that he wanted a divorce. Her licentious behaviour, abuse of his finances and refusal to perform the services 'befitting a viscount's wife', whatever that meant, had decided him.

'Since you have effectively deserted me for a bit of wartime spills and thrills,' he wrote, 'I cannot serve you papers. It would be too dangerous for my lawyers to chase after you. But I have instructed my man Markham to have our London property cleared of all your things.'

It was a poorly written screed, blots of ink everywhere. Clive liked writing even less than she did, that was for sure. But divorce was very hard for a woman to shake off. And 'licentious behaviour'? She hadn't put anything between her legs apart from the saddle of Roma's bloody motorbike. Perhaps that was what Clive was talking about.

'No great loss,' she murmured aloud, just as the vehicle came to yet another shuddering halt.

'What now?' Roma asked Stephens, not hiding her irritation.

'"What now" is that I have to point Percy at the porcelain,' he said, closing the van door and disappearing around the side.

'Vulgar fellow,' Sybil muttered.

'Sybil,' Roma said, her eyes suddenly beseeching, 'do you think—?'

They were interrupted by a WHEEEEE! then a dull thud and a sudden uprising of light on the road ahead. Carts, vans and horses scattered, people dashed about like ants.

Instinctively, Sybil grabbed Roma and flattened them both against the van seat, Roma grunting as her tailbone hit the gearbox.

After a few seconds, Sybil cautiously lifted her head.

'Another one!' cried Roma beneath her as a high note tore through the sky, descending in pitch.

So pretty, those shells, even when they were rending living things apart. And how warm Roma's body beneath her: each thigh so solid, the sensation of breast meeting breast ... and then another shell, right next to them. An explosion sucking all the air and sound, abrupt as a full stop.

'Where the hell is Stephens?' Sybil wondered. 'I hope that last one didn't get him.'

'Do you really care?' Roma was still beneath her, still warm, her breath tickling Sybil's neck. Her eyes were a pure colour like that river in

Switzerland before it meets the glacial stream near Lake Geneva. Sybil sighed and pulled herself up until she was kneeling on the seat. 'I'd better go see he's all right. Old Fritz seems to have taken a break for the moment.'

She did not see immediately, and then she did.

He … Major Arnold Stephens … was lying flat on his back several yards away from the van, his chest blown open by the shell, ragged ends of rib-cage sticking up. A black space where his internal organs had been blown out, half the intestines remaining, half in a bloody mess around him. The entirety of his innards, from neck to groin, open to public view. His face just about left intact, though part of his left jawbone had gone.

Sybil had never before seen the kind of injuries from which there could definitely be no recovery. She struggled not to be sick. Her teeth were chattering in her head. 'I'm not a society girl,' she addressed the mangled corpse, somewhat hysterically. 'I'm going to be divorced. So now you know.'

She called for Roma to fetch a blanket, or a covering of some sort. She did not try to shield the state of the man. Roma flinched only very briefly, a spasm of muscle at the corner of her mouth. Together, they dragged Stephens' body off the road and laid it in the ditch and covered his face.

'We'll tell them at base,' Roma said, 'once we finish our mission.'

It began to rain, gentle drops pattering on the ground, then firmer. With the runnels of water spilling into the ditch, Sybil felt her own will to move drain away. 'I don't know if I can do it, Romy,' she said, trembling.

'Of course you can.' Roma held out her hand, 'Come.'

Sybil took it but didn't move. She was crying hard. Roma stepped towards her, still holding her hand.

'I just found out today: Clive's divorcing me. And now this poor, boring man, dead like that when we were only speaking to him a minute ago. And this place is so muddy. And everyone's so rude. I shouldn't have come here. I hate the French. I hate the bloody French. Oh, Roma, what am I going to do?'

In an instant, Roma had her arms around Sybil's neck, and before she could think twice about it, Sybil kissed her. She tasted of salt and blood and the bit of Fry's chocolate Nevinson had given her that morning in Dunkirk. It was not a long kiss, but there was a flash of tongue, enough to seal intent. The rain fell on Sybil's jacket and shoulders, and she pulled Roma in close for a long moment.

'I'll tell you what you're going to do.' Roma's voice was, for once, ever so slightly shaky. 'You're going to get back in that van. And you're going to drive us to Nieuwpoort. Those were Major Stephens' orders. Now that he is dead, we must fulfil them.'

'I just …' Sybil could hardly speak properly for sudden happiness and fear. 'I … what about the shells—'

'For God's sake,' Roma said, kissing her again, 'just drive, Sybil.'

28

Eva stood on the deck of the ferry that carried passengers across the Solent, the channel between Southampton and the Isle of Wight. It was raining quite heavily, and everyone else had gone below. She knew from the temperamental look of the sky that it was only a shower, so she did not mind the rain on her face and hair, battering her clothes. She wore no coat and carried no umbrella, not having thought to purchase either after disembarking from the difficult journey across the English Channel (they had been narrowly missed by a German torpedo) or on arrival in Southampton.

She had spent the night at a guesthouse in town but had left first thing that morning. She had not slept much. She was too excited.

The rain began to clear as the ferry neared Cowes, and the sun came out. It felt warm on Eva's cheek, even on the ship, with the wind blowing. She pushed strands of wet, straight hair out of her face and licked the skin around her mouth. It tasted of rain, sweet and clean.

Cowes was pretty in the sun, dotted with little white sails where children and youths were taking part in a sailing regatta. It was strange to think of war ever touching such a place. And yet it had; when Eva disembarked, she saw that the streets and docks were full of men in uniform, men who looked lost and grim. A row of horse-drawn cabs waited near the ferry terminal. She got into the first one, drawing her wet shawl around her, hoisting her bag on her shoulder and clinging on to her small case until the handle slipped in her sweaty hand and the driver persuaded her to surrender it to the back, assuring her that it would be sent on ahead to the inn where she was lodging.

The driver knew where Osborne House was. East Cowes, just across the Medina river. The 'floating bridge' left every fifteen minutes. 'I'll just give him six shillings, ma'am, and all will be well.' Handing over the fare, Eva tried not to think of Charon ferrying people to the Underworld, as the horse trooped straight up the wide ramp onto the ferry deck. The entire structure moved along two chains held fast to each bank. As the boat rolled along its predestined route, Eva thought of the chains that held her own heart fast and that were pulling her across as surely as the actual ones.

They disembarked, still sitting in the carriage, and drove off. The road took them through East Cowes then out by the cliff. Eventually a pale yellow edifice with two towers, fussily crenellated parapets and many windows loomed up.

'Osborne House.' But Eva recognised it immediately.

'Are you sure you'll be all right?' the driver blurted as he helped her out and set her down on the ground, as if she were a light thing.

She looked up at him. 'Why shouldn't I be?'

He shook his head. 'A lady like you, in a place like that. On your own.'

'I'm visiting someone.' Eva's tone was sharp. So what if he was offended; he was not the first man to have spoken to her patronisingly on this journey. They treated her so differently when she was out of uniform!

'Well, if you're sure you're safe.'

'I am sure.'

'I'll say goodbye then. Good luck.' He seemed reluctant to leave, even after she somewhat sternly pressed a coin into his palm, but he drove off eventually.

The walk up the driveway was a long one. Eva was entranced by the series of split-level ornamental gardens, fountains with black stone statues and walkways on which men in blue pyjama tunics walked – or, closer to the truth, shambled and paced with ungainly steps. Eva tried not to stare at them, disturbed by their stiffness. They jerked like wooden dolls pulled about by some gleeful puppet master, oblivious to the beauty of the gardens that stretched back all the way almost to the Solent.

Closer to the house, Eva was distracted from its grim Italianate beauty by a commotion in the garden. A group of men in uniform were standing around a patient who had just risen from a bench, and one of the men was shouting at him and waving his fist. The shouting man was about forty-five years of age, good-looking, with a bristling moustache and a shock of brown hair under his blue hat, which was emblazoned with the red sash that indicated high rank, possibly brigadier.

As for the man he was taunting, he was, by contrast, quite wretched, his complexion sallow and wrinkled, and he had an odd posture, one of his legs quivering, his shoulders jumping, his entire body contracted into a comma of fear. He held his fists up to his cheeks and cowered. As a man he was quite finished. Eva was appalled to see the military men bully him – and what happened next shocked her to the core.

The brigadier reached out and pinched the patient's cheek, pulling the flesh with his thumb and forefinger. He laughed, or rather emitted a series of parcelled barks; his men all chuckled with him. The nervous man squealed and tried to put his arms over his face. But his tormentor only laughed more, shoving his arms away from his face, slapping him on both cheeks, pinching him again. His victim cried out in anguish and slithered to the ground, curling up in a ball and rocking back and forth, making an awful, high-pitched sound. The brigadier kicked him, just the once; then one of his companions followed suit, with a thin giggle.

'Stop!' Eva cried out, her voice strong and deep, strange to her. 'Leave him alone.'

The men turned around. She could see the surprise on their faces, that a young woman would challenge them. The leader looked up at her briefly and – there was no other way to describe it – dismissed her. A glance, a flick of the wrist, perhaps a little toss of his head. She was not worth speaking to. But it was more fundamental than that. His was a glance that could make people no longer exist. Eva knew in her heart that he would not hesitate to hit her. He was a woman-hater; she could see that instantly. But she had had enough of men in authority putting her down. Roy had put her through a lifetime of it.

Before she could say anything, a flock of nurses materialised and protectively surrounded the shell-shocked patient, comforting him. This was evidently an affront to the brigadier's pride. He proceeded to harangue them at length, using language Eva had never heard from a high-ranking army man. They saluted and apologised, hands nervously bouncing off their foreheads while still trying to care for the poor fellow he had insulted.

Eva shuddered and increased her pace to a brisk stride. It was the wrong time to get into such a business. She was there for one reason only.

A woman in a nurse's uniform with a few pips on the pocket was coming towards her, also briskly. Eva waved to get her attention, and the nurse approached with a wide, fixed smile, making a point of ignoring the ranting official, his fawning retinue and even his victim.

'Hello, sister. I'm Eva Downey. I'm here to meet Lance Corporal Christopher Shandlin.'

The nurse's face brightened. 'Oh, yes, I know that gentleman. He mentioned you. Do follow me in, Miss Downey, I'll let him know you're here.'

She followed the nurse inside to a vast parlour. The high ceilings were supported by slim Greek-style pillars of striated marble, and the curtains and sofa were made of the same sumptuous gold-coloured fabric. In the middle of the room stood a round coffee table with gold detailing around the side. A fire burned in the grate, which was made of a marble darker than that on the pillars, and a chandelier with far too many glass pieces for comfort hung from the ceiling.

'They're not all like this, the rooms,' the nurse smiled. 'We've kept this one for visitors. Unfortunately, some of the men get bad episodes, and having fragile items lying around … well, you know. You make yourself comfortable. You might have to wait for tea or coffee, I'm afraid – we're a bit low on hot water with that lot coming in.'

'Oh, that's fine,' Eva said. 'Thank you. By the way' – as the nurse was turning to leave – 'who were those men outside?'

The nurse looked nonplussed. 'Which ones?'

'The ones who were pinching that patient's cheeks. One of them wore a cap with a blazon.'

'Oh, there's a crew over from RAMC headquarters today, doing assessments. Brigadier McCrum is out in the garden measuring our fellows up. There's a medical board convening on Monday next. McCrum takes a special interest in such things. He'll be the one you mean.' A spasm of revulsion had crossed her face when she mentioned his name.

Measuring up, yes, that is one way of putting it, Eva thought.

'He has a fine appetite, or so they say, a great advocate of physical and mental health. Not got much time for "weakness of character", as he calls it. They'll be wanting soup and a bit of lamb for lunch, so I'd better make sure they're ready down in the kitchen. But first,' the nurse said, 'I'll find your friend.' She smiled and went out, leaving Eva alone.

Although she had done her utmost to dress nicely for this visit, Eva still felt awkward sitting down on the sofa, beside a fire that did not even begin to warm the enormous room. She thought of the man rocking on the ground. She knew shell shock, had seen the 'thousand-yard stare' from returning troops far too many times. But the fear in that man's eyes, his abjection in the face of McCrum's contumely – she had not seen that before, not even in Étaples.

And was Christopher like them? She had read his letters. They had seemed sane enough. But who knew? Was this what she had done to him? She shivered with guilt, a shiver that went through her body from her head to her legs and broke out a sweat on her skin. For a moment, she struggled with the urge to flee. But before she could, the door opened again, slightly more hesitantly, and all thoughts of flight disappeared.

She saw immediately that it was him. Older, paler, leaning to one side a little, but definitely him. She rose to her feet. Neither of them said anything. He had aged, no doubt about it, a lot in two years. The military barber had got hold of his fine dark hair and had given him a shorter cut, which made the grey more prominent at the sides. One of his temples was covered by nothing more than stubble, the line of shaving rough and irregular. Eva wondered how the barber could have been so careless. His cheeks were more hollow than before, making his eyes look large.

Those eyes, that now rested on her to the exclusion of all else. Those eyes showed awareness, not like the other men's eyes, not that frightening blankness. That was something, at least. Also, he was wearing something resembling an ordinary suit, a crumpled shirt with a loose collar and a red neckerchief. Not like those ghosts in their hospital blues. Perhaps he was all right.

Heaven knows what she looked like to him. A sight, probably, her hair a mess from drying in the open air, and her skin chapped from the wind.

'Eva,' he said. 'Hello.' He seemed not to know what to do with himself, whether to move forward or to stay where he was. He bunched his hands into fists and suddenly twitched in one eye, swallowing immediately afterwards. His face was working. For a moment she feared he was as fragile as that chandelier and that her presence was an India-rubber ball, about to bounce loose and smash everything.

Then he recovered. With a huge internal effort, or so it seemed to Eva, he collected himself, walked into the room and held out his hands, grasping both of hers briefly before letting them go. She could almost fool herself into thinking the first impression a dream, he seemed so urbane. She wanted to cry, seeing him like this and, well, just seeing him, full stop. 'It's good to see you, Christopher,' she whispered.

'It's good to see you too,' he murmured in reply. Then he cried out with what seemed a false joviality, 'Sit down, won't you? Tell me about your war. Tea's on the way, though you might have to wait a while. I gather you were already forewarned of that.'

'I don't mind.'

They sat down on the long sofa, facing each other, about two feet apart. As out of place as Eva had felt sitting there by herself, he looked even more ill at ease, his fingers tracing the pattern on the upholstery. Then he rummaged in his pockets and pulled out a cigarette and lighter. As he lit up, she recoiled at the sight of his hands. The cuticles on all his fingers had their skin pulled … no, ripped off, and sores clustered all around his fingernails, which were bitten down way past the quick. Furthermore, on the knuckles of each hand he bore deep, crescent-shaped cuts that had healed but left a trace of a red line across them. He must have inflicted those cuts on himself, with his fingernails, or, good God, maybe even a penknife. Some of them looked too deep and angry to be the work of fingernails. Her heart turned over, but she tried her best to look bright, indifferent.

Too late. Quick as a flash he saw the direction of her glance and immediately jumped to his feet, tamping his cigarette in the huge carved onyx ashtray on the mantelpiece. Then he sat down again, clasped his hands together and hid them between his knees. Eva thought the kindest thing she could do was pretend not to have seen.

'This place,' he said, wincing.

Eva laughed nervously. 'I don't know, it seems like a lovely building.'

'It's a lunatic asylum, and you know it.'

'Yes,' she said, 'but *you* seem all right.'

'I'm very far from it,' he said shortly.

Tea arrived, quicker than expected, served in an ornate bronze teapot on a tray.

'They ran out of gold at this point,' Christopher commented acidly as he poured the tea, which was served without milk. Unlike Eva, he added no sugar, and sipped infrequently. After a moment or two, during which they sat drinking tea and avoiding each other's eyes, both of them started speaking at the same time.

'You first,' he said.

'Oh, no, you should speak, please.'

Gripping the cup with both hands to steady herself, she hoped he couldn't see how nervous she was.

'Well,' he said, 'where should I start?' The words, so innocent, hung in the air. It was obvious he realised this himself, as he said nothing more. Where should he start, indeed?

'Wherever first comes to mind, I suppose,' Eva answered, with a self-conscious laugh. Christopher became agitated at this, picking at what was left of his cuticles. Eva tried desperately not to wince or intervene.

'It's been … quite brutal. I did things on the front line that were necessary, but, I fear, unforgivable.'

The words came out before Eva could stop herself. 'I'm not one to talk to about forgiveness.'

His entire demeanour changed, stiffened, his eyes darkening until they were small and almost black as obsidian. Eva's hand flew to her mouth.

He moved further down the couch, almost to the end, and fixed on her an accusing glare. Eva laced and unlaced her fingers, wanted to tell him how sorry she was. But Lucia's earlier warning rang in her head like a gong. To mention it now would be disastrous. It did not help that she felt more love for him than ever, seeing him opposite her, hurt, like an albatross with a broken wing. She wanted to take him in her arms and never let him go.

321

But, as for Christopher … she had no idea if he felt any sort of love for her at all.

'Let's go for a walk,' he said abruptly, rising from the couch.

29

To her surprise, he took her arm as they went outside, even though it was only to interlock his elbow with hers, a courtesy rather than a romantic gesture. He walked quickly; she stumbled to keep up before getting used to his pace.

'Still clumsy,' he remarked, not looking at her. 'Of course, there's not so much call for dancing these days.'

Eva said nothing, not wanting to shatter any détente. They walked for a while through grass still wet with rain, the traces of it dampening his trouser legs and soaking her hemline. On he walked, his profile set, the slant of the wind only making it seem sharper, as if it had shaped his cheeks. He had always been a thin man, but he had lost weight since Eva had last seen him.

She was about to make some anodyne enquiry after his health, but then Christopher started speaking. 'You said I could speak first, so I should, I suppose. I haven't been here all that long. Just since July the … 6th, I think? The trouble started on the 1st. Things got a bit busy, as I think you are probably aware. We were just getting off a supply train and preparing our stuff when they started hurling bombs at us with all their might, all raining down on us like billy-o. There were a few of us there; I was with Purcell, a private who was assisting me. I'd recently got my promotion, such as it was, and he didn't take kindly to it, believe me. Still, I shouldn't have laughed about the letters to his dog. That was wrong of me.'

'His dog?' Eva struggled to keep up with the conversation, and with him.

'He left the damned letter on the table. It was while we were training back in England. That was last year. God, the training was interminable; we were all bored out of our minds, so there was bound to be an upset about something petty. Anyway, I spotted the letter on the table in our quarters, and I thought it must be addressed to his wife. It said "Dear Emma" or somesuch, and I would have ignored it, but then it said she was a "heartless little dog". I wondered to myself if he usually addressed his wife in that manner, but on closer inspection it became clear he actually was referring to the dog. I won't repeat the rest of what I read. I don't want to embarrass the poor man's memory. I should never have been reading it in the first place. Anyway, when he came back, I teased him about it – cruel of me, I suppose, but I hardly cared at the time. Not very funny, though at the time I found it hilarious.'

'Why did you do that?' Eva said, starting to laugh.

'I was feeling rather bitter.'

Her laughter died as fast as it had started.

'Anyway, he never quite forgave me for that, but we muddled on. We were friends, after a fashion. It was always him and me, that was the nub of it. That's how they hook you in. Drill into you how important it is not to let your comrades down. I tried to stay aloof, but eventually it worked, even for me. I too am a "piece of the continent", as Donne would have it. So there we were, just off the train with orders to report to the clearing station when they began shelling us. Oh, God, Eva, it was a mess.' His voice faltered, then he continued: 'I saw people and horses running, but they got caught, and all of a sudden they transformed into bits of burning flesh, man and horse all mixed, floating down to the ground, little flames licking around each bit. I turned around to Purcell, and I remember him saying, face white as a sheet, "Gosh, getting a bit hairy now, Fritz is giving us a good pounding," and I responded – I don't know, "you don't say," or somesuch, not really looking at him, scanning the terrain to see when the next attack was coming. But he didn't say anything in response. So I turned around, and ...' – he started to shake – 'it must have happened without a sound, because I didn't hear a thing. Where Purcell had been a few seconds before were tiny fragments of flesh and blood on the ground. Just like that. Not even an eye.'

Christopher released Eva's elbow and brushed his hand briefly across his eye and cheek. Eva opened her bag to fetch a handkerchief, but he frowned and shook his head. 'No. Not that. I can't allow myself. If I let one crack perpetuate, the whole glass will shatter into a thousand pieces.'

Eva waited for him to continue without saying anything. He glanced at her briefly. 'You were always a good listener. I'd forgotten that.' Then he resumed: 'You never get used to it, you know. You pretend you do. You suppress whatever horrors you feel, but it's only ever an act of suppression. Each time it happens, it's like going to a bank and taking out more money on credit, knowing you have no collateral and that you'll have to pay it back some day, if you ever make it back to normal life. Or you will overdraw, and once you're overdrawn, why, you're done for. Account closed. The end. And now the bailiffs are coming knocking.'

'I'm not sure that normal life exists any more.'

'Perhaps, but really, Eva, is now the time for logical splitting?' he said irritably, sounding somewhat more like his old self. 'Anyway, to get to the end of my miserable tale, I took a ride on an ambulance to the clearing station, with some sort of idea of reporting what had happened. When I got there and tried to tell them, I don't know if what came out was English, but they took one look at me and sent me to the company doctor, who I imagine was busy enough with real problems that day. I can't remember a damned thing he said either. Apparently I talked and talked and he couldn't get a word in edgeways. Then something strange happened in my mind – I can only half-describe it: there was this chattering of voices, like children in a playground, only disembodied and far away, as if I were hearing them through some sort of drainpipe. Then everything was … dark with excessive bright? Do you remember that passage?'

'Yes, you made me learn it: "through a cloud / Drawn round about thee like a radiant Shrine / Dark with excessive bright thy skirts appear".'

'Precisely. Except I wasn't wearing skirts. That would have looked strange.' Christopher chuckled softly. 'Then … I fainted. Blacked out right there in the middle of the room. They put me into that category, what do you call it? You're in the field hospital, you know this stuff.'

'NYDN?' The letters tripped off her tongue, as pat as any poem he might have made her learn.

'Aha, yes! Not Yet Diagnosed, Nervous. That's it. Highly unflattering description, sounds like a hysterical spinster on a rest cure. But, you know, long before the Purcell incident I'd been on the edge, and it was the noise of those shells that caused it. Silence, then noise, then silence – and it takes a few minutes each time to register that it isn't you. Then to realise that it's someone else. And what it means. Then you see them as' – he waved his hands about – 'little bits of things.'

Eva did not say how often she feared it had been him.

'Then they brought me here. There's a psychiatrist I speak to most days. He tells me I'm making good progress, but I fear I'm fooling him. I fear I'm fooling myself sometimes. If everyone thinks I'm all right, I must be.'

'No,' Eva said softly, 'I can see' … *your hands* … 'you have a slight twitch.'

'Yes, that's one of the categories.' He counted on his fingers: 'There's twitchers, pissers, jumpers, mutterers and those poor chaps who soil themselves in terror. It's hard to be sanguine when you're surrounded by such wrecks of human beings and knowing you're a bit of a wreck yourself. A lot of men at the front were scared out of their skins, not of death but of the fear of death, if that makes any sense.'

Ar eagla na heagla. For fear of the fear. That was a phrase Eva had heard from time to time in Ireland. 'I had a suicide on my ward,' she said. She told him about the Munster Fusilier.

Christopher nodded in recognition. 'There were a few like that. More than the brass at HQ would ever like to admit. Mind you, I can't help thinking that everyone who obeyed orders was just as suicidal as your patient. I was never sure what I felt about the men who were shot for cowardice. Pity, mostly, I think. Many of them were just lads, not very well educated and totally naive about what war would actually be like. Poor bastards. Pardon my language.'

Eva had sucked in her breath at the mention of the executions. She had mentioned Cronin in a letter to Christopher. Would the name ring any bells? He had been at Loos – he might know all about it. To get him off that particular subject, she mentioned her encounter with Brigadier McCrum. Christopher's response was immediate. 'He's a bully. I knew people like him at school. They never really change, and they always make it to the top without getting their hands dirty.'

The path went close to the cliff, and Christopher moved to its seaward edge and hooked his elbow through Eva's once more, protectively. She allowed herself to be drawn closer to him – wished for it in fact. Then he stopped, and she stopped with him. Directly in their path lay the body of a seagull. It must have been dead for several days at least, for its body was torn open and insects were eating at it, their black backs shining in the September sun, while the head – eyes and skull long eaten out – was separated from the body by quite some distance. Eva was about to ask Christopher what he thought might have happened to the bird when she noticed that his eyes were ranging over the carcass. And then she saw what he must have seen immediately.

The gull's wings were spread open and surrounded by scattered feathers, some grey, but mostly white. Several floated along the footpath in the breeze. Christopher glanced at Eva briefly, then back down at the feathers. 'Lots of them,' he commented, 'lots and lots of them.'

His tone was casual, but Eva felt something plummet inside her and settle at the base of her belly, squat and hard. Meanwhile, he released her, deftly stepped around the dead bird and strode ahead at such a pace that she was hard pressed to catch up with him.

She felt an urge to tell him everything: about Joseph, yes, and how he had brutalised her so badly that she encouraged him to go to war so he

328

would leave her alone; about the desperate moments in Mama Leela's when she had called out Christopher's name and received no response; about everything that had happened to her since the day he had walked down the street and out of her life. No, call it what it was: since the day she had fastened that feather on him and sent him away. *Lots and lots of them.* She hated this tightrope of politeness but had no idea what would happen if she jumped off.

'Are you all right?' she said when she caught up with him, rather short of breath. He gave her a sour look and the lightest of shrugs. To her surprise, she felt a tug of impatience not unlike the one she had felt so often with Cronin. *For God's sake, make an effort.* She tried to shake it off, but Christopher noticed it. 'That was an odd look you had just there.'

'I was thinking of my husband.' The minute they were out, Eva wished the words back.

'Oh.' If he had been cold before he was now positively glacial. They made their way down the avenue to the centre of East Cowes in silence. They passed an ice-cream shop, and Eva gathered the courage to ask if he would like an ice; he murmured an unenthusiastic assent. She bought two, and, disregarding good manners, they ate them on the path as they walked, an almost tasteless dilution of water and aniseed. Christopher continued to keep a good two feet away from her, and she did not wish to urge him closer. The sun shone on the beach, a hard, bright light, but the bathing huts were almost empty, the drinks kiosks boarded up.

Later, in a café, they sat clutching cups of cooling tea. Christopher delivered a strange monologue, his voice unnaturally high-pitched, his entire body like a stringed instrument where the plucked notes were all sharp, and the strings in danger of breaking at any time. He spoke outwards, as if she were not there. Eva could not bear to look him in the eye, which was just as well, since he seemed once more bent on avoiding hers.

In the middle of his monologue, which was about this and that, again declaring Isaac Rosenberg the new poetry champion, damning Keats and Wordsworth and Hardy in increasingly hysterical tones, she shyly slipped the Rupert Brooke volume out of her bag and across the table. Anything to make him stop. 'I told you I kept it.'

'Yes, yes,' he said impatiently, waving it away and continuing to talk. She put it back in her bag.

His gestures were beginning to attract the attention of the other customers. Eva saw them looking and shaking their heads. She wanted to shout at them: 'He's not like those others! He's all right!' but she knew in her heart that it wasn't true. He was not all right.

After twenty more excruciating minutes, Christopher finally looked at her. It was not a friendly look. 'Let's get out of here, for God's sake.'

Eva was only too happy to comply.

They walked back up the hill and out into open terrain. The further they got from the crowds, the more Christopher relaxed, reverting to his usual slouch rather than the wired, puppet-like demeanour he had adopted in the crowded café. But as she drew level with him, Eva saw a bead of sweat run down the side of his neck. It had been wrong of her to judge. This outing had been a real effort for him.

He wiped his forehead with his hand. 'That went badly, didn't it? I don't know how to behave around normal people any more.'

'You were fine.'

'I was terrible.' He put his hands in his pockets. Eva said nothing; the only thing she could truthfully do was agree, and that seemed cruel.

'Your husband,' he said, abruptly changing the subject. 'You must miss him. To have your mind on him while walking with someone else.'

She was surprised at the injured tone in his voice. Had he not seen her face? Why had she mentioned Joseph? 'No. Well, I mean … we were … No, I don't miss him. I wasn't thinking about him for that reason.'

'Why were you, then?'

'You had mentioned some people who were shot for cowardice.'

'Ah.'

'He was one of them. They shot him when he failed to go over the top at Loos.'

Christopher gave a long, low whistle. 'Ye gods. But he was Irish, wasn't he? Why on earth was he fool enough to enlist?' She watched the thought cross his mind, then he looked at her with horror. 'You didn't make him?'

'No!' Eva shouted, 'I didn't. It's different there anyway. They see the feather as an English custom and don't care for it.' It was the first time either of them had mentioned the incident directly.

'But it was after marrying you that he signed up, yes?'

'Yes,' Eva said, reddening.

Christopher's gaze was that of a judge, and she strongly suspected he was finding her guilty as charged. 'I was angry,' she added. 'I hated him, he—'

'Don't start that,' he said quietly.

'What?'

'Blaming this man for the mess you've made of your life. And don't waste my time with tears either. Or a sob story about your mother. I'm not going to fall for that a second time. You hated him, is that right? So why did you marry him?'

'I—'

'Did you know Gabriel wrote to tell me of your marriage? Apparently it was announced in *The Times*. I had been up for twenty-four hours on marching training and then kitchen duty in some miserable camp out in Hexham when I got that letter. Can you imagine what that did to me after everything else you put me through?'

He was trembling violently, and Eva put a hand out to steady him, gripping his arm. He suffered it for just a moment before wrenching himself away from her. 'I had just about walked off most of my rage and thought of communicating with you again, to see if we could talk about what had happened. I knew you were under duress … But you didn't even wait! Did I mean so little to you that you could just waltz off and marry someone else? And so soon – permit me to refresh your memory on this point – after you humiliated me in public and sent me off to certain death?'

'No, no. You meant a lot to me. Mean a lot.'

'Words,' Christopher retorted, shaking his head, 'words, words. That's how you seduced me in the first place, wasn't it? Nice words and platitudes. Pity none of them meant a damn thing.'

Eva stood immobile, the stone of guilt hard in her belly. *This is what you have done.*

'But that's what you're like,' he added, with a nasty smile. 'You have one man in the grave and another in pieces. You're worse than your stepsister; at least *she* doesn't pretend to be nice. Oh, look!' – Eva had raised her hand in anger – 'You want to hit me? Go on then, why don't you?' Her arm froze. 'You know I shan't strike back.'

She let her hand drop to her side. 'I won't hit you,' she said quietly, trying to hide her hurt. She did not break eye contact, not for one moment. The wind made her eyes water – she blinked. She would not have him think she was crying, even though she felt close to it. Loose strands of hair beat her face.

'It doesn't matter what you do,' he said finally, in disgust. 'You're a worthless excuse for a human being. I thought more of you, but that was my mistake.' He turned away from her and stamped along the path, his shoulders hunched in a shield of hurt and anger.

Eva let him go and remained standing, a rolling, freezing fog of misery dancing around her, enveloping her close, even though the sun was bright, the sky clear and the sound so good that she could hear the distant echo of guns across the Channel. He had not forgiven her. And she could hardly blame him. In not so many words, Sybil had let it be known that what she had done was unforgivable – and Sybil had no selfish interest in the matter. Why on earth should *he* exercise forbearance? She didn't deserve it.

She thought of going back into town, but no; even if he hated her, she could not bear to be away from him. That was the God's honest truth of it. So she started to trudge after him, keeping him in sight, not caring whether she infuriated him or not by following him.

He stopped dead several yards in front of her.

He was coming back.

She saw him squint as he faced the sun, striding towards her in a way that brought her back to those days at The Links, but without any of the cheerful nonchalance he had displayed then. Now he was as grim as a rock. 'Give me that book,' he said abruptly, holding out his hand.

Eva clutched her bag close and shook her head.

'For God's sake, what earthly use do you have for it?' he shouted. 'Give it back!'

'I'll never give it back,' Eva said, shaking so hard she was almost unable to keep her composure. 'It was a gift, not a loan. I don't want to lose the only thing I have to remember you by.'

'Remember me?' Christopher was white-faced. 'For Christ's sake, I'm not dead yet!' He grabbed the bag and pulled it, and her, forward. Rummaging in it, his scarred hand pulled out the book in triumph. He raised it in the air, Eva frantically jumping up in an attempt to retrieve it from his grip. Then, with a creased, determined frown, he hurled it with all his might at the Solent.

Eva ran forward, but his throw had been athletic enough to dispatch *Poems* in a grand, balletic arc right over the cliff, much to the interest of a few cormorants perched on the rocks, and down into the sea below.

'You *fucker*!' She ran at him.

He grasped her arms. 'Eva, calm down or we'll both fall over.'

'You're telling *me* to calm down?'

'Yes, I certainly am. Here, keep still.' He tightened his hold on her. 'I've never met a woman who used such language.'

'I've never met a man,' Eva cried, 'who threw a perfectly good book of poems over a cliff just out of sheer cruelty.'

'They are *not* perfectly good poems. I told you already. They're trite and overcooked. I should never have given them to you. I don't want you to remember me from them. Look at me, Eva: I'm alive, I'm real! Why can't you remember this?' He took her hand and put her fingertips on his cheek. 'And this?', putting her other hand to his lips and licking the tips of her fingers. 'And these?', placing both her hands on his eyes. 'And this?', taking her hands and running them through his hair. 'And this?', pulling her in to him, grasping her hair, bending down to her ear and kissing it, following with more kisses down the side of her neck, kisses that were more like bites.

When he lifted his mouth to her ear once more, she heard his breathing, shallow and irregular. 'Do you think, when I thought of you, I gave a damn about poems? I just wanted this – and this – oh God—'

They fell into a long embrace, he kissing her wildly, pausing only to say her name, grabbing her hair, her shoulders, her waist, any part he could reach; she grasping his head and pulling it lower so she could kiss him ever more deeply, so she could feel from the vibration in his throat his sudden cry when she opened his lips with her tongue and met his. Oh, yes, it was sex, this thing between them, but it was more than that: it was hunger. She wanted to consume him, and he her. She wanted to forget everything she had done wrong; her desire was so white it would blank out everything. She wanted the impossible.

'Eva,' he said, over and over.

But she whispered into his lapel, his chest, his cheek, all the places where he would not hear, 'Forgive me, forgive me.'

30

That night, Eva dreamt she was once more on the Solent, this time by herself and in a canoe, the island to port and the mainland to starboard. The water was dazzling blue, the waves far smaller than they would have been in real life. The boat slipped easily along, always side-on, towards cliffs that never grew nearer. The air hummed with an air of peaceful, marine purpose.

She was woken by the smell of kippers frying, opening her eyes to the lumpen surface of a trowelled ceiling. A steady beam of light shone through the window and onto the shape her body made under the counterpane, symmetrical at breasts, knees, feet. The smell of fish cooking made its way through the closed door so Eva did not delay getting up and dressed: it had been months since she had eaten kippers.

In the dining room, a cheerful woman with a bandana knotted around her head told her that her porridge would be ready soon, kippers to follow. When the porridge arrived, it was really good, neither too lumpy nor dilute, heated through with milk and a touch of malt. Eva added a spoonful of honey and downed the lot in several mouthfuls. She was starving.

Once or twice she let the hot food touch the cut on her lip, or she worried at it with her tongue. She was a little bruised, and scraped, and the Lord knew what else. Ah, here were the kippers at last, with fried chunks of potato and a slice of Stilton on the side.

'Sorry for the delay, ma'am—' but Eva was already wolfing them down. She was filleting her second kipper when the woman came back. Eva wondered happily how she had known that 'more potatoes' was going to be Eva's next request, when she saw the envelope in her hand. The handwriting was huge and flowing, extending nearly to the edge. Eva did not recognise it. Then she saw it was postmarked from France and smiled wryly. She put down her knife and fork and wiped her oily fingers on the coarse hotel napkin before opening the envelope.

Before she had left on leave, Lucia had requested – no, demanded – that Eva provide news as soon as she had any. The letter contained one line: 'Dear Eva – major or minor key? – LP.'

Eva smiled and put the letter aside. She would reply to it after breakfast, and write to Sybil too, who had sent several letters since going up to the front, all breezy in tone ('the poor fellow driving our pigeon van came to a bit of a sticky end, but we rallied and got the thing to the church on time') and full of Roma, Roma, Roma. Eva's last to her had been just before she was due to leave for the Isle of Wight. Sybil had responded warmly but hinted at a 'bit of trouble on the home front' of her own. Eva wondered if the trouble was to do with Clive.

The letter to Lucia could be dispatched straightaway since it comprised one line: 'Major, I think. – E.' Back in her room, Eva licked the envelope and got it to stick, then ran her tongue over the cut on her lip once more. It was still a little sore. She splashed cold water on her face and patted it with a thin towel. In the mirror, a face older than her years looked back at her. Her chin was scraped raw from … well, the day before. Eva stroked it with her finger and scratched at the grazed skin. She had better leave that alone too. Then she licked her upper lip again. It was bleeding.

Mind you, she had started it. In the middle of one of those crazy, tormented and tormenting kisses, she had managed to wrench Christopher's shirt free of his braces and place her hand on his bare back, slithering it up between his shoulder blades, digging her fingernails into the flesh, squeezing the skin and clumping it in her hand. He had let out an unholy yell, followed by a half-suppressed swear word, before ordering her to get those claws away, thank you very much. She had tried to, but then he started pinching her, in very tender places. It hurt, and he wasn't stopping. He wanted her to hurt him back, he was goading her into it – and so she did.

Christopher had pushed her away and looked into her eyes, his own fathomless, lost. His cheeks were flushed, he was breathing heavily, and his sweat was pungent and hot. When she pulled him back into her arms, she could feel his shirt was damp, sticking to the small of his back. 'Wildcat,' he breathed, then, 'You know exactly what you're doing, don't you?'

Eva knew what he was implying, but didn't care. 'Oh? Should I stop, then?' she said prettily.

'Under no circumstances,' he growled.

And so they had started again, and then again, until, pressed against him, she could feel how excited he was – and she responded, making sounds she hadn't ever made before. Then she arched towards him, until once more he pushed her away and, gasping, told her to stop. 'Evie, I'm afraid I'll—' He didn't finish the sentence. He didn't need to.

After finally tearing loose from each other, unsatisfied, they walked back, hand in hand. A sexual haze had enveloped them both, stronger and more intoxicating than wine, making conversation as impossible as it was pointless.

Eva dried herself and picked up her watch, which was lying on the bureau. Christopher might be up now. She wanted to see him as soon as possible. It was another bright day, so she decided to walk to Osborne House; it was only two miles if she took the ferry and much cheaper than a cab.

Three-quarters of an hour later, she arrived at the end of the long avenue. As she walked towards the building, her attention was diverted by the spectacle, on a section of unencumbered lawn, of three rows of patients in plain pyjamas. They were following the gestures of a female instructor, aged about fifty, dressed in flowing green robes, her greying chestnut hair similarly flowing over her shoulders. She made deep, sweeping movements with her bangled arms, bending down and standing back up again in slow succession, her clothes billowing and ebbing in the slight breeze, all to the strains of the slow movement of Beethoven's Pathétique sonata from a gramophone on a three-legged table.

The men's attempts to imitate her were somewhat comedic, but there was a pathos in their comedy, so Eva couldn't laugh, not even to herself. She asked a passing patient, 'Excuse me, what are those people doing?'

He laughed shortly, through his nose. 'Them? They're doing eurhythmics, or so it's called. Some theosophist thing, dancing the demons away. Hunnish nonsense, if you ask me. Barmy.' He wiped his nose with his hand and walked off again.

Barmy they might be, Eva thought, but she saw none of the twitching, blinking and shaking of the other nervous patients wandering the gardens and corridors. Perhaps they were able to dance away their demons for a time, and, if that were true, the ridiculous-looking woman deserved a Victoria Cross.

Inside, the corridors were almost empty, bar the odd patient wandering around like a ghost. It took Eva a while to find any staff; as it happened, the first nurse she did see was the same one she had spoken to yesterday. She ushered Eva into a small room. Unlike yesterday, she was not smiling. 'I was wondering if you'd come,' she said. 'I'm afraid your friend Christopher Shandlin isn't very well today.'

Eva drew back, a cold shawl of fear brushing her heart. '"Isn't very well"? Why, what does that mean?'

'He'll be better by and by, or as better as someone like him can be. He's sleeping now, poor fellow.'

Eva sank into an armchair. Her legs felt wobbly. 'He was fine yesterday when I left him.'

'That's as may be, but one moment these boys can seem fine, the next' – she clicked her fingers – 'they're back in it again.'

'Can I see him?' Eva blurted out.

The nurse shook her head. 'That's not a good idea. Look, Miss Downey, I must speak plain. Last night he took a bad turn. He woke up shouting, delirious. It took three orderlies to hold him down. Three. Madness can make a man very strong, Miss Downey. We've already had to electroshock him once.'

Eva gasped, then tried to hide her horror. Doyle had told her what the shock treatments they gave to the soldiers were like. The stimulation of the brain caused the body to go into convulsions. 'Strong stuff,' he had said, clicking his tongue disapprovingly.

'So,' the nurse went on, 'I'm telling you now, so you can be informed. The sooner you realise he's too much to take on, the sooner you can leave, and his heart won't break quite as badly.' Here she sighed. 'That's what all the girls do. They don't know what it is they're dealing with, and when they do realise you don't see them for dust. And we pick up the pieces.'

Eva sprang to her feet, her cheeks hot. 'I'm not going anywhere!'

'They all say that,' the nurse replied.

'Listen … you … listen!' Eva could not stay civil. 'I don't care if he's mad. I love him, you see. I love him very much.' She was almost in tears.

'Yes, I do see.' The nurse's voice was gentler.

'I love him,' Eva repeated, for want of anything else to say, and because it was true.

'Then come back tomorrow. Come back, and we'll start again.' A smile broke out over the nurse's wintry face, catching the midday sun streaming through the open window, illuminating the down on her cheek. 'I know one thing for sure: he cannot wait to see you.'

A breeze flipped the pages of an open bible on a small mahogany tea table as the Pathétique crackled to a close and the clear call of the instructor declared the practice complete.

On returning to the hotel, Eva sat in the deserted lounge and closed her eyes; her earlier tiredness had returned, and all she wanted to do was sleep for a thousand years, sleep and cry, if it were possible to do both at the same time. She was offended at the nurse's suggestion that she would run out on Christopher, but, on the other hand, the little asides – 'his heart won't break quite as badly' and 'he cannot wait to see you' – could not but give her a thrill of pride.

At the same time, to think of his feelings laid bare like that, so exposed both in body and spirit, made something in her own heart crack a little.

It was not right that he be brought to that. To her surprise, she craved a cigarette. Back when Sybil was puffing away in the school dorms, Eva had thought it posturing, but she had begun to join the clumps of VADs hanging around outside the hospital huts, coils of smoke from their cigarettes dissipating in the summer air, as much for the communal moment as for any other reason.

She went back into the town to buy herself a packet of Embassy No. 1 and a box of matches. Smoking the first of them as she walked back, she reflected that she had spent the last year in a state of busyness, and today there was nothing for her to do but think and fret and smoke some more. She returned to the hotel and treaded through the little garden to the entrance. She would go up to her room and spend the rest of the day moping—

'Eva.'

Christopher was leaning against the wall outside the front door, his arms folded, just like that day outside the Swedish church.

He looked to be in a perfectly normal state, apart from his light-brown corduroy coat, which was far too big for him, and his shoes, which had thick blue laces. Institutional clothes, Eva guessed. His fingers were beating out some sort of rhythm on his arms, as if he were playing a piano exercise. But she knew him well enough not to be alarmed at that; it was simply not in his nature to be still for any length of time.

'Christopher!' she exclaimed. 'What are you doing here?'

'What sort of damn fool question is that?' he responded, with a smile.

'They told me you were unwell. They said—'

'I know what they said.' He betrayed a hint of agitation, digging into a capacious pocket and extracting a cigarette of his own, his fingers trembling a little as he lit it. Then he pursed his thin lips around the filter and exhaled. The smoke floated for a while in the air. 'I'm sorry,' he added, before taking a second puff.

'For what?'

'For dragging you into all this. I didn't think I'd crack up again, not so soon. I think it was ...' He broke off. 'Eva, what happened to me yesterday, when we were out walking, and I kissed you ...' He lowered his gaze to the ground. 'I don't know what came over me. I ceased to be human. I thought I knew passion, but that was madness ... madness!'

'You weren't passionate all by yourself,' Eva said quietly.

He threw the cigarette on the ground and stamped it out. 'No. The way you were with me was different to when we were together before. You answered my every gesture, and surpassed several of them.' A brief grin flickered across his face at the memory. 'I can tell that you know desire now and you didn't before.' He put up a hand as Eva made to protest. 'No, let me finish. Last night, I thought of him, your husband, then I fancied *I* was the one being dragged to the court martial, *I* was being blindfolded or having a bag put over my head or whatever and nearly pissing myself in mortal terror because I knew what was going to come. I need another cigarette.' His hands were shaking hard as he lit up, the scabs and sores around his fingers very noticeable.

Eva did not dare offer to help. It was all she could do to speak, lest there be a repeat of the rage he had shown her yesterday. 'I need to tell you this,' she said. 'There was no desire in my marriage. Not for one moment. Anything that happened was ... coercion.'

Christopher looked at her with suspicion, his mouth a thin line. It was as Eva feared: he did not believe her. 'After what I did to you, I was broken, do you understand? I knew you were lost to me, and, after that, all I could do was obey Catherine. You will tell me I am responsible for my own actions, and that's true. All I can tell you is I have never felt like this before. I have never behaved like this before with any man.'

He was silent, inhaling and then blowing out a long cloud of smoke. But some of the hardness had gone from his expression, his shoulders had relaxed, and, when he spoke again, his tone was softer: 'I thought I had some control, but then last night it all came back, memories like flying shards of glass. You opened the box,' he added ruefully. 'You opened the box.'

He pulled out yet another cigarette. 'Want one?'

Eva nodded, even though she had her own. He lit it and passed it over to her. They stood for a while, smoking in silence. A lone bee buzzed uninterested around the clumps of snapdragons near their feet. Too late in the year, probably.

'The nurse who spoke to me said they gave you shocks,' Eva said.

'Yes,' he said, 'they did.'

'What was it like?'

He reached for her hand. 'Painful,' he said, in a tone that conveyed as much. Then, after a pause, 'I didn't have anyone with whom I could speak of it, not even a psychiatrist, until later. It was hard, Evie.'

'I'm here now,' Eva said, adding glumly, 'if that's any comfort, which it probably isn't.'

Christopher slipped his thumb inside her palm and started to stroke it. 'Perhaps not, dear girl. Nevertheless, I'm very glad you're here.'

She looked up at him, knowing that she had a shaky, stupid smile on her face. But he was smiling too.

'I understand Dilys, that's Nurse Parvenor, warned you off me. Told you to get out while the going was good? As it is, I've no idea why you're still here.'

'I think you'll find I'm made of sterner stuff than that.'

'Good! I am glad to hear it. I'm not dead yet, just in the funny farm.'

Eva put out her cigarette and leaned against him. Christopher put an arm around her, and she felt at rights with the world again. That corduroy coat did smell odd, as if it had been left to gather damp, but beneath it lay his distinctive smell, which comforted her. She said, 'You do know that I stood up to Nurse Parvenor, don't you? Christopher?'

'I am led to believe,' he replied, in an amused tone, 'that your precise response was to tell her that you loved me.'

'Well, what if I did?' she said, blushing. 'It's not a crime.'

'It certainly isn't,' Christopher said with a laugh, adding, 'but it may well be a disease. That said,' putting her hand on his heart, 'I seem to suffer from the same problem, specifically with regard to you.'

'Silly,' Eva laughed, but she let him hold it there a moment.

He leaned towards her and touched her forehead with the lightest of kisses, then trod another cigarette butt into the ground. 'Eva, now that we've both acknowledged how we feel, do you think … ?'

He turned to her, looking rather anxious, his forehead lined and dappled by light and shade. 'I was just thinking after what happened yesterday. There's a logical next step, you know. Would you be offended if I suggested that sometime soon we might take it?'

Eva felt her heart beat a little faster and more unevenly, like a child playing hopscotch and skipping the cracks. He meant to go to bed with her soon, that was what he was saying. 'If you do,' she said, trying to sound calm, 'I owe it to you to tell you everything.'

And, in a low voice, so that the guests sitting on the stone seat next to them wouldn't hear her, she related the entire story of her return to London after Joseph Cronin's death, her unwelcome pregnancy and Sybil's and Lucia's help in dealing with it. Christopher said nothing to all this, but she saw him flinch, just as he had in the church porch years before, when her silence to a question had spoken volumes.

She found herself defending Lucia, though Christopher made no attack; it felt important to explain that the decision was hers alone. Still he said nothing, though he looked her in the eye. Finally, he looked down and said, even more quietly, 'That was a hard thing to go through on your own.'

An old lady with an unfinished book in the crook of her arm strode past. Her bookmark had a little tassel that bobbed up and down along the spine. She batted midges out of the way, which mystified Eva since she hadn't noticed any. 'You're shocked, aren't you?' she said, turning back to Christopher.

'Yes. A little.'

'I don't know if it affects things, if we—'

He waved that away. 'Evie. We all have our stories.'

She did not know how to take his response, whether to be offended or relieved.

'What I would like to do,' Christopher said at length, 'is to take you out tomorrow. Like an ordinary couple. And we'll talk about ordinary things.

I'll bring a packed lunch and Lord Northcliffe's finest newspaper, and we shall pore over it for gossip. Do you think we can manage that? Without the *Sturm und Drang*?'

'I'll be as ordinary as possible,' Eva said.

'You'll be lucky if you manage mediocre. Let's not be overambitious, anyway. I want to keep my head in one piece from here on in.'

Eva squeezed his hand and leaned up to kiss him on the cheek. 'I understand.'

'Tomorrow, then?'

'Tomorrow.'

18 September 1916

Dearest Eva,

It's time to tell you. I daresay you've already guessed and you've not sent me to Coventry, so perhaps you'll tolerate it in me. Suffice it to say, R. and I are head over heels in love, and I've given in to my true nature at last. (I really do hope this doesn't shock you.) He confesses he has loved me for quite some time but was waiting for me to catch up and realise it. Isn't that just like him?! Cool as a cucumber while I'm flapping about.

It is awfully unfair on C., now that I come to think of it, but he has matters in hand, and that's all I want to say about that for the present.

R. is bored with hanging about in Dunkirk and fancies a stint on the eastern front, so he is considering heading off with *another* war artist, to paint blood, mayhem and butchery with a bit of sunny weather. If he does, I'll be following him! I'm praying for you both too, you and Christopher. Still cannot for the life of me get used to calling him that. I'm scared he'll give me lines. Anyway. Do cease your lovemaking long enough to write to me! I'm burning to find out what's happened.

Love from,

Still your friend – I hope!

Sybil

Forwarded

14 September 1916

Dear Eva,

Why didn't you respond to my last letter? I know we've had our differences, but this is important. I have something I urgently need to tell you in person. Please write instantly and apprise me of a good time to meet.

Regards,

Grace Fellowes (Mrs.)

31

Christopher arrived at Eva's hotel at nine-thirty the following morning, with a full knapsack. He offered her his elbow as they walked out but was not long abandoning this chivalry and taking her hand instead, interlacing their fingers. He hummed discordantly, a sure sign that he was in a good mood. To Eva's enquiries as to where they might be going he gave a knowing smile and said, 'You'll see.'

For a while they made impassioned conversation on various topics, being much distracted by an argument about whether Thomas Wyatt had or had not written the first sonnets in English. A couple of hours later, with the sun not quite at its highest point, he said, 'Well, Eva, you had your confession yesterday. Now it's my turn.' *Oh, God, what now?* 'I don't know if I'm clean. At least I think I might not be.' At first Eva did not understand. Then she guessed: when he was in France, he had been with a woman.

'Was it … Did you go to the place? Where the men go?'

'No, it was nothing like that. Well,' he added shamefacedly, 'she worked there, but I didn't know that she did.'

Eva began to laugh, out of sheer relief. She had plenty of experience with treating gonorrhoea in the field hospital. She remembered Sybil once lifting a blanket and exclaiming in swift horror before dropping it again. Eva had had to step in and take her place. 'So, she was a prostitute.'

'No money changed hands!' Christopher was puce with embarrassment as he stammered out an explanation. He had been off duty and drinking in an Amiens estaminet with Purcell and a couple of others when the woman approached him. It was only later that he found out she was a stalwart of a 'blue lamp' brothel and had probably been with all the officers in the regiment. Word got out, of course, and they all laughed at him, though with a certain respectful tinge, given that he was an NCO and the officers' tart had condescended to sleep with him. No, he'd had no symptoms, and yes, he had taken some Protargol, which the MO had prescribed, but, still, he had thought he'd better tell her.

'Are you disgusted?' he asked hesitantly.

'Christopher, I've been working in a field hospital for four months. I might as well be disgusted at you for being human. As long as it isn't the syph, I don't care. Look,' she started to giggle, half covering her mouth with her hand, 'let's take things as they come. Anyway, I don't think you're in any danger if you haven't had symptoms by now.'

He gave her a grateful look. 'I'm glad you think so. But I promise I'll be careful.'

They reached the beach just before noon. Like the rest of the shoreline, it faced north and so received scant sunlight, and chilly winds blew across it. The steps down from the cliff path were tricky. Christopher had to take Eva's hand often, while also reassuring himself of his own balance. But when they got down to the sand it was all worth it. They were completely alone, under the shade of the jutting cliffs. Eva wasted no time in undoing her boots and stuffing her stockings inside them. She sifted the sand between her toes. It felt cold and heavy.

The ham sandwiches turned out to be rather good, with real ham and mustard, and no gristle to speak of. 'These are delicious,' Eva said with her mouth full, sitting on a rock. 'Did you make them?'

'I intended to,' Christopher said with a smile, 'but once I told Mrs Parvenor of my intentions, she told me not to go near the kitchen. Said I had a good chance here, and she wasn't going to let me ruin it. I was quite offended, you know. I'm perfectly capable of making a ham sandwich!'

Eva laughed. 'She likes you, Christopher. It must be your charm. I'm glad she didn't let you though: this is the nicest sandwich I've had in quite some time.'

They sat side by side and ate in silence, watching the sea advance and recede, seething, roaring and hissing as it trapped itself in rock pools and blowholes. Occasionally Christopher would catch Eva's eye, and a little smile would play about his face, and she would smile back at him.

Some time later, Christopher uncurled himself and rose to his feet, declaring his intention to go for a swim. Eva protested that they had no costumes. He ignored her and started to strip off his shirt. Pink-faced, she pointed at the waves. 'It's dangerous.'

'Dangerous?' He shot her a scathing look. 'It's 1916. Everywhere's dangerous.'

'You said earlier you wanted to keep me safe.'

'From my own depredations, yes. From life, no. Come swim.' He continued to undress; now he was unbuttoning his trousers. Eva had never seen a man naked in a setting not related to hospital work, not even Joseph Cronin, who had always had the forethought to assault her only once he had his nightgown on.

She couldn't take her clothes off. Not on a beach. He was asking too much now, surely he knew that.

But no. 'Come on, Evie. Nobody can see you. There's no one for miles.'

So first her shoes, then her lower undergarments, then her stockings. Although her dress was a simple calico shift, she claimed to need help undoing it, help which Christopher was happy to provide, lingeringly so, with lots of extra touches that didn't have anything to do with the task at hand. By now, he was completely naked, and she tried to ignore that fact as he worked on the fastenings. Then – *There!* – it was done, and she was as naked as he.

She allowed herself a glance at him, the subtlety of which he torpedoed with an amused stare in return.

There was an expression they used in Ireland, 'There's not a pick on him.' It described him perfectly. His arms and upper body were pale and spare, with sparse clusters of hair. His head stuck out like a bullet on a sinewed neck, and his ribcage was too visible for ideal health. Yet he was wiry and fit. When Eva allowed herself a glance at his lower parts, they looked perfectly ordinary. No sign of anything untoward, not much to see in fact under a shock of dark hair. Of course he noticed her looking, and of course he had to comment on it to the effect that she had not been so coy the other day.

Before she could reply, he took her hand, and they ran towards the waves. Eva winced at the small, sharp stones underfoot, but Christopher was relentless, pulling her with him so she had to run along the flinty seabed, the water first lapping at her ankles, then slapping against her knees, then off her feet and into deeper water, where he let her go.

She yelled from the sweet sharpness of the cold seawater as it hit her groin, chest and neck. *God, it is freezing!* For a few seconds all she could do was shout and flail, then she got used to it and let the waves bounce her around, not doing much more than kicking her legs to stay balanced.

She forgot that she was naked. She even forgot about Christopher. The sun was shining on the water like a million bright knives, and she turned ashore and raised her arms to it, as if it were a god.

Then she heard Christopher call her name and turned around. There he was, his hair flattened against his head, grinning like a loon. 'I told you you'd like it!' he declared, motioning her to join him further out. They swam into deeper water.

'Are you happy?' she called at him.

'Yes!'

'So am I!'

He splashed her, and she retaliated. They were like children. Then they were like seals, dunking each other and wrestling underwater. Then they were like themselves, drunk with the cold and excitement of being in the sea.

They stayed in the water for about twenty minutes before Eva decided she'd had enough and swam in towards the shore. She crouched down in the shallow water before springing to her feet, much to the enthusiastic approval of the man behind her. Eva blushed; she had forgotten the view she would be giving him. She ran up the beach as quickly as she could and put her wet backside on the tartan rug, folding her arms over her breasts and drawing her legs close.

Christopher bounded behind and sat down close beside her. His wet skin slid against hers. He slipped an arm around her shoulders and kissed her, putting his tongue in her mouth, licking some of the salt off her lips. It felt nice, but she was still chilly and so folded her arms tighter about her.

'Don't be shy,' he said, uncrossing her arms. 'Not now, not with me.'

She dropped them obediently to her sides and let him take first one breast, then the other, in his hands. He licked one of her nipples and she yelped in surprise.

'Salty,' he remarked. She tried to think of a sarcastic reply, but then he put his hands on her shoulders and laid her down on her back, pressing himself onto her and entwining his legs in hers. She felt his weight on her and the rug tickling her back, until she could no longer bear it and brought his head down to turn his lips towards hers. She held his head in her hands and kissed him without stopping so that he had to pull away to breathe. Then he scooped his hands around the small of her back down to her buttocks and lifted her towards him. When they came together like that, hip to hip and groin to groin, his flesh on hers, a madness overcame her, and she grabbed a fistful of his hair in one hand and once again dug into his shoulder blades with the other.

'There you go again,' he groaned. 'Jesus Christ, it wasn't enough to send me to war, you want to kill me yourself while you're at it.'

She cut him off by the simple means of kissing him again, then flipped him over onto his back so that her full weight was on him. 'You kill me first then.'

'Not likely,' said Christopher, adding ungallantly, 'I'm struggling to breathe as it is.'

Eva sat up. 'Very well then. I'll stop, will I?'

'The hell you will, come here.' They embraced and wrestled with each other again, and when she felt his hand between her legs Eva was at first surprised, then pleased. He asked her, in a harsh, breathless undertone, if she liked it when he did this with his fingers? And she said 'yes'. Did she like this, here, again? She said 'yes'. And again, here? She let her body answer for her. He must have known she liked what he was doing, because he put his full weight on her once more, and, with a pleasurable shock, she felt that he had put something else between her legs. She reared up to meet it. Feeling him against her, in her heightened state and in that certain way, was enough; a spasm of ecstasy coursed through her, her body forgetting all but the simplest imperative to unburden itself of a want she had unknowingly held inside herself for years. As she moved against him, in a half-sob he called out to her to be careful. Then he simply called her name, before making a sudden, loud cry, his head jerking repeatedly, then collapsing on her chest.

'Dear Kit,' she murmured, stroking his head.

'Darling Eva,' came the muffled response.

They lay there a while. Supine, she opened her eyes. Directly above her the chalk jutted out, the cliff spars the only interruptions to her view of a slightly cloudy sky. She heard nothing but seagulls.

Nobody came here. Of course, Christopher would have known that; that was why he chose the place to begin with. He had planned everything Well, almost everything. Eva looked at him lying there, his hair a spiky fan, his mouth half open – and laughed softly to herself. Poor boy! He was fast asleep. She ran her fingers across his cheek, but he did not respond or open his eyes. Against her breastbone, his breathing was shallow and regular.

After a few moments, the air grew colder, and goose pimples began to gather on Eva's breasts and arms. She sat up, letting Christopher's head rest in her lap, then put on his shirt, buttoning it around her breasts and leaving it loose at the belly and the collar. Donning her own underthings was more than she could manage without waking him up; besides, his shirt smelt of him. She pulled his coat over his body. He snorted a little, murmured something, then turned over so that he was facing away from her, bending his head towards his elbow, his hands bunched into fists in front of him.

Imelda used to sleep that way too.

Eva sang a little – probably as badly as he did – and continued to stroke his hair. The sun came out, went in, came out again, then faded behind a bigger cloud that seemed to overshadow everything. Eva shivered, but even though Christopher only had a light covering over his naked body, he had gone deep into a place where he was oblivious to the changing weather. One of Eva's feet went to sleep, and, even though it was agony, she stayed still, until Christopher opened his eyes once more.

'My God!' he exclaimed. 'Was I asleep?' He rolled back onto his hunkers so that they were eye to eye.

'Out for the count.'

'But I just lay down for a second. And then—' He hit his forehead. 'I never even—' He went pink. 'I'm sorry.'

'Sorry? What for?'

'You know what for.' He was mortified.

'You don't have to apologise for that!' Eva said. Then she added, in a gentler voice, 'I enjoyed you. Very much.'

'And I you, dear girl. Obviously too much.' Christopher looked down at his hands. 'It won't always be like that, I promise you. I won't leave you unsatisfied.' He took her hand in his and played with her fingers. 'Funny how things turn out, isn't it? A year ago I swore to myself if I saw you in the street I would look the other way. And now here I am, falling asleep in your arms like an infant.'

'I hope it will always be like that,' Eva said. 'You looked so peaceful, I didn't want to disturb you.'

'I was peaceful. The first time in … months, years. It was as if someone had wiped my mind clean with a cool, damp cloth. I haven't felt this way for … what, two years? You know, Eva, there's been no one, not since I walked away from you that day.'

'Apart from the girl in Amiens,' she corrected him.

'Apart from the girl in Amiens, yes. But that was physical. With you, it was – oh, what can I say? You know how it is for me, Eva.'

Eva dipped her head. 'Me too. I love you. Still. But you already know that, having been informed by the hospital staff.' They both laughed.

Then Christopher looked out towards the sea. 'I need to ask you a question.'

She covered herself with his coat. Poor man, she was now wearing nearly all his clothes, and he hadn't even noticed. 'What is it?' she said, after he was silent for a moment.

'You still carry that man's name. Cronin. Never mind what else you carried of his.'

'I never use it. It means nothing to me.'

He curled his fingers around one of hers. 'Wait, wrong finger.' Picking up the third finger of her left hand, he did the same thing. 'I know I'm not in the best of shape to be asking you this, but … I want you to have *my* name. Not his, not your father's, mine.'

'Is this … Christopher, are you proposing to me? Already?'

'What, you think this irregular?' he said with a chuckle. 'We were as good as engaged before everything went to blazes, and if you think, after everything we've been through, I'm going to get down on my knees for you, you have another think coming.'

'You are on your knees already,' Eva pointed out.

'Ha! You can say that again.' He laughed without bitterness. 'Look, Eva, I'm not going to put you on some pedestal after everything that's happened. You asked me if I could forgive you. I don't know, to tell you the truth, but I can't imagine living without you. That's all there is to it. Oh, sweetheart—' He pushed a loose strand of Eva's hair behind her ear. 'God willing, once this war is over or when they discharge me on health grounds, whichever comes first, I will find work again, and you'll study and become a right little bluestocking and drive me quite crazy, I don't doubt. So … will you, Eva?'

Eva put her face against his shoulder and murmured something.

'I'm guessing that's a yes?' he said, rather anxiously. 'I can't hear a word you're saying, and I want my shirt back.'

Eva straightened up. 'Yes!'

'Yes, you'll marry me?'

'Yes, you can have your shirt back.' She took it off and handed it to him.

'Well, that's not much use,' he said, grinning while putting his arms in the sleeves, 'that just makes me a single man in a shirt.' He glanced at her breasts. 'Would it be brutish of me to say those are sweeter and fuller than anything in Maupassant?'

'I've read that story,' Eva said, with cheerful indignation, 'and I'm not amused, not in the slightest. I've never breastfed a passing soldier in my life.' She wrinkled her nose. 'I suppose I have to marry you, don't I? If only because nobody else in the whole world would have an idea of what you were talking about half the time.'

They embraced again, and this time, with the help of a rather cumbersome 'rubber', which Eva had to help Christopher roll on – much to her embarrassment and his wolfish glee – this time, he was able to make love to her. At first, it was not as important to her as it was to him; for him it was important to know that the nervous shock had not rendered him impotent, while she had only bad memories of the act and how it had hurt her.

Towards the end of her marriage, her entire lower body felt frozen in an attempt to repel the intruder. She would have been happy never to have had to do *that* again. But to her glad surprise, it did not hurt this time. Perhaps it was because of what they'd done to her in that place. Or maybe it was because of that profound soul-longing she had for Christopher. Or maybe it was because he was older and more experienced than she was and was able to make it easy for her. Or maybe it was because it just felt right to have him there. Either way, she reached that delicious, white oblivion again – was beginning to recognise it – and let herself fall back on the rug, her eyes open to the white sky, her heart blown open. When they were both spent, she looked in his eyes. They were all pupil, dark as rock pools.

'Imelda died, Christopher.'

'I know.'

'How?'

'Because I knew the moment I first saw her that she would. They say someone visited the Brontë sisters and saw death stamped on all three of their faces.'

'But … that wasn't how it happened at all.' Even speaking about it, Eva felt her lips grow heavy and numb. 'She didn't die of tuberculosis. She killed herself.'

'Good God!' Christopher exclaimed with horror, raising himself on his elbow. 'How?'

'She was up in the Swiss Alps. It was a job getting her there, but Italy wasn't in the war then so it was just about manageable. She was already pretty ill; you had the measure of her all right. They did the operation, the one where they put those little balls in the space between the lungs, but it was a waste of time. The consumption had eaten away so much that she could hardly breathe. She couldn't take it any more. So, one night ...'

'It's all right, Eva. Take your time.'

'... one night, when everyone had turned in, she went out into the snow – it was the middle of winter – and walked in her nightgown until she fell down and died of cold. They found her in a drift nearly two miles away. They didn't bring her back to London. Father wouldn't pay the fare. She's somewhere in Switzerland, in a communal grave. I knew nothing about it until I got a letter from him a few months later. I'd written her about five letters that went unanswered. I was in Ireland by then, you see. Father said that everything had been taken care of and that "the family had attended to matters". I was her family! There was this stamp on the letter with the name of his firm and the date. I remember that: he date-stamped the letter to one daughter telling her the other daughter was dead!'

Here Eva broke off into sobs, and Christopher put his arms around her. Even in the midst of such overwhelming sadness, she felt oddly comforted by their wiry strength and the pattern of soft, dark hairs on the forearms.

She had been unable to talk about it before. The years of worrying, of protecting, knowing, without admitting to herself, that the disease would eventually take Imelda away … It had been enough telling Sybil that she had given Christopher a white feather. To tell her that it had all been for nothing would have been too much. And now: to realise he had known all along! 'You let me sacrifice you rather than say a word,' she said.

'What kind of man would I have been if I had?'

For the rest of the afternoon, they lay entwined, pulling various items of clothing over each other, drifting in and out of slumber, sometimes smoking. Eva ran her hand over Christopher's shoulder and down his long back. He was warm. Alive, alive, alive. She felt the welted skin where she had scraped him the other day and pressed the spot with her fingers, at which point he grunted in warning and held up his hand. She began to murmur an apology, and he mumbled that she was quite the wild animal, and so on, until he shifted his position again and, falling back into slumber, began to snore lightly.

At last, they put all their clothes on; at last, it was time to wander up the steps to the top of the cliff and take the long walk back to her hotel, Christopher insisting on seeing her all the way rather than leaving her at Osborne House.

They said little to each other now, only holding hands and exchanging the odd glance, then looking away again. The moon was beginning to rise in the east. A lovely calmness had washed over Eva, the rush of blood to her loins having dissipated all over her body. The night was still, the air humming, the moon becoming more solid and bright as the day retreated and the first blush of sunset began to spill into the sky.

When they reached the outskirts of the town, Eva felt as if that world were shrinking, the evidence of other people's commerce and lives crowding around them. No wonder Christopher was so skittish when they were in company. Why, he was nervous now, eager to leave her, though apologetic, dropping a kiss on her forehead and disappearing into the fast-encroaching night with barely a wave. But Eva didn't mind, because she now knew how much it cost him to be there, for her sake.

32

Since neither party felt inclined to be discreet about the matter, it did not take long for news of Eva and Christopher's engagement to spread. Eva wrote to both Sybil and Lucia to tell them. As for her family, let them read it in the papers as far as she was concerned. For his part, Christopher wrote to his mother and, with some trepidation, to Gabriel Hunter. 'I know his opinion doesn't matter a straw,' he confessed, 'but I am rather worried he'll be angry with me. If I'm unlucky he might get a whole book of sonnets out of it.'

'Will his anger change your mind?' Eva said. 'Because that's the only thing that's important.'

He laughed lightly. 'No. I'm committed now.'

The staff of Osborne House and some patients held a celebration. A long table was set on the small patio at the back of the building, where it would catch the sun. They even put up some bunting, which fluttered in the breeze. Mrs Powys, the Welshwoman who kept the general stores, donated some lemonade, as well as packets of sugar wafers and chocolate-topped buns, which the nurses set out on large dinner plates. Nurse Parvenor, who had warned Eva off Christopher, now took her hand and gaily escorted her to the table as guest of honour.

Small groups of men hung about, chatting and smoking. When Eva was introduced, they broke out into small smiles. They seemed a bit lost, uncomfortable in the presence of a woman who was not a member of staff. Eva was uncomfortable too, but that was because she was about to meet Christopher's mother for the first time.

'I can't put her off any longer,' he had told her. 'I've told her I'm a wreck but she says she doesn't care, she's got her train arranged, and she wants to meet you, and that's that.' He had laughed at Eva's expression. 'You've gone white.'

'It's just,' Eva had hesitated, struggling to find the words, 'what I did to you. I'd find it hard to look her in the eye.'

'Eva,' Christopher had said, dropping his voice, 'she doesn't know. I haven't told her a thing about it.'

'But why?'

Anger had flashed in his eyes. 'Why? Why do you think I didn't tell my mother some girl gave me a white feather?'

She had lowered her eyes. He was right.

'Look,' he had said, putting his hand on her arm, his tone more conciliatory, 'what purpose would it serve to say anything?'

And so they had left it there.

Eva had no knowledge of the woman other than the rather forbidding -looking photograph she had seen on the bookshelf of Christopher's old room back in Surrey. She took one of the wafers off the plate and started eating it, which was terribly rude, but she didn't care a straw. She always tended to eat when she was nervous.

Then she saw them, walking across the lawn, he waving at the assembled party, she holding something in both hands. She was as gaunt as him, with the same high cheekbones, but her hair, swept into a bun, was grey-blonde,

364

not dark, and her eyes were blue. They reached the table, and Christopher murmured something to her, gesturing in Eva's direction.

Mrs Shandlin immediately set down her cake tin, stepped forward and took Eva's hands, kissing her on the cheek. She wore a shawl embroidered with silver birds, and her expression was mobile and animated, nothing like the photograph. 'Miss Downey. What a pleasure to meet you at last.'

'Ma! I told you to call her Eva.' Christopher came up from behind, looking flustered. 'I was going to introduce you properly.'

'But there's no need,' his mother said, 'I've just done it.'

He shook his head and muttered something under his breath. Then, to Eva, 'Hello, dear girl,' with an attempt at a casual kiss, which lingered too long on her forehead, and a caressing hand across her back. In front of his mother, too, although she did not appear to notice, being engrossed in dividing the cake she had brought. Each section had been wrapped in wax paper so that she would not have to touch it with her fingers

Mrs Shandlin looked up at Eva. 'Would you like to try some, dear? I made it myself. Well, Betsy beat the eggs.' There was no little pride in her voice, and Eva immediately warmed to her.

'I'd love a piece,' she said, picking one out and putting it on a paper plate. 'Thank you.'

'She presses cake on everyone,' Christopher said. 'I'm the only person of her acquaintance who is not as fat as a fool.'

'In that case,' Eva replied, half covering her mouth, since she had already taken her first bite, 'you must have no sense of taste. This is glorious, Mrs Shandlin.' And indeed it was, soft and moist without being stodgy, tasting of coffee, walnuts and vanilla and a bit of ginger.

At the sight and smell of the cake, the other men began to gather around and pour themselves lemonade. They were so shy, Eva thought, so awkward in the company of women. Did they not have their own sweethearts back home? Then she remembered what the nurse had told her. It was too bad. If only their women had a little patience, or saw what their men had to go through, they would surely not run away. Why, there was Christopher, sitting beside his mother, laughing and smiling as if he were all right. It touched her heart to see them so relaxed with each other, to know that they had something she had never had with Angela. Now, one fellow, a well-spoken chap who wore five black ribbons in a fan on his back – it turned out to be his regimental flash – was turning to her, making polite and hesitant conversation, saying that he was glad for Shandlin, he was a decent fellow, and how had they met?

Christopher shot her a look of alarm, but what could she do but tell the truth? She provided as abbreviated an account as she could and was rewarded with a few wolf whistles and ribald comments. Mrs Shandlin listened with amusement.

'I'm never going to hear the end of it now,' Christopher muttered, head in hands.

'Well, it's not an ideal start,' Mrs Shandlin said, 'but it could have been so much worse. You could have ended up with—'

'Oh, here we go again.'

'—that dreadful woman—'

'She's talking about Miss Hedges,' Christopher explained to Eva. 'It's my mother's belief that the woman had her claws into me.'

'She was a predatory and self-interested creature,' declared Mrs Shandlin, 'and wouldn't look at you unless she wanted something from you. Why, she didn't say a thing when you enlisted. Every marriage and decoration mentioned in her little past pupils' book and not even the smallest sentence about you.' She made a face.

'Well, why do you insist on getting the bloody book, Ma? It always makes you angry.'

'Christopher, language.'

He rolled his eyes.

Eva was amused at this display. *The apple doesn't fall far from the tree*, she thought to herself. But Mrs Shandlin was kind to Eva, not peppering her with questions and apologising for the few enquiries she did make on the grounds that 'Christopher is *useless* at providing information.'

The sun came out, and the men swapped stories. Not from the lines of battle, but from home, about families and lawn parties and queer people they met at work – and someone nagged the Royal Welch man, Johnstone, to recite Browning's 'Home-thoughts, from Abroad', which he did in a faltering but clear voice. Christopher had to prompt him when he got to 'The first fine careless rapture!', which Johnstone repeated in a somewhat shaky voice. The first fine careless rapture – so long ago now, so far away!

After Johnstone finished, the assembly was silent for a moment, the only sounds being the clink of lemonade glasses and some shouts from inside the building where the more troubled of their fellows lay. Then Mrs Shandlin said, in a harsh tone, 'Time it was when we would gossip about the neighbourhood, we'd joke about who had died recently, and it was always my generation we were talking about.' She looked at her son. 'Now, it's yours.'

'Ma,' Christopher said quietly, putting his arm around her shoulders. 'Please, don't start.'

The silence began to hang dangerously in the air. Eva thought of the eurhythmics woman. 'Could we put on some music?' she suggested. A collective exhalation ensued. What to play?, Where was the gramophone?, Was it too windy? The conversation was back again, though it had a different quality now, less sweet and languorous than before.

Shortly afterwards, Mrs Shandlin took her leave of the party and invited Eva to walk her down to the driveway. 'No,' she held up a hand as Christopher rose to join them, 'you stay where you are. I'll see you tomorrow.'

'All right,' he said, 'but whatever you do, don't tell her the truth.'

Eva wasn't sure if he was addressing her, or his mother, or both of them.

They walked down the driveway together, their shoes making crunching noises on the gravel. Then Mrs Shandlin spoke. 'I wanted to give you some time together, you don't want an old woman getting in the way.' She smiled and dipped her head, in just the same way as Christopher did, and Eva felt a rush of affection.

'You're not in the way at all.'

'It's very brave, what you're doing, looking after Christopher. I can see how you watch him, to catch him should he fall. Oh, don't worry, you don't make it obvious. But you rush to his side every time somebody drops something, or shouts loudly. You are on alert, all the time.'

Eva was too overcome to answer. She knew all too well what Mrs Shandlin meant. Just the other day, when they had been walking through the town, a barrel had come off a cart, and the dray horse had reared up. Christopher had cried out, a high, unnatural scream, and had thrown himself to the ground. When he got up, he was covered in spilled ale and dirt from the street. She hadn't been quick enough to prevent *that*.

'It's been my life's work, Eva – may I call you that? – worrying about him. Especially since we lost Francis. I know he is putting on a front for me right now. He wants to shield me from the worst of it. But it gives me great peace of mind to know that he has somebody to take care of him.'

'I will do my best,' Eva said, 'I promise.'

Mrs Shandlin put her hand on Eva's arm. 'Don't lose yourself, though. He wouldn't want that, and neither would I.' She kissed Eva's cheek and walked away. She had the same walk as Christopher too.

That seemed to go all right, Eva thought, making her way back to rejoin the party. But when she got there, the men had all gone. Only Christopher was left, sitting disconsolately on the bench, one knee pulled up to his chin, the other loose and swinging restlessly, showing a trace of bare ankle above his sock. Around the table lay crumb-covered, discarded plates, while wasps crawled down the glasses, chasing the sticky residues of lemonade.

Eva ran over. 'What happened? Where is everybody?'

'McCrum.' The one-word reply was like a dagger to the chest.

'What about him? What did he do?'

Christopher rose. 'Let's go inside.' They moved to the room with the French windows overlooking the patio and sat down. 'He strutted over to the table with his array of flunkeys, and everybody jumped to their feet to salute like clockwork toys. Everybody, that is, apart from me.'

Eva felt her heart sink to her boots. 'Oh, Christopher, no.'

'Then he demanded that I salute. He didn't ask, mind you, just barked at me, as if it were his due and I were some delinquent child. Imagine someone so deficient in manners that they would demand a salute from somebody *here*, after all we've suffered.'

'And?' Eva tried to stop the shake in her voice.

'And? I refused, of course. I told him I had heard of how he'd kicked a man on the ground and that he didn't deserve my allegiance, or my respect. So he shouted blue murder at me for several minutes. Mentioned the Medical Board coming up. He's there as a "duration of the war" official, which is a bit of a joke, since he's hardly set foot beyond Rouen. The rest are doctors.'

Eva turned her face away with a cry of horror. 'Oh, God! I wish I'd never told you.'

Christopher took her hand. He was excited, almost febrile, boyishly defiant. 'But don't you see, Evie,' he said, 'this is my moment. Finally I behave like a man and not a slave. Do you remember that time when that *unco guid* of a stepsister of yours called me a coward?'

'Yes, yes I do. But Christopher, please calm down—'

'The bit that hurt most was, she was right, if for the wrong reasons. I thought about it often during training. I *was* a coward. I thought I could hold out, but the pressure from everyone, those rotten posters too … and then you gave me that feather and my resolve went to pot. I betrayed Francis when I signed up for this palaver, and I betrayed my own good sense. And now that popinjay demands my obeisance? While calling me a malingerer? No, no. This is as far as I go and no further, Eva.' His hands were bunched into fists and his entire body tense.

Eva stroked his back, her hand drawing long, even lines. 'Easy. Take it easy.' She tried to hide her dismay that in his mind such a futile, almost childish gesture against a powerful, dangerous enemy like McCrum could be a symbol of any sort of self-redemption.

'And that bitch Grace – I know what she thought of me. I won't take it, not from any of them, I'll not …' He was shaking; his entire body was consumed with spasmodic jerks.

Eva realised he was in the grip of full nervous shock and called out for help. But there were no nurses around. She put her arms around him and started to rock him back and forth, just as he had done for her that day in Southwark Park, two years ago. She whispered gentle words in his ear, saying the things she had wished her own mother could have said to her in all the intervening years, trying to comfort him, just as she had promised his mother.

But he was beyond help. He sobbed convulsively, gripping onto her as if she were a rock in the middle of a stormy sea, pulling at her blouse with his fingers like he were a child. She ran her hands up and down his back, stroking him the way she used to stroke Imelda when she had a bad night. But nothing calmed him. He was trying to say something, but it was lost in his anguish, which was all-encompassing, like a drowning wave.

Eva touched his forehead with her own so that they were face to face. Tears streamed down his cheeks, and his expression was all broken up like smashed glass. Some instinct prompted her to lick his tears with her tongue. That seemed to calm him a little. She whispered at him to breathe, to breathe normally, and … What was he saying? Eventually he was able to force it out: 'I'm afraid. Oh, God, I'm so afraid. I can't—'

'It's over now, darling,' she whispered. 'Soon they'll let you go home. You've done your part, and more. I'll take you home, my love. Nobody'll ever hurt you again, Kit, I promise.'

But he was inconsolable. He muttered broken sentences about there being no escape, that they were waiting for him, that they would catch him.

Still she called out for help, and still no one came, so she held him until his weeping subsided a little, the loud gasps turned into smaller sobs, until his twitching began to subside. Then she kissed his scarred hands and stayed with him until the pain and terror and unspeakable fear had gone out of his body for a while, or at least until his body was too tired to convey them any longer. She held him and said nothing, because she too was afraid.

The following day, Eva woke late, her hair sticky and tangled. Wind and rain soughed through the small crack in the open sash window. Yesterday had been exhausting. She had stayed with Christopher until he was totally calm, which took a while. After he stopped crying, he started talking gibberish, and she could tell he was reliving the horrors he had told her about. *This damned war!* She wanted to wipe away all the horrible things he had seen, felt, smelt and endured. She would have even wiped herself away, if it helped; all she wanted was for him to be right again.

What tore her apart was his apologising so often for his condition, when it was not his fault. She tried not to think too much about what might become of him in the civilian world. Would this trembling, frightened, distraught man ever be able to stand in front of a class of youngsters again?

Tomorrow was his mother's last full day on the island, so he would spend it with her. He would come to Eva's room at the hotel at nine in the evening and stay there all night, regardless of the rules. Even if they ended up just sleeping, it would be the first time they had said goodnight with their heads on pillows next to each other. She hoped he would be better by then.

At around seven o'clock that evening, Eva bathed, then dried her hair with a towel and brushed out the tangles. She applied cold cream to her face, starting at her cheekbones and working down slowly until all the white vanished into her skin. A quick dab of rosewater to her wrists and her toilet was complete. She dressed quickly, then sat on the bed and waited for her visitor.

By half past nine she was growing restless but did not want to move. Perhaps his mother wanted to talk about something. Perhaps she had heard about the white-feather incident. Somebody might have talked to her about it. These things got around. Eva began to sweat under her bodice.

She checked her watch. A quarter past ten. She could wait no longer. Downstairs, the concierge sat hunched at the desk. 'Did ... did anyone call for me?' she asked falteringly. The concierge jumped and snorted herself awake. 'No, not that I rightly recall. Nobody's come in.'

Eva retreated to her room and waited some more. Although she was too proud to check with the concierge every five minutes, desperation at last prompted her to ask one more time, at eleven o'clock, whether anybody had called. The irritated negative she received removed all hope.

Something must have happened.

She lay awake, the curtains open, looking at the varying patterns of the night sky. She was afraid that if she fell asleep she would miss his arrival – but by two o'clock natural body rhythms asserted themselves, and, against her will, she fell asleep.

She did not wake until the following morning, still fully dressed. Forgoing breakfast, she made her way to Osborne House, where she learnt that, in her absence, and in his mother's presence, the Medical Board, led by Brigadier Lionel McCrum, had convened early and without notice, had judged Lance Corporal Christopher Shandlin fit to serve and had sent him directly to the eastern front.

V

Singing It Straight

33

'If I have to stay here one more day, I shall go absolutely barmy.'

Eva watched Sybil trying to stretch her long legs out on her cabin bunk and failing. Defeated, she rolled onto her back with her legs hunched and her hands behind her head, looking out the small porthole at the overcast sky of a southern Italian winter. Rain flecked the glass; a storm was in train. The passengers on HMHS *Britannic*, all medical personnel supplemented by VADs, were immured in their cabins.

Eva merely sighed in response. What could she say? Captain Bartlett was a sensible man. If he thought it too risky to put to sea, then Sybil would have to wait.

'We'll never get to Greece at this rate. Which means you won't get to see Christopher.'

Eva did not rise to the bait. 'Nor am I likely to see him if we end up taking an unexpected bath in the Mediterranean. I'll take my chances and wait.'

'I still can't believe they shipped him off to Salonika like that. It's completely irregular.' Eva said nothing. They had been down this road before. 'No, it's jolly rotten, that's what it is. Do you mean to tell me that it was all down to that popinjay McCrum and that the three doctors were just yes men?'

'Perhaps they really did think he was fit.' Eva felt tired to the bone. 'Maybe he convinced them? He's very articulate.'

'Oh, Evie, darling,' Sybil said in gentle reproach. 'If even half of what you've told me about Christopher is true, he was manifestly unfit. Let's face it, he was never the most resilient of men, was he? Always at least flirting with a nervous breakdown as far as I could see. *Augh!*' as the *Britannic* pitched suddenly, 'Blasted ship! It's supposed to be in the harbour.'

The ship was actually supposed to be halfway across the Ionian Sea, en route to Greece to pick up wounded soldiers from the eastern front. It had left Southampton on 12 November and stopped in Naples on the Friday to refuel. They should have left on Saturday morning, but it was now midday, with no sign of any movement, and tempers were getting frayed.

'I agree with you, Sybil. He was unwell and frightened. But there was nothing I could do.' Eva wished Sybil wouldn't keep bringing it up. For her, Christopher's redeployment was an injustice to be championed, but for Eva it just hurt. To remember how she anticipated him coming to her that night – the bath, the rosewater – then the morning's news and the look on Mrs Parvenor's face. And to think of poor Mrs Shandlin, having her son taken away like that, manhandled into a troop carrier with ten others. Mrs Parvenor told Eva over cups of hot, sweet tea that Christopher's mother had left immediately. Eva could not blame her; she herself packed up as soon as she could.

Telling Sybil what had happened had been difficult. When they met at the station at Boulogne, her first question was, 'Why the long face? I thought you were engaged.' Eva explained, her lips feeling as if they had been numbed with proof alcohol. Sybil had been outraged, then had gone into action.

'Where did you say it was they've put him? I bet it's Salonika, that's where Henry Lamb is stationed.'

'Henry who?' Eva's head spun.

'He's with the RAMC, has been there since September. He's another of those painter chaps Roma hangs around with. Pretty good, by all accounts. Roma's going over to accompany him, but it's all for show. He'll be doctoring, not painting, and she'll be filing copy to Reuters like a proper reporter. It's the only way she can get around the nonsense of being accredited by the War Office. I've applied for a transfer. I'm not spending this winter away from her.'

Ah, Roma. Eva allowed herself a small smile. Whenever Sybil had some sort of wheeze on the go, one could usually rely on Roma's being the reason behind it.

'You should come too.' Sybil put her hand on Eva's shoulder. 'We stuck it out here through all the rotten bits. We deserve a break. I miss Roma like hell – and you're engaged now, Eva. Your place is with Christopher, or as close as you can get. Come with me.'

Eva had needed little persuasion. When the transfer was granted, she wrote to Christopher that they were crossing on the *Britannic*. He replied quickly to tell her to watch out for the handsome Italian stevedores. He was bored, he said; it was all short intervals of aggression broken up by days of tedium. His writing was sometimes shaky. He missed her very much. He would say more, but … Yes, Eva knew. Everything was censored.

The ship rolled again and nearly tipped Eva off her bunk. She dropped the letter she had been reading and bent over the bunk edge to retrieve the single page. It was the first sent after he left the Isle of Wight, dated 5 October, and postmarked Folkestone.

Beloved Eva

As you have heard, I have been redeployed to

Serve on the eastern front. Have no idea where

They are taking us, but believe it is near Salonika

And we are leaving directly. Being with you was blessed

Respite in the midst of chaos and I love you

Dear girl, with all my heart. Yours, always, Christopher

Shandlin

On Sunday the weather cleared slightly, and Captain Bartlett wasted no time. Under full power, the *Britannic* headed east. As they neared Greece on the Monday, the air became noticeably warmer. Hard to believe in November, but, as Sybil said, 'That's the Med for you, darling.' Below decks, the nurses started opening the portholes to let the air in to circulate around the wards, a welcome antidote to the stuffy heat and smell of medicaments.

Tuesday dawned in similar fashion. Sybil was one of those morning people who bounced out the moment the ship's bell went off, but Eva lingered abed. The throb and drone of the engines made her feel sleepy, and she fell into the kind of sweet oblivion that only occurs when one sleeps at a time one shouldn't. Soon she would get up—

THUMP!

Eva cast her blankets aside immediately and put her feet on the floor, just in time to be thrown backwards as the ship lurched violently. 'What was that?' she called out, rubbing her skull, only to hear commotion everywhere as voices in the corridor shouted and warning horns began to sound.

She pulled on her uniform, left her cabin and joined the ranks of RAMC staff and nurses all making their way to their posts, as they had been instructed to do in the event of an emergency. 'Is it another storm?' someone demanded to know. A male voice replied, 'I think that's a storm called "German submarine",' which was in turn loudly contradicted by several others. Nobody knew what was going on.

Eva passed a VAD who was sobbing, 'We're going to drown, we're going to drown!'

'We're *not* going to drown,' Eva comforted her. 'The ship has many watertight compartments. Even if one fills up, it won't sink.'

'Oh, yes, the watertight compartments,' an older nurse said sarcastically. 'Now where have we heard that one before?' She was talking about the *Titanic*.

'They've added extra ones since then,' Eva said shortly, putting her arm around the younger girl's shoulder. 'Don't worry, Dorothy. The water won't reach us.'

'It might do,' the older woman said, 'if anyone has left portholes open.'

'Oh, Christ,' Eva exclaimed, realising.

The woman's prediction was confirmed by the ship's suddenly listing far to starboard, amid screams, and pipettes, trolleys and plates crashing onto the floor. Then the call came to prepare the lifeboats. So, it was official. They were going to abandon ship. She looked around for Sybil but could see no sign of her. Then she remembered something else: she had left her letters in the cabin. All of them. *I need to get those back*. She about-turned, elbowing all the staff who were frantically moving in the opposite direction.

By now the ship had listed so far to starboard that it was impossible to see over the port deck. The smell of bilge water and sulphur was overwhelming. Eva wanted to be standing on a level again. But she could not leave without her letters. She could hear the roar of the engines at full steam and a tugging, which felt like an attempt from the bridge to turn and head towards the land, but how could the captain steer a ship filling with seawater and leaning to one side? Surely he knew he hadn't a hope?

The water was coming up along the corridors, lapping at Eva's feet and soaking her skirt, as she navigated her way back to her cabin. She retrieved the letters and stuffed them in her apron pocket, then tightened her sash around her head and headed back out. She was alone below decks as the wash gurgled up and down, but then, at the end of the corridor, at the top of the ladder, she saw Sybil.

'Where the blazes have you been, Eva? They're lowering the lifeboats.'

'I had to get my letters,' Eva said.

'You lunatic!' Sybil cried. 'Fat lot of good they'll be to you if you end up at the bottom of the sea. You want to be alive for him, not dead for keeping his letters, you absolute fat chump.' She ran down towards the aft port side, where a crowd gathered around three lifeboats.

'Sybil,' Eva called, 'I thought the lifeboats were for'ard.'

'Oh, just shut up and be grateful they're here at all!'

The first two were full, and they secured seats in the third, in among a group of doctors and just two other nurses. All they could do now was wait to be lowered. This was not done smoothly. The boats flew down the listing side of the ship, roughly jolting everyone inside. They stopped suddenly a few feet away from the water. One of the women screamed, and Sybil held on to Eva's arm so tightly that her fingernails almost drew blood. Finally, they touched the water and the ropes were released.

Then they heard shouting. Another officer had appeared, calling out, 'Stop lowering the lifeboats! Who is responsible for this? We said *no lifeboats*. My God, can you not see the engines are still at full power?'

The blood drained from Sybil's face. 'Eva, what is he saying?'

Eva could not speak. She pointed at the stern. The *Britannic*'s propellers, half out of the water, were still spinning, their massive steel blades slicing the churning water. Towards them drifted the other two lifeboats, and their own, the current relentlessly bearing them along. They had no oars to row their boats away.

'Oh, Jesus,' Sybil said, 'we're done for.'

'Shall we jump out, Syb?'

'No, you fool, look.' Sybil's voice was taut with fear. A man and a woman had jumped out of one of the boats, but the sea carried them sternwards so quickly that they soon stretched their arms out and were hauled back on board.

They could hear screams as the two boats ahead of them drifted towards the whirring, driving propellers. 'Something has to happen,' Eva said, feeling vomit form at the back of her throat. 'The captain will turn them off.'

Sybil shook her head without a word. The first boat was only feet away, the poor people on it screaming and screaming. Then it was closer still, then closer, then—

Eva felt a heavy pressure on her arm that nearly knocked her off her seat. 'Don't look for God's sake!' somebody shouted. Eva, her face towards her knees, did not look. But she could hear everything. When she raised her head once more, the first boat was a boat no more, just broken bits of floating timber. The foam near the propellers had turned crimson with blood, and bits of bodies lay on the surface of the water, some still bearing signs of rank and uniform.

Instinctively, she crossed herself. For all she had seen during the Somme, nothing matched this carnage.

It was not over. Not yet. Now the second boat was meeting its fate. This time Eva did not avert her eyes. It was a fate that would soon be her own. It was unmentionable, unthinkable, what they endured in those last, grinding seconds. Hearing the death agonies, seeing them suffer what she and Sybil were about to undergo, made Eva feel weak and nauseous in her belly, loose in her bowels; she cried without restraint.

This is the last minute of my life.

She realised that she was vomiting, pale green, almost liquid stuff, down the front of her tunic. She saw a wet patch on Sybil's thigh, her mouth round in a noiseless O – at least, Eva could not hear its sound, her own fear gripped her too tightly to be aware of much outside her own heart beating powerfully in her chest. She knew, she could feel, from the sudden heat on her legs and feeling of release, that she too was wetting herself, but she could not prevent it, the terror was stronger than anything she had ever felt before. Her very bowels would loosen in a moment.

The last thirty seconds.

She gripped Sybil's hand as their boat swung away and back towards the wash of the engines. And now the dark shadows of those propellers were casting themselves on them.

Oh, God, please let it be fast.

Away and back, away and back.

Ten seconds.

And then something in Eva began a warrior shout, a hoarse yell. As she drew close to the propellers, the shout grew louder until she was roaring like a soldier going over the top, ready for the German guns—

The propellers stopped. The noise of the engines vanished. There was only the sound of the waves, the shouts from the other lifeboats and the creaking of a distressed ship at sea.

Sybil released Eva's hand. The wild thud of her heart began to slow down. They both looked at each other.

'Christ,' Sybil said, with a shaky laugh, 'we're alive.'

'Don't say that,' Eva said. 'It might start up again.'

Sybil shook her head. 'Oh, my God, I'm a mess. Don't look at me.'

'I think we all are.'

One of the men stood up, causing the boat to lurch from side to side. Eva noticed with some relief that his trousers didn't look too clean either. With all his might he pushed against one of the propeller blades, causing the boat to shoot several feet back out to sea, where the waves brought it safely away. A sigh of deliverance rose from all the passengers in unison.

The ship sank, of course. It had taken on too much water to stay afloat. The speed at which it went under was frightening. Fifty minutes after impact the stern finally vanished into the sea with a terrible, roaring sound, like water going down a giant plughole.

By then, all the dead and injured had been gathered up and laid out on the pier at Korissia, the nearest harbour. The locals were kind, though they did not speak the same language, and offered fish and fruits. But Eva could not stomach a thing. The sight of some of those bodies, people she had known to speak to, brought fresh tears to her eyes.

There was no time to change from their sodden, filthy uniforms; she and Sybil went to work, caring for the injured, dressing the wounds and stanching the worst of the bleeding. To one pale-faced man who had lost both legs and was bleeding to death, Eva was tempted to administer a small, painless nick to the main artery to help him die quickly and without pain. She did not, of course, but rather did her best to save him. He died anyway. Others, though horribly mutilated, were more fortunate. They would survive, but the injuries they had suffered as the propellers sliced through their limbs meant that their lives were for ever altered.

The young officer Eva was tending to, his clothes around his pelvis and legs dark with fresh blood, began to make that familiar, rattling noise Eva knew and dreaded. He too was lost. A hand rested on her shoulder. 'Downey, you have done enough. Leave that poor man, he is beyond help. We have arranged transport to the mainland. Come with us.'

They were conveyed to a hotel in Palaio Faliro, just southeast of Athens proper, where finally Eva and Sybil could get rid of their uniforms, which were by now in a disgusting state. 'They'd better boil it before I wear it again,' Eva remarked to Sybil, who responded, 'Boil it? Burn it, more like!'

There was just one bathroom on each floor, and the water was lukewarm, but it was so warm outside, even on a winter evening, and Eva was so glad to be able to scrub herself down, that she didn't mind.

When she had cleaned and dried herself, she didn't bother going down for dinner but returned to her and Sybil's shared room and carefully placed her letters on the nightstand before throwing off all her clothes and falling into what seemed like the softest, whitest bed she had ever been in, although in reality the sheets were worn and yellowed, the mattress hard.

A cool breeze blew on her forehead through the louvred shutters as she slept at last.

34

Sybil patted her belly and leaned so far back in the wicker chair that she nearly lost her balance. 'My stars, Evie,' she said, 'I am absolutely stuffed.'

It was no wonder. They had been sitting at the terrace for the past half hour, enjoying a late breakfast of olives and feta cheese, cold cuts of meat with dips of yoghurt and herbs, followed by strong black coffee and *loukoumades*. These last were little balls of light pastry dipped in sugar and rose-water, and Eva and Sybil could not get enough of them, summoning the waiter back for more, licking the syrup off their lips and fingers.

Their hotel looked over a busy road, and beyond that there was a beach where the sea glittered. Faliro lay barely two miles from the Acropolis, but neither Eva nor Sybil felt like sightseeing. Some of their colleagues had gone to work in the Russian hospital in the city, but, after the rescue work they had done, Eva and Sybil had been assured that they could rest for a day.

Eva was starting a new letter to Christopher to tell him about their ordeal, though her reluctance to write down the more distressing parts as well as constant breaks to scoff more *loukoumades* did not help her in its composition. Sybil was fretting about Roma, who was due to arrive in Piraeus later that day, having talked her way into being included on a Canadian troopship, the RMS *Andania*. 'It's just that after yesterday, and the *Galeka* just a month ago … I'm a bag of nerves. If anything should happen to her …'

'Stop worrying, Syb, I'm sure she'll be fine. You'll see for yourself.'

A girl in white slacks appeared on the terrace. 'Downey! Faugharne! The Matron wants to see you.'

Eva set a half-eaten *loukoumas* back down on the plate, while Sybil put her hand to her mouth. She had gone quite pale.

'Whatever for?' Eva asked the girl.

'I don't know,' she shrugged. 'Just that she wants to see you as soon as possible.'

When she left, Sybil leant over to Eva and said in an anguished whisper, 'Oh, ye gods, Matron knows about Roma and me. She's been funny with me ever since we got in. She'll tell the War Office and get us kicked out.'

'Sybil!' Eva wanted to give her a good shake. 'For heaven's sake, her ship just sank! She's probably trying to get a headcount. I doubt she knows who Roma is, to be frank. She's the kind of person who thinks Lesbos is a Greek island. Which it is, of course. She might even bring us on a trip there if we're lucky.'

'I really don't want to see her,' Sybil whimpered.

Poor Sybil, so unlike her usual self. 'You're making a mountain out of a molehill. The matron doesn't know what you do behind closed doors, and, anyway, what if she did? It's not illegal.'

'If it comes out in the divorce court,' Sybil said, through gritted teeth, 'whether it's legal or not will be the least of my problems, believe you me. I just can't shake the feeling that something terrible has happened.'

'Everything's fine,' Eva reassured her. 'Honestly, Syb.'

*

Matron Dowse had been installed in an office near the docks, a few minutes' walk from their hotel along the coast road. The sea glistened and
roared in the near distance as the sun warmed their backs. Small fishing boats moored here; the real business of troopships was at the port of
Piraeus, further along the bay. Although she appeared to be very busy, with
a noticeboard full of maps and pins behind her and an assistant tapping
away at a typewriter at an unbelievable speed, Matron Dowse rose at once
when Eva and Sybil came in.

'Which one of you is Downey?' she asked, with a frown.

'Me.' Oh? What had she done? Though at least Sybil was off the hook
now, after all her complaining.

'I have received a communication from my opposite number in France,'
Matron Dowse said. 'She had some important information I need to pass
on to you.'

'Eva, I'll wait outside,' Sybil said, scarcely bothering to disguise her
relief.

'No, stay!' Matron Dowse's voice was so sharp that Sybil jumped, and
Eva felt a strange tightness in her chest. 'Please,' she added, in a softer
voice, 'it would be better if you both were here.' She motioned them to sit
and did so herself.

'Well … all right.' Sybil, bemused, took the chair beside Eva. The chairs
were wicker, like at the hotel; Eva could feel the pattern through her dress.
For some reason, she did not want to look into the matron's eyes.

'I'll come straight to the point,' Matron Dowse said. 'Downey, I understand you know a Lance Corporal Shandlin from the 1/2nd London
Division? Currently on transfer to service in Greece?'

'Yes,' Eva said, in a voice that was not hers, though it sounded like it. 'I do know him.'

'Your matron in France received a notification yesterday from his commanding officer, Captain Bailey, and she passed it on to me. I am very sorry to tell you that' – for a moment the ceiling roared into the walls and Matron Dowse's voice boomed and echoed – 'while being called to evacuate two wounded officers from Tumbitza Farm, he came in the way of a falling shell and was killed instantly.'

Sybil swore in the name of Jesus.

Eva did nothing. She did not move or speak. She heard the words, but could not take them in. Matron Dowse's hand, clean, stern and bony, reached for hers. 'I'm so sorry, my dear.'

'Thank you,' Eva said, like an automaton. Because that was what one did when people offered condolences, one thanked them.

'Captain Bailey found some correspondence in Lance Corporal Shandlin's personal effects. He saw that it was very … affectionate. Pardon the intrusion, but he needed to establish whom he should let know. He has promised to forward them on to you and also offers his own condolences.'

Sybil was crying now, openly and loudly. 'Oh, the poor bastard. He should never have been there, and now he's dead!' Matron Dowse looked unimpressed. It was not done to make such noise. Eva was doing better, evidently.

Her breakfast churned in her stomach. She thought she would throw up, but all that repeated on her was sweetness. Those *loukoumades* … 'Is he—' she could not finish. Her throat was drying up, closing in. *Hurry, Eva. The matron has important things to do. See that stack of papers on her desk? And you still have to write that letter. No. You don't have to. He will never read anything you write again.*

'Was he—?' the matron kindly prompted her.

Eva ignored the prompt. 'Is he … whole?'

Matron Dowse supported her chin on her hands. 'Why, what do you mean, my dear?'

'The shell that hit him. Is he whole or is he … damaged?'

Sybil gave a low cry of agony. Matron Dowse's face softened. 'Downey, he was hit directly by that shell. It was instantaneous. At least he had that blessing.'

'"Blessing",' Eva echoed.

'Yes,' Matron Dowse said. 'Compared to what many endure, it *is* a blessing.'

Eva remembered a voice once telling her something, a voice that now had no existence: '"tiny fragments of flesh and blood on the ground. Just like that. Not even an eye."'

The plain earth floor rose up to meet her, but Sybil's hands were faster. From far off, further than the sea in the bay, Matron Dowse's voice rushed in like a wave and then receded again. Eva could hear her own surname, but barely anything more.

Sybil held her tightly around the shoulders. 'It's not fair,' she said to no one in particular.

Matron Dowse nodded in agreement. Her mouth drooped a little, the lines around it deepening. She was altogether plain, with small eyes and coarse cheeks, but the fullness of her lips gave her a motherly look. 'It's not, no. I never get used to delivering news like this.'

'It's especially hard for Eva. They went through so much …' Sybil's face began to crumple. Matron Dowse pursed her lips; she had dealt with quite enough emotion that morning. 'Will you be all right, taking care of your friend?'

It was a tactful but clear dismissal. Sybil turned to Eva, still slumped in her chair. 'Evie,' shaking her gently, 'Evie, I need to take you back to the hotel.'

Eva did not prevent her, but Sybil had a job lifting her to her feet. *God, she weighs a ton.* Then Eva said something, but it came out all garbled. 'Yes, what are you trying to say?' Sybil said.

'They sent him back.' Her words were still indistinct. Sybil saw her swallow, her lips trembling, then her eyes lighting up as if someone had ignited a white flame: 'They sent him back because he didn't salute an officer. He wasn't well. And they still sent him back. They murdered him.'

'Eva—'

'I will never forgive them,' she said softly, then, in a roar, in a low, hoarse scream that blasted beyond the hut's wooden walls, making Sybil clutch her chest and nearly fall over in fright, forcing nurses promenading along the water's edge to stop in their tracks: '*I will never forgive them!*'

'All right,' Sybil murmured when her heart had stopped hammering, 'we'd better get out of here. C'mon.' She dragged Eva out into the sun. Why was it so bright? The sun had no business shining like that in November, right in their faces. Eva just closed her eyes. People stared. 'Go away, will you!' Sybil cried, not caring if they were Greek or British. 'Mind your own business.'

The walk back to the hotel felt like the longest of Sybil's life. Eva was so inert that it was like hauling a sack of potatoes. At first Sybil murmured gentle words of encouragement in her ear, but she stopped when she realised how pat and foolish she must sound. *By God,* she thought, *now she really has lost everything.*

On the road, all was busy. Men had disembarked at Piraeus and were finding rooms, men in khaki with chevron patterns on the upper sleeves of their jackets. Canadians. So much life and brash noise, and Eva vulnerable. Sybil feared for a moment that they would injure her by their very existence, though common sense told her that Eva was beyond being hurt. Then she spotted a solitary female figure, poised and quiet.

Roma and Sybil locked eyes. Sybil returned her look with a slight but firm shake of her head. As she toiled along Poseidon Avenue with Eva, she looked behind: Roma was several yards back. Even though they were moving slowly, she did not catch up but followed them at the same distance.

Sybil brought Eva to their room and knocked her out with a heavy sedative. Carefully she pulled the sheets up to her shoulders, dropped a quick kiss on her forehead and left. She badly needed to find Roma, to feel her strong, slight body close to her own … and there she was, standing in the corridor, her room key in her hand.

When they reached Roma's room, Sybil slammed the door behind them. The sound echoed all through the building, and someone shouted from a downstairs room. Before Roma could protest, Sybil pulled her down onto the narrow bed, divesting her of her skirt and pulling off her own with jerky, violent movements. Then she tore at Roma's blouse, pushing away all the layers until she laid her hand on the small breast with the disproportionately large nipple she had admired with slow tenderness before but now pressed hard with her thumb. Then, without preamble, she mounted Roma and started to finger her, pushing her underwear out of the way. She was in charge, and not inclined to be gentle.

'Sybil.' Quiet but firm. 'What are you doing?' Roma was looking right up at her, into her eyes, with the slightest hint of reproof. That hint was enough to stop Sybil in her tracks. How could she? She stayed there a moment, swaying over Roma. Then, feeling a burst of shame opening inside her like a flower, she began to withdraw her fingers, only for Roma to tighten around them, the briefest flick of a powerful muscle. 'Stay where you are.'

'But …'

Roma pushed her hips forward, arching up to allow Sybil to get deeper still. Her eyes closed, and her lips parted as she sighed with satisfaction. Then she lowered herself back down and opened her eyes once more. The edge of her underwear was light and loose, barely brushing against the back of Sybil's hand.

She said, 'What's going on, darling? No—' as Sybil made to pull out again, 'I told you. Stay.'

Sybil found her earlier boldness disintegrating. She breathed shallowly. 'We had some bad news today, Eva and I. About Christopher Shandlin. I don't know if I told you about him, he's …'

'Sybil.' Again that hint of reproach. 'Of course I know who he is.'

'Well, he isn't any more. He's bloody dead!' Sybil inhaled back a strangled sob. 'Poor cranky old bastard, he never harmed anyone, and now he's blown to bits by a shell, and Eva's life is ruined. What's it all for, Romy? I don't know any more.'

Roma reached her hands up to Sybil's shoulders and slowly pulled her down. Their kiss was long, soft. She tasted clean. Sybil felt her tears dampen Roma's cheek, and the intimacy was nearly too much; she began to cry. Her fingers were still inside Roma, moist and warm.

'I am so very sorry, Syb. For her and you. He taught you too, didn't he?' They lay like that for a while, Roma stroking Sybil's back as she wept, until the stroking became something more rhythmical, her desire waking up again, and Sybil responded, first with a delicate touch of her thumb against Roma, then by raising herself with her free hand. Sliding out her fingers and pulling off her own underthings, Sybil made Roma understand, hoarsely, that it was *her* turn to use her hand – *Oh, please hurry!* – then let herself feel it coming, in a descending column through her. It wasn't the thing itself, but the closeness of it approaching, and then she did come, and she thrashed like a fish on a boat, nearly hitting the ceiling, rising like a ship on the horizon and forgetting Roma far down below, forgetting not to make a sound, forgetting war, forgetting herself. The sun lit her up as her head fell back, her arched neck bathed in light, the tears still glinting on her cheeks, giving her hair an intense, aureate glow.

Sybil collapsed beside Roma, who gazed at her with bewildered affection. Spent, Sybil drew her knees up and curled herself as if she were waiting to be born all over again.

It was a while before Roma spoke. 'How is Eva?'

'She's asleep. I was there when they told her. My God, it was as if her soul flew out of her body. Right there and then, I saw it.'

'How awful,' Roma said, with a shudder.

'And now I've come to you, and I've left her alone, because I'm too much of a coward to bear it.'

Roma's eyes were wide and light blue and looked innocent, even after everything she and Sybil had seen and done together. 'Then you should go back, my love. I'll be here tomorrow. I'll always be here. I promise.'

Sybil pressed her entire front against Roma's. The smell of the two women after love was strong and salt-sweet. Her voice was subdued. 'No, you won't, darling. You know that. Everything ends. Just promise me tomorrow.'

'I promise,' Roma repeated. Her lips tickled Sybil's ear, her warmth was close. They came together one more time before Sybil slipped out and returned for the long watch over Eva.

No, not that. 'If I let one crack perpetuate, the whole glass will shatter into a thousand pieces.' But it is too late, the glass is shattered. Bits fall, raining out of the sky, cutting the face of anyone who looks up. The sky is glass, raining more glass; the glass falls into Eva's heart; she is the Snow Queen. If she could weep, her tears would be glass too. Her cheeks would bleed from it.

In the Russian hospital in Athens, where she is expected to continue her duties looking after refugees and the wounded of the *Britannic*, Eva does not sleep. On her first day on the Isle of Wight, she had lied to Christopher: *You were fine.* And he had responded, the familiar irritation in his voice (which she will never hear again): *I was terrible.*

You are fine, fine, fine. You do your bit. No room to be insane in the midst of all this insanity. Far below your feet the wheels of the war machine thrum like those giant propellers on the *Britannic*, waiting for you to trip, fall and be crushed. You cannot get off this moving machinery. You have nowhere to go.

And still her limbs are strong, her heart steady. A warm September afternoon in 1914, with Christopher, in Southwark Park, her head against his chest, hearing his heartbeat, reassuring, firm. Now his heart has been blasted into pieces, along with the rest of him, while hers could go on another fifty years. Why is it so resilient? Why will it not stop? Why will her mind not stop? She is so short of sleep, her hand shakes and her eyelids twitch, and yet she continues – continues. Then, finally, one evening, as monks nearby chant the Greek doxology, the emptiness of the Kyrie's perfect fifths, the relentless drone of the bass – then, like a felled tree, she falls.

Now people intervene. She is brought to a bed in the corner of the ward where she was working. A young girl with a veil who speaks little English sedates her. But her dreams, which flit through her mind like motifs and musical phrases, will not let up. Matron Dowse at her desk, chin on hands, saying, 'Do you know a Lance Corporal Shandlin?' until the propellers move through her face. Suddenly, her cheeks, eyes, mouth are sliced and chopped and flying in all directions, spotting the walls and desk with blood and lumps of flesh. And still that face, now a blood-drenched skeleton with sodden flesh still attached in parts, clack-clacking its jaw: 'He was hit directly by that shell. It was instantaneous.' Then she is a child again, in St Peter and Paul's in Cork, her mother and Imelda by her side, the Palestrina floating from the nave, ribboned and looped, like a Gavioli fairground organ. Light spills in from the window. At last Angela is fully remembered: her smiling face, its jowls and dimples, expands until it fills Eva's vision. What she has longed for.

But, 'No,' Eva says, a jagged piece of glass in her throat. 'You're too late.' And Angela's face melts into the dark, replaced by Catherine's. Her smile is a thin smack of complacency. Her mouth opens, a black underwater cave to trap fish. ''Twas always going to be me in the end, you know. I told you I'd break you, now I have. That'll learn you.' Catherine's laughter is horrible. *Horresco referens*. Eva screams. No sound comes out. She wakes suddenly to find herself banging her head repeatedly against the wall, the pain bouncing along her skull, then voices calling out, firm hands grabbing her upper arms, securing her. Everything goes black.

When she woke again, the room was bright. And empty, apart from herself. The walls were painted warm brown, like fresh mud. Someone had removed her dress, and she was wearing a pair of pyjamas that felt like straw on her skin. Her buttocks felt slimy on the mattress; with a nascent horror, she realised that she was menstruating. Why would the whole apparatus not shut down?

'Eva.' Sybil was on her left, out of her vision.

Eva wearily moved her head. 'Sybil.' Her voice felt like the wind in the joists of an abandoned building. 'What's the matter with me?'

'You're in shock, darling. You need to eat. Keep your strength up. Please, Evie.'

'Keep my strength? Whatever for?' Eva said, collapsing back into the pillows.

'Because we need to take you back. Matron Dowse has made arrangements. You're going tomorrow on the *Aquitania*. To England.'

Sybil's face looked wrong, as if Eva were regarding it through the wide end of a telescope. It made Eva's head hurt, looking at her. 'I don't think I can work—'

Sybil took her hand. Her fingers felt absurdly warm. 'Evie. Nobody will make you do anything you don't want to. I'd come over with you but I'm not due leave. You can stay at the flat as long as you like: Clive won't bother you. I'll be back in London just before Christmas.' She dropped her voice. 'We want to help, you know. I'm worried about you. So is Roma.'

'I'm sorry,' Eva said, not knowing how else to respond. There was an odd pattern on the ceiling, she noticed, as if a glass of red wine had spilled upwards and left a splodge.

'Darling, don't be silly, nobody's looking for an apology. It's a rotten shame, what happened to Christopher. It really is.'

'Yes,' Eva said, but she could not keep focus. It was as if a piano were collapsing in her head. 'Why am I bleeding?' she said.

'What?' said Sybil, then, understanding. 'Oh. Because that's what a woman does. Unfortunately.' She made a face. 'I can get someone to help clean it up for you.'

Life mash, Lucia had said, when Eva told her Christopher had gone to war. Eva had asked her what it meant, and Lucia explained it was a patois expression, meaning everything was messed up and broken. Meaning life was cruel.

'*Life mash*,' Eva whispered, closing her eyes, feeling ever more blood leach out of her.

On the *Aquitania*, the fog in Eva's mind began to clear just as the weather worsened. The Atlantic waves were malign grey-silver, the ship's passengers' faces a similar hue. On deck, the December wind howled. Inside, the cabins stank of puke and ordure.

The ship was packed with the wounded from the eastern front. Many were nervous about German attack. Eva wasn't. No German had hurt her, no German had browbeaten her into giving the man she loved a white feather, and no German had sent him back to the front.

A chaplain took a shine to her. Eva tried to tell him that he should administer to his patients instead, but he would not be put off. He had a round, moon-shaped head and a habit of chewing when there was nothing in his mouth. 'Better to remember how he lived than died, my dear,' he intoned, his hand sliding onto Eva's knee, his mouth making an odd noise as he compulsively masticated, 'and that he's gone to a better place.'

She tried, and failed, to explain that for her it was not a passing irrelevance that the body she had loved had been violently torn to pieces, or that Christopher had had to experience this dismembering, eviscerating, tearing even for a moment. 'I'm alive, I'm real,' he had said. But now the arms that had held her when she told him about Imelda's death were gone; the teeth that had caused the cut on her lip, a cut which had since treacherously healed, were gone; there was nothing left of the face that had fallen when she put a white feather in his lapel, or of the sudden, wide smile when she did something that surprised him, or of the hands that had pulled the Rupert Brooke out of hers and thrown it into the Solent. All those memories gathered in his brain, all those thoughts about her, good and bad, were now blown everywhere, grey matter fallen in a wet shower on dry earth. *Not even an eye.*

'Excuse me,' she interrupted Moon-Face. 'You're wasting your time. I don't believe in Heaven, and I don't believe in God. There is no immortal soul, it's all tommyrot. There is no "better place". We are nothing but temporary structures: viscera, bones and skin stretched across them. And some of us are blown apart, while some of us remain intact until we rot.'

The chaplain stammered, offended. 'Now, my dear lady, if your fiancé were here—'

Eva bounded to her feet, knocking his hand off her knee. 'If Christopher were here,' she said, 'he would not abide you. He would throw you overboard and feed you to the fish. Go away, and take your bible with you. I want nothing more to do with any of you people, ever again.'

35

Grace Fellowes stood outside the row of grand houses, looking up at the unblinking windows. The wind blew at the pram, and Dolly, warmly wrapped up inside, grew fretful, as seemed to be her wont, no matter what Grace did for her.

Her maid had no idea that they had gone out. Nor did she know that Grace was not coming back. She had just left her husband. She did not leave a note. There was nothing she could say against Herbert. He had never said a cruel word, nor laid a finger on her. He refrained from medical talk at the dinner table. He had done his bit, suffering a convenient wound at a convenient time. And he had not, as far as she knew, committed adultery, so she could not sue for divorce.

Instead, she chose to leave. She had a ticket for the mailboat, the RMS *Leinster*, booked for nine sharp the following morning. There was only one loose end she needed to tie up: Eva.

The bitch hadn't answered a single one of her letters, fancied herself too good for her now, Grace supposed – then she felt ashamed to have supposed it. After a lifetime of apologising for her mother's ignorance, Grace was appalled that she carried around the same resentments, in spite of her efforts to scrub her mother out of herself. Certainly, if she were in Eva's position, she would have chucked all the letters in a bonfire.

On the matter of Eva's unwise relationship, however, her conscience was clear. Never would she forget the sneer that ill-mannered fellow had fixed on her when they first met. Intellectual poser, making a mock of her beliefs, flaunting his refusal to fight as if he deserved a medal. It was nothing but inborn mental weakness. He was damaged goods, she could tell, from that odd look in his eye; rarely in her life had she disliked anyone as much. But Eva …

It might have never have come to light if Mother had left her and Herbert alone. But with Imelda in the grave and Roy preoccupied with Irish affairs, Catherine would phone the Fellowes household day and night, haranguing Grace with endless requests and impositions. Ignoring the telephone was not practical; as a doctor, Herbert needed to make and receive calls.

Grace stopped rocking the pram for a moment and put down her case to tighten the belt of her high-collared wool velour coat. In one of the windows, she could see activity, a chambermaid stripping the sheets from a bed. She knew which doorbell to ring. She knew exactly where Eva was. But indecision kept her still.

She had been as officious as you like when seeking her sister's whereabouts. Demanding answers from the matron in France in the name of 'family', then a convoluted line of enquiry via Salonika and eventually a quick trip on the train down to the Destouches residence in Kent. An under-butler with a snotty tone had sent her packing, but not before she had obtained the final address she needed. Now she could tell Eva the full story. Eva needed to know.

It had all come out by chance. After one phone call too many, Grace had stormed down to the old house in Wellclose Square to have it out with

404

her mother. She had burst in and told her: no more, she would not be constantly pestered in her own house, she was a married woman now, and it wasn't fair.

And all the time, a small smile played about her mother's face, flickering like a hell-flame. She was only waiting for a pause in the conversation to say it at last: 'Grace, Roy Downey is your real father.'

Grace had frozen to the spot.

His marriage to Angela had been over in all but name for a long time, Catherine said; he never went to visit his wife of a night, but it was not unknown for him to visit *her* during the day when Angela was out paying calls. Angela Culleton as was, that dumpy article of a piano teacher, whom she had to address as 'Ma'am'! But she made sure that Roy would have something to remember his loyal servant by. 'That was you, Grace,' Catherine had said, with a craven smile. 'The apple of me eye, you were.'

By now Grace's gut was surging, but she knew she would stay to hear the end.

Roy played false, Catherine said. There was nothing between him and Angela, he said, nothing true or meaningful, but then Mrs Downey began to be sick in the mornings, and soon the news was announced that she was expecting. It was just a one-off, a terrible mistake, Roy told her, time and time again. Did Grace have any idea, Catherine asked, how it felt to have the mistress of the house patting her belly while her belly swelled too, with the same seed from the same man, while she had to keep going with her sham of a marriage to that drunk Nelius Connolly, till he had the decency to die when Grace was two? What it was like to see the evidence of Roy's infidelity right there in front of her?

Grace stopped her. 'He was married to her. Not you. You were the one he was being unfaithful with.'

But her mother refused to hear a word. On and on she went about the shame of his infidelity, the constant humiliating presence of his infidelity, his infidelity this, his infidelity that, until Grace broke in, her voice like the edge of a knife: 'You are speaking of Eva, and I am now to understand that she is my blood sister.'

By the look on her face, it was clear that Catherine knew she had made a mistake. 'And Roy … Roy is my father.' Now Grace was shaking. He too had known. Grace rushed to the bathroom and vomited in the sink. In the doorway, Catherine's anxious shadow hovered, just as it had that day when Grace had flung Eva against the wall and cried, 'Him or Imelda?'

'I couldn't tell the truth,' she whimpered. 'I wasn't going to let them look at ye and think ye were a bastard. He was good to me, Roy. There was no question who was your father, but, d'you see, I could never tell. And then that Eva was born, and she wanted all of yer daddy, and I had to make sure you had your bite of the cherry. I wasn't going to let her take away everything you deserved, just because you were born the wrong side of the bed. I fought for you, Grace.'

Grace stood up and wiped her mouth, running the tap until the repulsive mess began to spiral down the sink. Only then did she reply: 'No, Mother, you didn't. You lied to me – and you used me. You're obsessed with Eva, always have been, because she's living proof that my father was with Angela too. It must have been hell for you, seeing her every day, a constant reminder of his wife.'

Catherine's eyes filled with easy tears, but Grace was not finished. 'He was doing the two of you, the wife and the servant. That's why you kept punishing her, wasn't it? Pretending to give a damn for me.' Then, a sudden realisation: 'And it's why you insisted Eva marry that awful man Cronin? Pure spite. God,' Grace declared, 'you are vulgar, vulgar, vulgar. You make me sick.'

Those were the last words she ever addressed to her mother. The minute she got home to Shoreditch she had the maid run her a bath and scrubbed herself nearly raw. She was unable to stop crying. It took hours for her to pull herself together enough to write to Eva. She hardly expected a response, and she didn't get one. Eva had one power over her, the power of withholding, and God did she use it.

But now the time to tell Eva had arrived. Grace pushed the pram with renewed determination, preparing to cross the road.

And then she saw a figure at one of the windows.

No question but it was her, clear as day. Not looking down, but away. Grace remembered something Herbert had said to her: that the first time he met Eva, when he'd driven away from the house, he had seen her figure in the window, just as Grace did now. 'Like a mannequin,' he'd said. 'Too fat for a mannequin,' Grace had replied, but now, when she saw the still figure, she knew what Herbert meant. It was not like seeing a living person: there was nothing in that face, nothing at all. It frightened Grace, that blank look.

'There's nothing I can say to you, is there?' she whispered sadly.

Spots of rain began to fall on the pram cover. Grace shuddered and pulled her coat around her again. It was madness to think she could reach Eva. And, more than that: it wasn't fair. *What were you hoping to get out of this?*

Grace admonished herself, *forgiveness?* Because there was no way in hell Eva would ever forgive her for pushing her to pin the white feather on that Shandlin fellow. *Probably*, Grace thought, *because Eva has never forgiven herself.*

No more of that. Grace would not delay; she would continue on her way to Paddington Station for the train to Holyhead, where she and the baby would stay overnight before travelling to Kingstown in the morning. The journey had been a long time coming: letters had been flying back and forth while Herbert had been in his consulting rooms. Since her mother's revelation – no, further back, since she had become disaffected with the life of a doctor's wife in East London and had read about the Easter Rising in the papers, she had thought more and more about the roots she had so long disowned and had come to the conclusion that her race had been the victim of massive injustice.

She would spend that Christmas and all Christmases thereafter in Ireland. She was taking up membership of Cumann na mBan, the women's wing of the Irish Volunteers, having been given a letter of introduction from Mrs Charlotte Despard, with whom she had entered into a friendly correspondence. The sister of General John French, who had led the Old Contemptibles into battle in 1914, Charlotte had gone very far the other way, turning Fenian and supporting the workers during the Dublin Lockout. She was also a raving suffragette. Eva would have approved.

Grace Fellowes had no more time to lose worrying about the past, because Grace Fellowes was no more. She had a new mission and a new name: Gráinne Ní Dhomhnaigh. From now on she would serve neither King nor Kaiser, but Ireland.

*

Eva had the flat in Cumberland Place almost to herself, apart from a house-keeper who came in three times a week. During those solitary days, she could not set her mind to anything. She was gripped by a profound listlessness. Day after day she would wander the rooms like a ghost and then stand at a window, looking out at Hyde Park, watching the figures on the path below: matchstick men and women, some with prams, some selling flowers, some singing Christmas carols. Faceless, all of them. There were days she stood like that for hours at a time. She tried to write another letter to Christopher's mother – she had received no reply to her first, posted when she had disem-barked at Southampton – but tore up each effort. She did not know what to say. So many dead now: Christopher, Imelda, even David Wentworth Hopkins while a prisoner of the Turks at Kut-al-Amara, poor child.

Soon Sybil will be back, she thought.

But then Gabriel Hunter called, and Sybil was not there. Eva had to face him alone.

He stood at one end of the room, Eva at the other. She had not seen him since that day in the field hospital. He had survived his injuries, and was still beautiful, with his winter coat and summer blazer, his berry-red lips and Myrurgia cologne, the tobacco scented traces of which filled the room.

He wasted no time. 'You have caused enough hurt, enough damage for a million lifetimes. You gave him a death sentence.'

'Mr Hunter,' Eva said falteringly, 'please—'

'I won't please,' he said angrily, 'to suit you. Why should I, after what you've done? You were the ruin of him, and I warned him. I warned him!' He spoke with real anguish, and when Eva looked up, she saw he was close to tears.

'We both loved him,' she said, feeling a brief flare of compassion for the angry man opposite her. But from the way he coloured and glared at her, she realised that she had made a bad move.

'Your "love", as you call it, was a mere fiction,' he said coldly. 'You took a classroom crush and made it into much more than it really was.'

'That isn't true. We were lovers.'

He looked at her with disgust. 'Typical woman, all manners and artifice on the surface, but underneath you are all little alley cats. You are lying, Miss Downey, and I can assure you that nobody of consequence believes for one moment that what you had with Christopher amounts to a hill of beans. He didn't love you, and he didn't respect you.'

'He did! You said so yourself, remember? And he proposed to me,' Eva countered.

'Really?' Hunter was smiling now. 'I don't remember saying anything of the sort. And I don't see any ring.'

'He didn't … he couldn't …'

'I don't suppose you've read my recent in *Blackwood's*? Of course you haven't. Women like you only read the requisite minimum to seduce men. I have a poem, part of one. It's called "The Dove", and I imagine it will be quite famous in time. It's dedicated to him. I am the one who will write about him, and celebrate him. Christopher won't be forgotten, I'll make sure of that. And I'll name you, you bitch. I'll drag you through the mud for what you did.'

'I may have hurt him, but I loved him!'

'I don't think someone like you could know the meaning of the word.'

Eva hadn't intended to show him Christopher's acrostic, which she had on the table, but his manner was so maddening she could not stop herself. She unfolded it and pointed to the words. Hunter smiled nastily and whipped the letter out of her hand, tore it down the middle and threw both parts in the fire, which had been dying peaceably in the grate but now flared to life.

'That's not Christopher,' he said calmly. 'It's just some fancy of yours. Now I've put it where it belongs.'

It was then Eva quite forgot herself, and Hunter won, for she flew at him, scratching at his cheeks, growling and baring her teeth. He restrained her with disdainful ease. Eva wrested her arm free of him and pushed him into the hall. 'Get out!' she shouted. 'Get out of this house, before I throw you out!'

'It isn't even your house,' he shouted through the door, as she attempted to push it to. Then he wedged his foot in the crack. 'I'll tell you one last thing. I spoke to Lilian Shandlin. We're great friends, she and I, I've often been to her home. I enlightened her about what you did to her son, about that white feather. And do you know what she said, dear Eva? She said, "God is unjust if that girl dies a quiet death."'

So that's why Mrs Shandlin had not replied to Eva's letter. Hunter had got there first. 'If you don't believe me, you can ask her yourself. Though I wouldn't advise it.'

Eva shook her head. 'I believe you,' she said dully. But he had already gone, the door shutting behind him with a curt click.

Sybil arrived in five minutes later, with Wilson in tow. 'That bastard,' she exclaimed, all suitcases and damask-rose perfume. 'I knew he'd come from here. I saw the revolting smile on his face as he crossed the road. Oh,

Eva, no, please don't cry, try not to, darling.' But she might as well have told the wind not to blow, or the rain not to fall, or the war not to keep on raging. Eva wept in Sybil's arms, wept and howled. She called the name of the man who could never answer.

Sybil swore she'd have that Hunter's guts for garters if she ever saw him again. 'McCrum is his uncle, you know, on his mother's side. So if anyone's to blame for what's happened, it's *his* people.'

Eva did not hear her; all she could think of were Lilian Shandlin's words. They rang in her ears as she sank to the floor, and nothing, nothing, could cancel them out.

36

May 1917

How strange, Eva thought, that she should return to Eastbourne of all places to see things through. To take the same train as on that autumn day in 1913, to get off at the same station. Then to hire a bicycle and cycle to The Links, for one last bittersweet look back.

But the debutantes were gone, and there was no sign of Miss Hedges. The whole place had been requisitioned as a unit for wounded officers. The patch of laurels where Christopher and she said the first of many goodbyes had been cut down, and the lawn now stretched out without interruption as far as the netball court. The lines on the court were blurred and scuffed, and the net hung limply. When a figure in white came across the lawn, Eva did not wait to be asked what she was doing there but mounted the bike and sailed off once more.

She cycled the few miles back into Eastbourne then went right through the town, skirts flying, ankles on display to all, heading west along the South Downs to Beachy Head. An hour after she left The Links, almost at the headland, she abandoned the bicycle, flinging it into the grass near a stile, its pedals spinning uselessly.

The sun was high in the sky, and the long grass on the clifftops brushed her ankles as she walked. Spring was late with a vengeance, and the fields

413

were dotted with forget-me-nots, buttercups and loosestrife. Spontaneously, she raised her arms to the sky. She felt more light-hearted than she had in months.

Nearer the cliff edge, the ground was covered in scree and chalk. Eva looked down at the beach five hundred feet below. From such a height, she could barely see the rocks. It was easy to imagine that they were skulls, washed back from the marshes of Flanders and the fields of Picardy and dumped at the bottom of the English cliffs.

In a moment now it would be time. Time to put all her energy into the run. You can't do these things more than once, and you have to do them properly. She remembered how hard Christopher had thrown that little book; it must have taken all his strength …

Then, along the stretch of the cliffs, she heard the ting-ting-ting of a bicycle bell and what sounded like someone shouting.

Oh, for God's sake, day trippers. Just what she needed. The closer the figure got – it was a lone woman – the more familiar she looked. Eva realised that it was the same bike she had dumped at the stile, and by the time she realised that the woman had stolen it – she laughed at the absurdity of her outrage – the stranger was one no longer but had resolved into the form of Lucia Percival.

'*Cha*, I am very sweaty after that sprint,' she exclaimed, dismounting and putting the bike on its stand. 'Whew! You were just about to run for that cliff, weren't you? I could see it in your shoulders. I thought I was too late.'

Lucia was not lying. The armpits of her calico dress were stained, and sweat was running down her forehead and neck. She clung onto the bicycle.

She was not looking that well herself, wan and haggard, out of breath from exertion. Her chest rose and fell, and she put her hand on it. 'I wanted to see you. I needed someone to talk to. Your friend Sybil just said that you'd gone to Beachy Head. She was in a rush out the door. Well, she was not worried, but she doesn't know about suicide, and I do. So I went after you. No sign of you on the train. Thought I'd missed you.'

'That was very good of you,' Eva said, trying not to sound cold, 'but there was no need.'

'People like her don't understand,' Lucia continued, as if Eva had not spoken, 'that some of us feel at the outer, higher ranges of life. Everything is brighter and crueller. We feel the full experience; most people, only half. How can you even listen to Wagner, for example, let alone sing him, if you are not born that way? I knew here,' she thumped her chest, 'that you were not out for a pleasant walk. *A mi fi tell yu*, just a few weeks ago they pulled me out of the river Clyde after I had tried the very same thing and nearly succeeded.'

'Lucia!' Eva said, with genuine surprise.

'I was in sad, sad straits – I will tell you presently what it was all about – and had made up my mind to be swept away out of reach of human cruelty for ever. So I went down to a certain spot and walked straight into the water. It was so rank and cold. I had to keep telling myself I was about to die and that the water quality was not that important.' She laughed bitterly. 'The strange thing was how aware I was of the beauty even in that filthy place. Glasgow was clothed in fog, but as the water lapped around my chin I saw the lights of a ship emerging. It was like a painting. Then I lost my footing; before I knew it, I had been carried out to a place beyond

415

my depth. My hair was all loose and spread across the water as I sank. My clothes were helping me sink too. Then water poured into my mouth, and I could barely keep above the surface long enough to breathe before I was under again. I felt fear, but from a long way away, you understand? I was beyond everything. It was neither good nor bad. It just was. I was drowning, then, you see, good and proper.'

Eva became aware that Lucia was walking her further away from the cliff edge, slowly, bit by bit.

'But you didn't drown.'

Lucia shrugged. 'Oh, I got rescued. Some captain from a tugboat pulled me out and told me not to be such a damned fool. I puked river water all over his shoes, and then he propositioned me. I had to turn him down.'

'I see,' Eva said, laughing in spite of herself. Then, 'Why did you try to drown yourself?'

'Keep walking with me, and I'll tell you.'

Eva let Lucia steer her safely inland. It was only now, as the magnitude of what Lucia had guided her away from dawned on her that she began to feel a bit dizzy and tight around the chest. The light-hearted detachment that had buoyed her over the past few days was beginning to fade. She hoped Lucia would keep talking. She was not ready to face her own demons yet.

'I had a son,' Lucia said, her voice choked. 'And they took him. Just a few weeks ago.'

'Oh, Lucia!' Eva said in gentle horror, taking her arm.

'I tried to hold on to him, but I couldn't.'

In fits and starts, occasionally overcome by grief, she told her story.

Mackenzie had finally made his move. Lucia had discovered her pregnancy when she could no longer hold a long phrase in her singing practice – 'By then, everyone else had noticed, but I was naive!' Mackenzie's mother was crashingly ambitious for her son, and, as Lucia put it, 'She already had a plan for him, and a quadroon child was not part of that plan. Nor a mulatta mother! *Zugzwang*!' Powerful connections meant that Lucia found herself shipped to a large mother-and-baby home in Morpethswade in Glasgow, where she was kept until the baby was born.

'I nurtured a hope that if the child had dark skin the Americans who buy the children for adoption would not take him. You know, they have great race prejudice in America. But barely three days after he was born, those nuns, those vultures, they came for him. I had him at my breast ... I clung onto him as long as I could ... I begged them, I screamed at them, please, but they said "no, no, no".'

She was there, right in that moment, Eva saw. Her mouth was open, tears streaming down her cheeks, an agony so raw imprinted on her face that Eva could hardly bear to look. She maintained the lightest of touches on Lucia's arm, enough to remind her that she was in the present, no more.

Finally Lucia collected herself with a strangled sob. 'I called him Dominic. It means "belonging to God". It was after this priest I met at the home. Heaven only knows what he's called now.'

'And this priest – did he help you?'

'Oh, he fell in love with me. But he was *nyaamps* when I needed him.'

Eva could not help grinning. This refrain of Lucia's was becoming somewhat familiar.

'That is why I looked for you. I thought ... I am alone here, you know,

now Dominic is gone. I look different from everyone else. I *feel* different too. You have heard me sing: I am a natural soprano, I could sing in an opera! But on my own? Na, all the doors are shut. Let me be plain, Eva, I need someone to hold them open for me. Otherwise, I might never see Dominic again.'

'I can hardly open them myself, Lucia. But I will try for you.'

Something in the air between them, a hard, nervy tension, had dissipated. The sun had wound its way around to the west and was getting in their eyes. Lucia adjusted the brim of her hat; Eva had none, so she just squinted.

'At least he is alive,' she said. 'If you have nothing else, you have that. He is alive and cared for.'

Lucia turned to her, her hat brushing Eva's hair. 'Yes … I heard.'

Eva shrugged. 'It's a common enough tale.' If she said that often enough, she might believe it.

Lucia shook her head, frowning. 'Sybil told me to be gentle with you because you'd lost your Christopher man, but she said it was because he was sent back when he shouldn't have been.'

'What difference does that make?'

'It make a whole deal of difference. Eva, what happened to him was improper.' She put her hands on Eva's shoulders. 'I know injustice. I know it does not go away like normal sadness. It eats and eats at you, until it consumes your spirit whole.'

Eva began to shake. This is what she had feared, the return of all those feelings. The anguish was as acute now as it had been last November. Time had put no rust on the iron, only sharpened the blade. Only the promise of suicide had lulled the horror for a while.

'But be not afraid,' Lucia added, seeing her upset. 'Because God is always there, and He watches over us all. In His name justice will be done. That I am sure of.'

Eva couldn't believe her ears. After a half an hour of talking nothing but good common sense, Lucia was reciting this sort of claptrap. She laughed, and her laughter had a trace of scorn.

'After all you have been through, Lucia, how can you insult your own intelligence, let alone mine?' At the hurt look on Lucia's face, she felt a brief, hot flash of regret, but carried on. 'If God were truly all-loving, He would have stopped those women taking Dominic away from you. And He wouldn't have stopped the propellers on the *Britannic* when our boat was heading for them. I would have been cut to bits, and I'd never have known what it felt like to have lost Christopher. He was already dead for several days by then, and I need never have known.'

Lucia kept walking. 'You know,' she said, in an almost dreamy tone, 'we say in Jamaica that after a man dies, his spirit, which we call his *duppy*, wanders the earth for nine days. When my father died, we left his study just the way it used to be, and on the ninth night we laid food out on the desk: jerked pork, kedgeree, chicken, sweetened coffee and a bottle of Jamaican rum. They say the *duppy* eats a proper meal for the last time and then goes to the grave, and we put a cross on the door to make sure it never comes back.'

Now in front of them rose the Belle Tout Lighthouse. The wind was light and fresh with spring. In spite of Eva's turmoil, it felt refreshing.

'He stopped those propellers for you, you know.'

'What?' Eva said.

'That was him. Your Christopher. His *duppy* saved you.'

'Lucia, that's … that's nonsense.'

'It is *not* nonsense!' Lucia cried, impassioned. '*Cu yu*, what else could it be? Only gone a few days, he was not at rest! I am telling you, Eva, it's his doing. He wants you to live, star. He wants you to go to Summerplace and study with the bluestockings.'

'Stop it, Lucia,' Eva said, near tears. 'That's cruel. Superstition, that's all.'

Lucia put her hands on Eva's shoulders again. Her voice was very tender. 'He was there, and he saved you. I know it.'

Eva tried to protest again, but something in her heart came loose, like one domino knocking over a row. Lucia's face was suddenly a warm, brown blur. She was aware of falling forward, of being supported, as she wept, tumultuous sobs that seemed to tear her body apart. 'I miss him. Oh, God, I miss him so much. It's not fair.'

'I know,' Lucia murmured. 'I know, sweetheart.' Then, into Eva's ear, 'He loves you. He loves you. He's here.'

'No, he's not,' Eva wiped her eyes with her fingers, 'and he shouldn't be. It's my fault he's dead.' Lucia raised her eyebrows in query but said nothing. There would be time, they both knew it, now that Eva had been talked back from the edge.

They turned from the lighthouse and walked back to the bicycle, which had fallen over, much to Lucia's irritation. She expended several patois swearwords righting it. Then they returned to Eastbourne along the wide cliff path. Eva was still crying, quietly now, but openly. Lucia was singing melodies here and there, wheeling the bike, pacing her walk by her breath.

They repaired to the station teashop to wait for the five o'clock train to London. Eva, by now composed, procured tea and plum heavies from the bored proprietress, while Lucia tactfully and quietly bought the ticket for the return journey which Eva had failed to purchase that morning.

'Eva,' she said at length, 'forgive me if I'm prying, but … Hey, am I allowed to do this?' She was dipping her cake into her tea.

'I don't see why not,' Eva said, 'except that it will all fall into the tea. You need to use a biscuit.'

'*Cha*, whichever, it's all the same to me. My tea will be a little sweeter, that's all. Anyway. You said something earlier – that it was your fault he's dead. What did you mean by that?'

Eva put her teacup down but didn't say anything for a moment. Then she raised her eyes to meet Lucia's. 'It was my fault.'

The train pulled out of Eastbourne. The compartments were on the land-ward side, and the setting sun made Lucia look like a gold-bronze statue. She was deep in thought. Eva, meanwhile, was waiting for her to respond to what she had told her. There was no hurry. She had nowhere special to go.

Finally Lucia spoke. 'I have a lot of difficulty running this through my mind.' Eva nodded. 'But I do have some thoughts.'

'Go on.'

Lucia took off her hat and leaned forward, her chin in her hand. 'This Gabriel Hunter man, he's mighty angry. Drag your name through the mud, eh? Can't wait till the war finish, *nuh*, he must rewrite history now? Well, you can do three things. One, jump off a cliff. That you are not going to do. No.' She shook her head emphatically. 'Two, let him do like he threaten. Stand by while he tells the world you're responsible for killing your Christopher. And make sure everyone forgets about the man who sent him to Salonika. Always blame the woman, not the system. Three? You fight.' She took Eva's hand in hers. 'There is nothing you can do for Christopher any more. He's gone. But you *can* tell your truth and sing the song straight, not crooked. So, Eva, which will it be?'

The sun vanished as the train roared into a tunnel. Cold air streamed in the open pane. Lucia reached up and shut it with a smart thud. For several minutes, Eva sat mute. Every sound, every sensation was amplified in that dark space. When she spoke, her voice was low and firm. 'I'll fight. Yes.'

The train left the tunnel and steamed into the Sussex countryside, lit up by a shaft of brilliant light as it continued its journey back to London.

Acknowledgements

The Pico group, who saw snippets of a very rough draft and kept cheering me on; Helena Mulkerns; Conor Kostick; the Irish Writers' Centre and Novel Fair 2013; June Caldwell; Arlene Hunt; Mary Conroy and Orlaith Mannion – we found the name at last! – Myrhad Lanigan for the gift of Adam Hochschild's *To End All Wars*; my late grandparents, Brian and Nora Boyle, for their belief.

My wonderful agent Svetlana Pironko; Michael O'Brien and The O'Brien Press for taking a chance on me; Emma Byrne for a stylish and evocative cover. A very special mention goes to Liz Hudson, who went above and beyond the call of duty in her commitment to editing this book.

Writing this novel meant much reading: I particularly acknowledge among the many works consulted: Vera Brittain's *Testament of Youth*; William Moore's *The Thin Yellow Line*, which dealt exhaustively with the subject of military 'cowardice' in the First World War; and Zora Neale Hurston's wonderful *Tell My Horse: Voodoo and Life in Haiti and Jamaica*.

My thanks also to Nina Panagopoulou and Athena Andreadis for queries about Greek language and culture; Keith Graham for architectural tips; Tony Wade, historian and leader of Back-Roads Touring; the Imperial War Museum; the Tyrone Guthrie Centre in Monaghan; the Palazzo Rinaldi residence in Basilicata, Italy.

Finally, to Jonathan O'Neill, whose support and encouragement made this possible – my thanks, with all my heart.

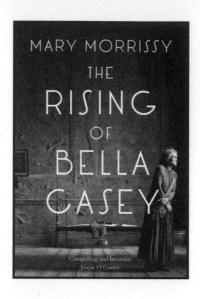

From a piano abandoned on the strife-torn streets
of Dublin at Easter 1916, Mary Morrissy spins
the reader backwards through the life
of enigmatic beauty Bella Casey, sister of the
famed playwright Seán O'Casey.

'Elegant and unadorned at the same time ... an intimate portrait of a
woman and a depiction of Irish history at its most extreme ... a wonderful
book from one of our finest writers.'

Colum McCann

'One of the most intelligent, well-written and well-researched
historical novels I have read. Mary Morrissy is the Irish Hilary Mantel.'

Eilis Ní Dhuibhne

'Mary Morrissy has a genius for lifting characters out of the dim
backgrounds of history and brilliantly illuminating them ... she evokes
the rich Dublin world of the plays of Seán O'Casey.'

John Banville

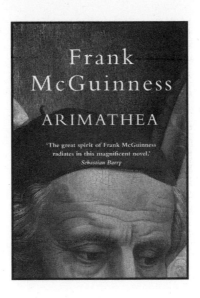

It is 1950. Donegal. A land apart. Derry city is only fourteen miles
away but too far, mentally, for people to travel there in comfort. Into
this community comes Gianni, a painter from Italy.
A book of close observation, sharp wit, linguistic dexterity – and
of deep sympathy for everyday humanity.

'The great spirit of Frank McGuinness radiates in this magnificent
novel. Myriad voices converge on one glistening core; it is a high-wire
act earthed in the deepest humanity.'
Sebastian Barry

'Poetic and strange, elemental and truly original, Arimathea engages
fearlessly with the mysteries of art and love.'
Deirdre Madden

'A work of passion and truth, in which imaginative daring is matched
by deep psychological insight.'
Declan Kiberd

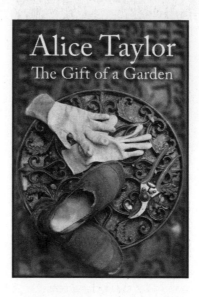

Alice Taylor
The Gift of a Garden

Alice's garden is her refuge. Inherited from Uncle Jacky, she introduces
the great variety of plants and objects she has gathered – everything,
of course, with its own unique and fascinating story,
brought to life by a master storyteller.

'reading Alice is like being pushed in the small of the back off a rock
into a deep warm pool … she gives one the exhilaration of being in
the presence of a real writer and her skill is so accomplished
that it appears effortless.'
The Western People

'the joy of gardening unearthed by Alice'
Evening Echo

'will provide restful reflection for many'
Sunday Independent

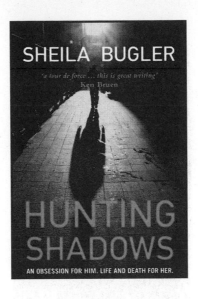

A tense thriller that stalks the urban streets of southeast London
and the bleak wilderness of the North Kent coast,
Hunting Shadows introduces the forceful, compromised
police detective, DI Ellen Kelly.

'Wonderful characterisation and a gripping plot. DI Ellen Kelly's
mourning felt so tangible that it was heart-wrenching. This debut
pulled me in straight away and I was hooked! A book that has stayed
with me long after the reading.'

Crimesquad

'Terrific … compelling.'

Irish Examiner

'Truly a tour de force. Imagine a collaboration between Anne Tyler and
AM Homes. Yes, the novel is that good. This is great writing.'

Ken Bruen

'A most assured debut.'

crimefictionlover.com